STAR TREK™
PICARD
ROGUE ELEMENTS

STAR TREK™

PICARD

ROGUE ELEMENTS

John Jackson Miller

Based on *Star Trek: The Next Generation*
created by Gene Roddenberry
and
Star Trek: Picard
created by
Akiva Goldsman & Michael Chabon
&
Kirsten Beyer & Alex Kurtzman

GALLERY BOOKS
New York London Toronto Sydney New Delhi Sigma Iotia II

G

Gallery Books
An Imprint of Simon & Schuster, Inc.
1230 Avenue of the Americas
New York, NY 10020

This book is published by Gallery Books, a division of Simon & Schuster, under exclusive license from CBS Studios Inc.

First Gallery Books hardcover edition August 2021

GALLERY BOOKS and colophon are registered trademarks of Simon & Schuster, Inc.

Interior design by A. Kathryn Barrett

Manufactured in the United States of America

10 9 8 7 6 5 4 3 2 1

Library of Congress Cataloging-in-Publication data is available.

ISBN 978-1-9821-7519-1
ISBN 978-1-9821-7521-4 (ebook)

To James Mishler,
for always adding +1
to my Wisdom score

Our torments may also, in length of time, become our elements.

—Mammon
Paradise Lost
John Milton

There's no such thing as good money or bad money. There's just money.

—Charles "Lucky" Luciano

HISTORIAN'S NOTE

The events in this story begin in 2391, four years after the death of the Romulan star and one year after the events aboard *U.S.S. ibn Majid* that resulted in Cristóbal Rios leaving Starfleet.

☿ ♃ ♂ ♄ ♀

—2391—

THE WRETCHES OF THE SEA

In which **Cristóbal Rios** *meets a mermaid—*
and takes it on the lam

1

KRELLEN'S KEEP
VEREX III

"Look, I don't want to be a killjoy, but are you gonna sit in that chair or marry it?"

The black-haired customer ignored the starship dealer's yammering. His focus was fully on the seat before him. It didn't look comfortable. Ebon and gray like the rest of the freighter, it appeared to have been built to serve its purpose and nothing more. But Cristóbal Rios regarded the furnishing with reverence, his hands noting every contour.

A captain's chair was a captain's chair.

He heard the nasal voice behind him, again: "Pal, are you all right? You've been standing there a long time."

"It's *been* a long time," Rios mumbled. *Too long.* Without looking back, he asked, "What's the cargo capacity?"

"Plenty. Ninety thousand cubic meters."

"It's a freighter, not a concert hall." Rios turned to face the speaker, the shorter of the pair of starship dealers who had been showing him around the vessel. "Listen—what's your name again?"

"I told you. Twice!"

"Listen, Mister Twice, if you don't know an answer, don't bullshit me. It won't help you make the sale."

"Smart guy's got a mouth," the short one called out to his partner.

"Don't be rude," the reed-thin man said, stepping forward to intercede. "This is Burze—and I am Wolyx, at your service." Wolyx doffed his hat.

Both he and his huskier colleague wore brown slacks and white shirts, but while Burze's sleeves were rolled up sensibly, Wolyx's were buttoned, as was his collar. He wore a tie, to boot. It seemed to Rios an odd choice for Verex III, a barren bit of nastiness where even midwinter was oppressively hot. "Don't you sweat, Wolyx?"

"Oh, no. Not in here." Wolyx lifted his arms in a flourish. "Why would I? This ship is paradise itself. Risa every day."

"If you think this is Risa, you stayed on the wrong planet."

"Quite amusing, sir." The balding trader attempted a smile that Rios found wholly unconvincing. Then he gave up and fanned himself with his hat.

Burze rolled his eyes. "We don't have all day. Have you seen enough?"

"I've *smelled* enough," Rios said. He winced as he took another whiff. "Did something die in here?"

Burze giggled; Wolyx hedged. "It's just this planet, Mister Rios. You've been outside. But in here, all you need do is cycle the air for a minute and—"

"Paradise. I got it."

Rios glanced out the forward port at the parking area. Verex III's volcanic seams vented enough that ground fog was ubiquitous, but he could still make out a number of ships by their silhouettes. One, he noted, was absent: the shuttle that brought him had barely stayed long enough for him to get his duffel out of the hold.

It wasn't wise to linger long at the spaceport, even in daylight, the pilot had said. "*Especially* not then. They can see you coming."

The Federation might be a post-scarcity society, but Verex III was not in the Federation, and possession was doubly implied in the name of Krellen's Keep, the planet's largest outpost. It was also the biggest bazaar in the sector when it came to used starships.

Burze tugged at Rios's arm. "Don't bother looking at that junk out there. We told you, this machine is just what you want. It's a beauty."

Wolyx quickly agreed. "It has everything you could imagine."

"Yeah, it's strewn all over." Rios turned again to look at the debris spread all across the ship's upper level, stretching all the way back to the warp engine. Discarded containers, broken ceramics, parts of some ancient farm implement—even a stuffed Klingon *targ*. And that was nothing next to what he'd seen below on the galley and cargo decks. "Did a chimpanzee program the replicator?"

"A *what*?" Burze asked.

"Which part haven't you heard of?"

"Listen, buddy—"

Wolyx intervened again, nearly stepping on Burze's shoe. "The ship has a very fine replicator. And not one earthly simian."

"Then what about all the junk?" Rios asked.

Burze snickered. "The—uh . . . *former owner* wasn't available to remove his stuff."

Seeing Wolyx shuffling uncomfortably, Rios blinked. *Okay, maybe something* did *die in here.*

Wolyx recovered and grinned. "We simply didn't want to wait to put this little wonder on the market. Consider the rest . . . a *bonus*. A treasure at every turn."

"Free crap. I get it. Is the reason it was carrying so much on board because there's a problem with the towing system?"

"Oh, this model comes with state-of-the-art couplers designed to connect to a variety of cargo modules!"

"Do they still work?"

Wolyx's grin wilted a little. "They require a little service."

"No towing system."

Burze threw up his hands. "When you're done jawing, I'm waiting outside." He passed his partner on the way. "Call if this jerk wants to do more than complain."

As Hard Sell headed downstairs, Soft Sell started in again. "Forgive my associate," Wolyx said. "But I'm sure you'll agree, this ship—this *yacht*, really—is perfection. It's not missing a thing."

"It is," Rios said.

"Impossible!"

Rios gestured to the empty space ahead of the command chair. "Control panels."

"Ah. The Kaplan F17 Speed Freighter captain's interface is holographic. It only appears when authorized."

"I'm not an idiot, Wolyx."

"Of course not. I didn't mean—"

"Authorize it."

"Oh." The dealer shook his head. "No, no, they don't like me to do that."

They? That would be whomever it was that Burze was waiting with, Rios imagined. He upturned his palms. "I said I had to inspect the bridge. Without the interfaces, it's just some chairs and a window. It's an observation lounge."

"Surely, it's more than—"

"I'm not paying for an observation lounge, Wolyx." Rios turned over his hands and lifted them into the air before him. He held them there, fingertips poised over nothing. He shot the dealer ten percent of a smile.

Well?

Wolyx considered for a moment. Then he repeated his own name, followed by a curious phrase: "*The hoard, the hoard, the journey's reward.*"

At those magic words, glowing holographic control interfaces appeared suspended in front of the command seat. Rios glanced at them for a moment before sitting. "Nice passphrase. What is it?"

Wolyx clasped his hands together. "Oh, I chose that. It's from *The Songs of Uthalla*, an Orion classic."

"Sort of 'open sesame.' "

"Oh, you know *A Thousand and One Nights*!" Wolyx's voice bounced. "That phrase probably first appeared in Antoine Galland's version—though I prefer the newer one by Wu Hezar."

The people you meet, Rios thought, his fingers dancing over the glistening controls. "You read a lot, Wolyx?"

"Every chance I get—which sadly isn't often in my trade. But my people take books very seriously."

More than one part of the comment puzzled Rios. The dealer looked human, although that didn't really mean anything. And it was much more common to hear people referring to stories, rather than books. The physical media still existed, to be sure, but for many they were a curio.

Rios included.

"There's another line," Wolyx said, pacing ahead of the navigator's station. " 'For the ship is my castle, this chair my throne.' Now, that really puts into perspective how important—" He stopped as he noticed his listener. "Er, what are you doing?"

Rios allowed the ship's awakening systems to answer for him. He felt the hum through the command chair—and he liked seeing indicators coming online on the display panel of a class of ship he had never piloted before.

No, no rust there.

Wolyx stepped before him and waved his hands in alarm. "Mister Rios, I'm not authorized to allow you to activate the ship."

"You literally *just* authorized me to activate the ship."

"Yes, but that was so you could see there was a console, not to—"

Rios punched a holographic key, and the hum became a thrum, reverberating faster and faster.

"Really, I can't—" Wolyx said, only to be interrupted by a chirp from his personal comm unit. Flustered, he answered it. "What?"

"It's Burze. What's going on?"

"He's started the ship."

"I can see that, moron. Who started the ship?"

"*He* started the ship!"

Rios lifted a finger in the air to correct: "He's *flying* the ship." The freighter lurched off the ground, causing Wolyx to lose his balance—and to drop the communicator. "You might want to find a seat," Rios said.

While Burze ranted inaudibly over the fallen comm unit, Rios peeked outside to see several individuals advancing. Whoever they were, they quickly thought better of it. The freighter's warp nacelles extended well forward from the ship, like a javelin in each outstretched hand; as Rios rotated the ship, everyone on the platform retreated for cover.

Sprightly. The word had been in the sales description he'd been sent, and Rios had found it an odd choice for something that hauled cargo; obviously it had been written by Wolyx rather than Burze. Rios found it to be apt. The freighter spun a full rotation one way and then another as he gained altitude—all while the dealer fumbled alternately for his communicator and his hat. Verex Prime cut through the haze, stabbing light onto the bridge.

"Mister Rios!" Wolyx declared, clutching in vain for an armrest of one of the forward seats. "Descend immediately!"

"Okay." Rios slammed the virtual yoke and hit the throttle, angling downward toward the rock-hewn structures of Krellen's Keep. For a full kilometer, the freighter buzzed just above the ground, startling passersby and barely missing several hovering transports.

He worked the controls swiftly, banking back and forth as he searched for a path to space. Air traffic here, skybridges there—and the freighter, weaving below and between. There were minute performance flaws, little divergences from Rios's expectations. He mentally cataloged them but did not ease back. After another kilometer, he spotted the open sky he was looking for.

There's a genie in this bottle, Rios thought. *Let's let her out.*

2

Verex III

The freighter blazed forward and upward, ripping so near to a towering structure that it scared half the roosting avians right off it. The other half of them took flight a second after that, terrified by the sonic boom.

Wolyx, who had managed to steady himself against a support, was in motion again, too, on a stumbling journey in the worst possible direction: aft. That way led to the open well to the galley deck, and certain injury. He got no closer to it, though, as Rios's arm shot out, allowing him to grab the dealer's tie. He reined the older man toward him before glancing behind him and to the right.

"Chairs," Rios said. "I can't give you a fancy quote about them, but they help."

Gulping, Wolyx composed himself. "Very well." He stumbled to a seat—arriving just in time to be thrown into it as Rios shifted from thrusters to impulse.

The freighter tore from the Verexian atmosphere into space, where a convoy of incoming transports coasted. Rios angled the ship toward them and accelerated. Before the vessels' pilots could react at all, the freighter neatly bisected the caravan. Rios then saw another target, one of the planet's silvery moons. He made for it.

The ship was rounding the airless globe at an elevation of thirty meters when Wolyx's comm unit skittered past his feet, striking the left side of the command chair. Rios scooped it up. Hearing its chime, he answered. "How's it going?"

"Wolyx!"

"Not Wolyx. It's the other guy."

"You!" He could practically see Burze splutter. *"You stole our ship!"*

"Test flight."

"Test—?" Burze shouted louder. *"Do you know who you're dealing with? We don't* do *test flights! You come back here right now, or we'll—"*

Rios lost interest and pitched the communicator toward Wolyx. "It's for you."

The dealer juggled the unit for a moment before letting it fall. It clattered away as the freighter lurched, and Wolyx appeared to decide to let it go. As the freighter cleared a lunar mountain it had been racing toward, he spoke again. "You—uh—have flown before, I take it."

"You get a lot of first-time buyers for ships this size?"

"Not one."

Another topographical near miss, and Wolyx went silent.

One test led to another—and another. The freighter was hurtling in the direction of Verex's primary sun when its sensors detected four approaching contacts. They were massive: dreadnoughts, of the sort Orion pirates used to fly. Rios had seen a few going about their business earlier; now, they seemed alive to his actions.

This time it was the ship's comm system that chirped. The person that appeared on one of the panels on the holographic interface was not Burze—and not happy.

The caller hadn't gotten a syllable out when Rios spoke. "Busy," he said, ending the transmission and gunning the freighter in a screaming arc around the star.

Rios delighted to see the dreadnoughts moving to intercept him. They were the exact kind of craft that might prey on freighters in space unprotected by the Federation or other powers. He figured a deliberate close encounter with one or two of them would be instructive, and he moved to make it happen.

It told him what he needed to know. *Not perfect—but potential.*

Nobody had opened weapons on him, yet, suggesting either that they valued Wolyx—or the freighter. From the dealer's woeful moaning, Rios figured it was probably the latter. He started keying in a quick series of calculations. "Those your people?" he asked.

Wolyx groaned something like an affirmation. His voice creaked. "You—you're not going into warp, are you?"

"I'm sure acting like it." Glancing over, Rios could see the trembling dealer lose what little color he had.

He then directed his attention back to the glowing machinery far behind him in the freighter: the warp core, brightly visible through the field of bric-a-brac. He turned again to the interface, his fingers hovering over the virtual switches that would send the freighter somewhere else—

—and then he dismissed the screen, calling up the impulse controls. The freighter spun quickly and reversed course, lancing between two pursuers and beginning a rapid return to Verex III.

"Oh, no!" Wolyx cried as Rios slammed the freighter against the planet's exosphere, shaking the ship's contents and occupants. Rios braced himself in the chair as he guided the vessel downward through a sea of flames. He didn't know whether the dreadnoughts could make planetfall, but he was pretty sure they couldn't do it *his* way—and he wanted a few extra minutes to himself. He got them, banking the freighter toward Krellen's Keep as soon as it cleared the clouds.

Four minutes later, the ship was on the hazy tarmac—and so was Rios. The freighter's main physical accessway was a loading ramp leading from the lower deck, midpoint starboard; he didn't imagine it got a lot of use, given the cargo transporter he'd seen earlier. He stood at the foot of the ramp and gazed up at the ship, taking stock.

More of the drab gray, and a lot of it—its outboard nacelles likely spanning from goal to center spot on a regulation football pitch. Angry angles jutted from its stern like great metallic fangs; a contribution to aerodynamics, he imagined.

Strolling aft, he did a double take. He counted twelve impulse and thruster ports on the rear of the fuselage, well over what was necessary for a transport of its size. He couldn't believe it was all standard to the model; someone believed in overkill.

And he could easily see a way to add even more.

Movement to the side drew Rios's attention. Wolyx's hat tumbled down the ramp. The dealer followed, clearly a shambles. His necktie had migrated somewhere around his neck, and his face was frozen in a puffy grimace that nearly gave him the look of a frightened Denobulan. Wolyx followed his hat onto the platform, only to stare blankly at it as it stopped.

When he finally looked up and around, his voice was eerily calm. "This isn't the landing pad we were at."

"Sorry. I wanted some more time to look." Rios gestured into the ground fog. "At least I got the right city." He picked up Wolyx's hat. "Here."

"Thank you." The dealer took it—and tried to locate the knot in his tie with his other hand. He appeared to be searching for words, as well, when Rios spoke first.

"It's kind of an odd duck."

"A what?"

"The whole thing." Rios gestured above. "Big nacelles are a damned nuisance to drag around in the wrong atmosphere—the Klingons are smart to avoid them. And the designers clearly think that seeing to port or starboard is overrated. Good thing it's got sensors, because peripheral vision from the cockpit is zilch."

"You—uh—didn't seem to have any problems up there."

"I don't tell anyone my problems."

Seeing Wolyx's discomfort, Rios decided to make an exception. "The mix is off on the cryogenic deuterium before it goes into the impulse reaction chamber—probably using the wrong sequestrant. Something's buggy in the accelerometer grid, too—it's showing up as a little lag in the RCS response. Probably hasn't been recalibrated once since it left the yard. Nobody ever bothers." Rios scratched his beard. "It handled that angle of assault on re-entry better than I expected, but it still shakes too much. It can use some punching up."

"Punching up."

"Yeah. It's okay. With work—a *lot* of work—it's good."

"Good." Wolyx looked down at his hat and laughed, seemingly in spite of himself. "What's the line? 'Her destiny depends on the power of another.' "

Rios looked at him, a little startled. "What'd you say?"

Wolyx repeated the line. "It's from another story—I don't remember which one. I think it was about a statue or something."

Rios stared up again at the ship. "No. *La sirena*."

"Come again?"

"A mermaid," Rios said. With more reverence, he added, "*A mermaid has not an immortal soul, nor can she obtain one unless she wins the love of a human being.*"

"Ah!" Wolyx snapped his fingers. "Christian Andrews!"

"Hans Christian Andersen. It's from—"

Before Rios could finish, a much deeper voice called out, "Are you a trader, or a poet?"

"He's neither," Burze said, rounding the nacelle. "He's a chiseling pirate!"

The dealer was accompanied, Rios saw, by a much larger companion, similarly dressed.

"Stealing ships is no way to act," the deep-voiced newcomer said as he advanced toward Rios.

Burze stepped to the side and pointed. "Paste him good, Dinky!"

Rios stared. "*Dinky?*"

Wolyx yelled—but Rios didn't hear what he said, as something hit him in the back of the head. He stumbled forward but stayed on his feet, turning to see that "Dinky" was only one of several approaching assailants, all similarly proportioned.

Rios was just dazed enough to wonder if they also had incongruous nicknames—

—but that stray thought vanished as the nearest one pounced. Rios took a step to the side, dodging the bruiser. From his new position, he delivered a punch to the side of the goon's jaw. Then it was time to move, as someone else tried to return the favor.

"Stop! He's a customer!" Rios heard Wolyx's cry this time, but his attackers either didn't hear or didn't care. One against four—or six, going by mass—was a ratio he'd faced in the past year, and it had usually ended badly for him. But this time he was sober, and the scrap went on for a good thirty seconds before they cornered him against one of the nacelles.

Rios wiped the blood from his face with the back of his clenched fist and smiled. "Had enough?"

They apparently had, because the weapons came out, one by one. Disruptor. Phaser. Blackjack. Revolver.

Revolver?

Rios knew weapons; he'd even collected them back when he had a place to put them. But that particular firearm made him take another look at how the heavies were dressed. These weren't garden-variety thugs at all. No, these were a very particular and peculiar sort, almost too improbable to exist and yet nonetheless very real, and capable of killing him.

Or rubbing him out.

He glanced over at Burze and Wolyx and chuckled. "I should have had you guys at 'killjoy.'" He turned back to face the weapons. "How are things on Sigma Iotia?"

Founding "Godfathers": The Iotian Paradox

D. S. Whalen, Starfleet Academy Press, 2368

(Excerpt from the introduction)

Sigma Iotia II and its denizens have long inspired both wonder and bafflement in others. Writing today, in the centenary year of James T. Kirk and *Starship Enterprise*'s visit to the planet, the "Iotian phenomenon" has only grown more intriguing.

The Iotians are far from the only species in known space adept at quickly assimilating new technologies, and it would be difficult to find any world in the Federation where the cultures of isolated tribes weren't contaminated—or worse—by contact with outsiders from other lands. But nothing compares to the Iotians' swift and total adoption of the language, modes, and values peculiar to a vanishingly brief time period on another planet—and even less explains the determination to cling to many of those traits long after their otherworldly origin became common knowledge. In the informal words of Bakinski, the Iotians are now "in on the joke," yet seem completely unbothered by it.

The sequence of events that made it all possible is infamous, yet has never lost its ability to shock. Stretches of chaotic, planetwide violence had been common for Sigma Iotia II; its factions were numerous, small, and ever changing. Familiar fault lines that divided other planetary populations such as species, race, geography, language, and class do not appear to have been barriers for ancient Iotians, though our understanding of that time is sorely limited. History requires institutions to survive long enough to record it. The Iotians never gave any the chance.

No, they were too busy fighting over matters non-Iotians would consider whimsical. Warfare over negligible, even nonsensical differences may sometimes be found on worlds with an overabundance of leisure time, but the Sigma Iotia II of old was not a world of plenty. Not until the Earth ship *Horizon* visited during a period of relative calm in 2168—and left behind a collection of books.

Whether they were left intentionally or not remains a matter for speculation, since the *Horizon* was lost. What is known is that the assortment included, among several guides for planetary improvement, a book called *Chicago Mobs of the Twenties*, which the Iotians took to be just one more instruction manual. A glance at the work easily explains the error. The oversized 1992 hardcover volume—of which the *Horizon* copy appears to have been the last surviving specimen—overflows with details, and is lavishly filled with illustrations of period fashions and technology. Its catalog of expressions from the era is so exhaustive that today's researchers still refer to it to decode ancient texts and recordings. Where else would one turn when hearing that a tomato's new oyster fruit was the bee's knees?

Most significantly, *Chicago Mobs* contained a detailed description of the power relationships and many of the practices employed by criminals in Midwestern North America in the 1920s. The other *Horizon* volumes held much knowledge, but nothing whatsoever about how society should be structured. What better model, then, than a book detailing the years when criminal behavior in the United States went from being disjointed and independent to organized and hierarchical?

It is no coincidence that, while the Iotians duplicated "the Book" millions of times for mass distribution, the very earliest identified reprints appear to have been the ones holding places of honor in every faction boss's headquarters. Indeed, it might have been the only kind of magna carta the Iotians *could* have adopted, since it showed how their past propensity for violence could be made to function as part of—and I use this term with all irony—good government. "The book glorified as it codified," Ambassador Spock later said. "It suggested that when random violence became targeted, influence flowed to the ones doing the targeting. The Iotians found order—of a violent kind."

The Earth period inspiring the Iotians was indeed savage, as this author painfully found a few years ago in a holodeck accident that gained some notoriety. So, too, did the Iotians remain murderous for the next century, with the distinct change that the tribes involved grew both in size and cohesiveness. Told that "turf" was a thing worth fighting for, Iotians warred over something rather than nothing. It was their first collective agreement.

While encyclopedic in many ways, *Chicago Mobs* gave little attention to certain crimes its subjects were involved in; perhaps the editorial strictures of 1992 were more puritanical. "Bathtub gin" flows freely through its pages, for example, but narcotics do not appear at all. And while the era's retrograde gender roles are covered, the mechanics of sexual exploitation are not, leaving Iotians to interpret vice within their own species' context. *Enterprise*'s crew encountered streetwalkers who practiced no trade and gun molls who never said anything. "They just stood around as if posing for a picture," Leonard McCoy later said. That is exactly what they were doing, we now know: mimicking images seen in the Book, and no more.

The omission of such matters was fortunate for the Iotian people, because they certainly invented everything else they needed to make their other crimes possible. Hard currency. The firearms they used to steal it. The automobiles they used to carry it. The playing cards they used to gamble it away. And, of course, there was alcohol—though there was no governmental force to impose Prohibition, and little evidence that the chemical compound impacted Iotian biology anyway.

It was this state of affairs that confronted Captain Kirk in 2268. His gambit, achieving planetary peace by positioning the Federation as a rival criminal "outfit" demanding tribute, had many critics then, and certainly no modern captain would dare attempt it. The wrongs *did* combine to make a right, as Kirk had hoped, but it became a close-run thing due to another equally infamous blunder. The abandonment—definitely accidental, this time—of a personal communicator by a member of the *Enterprise* landing party.

The speed with which the Iotians came to understand its transtator technology and subsequently find their way to the stars could have led to disastrous consequences, especially as the species came to realize that *Enterprise*'s frightful weapons were not magic, but something they could wield themselves. Imagine the acquisitiveness of the Borg, but only a few years removed from completely random violence and organized into paramilitary units. The Chicago gangs aspired to Roman legion-hood, after all. The result could have been catastrophic.

That it did not happen was thanks to skillful work by Starfleet's second-contact—actually, *third*-contact—personnel. As Kirk's appointed leader came to understand what the "Feds" really were, he also learned what they were not: "chumps" ripe for criminal exploitation. The Federation's economy was not based on financial gain, and the bulk of its territory separated the Iotians from regions with systems more to their liking. The Iotians might prize "easy pickings," but none of their neighbors had pockets to pick.

With little to reward expansion, the Iotian Syndicate—as the new regime was called—managed to keep most of its people home, forming a society that grew less violent, as the *Enterprise* officers had hoped. Some would-be rival gangs departed the planet, but the diaspora in fact worked to stabilize the culture, leaving the majority of Iotians free to become peaceful and productive members of the galactic community.

A most confounding mystery remains, however, among both the expatriates and those who never left. Despite their imitative gifts and exposure to the greater universe, most Iotians remain devoted to the sartorial fashions and speech patterns learned from the Book—with those who emigrated clinging additionally to the practices it described.

This, the paradox of this work's title, will be fully explored in later sections. Several decade-long cultural studies are examined—as are some of the biological-based explanations. Significant space is also devoted to examining the contentious "Born Krako" theory, which poses that Iotia's bosses, underbosses, captains, and soldiers correspond to distinct pre-existing subspecies who mentally imprint on the actions of those of higher genetic rank. Critiques of that theory are also covered.

Cultural historians tend to avoid simpler answers when more nuanced ones are available, but "the Iotian Paradox" may come down to a basic matter of taste. When I recently put the question to the current syndicate boss, he answered, "Ain't it easy? We just like the suits!"

3

KRELLEN'S KEEP
VEREX III

The room had modern climate-control equipment, but the Iotians had installed ceiling fans anyway. Rios had spent long minutes puzzling over that one as his eyes followed the blades round and round. The rest of the world had been spinning for him for the better part of an hour, so it matched nicely.

That Rios was only roughed up and not dead owed to a call Burze had received at the landing pad. The goons had used an antiquated method of delivering him here: a replica of an early twentieth-century automobile, likely fabricated in the same faraway facility where the Iotians got their ceiling fans. Earth's early astronauts were pikers; they had only taken a cart to the Moon. The Iotians had carried their jalopy billions of times as far, apparently just so they could drive over every pothole in Krellen's Keep. Rios had felt each impact while locked in the trunk. There weren't many Romulans left in the torture business anymore, but they could learn a thing or two from the Iotians.

He stood now only because of the thugs on either side of him, who were holding him up. Dinky, the walking tank, was one. The other, an edgy youngster skinnier than Wolyx, apparently answered to Stench. And he didn't like to hear about it—least of all from Rios, who, having nothing better to do, brought it up every few minutes.

"So, kid, if Stench is your real name, what do you do for a nickname? Stinkles?"

"Shut your mouth!"

"No, I'm interested. You're Stench, he's Dinky. Does your society balance descriptive names and ironic ones? An equal number, is that it?" He glanced at the dolt on his left. "Or does Dinky refer to something else?"

The bruiser smacked him with the back of his hand.

Rios felt it—but shook it off. "Hey, I'm a guest here. Just trying to learn."

Burze, waiting in front of a large closed door with Wolyx, snarled. "That's enough out of you!"

"Why don't *you* guys have nicknames?" Rios asked. "Miss a meeting?"

"This is ridiculous." Burze threw up his hands and jabbed at a button on the wall. "C'mon, answer!"

Wolyx, who had spent much of the last hour pleading for mercy for Rios, stared nervously at the door. "You shouldn't do that, Burze. We were called. They know we're here."

Burze rolled his eyes. "We wait for a break, it'll be next year." He pushed the button again.

Wolyx's expression went from worry to sadness when he looked at Rios. "I'm truly sorry. I've tried to tell them that you didn't mean any harm."

"I know," Rios said, and he left it at that. One kindly captor more or less wasn't going to matter much in the end, and it was no use hoping for a rescue. Not out here.

Verex III sat in a region that had once been known as the Borderland, a lawless territory long plagued by roving Orion syndicates. The creation of the Romulan Neutral Zone nearby had resulted in more Starfleet patrols, lending some stability to the area for a couple of centuries. But the destruction of the Romulan star had put everyone on the move—and travelers always attracted opportunists. It took many local planetary societies less than a decade to return to the bad old days—and without the urgency of the Romulan military threat, the Federation's commitment to the region had dwindled.

That was no surprise to Rios, who knew that the Federation wasn't the moral arbiter of the galaxy, no matter what it pretended to be. Neither was Starfleet; his own recent experiences had brought that truth painfully home to him. It was the reason he was in the market for a starship of his own in the first place. But even in the best of times, he doubted the Federation had ever gotten one of its citizens out of a jam on Verex III.

He'd been warned: *"The last time a Starfleet vessel dropped by, Jonathan Archer was commanding it."* He didn't know if that was a joke or not, but he had to face facts. Unless he thought of something fast, he was likely to wind up incinerated, encased in concrete galoshes, or whatever the hell these weirdos did.

"Come on, come on," Burze said, punching at the button again. Then he saw Rios staring off to the side. "What're *you* looking at?"

Rios nodded to the stand on the dealer's left, where a cigar had been smoldering in an ashtray full of butts. "Can I have a smoke?"

Stench chuckled. "We're not up to last requests yet."

Wolyx faced the table. "I'm not sure you really want one."

"You have no idea," Rios said. There were several more cigars going in other trays in the room, and the smell had driven him to distraction. "Give."

"If you insist."

As Wolyx found a box in a drawer, Rios thought quickly. He wasn't worried about the punk on his right, but he wasn't likely to break free from Dinky's hold without a weapon. He hadn't wanted to consider biting the guy, but having something on fire clenched in his teeth gave him some options.

But before any of that, he wanted a puff. He watched as Wolyx fretfully clipped the end off a stogie.

"Good man," Rios said as the dealer placed the cigar in his mouth. "A light?"

"I *really* don't think I should, Mister Rios."

"Wolyx. They've got my arms. Where am I going to get a light? Come on."

Wolyx sighed. "If you say so." He produced a lighter and ignited the cigar.

Rios inhaled—and choked. "*Madre de dios!*" Wincing, he spat the vile thing to the floor. "*That's awful!*"

His violent coughing joined a symphony of laughter from the other goons.

"We don't smoke," Wolyx said as he ground his shoe on the cigar.

Eyes watering, Rios glanced from one ashtray to another. "Then what are all those? Incense burners?"

"More or less," Wolyx replied. "The Book described the practice of smoking—and the value of smoking implements as merchandise. But our planet grew nothing usable, and what we discovered offworld disagreed with us. The paraphernalia is used now more as decoration—as motif."

"Well, good for you," Rios said. He still wanted a smoke.

He also wanted to kick himself. This was just the kind of stupid jam he'd been getting into for nearly a year. He'd only come to Verex III through the intervention of a friend who wanted better for him than he had lately wanted for himself—and now he'd blown this up, too. All because—*why?* A couple of merchants weren't going to let him do exactly what he wanted?

How did one go from a regimented life to a total flameout so fast?

The answer was not in the concrete floor, no matter how long he stared at it. More minutes passed, with his captors discussing in detail what might happen to him—and Burze pressing the button to no avail. But there were more sounds from beyond the door: horrible screeches, almost bleats of pain of a kind Rios had never heard before. It set Burze and pals laughing again, while Wolyx swallowed uncomfortably.

Okay, maybe it does help to have a friend, Rios thought. It was time to make a different play, one he'd been avoiding. "Wolyx, you remember where I arranged to meet you guys, right?"

"Outside the Tellarite mining dock at the spaceport."

"Right. I left my duffel at the Traveler's Aid office," Rios said. It was the only place he trusted. "Contact them—and have them send it here."

"What, are you trying to call your buddies for help?" Burze said. He laughed. "They won't come—not here. The Tellarites know who we are!"

"No help. I just want my bag."

Stench was his jittery self. "What, have you got a weapon in there?"

Rios thought about how to answer. "Nothing that would be any use here—except maybe to straighten this mess out."

"Fine. Then *I'll* get it," Burze said.

"Nope. Wolyx gets it—or nobody. I set up a code word with the office. You remember what I called the ship, Wolyx?"

Wolyx stood stone-faced for a moment, before brightening. "Yes!" Then his brow furrowed. "But I don't remember what it was in that other language you used."

"Standard will do fine."

Stench shouted at Wolyx as he started walking, communicator in hand. "Hey, nobody here agreed to this!"

"I did. I'll be back," Wolyx said. He was out the door in seconds.

More time passed, during which Rios felt rumbling through the floor. Something industrial was going on elsewhere in the building—likely beyond Burze's precious door. None of it boded well.

Neither did Wolyx's face, when he returned, crestfallen. "I called—but I don't think they believed me."

Burze sneered. "Of course not. I told you, they know who we are."

"You gave them the code word?" asked Rios, alarmed.

"I did everything just as you asked." Wolyx hung his head—and a moment later, a clanging noise jolted everyone to attention. The metal door Burze had been waiting beside went into motion, rattling upward into its frame.

Dinky and Stench jolted Rios into motion. Burze smiled. "You're in for it now, smart mouth."

"I'm sorry," Wolyx said.

So am I, Rios thought.

4

Krellen's Keep
Verex III

From his captors' chatter and the horrific sounds he'd heard, Rios had expected he was heading into an abattoir—but there were no meat hooks in sight, or even a single bloodstain. Instead, the cavernous space the thugs shoved him into resembled a large counting room.

Or rather, he considered, what the Iotians *thought* a counting room looked like. Hanging lamps illuminated more than a dozen tables, each of which held mounds of multicolored coins, gems, and credits. Rios figured they were the hard currencies of dozens of powers, on Verex III and off, whose current and former residents made their way through Krellen's Keep every day.

He'd expected to see at least some gold-pressed latinum, by far the most popular means of exchange for trade outside the Federation. None was in sight. Maybe it was too dear to be entrusted to the counters, a platoon of Iotians in shirts and ties tabulating feverishly away as their so-called "cigars" burned in trays. Three toughs with old-fashioned machine guns kept an eagle watch on the workers.

Through a yawning portal farther to the rear, Rios saw what must have made the machinery sounds he'd heard: old-fashioned forklifts moving goods about a warehouse area. Material acquired in the Iotians' rackets, he imagined. It was a wonder anybody shipped anything through the spaceport at Krellen's Keep.

Finally, there was the tall figure in the middle of the counting room, directing it all. Rios hadn't seen any images of women from Iotia; going off what he'd seen in pictures from early twentieth-century Earth, he'd imagined they mostly wore skirts or dresses. Instead, this woman wore a shirt and button-down vest with loose-fitting slacks that allowed her to walk quickly from station to station. Her golden-brown hair anchored a beret that Rios assumed had to be pinned on, because it never slipped once as she whirled from table to table, a dictatorial dervish issuing commands.

She gave orders to the messengers lined up to see her. She gave orders to the bean counters, who apparently needed constant lessons in exchange rates and remedial math. And she gave orders to people somewhere else, via the two different comm units she held, one in each hand.

"—don't care *what* his sainted mother says about him," she said into one, her voice sharp. "We're not running a charity here. He makes good or it comes out of your end. Savvy?"

She switched to the other. "No. I said nineteen, and I meant nineteen. With ears like yours you'd think they worked!"

Back to the first. "Why are you still talking? Get to it!"

Then to one of the counters nearby: "I see what you're doing. You're supposed to count the gems *here*, not later at home!"

There was a flinty edge to her voice, Rios thought, a rat-a-tat-tat to her cadence. Metaphors involving knives and guns came readily to mind around the Iotians, but there was a reason for that. They fit. One of the armed guards already had the accused pilferer in a headlock, causing rubies to tumble from beneath his sleeves.

"Time for your break," the woman curtly declared. Judging from the culprit's wailing as he was dragged into the warehouse, Rios assumed she wasn't referring to a stop for coffee.

From the new arrivals' vantage point on the periphery, Burze called over to her. "Hey, *Ledger*! We got something for you!"

"Who let *you* in?" She didn't look back to see who it was.

"You just did!"

"That was thirty seconds ago. I'm busy."

Wolyx spoke up, his voice shaky. "It's important, Miss Ledger."

"Blow, d'you hear? And call me 'miss' again and they'll find you floating in the nearest body of water."

"That might be a few systems away," Rios said.

The woman they'd called Ledger slammed the comm unit in her left hand on the desk. "All right, who's the—" She stopped midsentence when she beheld the prisoner. "What on Earth?"

"Odd expression," Rios mumbled.

She started toward him. "Well, look what the cat dragged in!"

"And there's another." He looked beside him to Stench. "They have cats where you come from?"

"Shut it," the kid said under his breath, his hold tightening as the woman approached. It was clear that whatever sway she had over the counters extended to the thugs.

A moment later she was practically in Rios's face. Lively hazel eyes looked him up and down. "What cave did they snatch *you* from?"

"He's Cristóbal Rios," Wolyx said. "He's a customer!"

"Customer, my eye," Burze corrected. "He's a crook. This crumb tried to glom the Kaplan over at pad eighteen!"

"I know the story," Ledger said, still eyeing Rios closely.

"He didn't get away with it." Burze pounded his own chest with his fist. "We nabbed him!"

"Applesauce! He made suckers out of you saps."

Rios laughed at her.

"What's funny?"

"I just can't believe you're for real. I mean, I took the class like everyone else—"

"Class? What class?"

"*Classes*, actually. Nobody leaves the Academy without knowing about Iotia."

"*Academy?*" Wolyx blurted.

"Yeah, you're all part of the first lesson on the Prime Directive," Rios said. "Then sophomores get you again in Second-Contact Practices. I didn't take the senior seminar—one chapter by Whalen was plenty. Guy loved to clear his throat."

Wolyx seemed starry-eyed. "Yes, it makes sense now. You didn't tell me you were in Starfleet."

"That's because I'm not."

Burze blew up. "Why are we mollycoddling this guy? We should have given him the bum's rush at the start."

"There it is," Rios muttered. "I knew that one was coming."

"What one?" Ledger asked.

"*Bum's rush.* Are you going to tighten the screws next? Or put me on a meat wagon?" He smirked. "I'm loving this."

Dinky shook him by the arm so hard that Stench lost hold of Rios entirely. "Can we bust him up now, Ledge?"

Stench spoke up. "Yeah, let us take care of him. He's been asking for it all day!"

"Have not," Rios said. "I've been asking stuff like, in the unlikely event Stench here ever procreated, would his kids be named for their flaws? Or is the ironic name thing recessive?"

"Shut up!" the kid yelled.

Ledger didn't seem amused. "Full of himself, this one." She waved Stench off before turning around and marching back into the counting area. "They call me Ledger, Mister Rios. Do you know why?"

"Because you got luckier than these guys?"

"Because I keep tabs on everything." She picked up a padd, one of the few modern devices Rios had seen in the room. "I've got better things to do than babysit these dewdroppers, but freighters aren't cheap. Nobody's going to make off with one on my watch—even if they do know Raffi Musiker."

Another former Starfleet officer, Raffi had set up Rios's visit to the bazaar on Verex III, but she hadn't told him anything about the people he'd be meeting. He'd assumed they were peculiar characters; so many of the people she knew were. Raffi wasn't much better. But she hadn't said anything about her contacts being from Iotia, which suggested to him she hadn't known that fact.

How could anybody *not* mention these twerps?

It didn't matter now. "That's right," he said. "Raffi vouched for me. You know her?"

"Never met her," Ledger said. "But she rates with the big cheese somehow—which is the only reason my salespeople took your meeting." She gestured to the hoods holding him. "Looks like you also met the delinquency department."

"They're definitely delinquents."

"Cute." She turned and began shuffling through material piled on one of the tables. "I've got things to do. You really expect me to believe that was just a joyride?"

"I came back, didn't I?"

Burze sneered. "Only after the dreadnoughts got after him!"

Rios glowered at him. "They didn't stop me."

"I noticed that," Ledger said, looking up. "Words will be spoken to the relevant parties."

"Those were heavy cruisers," Rios said. "What are *you guys* doing with those?"

"What do you mean?"

Burze figured it out. "He thinks we're small-time."

"Small-time?" Stench erupted. "You're dealing with the Convincers, pal!"

"*The Convincers?*" Another new one on Rios. "Sounds like a debate club."

Ledger looked to the gun-toting guards, now flanking her. "Show him what a Convincer is." At her command, they sprayed the ceiling with automatic projectile fire. "Some club!" she shouted over the din.

Whatever response she'd expected from Rios, he didn't give it to her. Instead, he just stared at the ceiling, which was now raining dust from multiple holes. "What was the point of that?"

"It makes an impression!" Burze shouted.

"Certainly with your upstairs neighbors."

"We don't have any."

"Not anymore." The patch of ceiling anchoring one of the ceiling fans gave way, bringing the whole assembly crashing down onto a table, scattering both coins and the people counting them. "I hope you get those fans in bulk," Rios said.

Ledger shot a withering look at the fool who'd shot down the fixture—and gave the next one to Rios. "You think this is a game."

"That's the word," Rios said, glancing about. "It's *all* a game, your whole thing here. Why rob when you can replicate?"

"You Feds have done that slogan to death back home. But you know very well there are things that can't be replicated—and others for which people will accept no substitute." She crossed her arms. "It's why we need freighters—and even where you come from, nobody's just going to give one to any loser who comes along."

Rios knew there was truth to that.

"So you come to us," she continued, again brandishing the padd. "But you show up with no money—and from the records I see here, you have no assets anywhere else at all."

His eyes widened. "You can check that?"

"We're a financial institution, like any other." She waved the padd. "Says here you *were* once in Starfleet, but never served on any ship at all, as near as I can tell."

Rios started to say that wasn't true. That he'd served on *U.S.S. ibn Majid*—that he was her second-in-command, in fact. But there was a reason that wasn't in the records: the same reason that had brought him here, without prospects and practically without friends.

And that reason looked, here, to be the end of him. "I think they bounced you," she said. "So you came all the way out here, thinking you could rook some poor yokels out of their property in order to keep playing officer." She snapped her fingers, summoning one of the other gun-toting guards. "There's no evidence you were here to deal—which means you're here to steal."

"I told you, I was just testing the ship. You—"

Another sequence of bellowing squeals came from somewhere beyond the warehouse, reverberating throughout the counting room. A few of the counters shifted in their seats but otherwise kept on working. Was it the gem stealer, meeting his end? Possibly, but it didn't sound human—or Iotian.

Either way, Rios didn't want to find out. "A test flight. All it was. Wolyx, tell her." Rios looked over, only to see that the dealer had stepped away sometime, perhaps during the earlier commotion. "Wolyx?"

"Tough luck," Burze said. "Looks like he—"

Rios interrupted. "I swear, if you say he took a powder, I'll strangle you with your tie."

"Good luck trying." Burze smiled toothily as the gunman approached. "Think I'll stick around. This'll be fun to watch!"

5

Krellen's Keep
Verex III

So this is the abattoir, Rios thought as blood squished beneath his boots. *I didn't think they'd be so literal.*

Here were the hooks on the ceiling he'd imagined earlier, many of them suspending limbless bodies so rent he wasn't able to tell what species they'd ever belonged to. Rivulets of crimson liquid streamed from them, some of it pooling in enormous ceramic vats that sat atop wheeled dollies. The problem was that the Convincers had more bodies than vats, which meant the red rain just added to the centimeter-thick sheen coating the floor.

"You guys ever heard of a mop?" Rios shouted. But whether his captors had or not, there was no sign they had heard *him*—or anything else—over the screams.

And such screams. Inhuman, because they were.

These were the sounds he'd first heard three rooms away in the waiting area through a thick metal door: the death cries of countless five-legged hairless ungulates, tumbling haphazardly down conveyor belts from truck trailers parked side by side at a back entrance. The howling creatures, each as tall as Rios, disappeared into a colossal black machine. The monstrous contraption thundered away, dueling the animals with decibels until they could be heard no more.

When the device finished with a load of the creatures and its internal motors spun down, Rios half expected a mechanical belch. Instead, metal doors on its backside opened, disgorging the results of the slaughter onto the mound of charnel already on the floor.

It was then that Rios saw them. Shirtless individuals plodded into view from either side of the machine. Each carried a sturdy staff with a hook on the end; Rios thought they looked like the pike poles he'd seen in old images of logging and fishing. Wordlessly, they began poking at the kill. Rios could barely tell that the workers belonged to several different species; that was because they, like the carcasses they plucked from the pile, were completely drenched in blood. Indeed, the haggard expressions they all wore seemed to unify them as members of a new race: prisoners of hell.

Dinky shoved Rios forward, causing him to lose his footing in the slop on the floor. The thugs laughed as he went down with a disgusting splash.

This is it, then. But in getting to his hands and knees, Rios noticed that the gunman Ledger had dispatched with them wasn't pointing his weapon. "What, you're not going to kill me?"

"You *want* us to kill you?" was Burze's snide response.

"No, I'm good." Rios looked back to the loading dock, where another truck was backing toward the landing. He could see through its slat-paneled tailgate more of the creatures, bleating like mad as their sensory organs registered what they were approaching. "What are these things?"

"Out of luck," Stench said. "The Verexians call 'em zylladons. There's a native bunch that raises them."

Back on his feet, Rios made a futile effort to flick the blood from his hands. "Didn't think you guys would be into rustling livestock. Did someone leave you another book when we weren't looking?"

"Naw," Burze said. "The tribe uses these things to pay us for protection. Ledger figured out that the blood is nectar to the Klingons." He pointed to one of the vats being wheeled out by a worker. "Even better, it's illegal in Klingon space."

"Bootlegging blood hooch," Rios said. "Okay, that tracks. Ledger thought of this?"

"Yeah, she's got all kinds of little side hustles."

Stench chortled. "Maybe too many!"

Rios watched the latest truck back up well to the right of the slaughter machine's intake, allowing laborers access to the contraption's innards. He couldn't imagine a worse job than doing dental work on the thing immediately after a meal. "I assume your ships have transporters," he said. "Why don't you just beam the animals here?"

"The tribals flip their lids when we use it," Burze said. "And what do you care? Driver's gotta make a living. You trying to take a lug's job, now?"

"This one's *got* a job," growled the gunman, who hadn't spoken until now. Rios thought the guy sounded like an elephant was sitting on his vocal cords. He prodded Rios to a spot where weary laborers used their pikes to hang the zylladon carcasses on the hooks above. "Get him a pike."

So that's it. "How long do I have to do it?"

"Until you drop," the gunman said.

"So it *is* a death sentence."

Burze looked to his colleagues. "On the way to the freighter, this guy barely says a word. Now he won't shut up."

A laborer offered Rios one of the poles. He looked at it—and then the worker, with sudden recognition. Somewhere behind the smeared blood and the beleaguered expression was the money counter Ledger had banished for stealing. Rios swallowed. *Not thirty minutes here, and the guy already looks like this?*

He had no intention of sticking around that long—not now, when the Iotians had finally made the mistake he was waiting on. More than one, in fact. He glanced over at the truck that had arrived. The driver had apparently taken a break, leaving the door open and the motor running. *Yeah, that'll do.* Rios wasn't entirely sure how to operate it, but he had driven many vehicles. How hard could it be?

Rios dried his hands on his backside before taking the pike. Then, with one bushy black eyebrow ever-so-slightly raised, he looked over at Burze. "No other way, huh?"

"Get on with it!"

Fine. He tromped a few steps through the blood and pierced one of the corpses with the tool. Once he liked the hold, he heaved upward on the pole with both hands, lifting the body. He turned partway, giving every indication he was headed for one of the hooks over the vats. Burze and Stench guffawed to see the Convincers' new employee in action.

His service was short. Rios pivoted quickly and extended his arms, allowing the pole and its grisly cargo to serve as a sort of weapon he was familiar with: a flail. The carcass wasn't light, and the effort it took was immense—but the effect on the thugs was greater. The body slung wide, showering Burze's face with blood, midlaugh. Its arcing journey continued, causing a panicked Stench to stumble backward. His ass landed squarely in the guck.

Rios continued the rotation with a twist of the pole that caused the zylladon's body to slip free from the hook. The macabre missile struck Ledger's gunman in the chest, causing him to drop the machine gun. Seeing Dinky heading toward him, Rios slung the pike itself. The giant dropped—and so did Rios, making a running slide through the scarlet goo. It ended with him on the ground near the far wall—and in possession of the fallen automatic weapon.

"Get him!" yelled Burze, rubbing his eyes, still blinded from his faceful of blood. Rios could see fine. Stench and Dinky were going for their shoulder holsters, while more gorillas, likely the room's usual watchmen, were on their way in.

Rios had already decided spraying the air and ceiling wouldn't do much to unnerve thugs who saw such displays every day. Instead, he took aim at the ceramic vats lining the far side of the room and fired.

The sides of the containers gave out instantly under the onslaught, issuing a torrent of blood toward the center of the room. Rios paused his fusillade for just a moment so he could target the stacked cases of bottles he'd seen farther away—and closer to the entering guards. More vital fluids for the floor—but also a spray of glass.

The initial Iotian charge rapidly turned comical. Whatever taste for blood the toughs might have had didn't extend to being showered by it—and they certainly weren't as nimble when ankle-deep in it. "Wrong shoes, *amigos*!" Rios called out as one after another slipped—but he wasn't staying for the fun. Instead, he turned and ran toward the parked truck.

The returning driver, seeing him charging with the gun raised, yelled in panic and leaped out of sight. But Rios had a different target in mind. He fired at the chains sealing the back of the truck—and dove to the side himself as the gate flew open, freeing its terrified cargo. Dozens of terrified zylladons surged forward—and finding the vehicle out of position with the killing machine, leaped across the loading dock and streamed into the warehouse.

Rios had his own counterassault going, but it wasn't done. Enslaved workers, initially fleeing the stampede alongside the Convincers, remembered the pikes they carried and recognized their chance. Having stepped onto a ledge to avoid the charge, Rios saw his own opportunity. He gingerly stepped off the loading dock into the now-darkening street and made for the truck's cab.

The motor was still running: more luck. Taking his seat, he paused, heart racing, as he confronted the controls. He knew what some of them did—but the particular arrangement here came as a surprise. One lever beside the steering column stuck out as a possible gearshift—or was it the parking brake? Maybe both? Clutch, brake, throttle—but in what order? Was the Ruckstell transmission being used then? It was a hell of a time to think back on automotive history.

He put down the gun onto the seat beside him and jammed one of the sticks forward, only to hear an angry grind. His stomach fell with the realization that the Iotians might not have aped any particular model—that what he remembered of early automotive controls might not be of any use. How much detail was in the books they had, anyway?

I really should have taken that senior seminar . . .

"That's enough," declared a voice from outside. Rios turned to look into the muzzle of a pistol—and behind it, the furious eyes of Ledger, standing on the road beside the truck.

Rios's hand moved toward his own weapon, only to see another gangster pointing a gun through the passenger window. Rios thought to jam on a random pedal on the floor to see what happened, but it was too late. Both doors were now open, and his weapon was being plucked from the seat.

He looked down at Ledger and flashed a weary grin. "Sorry, no riders."

"You're a laugh riot. Down."

6

KRELLEN'S KEEP
VEREX III

They had him again. Only this time, he was out in the alley behind the Convincers' warehouse, standing in the twilight amid what were probably the only metal garbage cans on Verex III.

A few more hours of this, Rios thought, *and I'll have toured the whole city block.*

Only he didn't expect to have that time—not given the warpath Ledger seemed to be on. She'd apparently emerged from the counting room through a different exit, missing all the fun—but the blow he'd dealt to local Iotian fashion said plenty. All the underlings who emerged from the warehouse to confer with Ledger had gone from dapper to damaged. "Did your Book have a chapter on—what did they call it—dry cleaning?"

"That's enough from you," Ledger said. "Besides, I've never even read the damn thing."

"No? I thought that was a membership requirement or something."

"Earth has a slew of important books. How many have *you* read?"

"Never have the time."

"I wouldn't make any plans if I were you."

Rios watched her place her pistol in her small handbag. "I was surprised to see you. They told me you never do the dirty work."

"I've never been this mad. Do you have any idea what you've done to this operation?" Padd in hand, she ticked off the items. Massive damage had been done to the blood hooch inventory, of course, but the stampede had made it into the main stockroom, extending the destruction. The worker rebellion had been put down, but several had escaped, as had many of the zylladons. And some others of those had made it as far as the counting room.

"Did you know zylladons ate Tikatian banknotes?" Ledger asked.

"No."

"Neither did we!" She called forth a couple of fresh gunmen and pointed to the intersection up the way. "Take him for a walk."

Rios glanced in that direction. "You're going to kill me in the street?"

"That's how you send messages, sailor. Where people can see them."

"What message?"

"*Don't cross the Convincers!*"

"My body will say that? Shouldn't you leave a note?" He looked to the gunmen—and into the soiled, angry faces of the toughs he'd humiliated, looking for any out.

Dinky did raise an issue. "Ain't he the pal of the boss's friend?"

"My job, my decision." Ledger looked to Rios. "That concludes our business. On your way."

Burze, an unsightly mess, laughed. "Last call, Charlie!"

"What is it with the names around here?" Rios asked as they prodded him forward.

He was only a few meters into the deadly march when a motorcar screamed around the corner. As it was heading directly toward them, his escorts raised their weapons. "It's a hit!" one yelled.

Rios gawked. "A what?"

"You think we're the only Iotians here?" Seeing the vehicle stop, the guards trained their weapons on it.

"Wait!" Ledger shouted. Rios saw she'd moved to a position of cover. "That car's one of ours!"

The vehicle's door opened and its driver emerged, hands up. "Stop!"

Rios brightened. "Wolyx!"

Once he was certain he wasn't going to be shot, the dealer reached into the back of the car. He pulled out a long duffel bag with a Starfleet logo.

"My stuff," Rios shouted. "You got it!"

Wolyx hobbled toward them, using both hands on the strap to move the heavy bag. Rios was glad he hadn't brought his trunk.

"I got a message earlier from the Tellarites," Wolyx said excitedly. "The holdup wasn't what I thought. Their transporter's broken. They needed me to pick it up!"

"*Gracias*," Rios said. "You're a lifesaver."

"Don't speak too soon." Ledger put her gun away again and advanced. She gestured to Stench. "See what he's got in there."

Rios watched as his clothing and other personal effects were tossed onto the street. When the punk revealed a cigar box, Rios called for it to be brought over. "I know you guys don't smoke, but you might want to see this."

Ledger broke the seal and opened it. What she saw caught the waning light—and her rapt interest. "Gold-pressed latinum. That's the stuff, all right." She ran her fingers across the tightly packed bars. "So you *were* here to deal."

"Of course. I just wasn't going to carry this on me. This place has a bad reputation."

"Yeah!" Burze yelled with pride.

"Shut up," Ledger said. She studied the box's contents, appearing to do some mental arithmetic.

"It should be a little more than the down payment you messaged me in the invite," Rios said. "I need to keep something for incidentals, of course."

Ledger closed the box. "No."

"What do you mean, no?"

"We only sell on time to people we trust. That's not you, not anymore. Your price is higher." She handed the box to Wolyx. "I have no confidence that you'll make good on the rest—and that doesn't even get into the cost of the damages." She nodded to the box. "But if we keep part of this, we're more than made whole."

Burze smoldered. "*Part?* Come on. If we kill him, we keep the whole thing!"

"*You* might, but you're not in charge," she replied. She faced Rios. "No, if you want to do business, I'd need a sweetener. This isn't enough."

Rios frowned—and then looked over at the duffel, which Stench had abandoned once the latinum had been found. "Wait," he said. "There's something else."

She grinned, expectantly. "Another box?"

"Not quite. May I?" Rios got permission to complete the search. It was easy to find—quite the largest thing in the bag, giving it much of its weight. He withdrew the bundle with care and unwrapped it on the street.

"He's got a blade!" Stench shouted.

"It's sheathed," Rios said, standing up with the ornate scabbard. He held it in both hands and walked toward Ledger. "An antique. Very valuable."

Ledger looked skeptical. "We're not junk dealers."

"Yeah, I heard. Just look."

She took it from him and looked over the sheath and the handle, both of which had the letter *R* engraved in them. "Nice. Precious family heirloom?"

"Not my family—but it has been around. I think it was awarded to Captain Galvarino Riveros."

"A reward?" Her eyes narrowed. "What for?"

"Victory in the Battle of Angamos—in the Pacific War."

She deferred to Wolyx. "Was that an important one?"

Startled to be called upon, the dealer spoke up. "Yes, it was one of Earth's biggest wars—a few years after the Book, I think. There are a lot of good stories set during it. A fine one about a captain and some strawberries—"

"Enough," she said. But the information caused her to look on the sword with heightened interest, and she turned it about in the light. "Huh."

Rios realized Wolyx had just made a mistake about Earth's history, but he wasn't going to correct him. Not when the error had given him something he could use. "It's all that's left of my collection—I didn't want to part with it. It's priceless."

"Everything has a price." But as she brandished the sword, she appeared to think better of it. "It's really valuable? You're not trying to flimflam me?"

"I don't know the meaning of the word."

She snorted. "You're no angel."

"No, I really don't know the meaning of the word." He shrugged. "You throw me with something about once a minute."

"*Bushwa!*"

"There you go again," he mumbled. "That was about fifty seconds early."

Ledger nodded gently. "We may have something here."

Wolyx took a shaky step toward her. "Begging your pardon—but you can't take his sword."

"Oh, yeah?" she asked. "Says who?"

"Captains never give up their swords. I've read about it."

"He's not a captain of anything, yet."

Rios's eyes narrowed as he looked at the weapon. It was true. He wasn't a captain—and hadn't gotten to be one, either, in Starfleet. He'd already decided there was only one way to fix that. "Take it."

Ledger passed the sword to an underling and faced Rios again. "Tell you what, sunflower. To prove I'm a sport, we'll check out what it's worth. Somebody's gotta know about this Battle of Angrymoose—"

"Angamos."

"Whatever. We'll call it collateral. And if you make good and pay the ship off, you can have it back."

Likely story, Rios thought. "And if I don't make good?"

"You'll get it back," Stench said. "Maybe *in* the back." Burze and several others laughed.

But not Ledger. "Wolyx, give him the freighter's command codes—and the payment schedule. Set him up on the longest term we do."

"How long is that?" Rios asked.

"Your whole life."

"Not the life of the ship?"

"Well, if you lose the ship, you won't be able to pay—"

"—so it's basically the same thing. I get it."

Rios rubbed the back of his neck, finally fully feeling the weight of the day's exertions. Yet somehow he cracked a grin. "Pleasure doing business," he said, bowing to Ledger. "You absolutely lead the class in starship dealerships run by refugees from a time warp."

"Make tracks before I change my mind!"

Rios did exactly that.

7

LA SIRENA
DEEP SPACE

"Did this thing carry wild animals?"

"Is that a rhetorical question?" Raffi Musiker asked.

"Not really." On his hands and knees, Rios bore down hard with a scrub brush, trying to banish a meter-long smear of something foul from the deck. It was one of many scars and blemishes he'd discovered after rearranging the previous owner's junk. He had no idea what they were from; he only knew that every item he moved revealed the stains of something else. "Whole ship's a mess, Raffi. And it's not that old."

"Neither are we, but we've still got the scars."

Raffi's voice resonated crisp and clear over the freighter's comm system. Rios assumed she was back on Earth, but he never really knew with her these days. He had kept away from everyone and everything following his departure from Verex III; that was the way he wanted it. But Raffi had helped set him up, and that had more than earned her the right to break his solitude.

And to make suggestions. *"You ought to be able to run some kind of disinfection protocol."*

"That's Starfleet talk."

"Does swabbing the decks make you feel more like an ancient mariner?"

"No, but it's also not that simple. I've got to see the decks to clean them. Half the ship's volume is the old owner's crap."

"I'm surprised the sellers didn't clear it out."

"I'm not." He looked up. "And thanks for warning me about those people, by the way."

"Warning? I didn't—"

"It's sarcasm. The Iotians nearly gunned me down in the street."

"Oh, pffft!" she said, and he could almost see her blowing her hair out of her eyes in exasperation. *"Iotians are pussycats. Didn't you read Whalen as a sophomore?"*

"Only as much as I had to." Rios snorted. "There's a difference between knowing circuses used to have clowns and having a bunch of them beat the hell out of you."

"Did they do that?"

"Which time?"

"Oh." A pause. *"You seem to have survived."*

"Regrettably. How do you know those idiots?"

"Intel days. We had an agent the Romulans were taking to a Reman mine. We grabbed the transport. We freed an Iotian VIP in the process."

"Sounds classified. Should you be talking about this?"

Rios listened as she laughed long and hard. *No, she would not care.*

Raffi had been someone. No—*Someone*, with a capital letter. She was already a lieutenant commander specializing in intelligence in 2381 when Admiral Jean-Luc Picard tapped her to assist with the mercy mission of a lifetime: relocating nine hundred million people threatened by the impending Romulan supernova.

But it had all come to nothing following the destruction of the Utopia Planitia Shipyards on Mars. Starfleet's aid was withdrawn, leaving the remaining nongovernmental organization relief operations like the Sylvus Project and the Interspecies Medical Exchange hopelessly overmatched. The failure had left a stain on the Federation's reputation more indelible than any Rios had encountered on *La Sirena*'s deck.

It had done even greater damage to Raffi.

Rios had won his post aboard *ibn Majid* in the post-calamity period, and while disappointment had lingered in the air, he hadn't let it cloud something he'd worked so hard to achieve. That made his first encounter with Raffi, while he was serving on the *ibn Majid*, all the more startling. He'd known of her and respected her service. Yet the woman he met was completely different, driven to search for answers to—

—*to what?* To questions she could never quite verbalize to him. A sense that something had been amiss about the entire Romulan debacle, perhaps—that some person or persons existed on whom the blame truly could be assigned. Rightful indignation had bred pointless paranoia.

By then, Raffi's credibility was in tatters—and she'd insisted on ripping at the rest with her actions. Rios and his *ibn Majid* shipmates had pulled her out of a jam she'd gotten into with some underworld characters in the former Romulan Neutral Zone; she'd claimed to be chasing a lead, but to what, she could not—or would not—say. From several accounts, she'd been involved in many such incidents since leaving Starfleet.

Rios still felt sympathy, so when they ran across each other after his own forcible separation from Starfleet, it made sense that they'd begin talking. Their occasional discussions, all remote lately, almost made him feel normal.

Almost.

"Sorry," she said, punctuating a long pause. *"Thought I heard something outside. Where were we?"*

"Iotians."

"Yeah. So one of the other prisoners I rescued was someone to the Iotians—which made me someone to them. These guys are big on loyalty."

"Wonder where they got *that* idea from."

"It landed you the interview. I'd never actually met the person in charge—just a name on the screen. Boss Arkko."

"Yeah, you wrote me. So important his name rates an unnecessary *k*."

"You didn't meet?"

"No, I only saw the troops—and an accountant who was a real piece of work. It's just strange to see it up close. I'd have thought they would have dropped the whole gangster shtick by now."

"People pick and choose what they want. Neither one of us has been near a shtetl, yet we'll use a word like shtick. *It's expressive."*

"Original Iotian must have been a pretty damn dull language if they're sticking with this." He thought for a moment. "There's another thing: except for the lead money counter, they were all guys. I thought for a moment there weren't any Iotian women."

"Kirk met some. Maybe they're too smart for the whole act."

"No idea." Rios shifted his area of operations, toppling a pile of empty cans in the process.

Worlds away, Raffi heard the clatter. *"The Iotians aren't back, are they?"*

"If they were, they could carry this shit away with them."

"If the stuff is useless, why haven't you dumped it? Vaporized it? Beamed it into a sun?"

"I've considered it. I'd just hate to atomize someone's beloved pet." He looked over at the stuffed *targ*, sitting kingly atop a pile of mildly sorted debris. "There's still one door I haven't been able to get open."

"Ooh, maybe the former owner's in there! Ought to be getting pretty rank by now."

Rios sighed. "On this ship, I wouldn't be able to tell." He looked to the overhead, where Raffi's voice was emanating from. "You could see it if you liked—and I could see you. Holo-emitters all over the ship. Sure you want to stick to audio?"

"I'm not getting out of this chair today."

"But that's the point. You don't have to. You can follow me around wherever I go."

"I'll pass." Then, lighter: *"Why are there holo-emitters on a freighter?"*

"The Kaplan designers expect small crews. A captain's gotta take calls wherever he is. On top of that, it's got a concierge package."

She'd heard of it. *"The replicator is networked with the transporter."*

He spoke in a faux formal tone, "Ask for something, milady, and it shall appear."

"Tell it to make me a martini."

"Would if I could." He wiped sweat from his brow before returning to work on a greasy skid mark.

"*Love those concierge packages. They were trying to make things as autonomous as possible.*"

"Are you saying that freighter captains are insufferable pricks nobody would want to be around?"

"Present company excepted, I'm sure." She laughed. *"Maybe you could use the system to clean the ship."*

"I've beamed some stuff around, but I'm not parking a junkyard in the pattern buffers."

"You know what I think? There's going to be some treasure in there."

"That only happens in stories I never have time to read. Trust me. I've found a working record player—that's it. The rest is all dunsel."

"And the ship itself?"

"Better." He stopped scrubbing and looked up. "I feel like we ought to switch places. You paid for this thing."

"Oh, no. I told you to forget it. It was found latinum."

"Is that so?"

A pause. *"Yeah. I'll just say I got it—and I didn't like having it around."*

"Sounds like me and an open tab."

"There's that. But also . . ." She trailed off.

"Yeah." He didn't need to hear the whole story.

"Besides," she added, *"I'm done with traveling."*

"Forever?"

"For now."

The signal went silent for several seconds, during which he chucked the scrub brush and stood. When he heard her again, her tone had changed. *"I never asked. What did you name the ship?"*

He looked around. "*La Sirena.*"

"The mermaid? Goes with the tattoo, I guess." He'd just gotten it when he'd seen her last. *"You never told me the significance of that."*

He felt for it on his arm. "Just woke up with it one day."

"The ink, or a mermaid?"

"Guess." He began to make his way forward. "To be honest, it was a clerical error."

"Somehow when you say that, I believe it."

"It's true. There was a bartender who was into Greek mythology—told me about Odysseus and the sirens. I must have gone after that to get inked. But the Greek sirens weren't mermaids. That got added to the legend later."

"You could have had it changed."

"Mermaids are prettier." He walked through a cleared space he'd created. "I looked it up afterward. Read a little bit of the fairy tale. The Danish one."

"You only got to that now? I was seven when I read that."

"Instruction manuals were my thing. It's where I learned to open doors." Seeing the jammed doorway, he opened his hand and spoke to the air. "Screwdriver."

The freighter's sensors heard the word and saw his gesture—and imputed from them an instruction. Less than a second later, replicated atoms whirled into being, depositing in Rios's clutched hand a perfect combination of vodka and orange juice.

"Great," he muttered. He took a swig anyway.

"Hey, is that my drink order? I paid for that damn ship."

"Sorry, interference. Can't hear you." He gulped a lot more before ordering the ship to dispel the beverage. "Still some bugs to work out." He resumed his previous posture. "Flathead screwdriver. Two-centimeter tip. Two-decimeter shank."

The correct tool materialized in his hand. "The system likes blue handles for some reason," he said, positioning the sharp end in a slot he'd worked into the jamb of the stuck door. A few wiggles, and it held firm. He spoke to the air again. "Sledgehammer. *Not the song.*"

A flash of light, and a formidable implement appeared at his feet. "Don't mean to bore you."

"No, this is the most excitement I've had all week. What's going on?"

"A man has had enough." With a mighty heave, he lifted the sledgehammer and swung it mercilessly against the screwdriver. The tool didn't move, but neither did it break.

Raffi, wherever she was, called out. *"Oh, dear. Sounds like you're not going to get your damage deposit back."*

"I'm not doing anything to their ship that they didn't try to do to me." He swung the hammer twice more—until a terrible crack announced that the screwdriver had created a gap between the automatic doors. "Delete sledgehammer, add crowbar." One tool turned to another, and he went to work on the opening.

"You're opening the vault. More adventure than I thought I'd have today."

It only took a few seconds to pry the doors open.

He whistled, and Raffi heard him. *"What is it?"*

"Jesus."

"He's in there?"

I wouldn't be surprised, Rios thought. More useless garbage, stacked to the overhead and packed wall to wall. No wonder he couldn't get in: he expected the mass of it must have mashed against the door during his Verex III aerobatics, damaging the door mechanism somehow. He could barely see any light in the room.

He dropped the crowbar, defeated.

Raffi heard it. *"Cris, are you all right?"*

"It's fine. Just even more crap." He knelt before the mass of rubbish. "I think the last owner might have had an untreated condition."

"Or maybe this junk is from two owners ago, and that's where the last owner stashed everything. Like Tut's tomb, but a time-share. Every owner will fill a new room."

"Joy. Glad you're having fun." He scowled. "I'll dump it all somewhere—when I need the space. I've managed to go three months without going in."

"Wait—what?" Raffi sounded astonished. *"Did you say* three months*? I thought you just bought the ship."*

"No, I did that right after we last talked—when you sent me the dealers' contact info."

"I didn't give you enough to buy the ship outright. How often do the Iotians want their payments?"

"Once a month. They're very old-school." The moment after the words came out of his mouth, he couldn't believe he'd said it.

"And how many payments have you missed?"

"This week will make . . . *all of them*."

Alarm rose in her voice. *"Haven't you been taking jobs? Cargo? Fares?"*

"Can't. No room."

"But how will you pay for it?"

He scratched his beard. "I haven't given it any thought."

"You're not making sense."

"You love it when people say that to you." He forced the doors to the crammed room closed and turned to look again on the upper deck. He saw only the former crews, whoever they were, and wondered whether the ship would ever truly be his—even if he could pay for it. "She's not ready, Raffi. *I'm* not ready."

A pause, during which he thought he could hear her sigh. Then, tentatively: *"Cris, you never did tell me what happened between you and Starfleet—"*

"Nice chatting, Raffi. I may be hard to reach for a while. *La Sirena* out."

8

La Sirena
Deep Space

Captain's Log: There will not be a captain's log.

Rios ended the entry, satisfied—or as satisfied as he ever got. His evening meal after Raffi's call had consisted solely of summoning a few more of the screwdrivers—the liquid kind. It wasn't his kind of drink, but he hadn't eaten all day and reasoned there was nutrition in the orange juice.

The novelty wearing thin rather quickly, he moved on to his old standby. Chilean aguardiente was half alcohol—*what even was the point of synthehol?* His favorite variety was seasoned by walnuts and almonds. Food and drink all at once. That was good enough for him.

He stumbled around the deck, bottle in hand, wondering what the brewmasters, vintners, and distillers of the universe thought of replicators horning in on their trades. Jesus—who was indeed not in the storage room—was said to have turned water into wine. What did the wedding caterer think of that? And what about the local bakers and anglers whose sales were impacted when their loaves and fishes were duplicated for the masses? Did such things even matter now, in a world where everyone had the power of matter creation? It was a wonder to Rios why anyone even bothered to—

—to what? Rios rubbed the side of his face and burped, having no recollection of whatever grand thought he'd been entertaining. He was at once sure that it had been of vital importance, and that it couldn't possibly have mattered. He staggered toward the wide opening to the galley deck, where he knew a lovely railing awaited.

It was as he remembered: cool to the touch, and supportive by nature. It had never let him down. The aguardiente, however, had abandoned him—or at least he couldn't see any more of it in the bottle. Rios threw the container over the railing and smiled as it sailed into the mess area. It shattered against the table.

"Clean that up," he declared—and smiled again as the larger shards disappeared in a flash of light. "You're damn right. I'm the captain!"

He stared down at the deck below. Yes, of course he could have gotten rid of some of the debris onboard in the same way, as Raffi had suggested. All the bric-a-brac could easily be broken down to component atoms, for repurposing somewhere in *La Sirena*'s systems or expulsion. The will to do it had never materialized.

The ship was already freedom, and that was all Rios had wanted in the first place. It was the only reason he had bothered with the Iotians at all. He'd gotten what he wanted from them, and he'd made enough warp jumps to ensure they'd never find him. That was that. He wasn't about to move until he was damn good and ready.

Life as an unregistered pilot, "off the books," might appeal to some; that was clearly what Raffi had thought he wanted when he first expressed the desire for a starship. But Rios had already *had* a starship. A real one.

He no longer knew whether the *ibn Majid* existed at all.

No, he wasn't going to tell Raffi what had happened the year before. He would never be able to tell anyone. That had been a condition, and they had made sure he abided by it.

And "they" was the very Starfleet he'd loved. Or once had.

He could still remember it all. The pride of scoring the post of first officer—and the honor of being able to serve with a captain like Alonzo Vandemeer, who taught him more about starfaring in a short time than he could have learned from a roomful of Academy instructors.

And he could remember that day, and how excited he had been when it began. A first-contact situation. A chance to make history. A memory to be prized for years, to be described at bars to envious colleagues and to rapt new recruits decades on. The two aliens had come on board, and—

No.

He still couldn't think about it. Not even now, not even hammered. It was too horrible. And everything that had come afterward just compounded it, made it even more personal to him. He had been forced to leave, forced to lie to protect the careers—and maybe even the lives—of the crew. Yet they never learned of his sacrifice. Instead, they blamed him for the upheaval in their lives.

They needn't have bothered. He already spent enough time blaming himself.

"Definitely not the night to go there," he said, staggering off to his quarters to hit the head.

Minutes later found him back on the bridge, trying to figure out what chair he wanted to sit in. There were so many, and he wasn't feeling like playing captain tonight. At last, he snapped his fingers and chose. He slouched toward the navigator's chair and collapsed.

"Aye, and I'm the navigator," he called out in his worst Irish accent. "Whisky, if you don't mind!" The bottle materialized atop the console, alongside a glass. He always ordered from the Emerald Isle when he was in this seat. It also helped that the control station was real, as opposed to the captain's virtual one. That one was no good at supporting bottles at all.

He lifted the glass, which he hadn't asked for, and turned it in his hand. *Maybe it's the ship telling me to slow down.* If it was, the suggestion wouldn't do any good. He poured himself what he fully expected would be the first of a series.

Rios leaned back and held the glass between him and the forward viewport. From outside, the light of the nearest stars shone through the transparent container in his hand, blossoming outward as he turned it. *Spirits—through spirits.* It wasn't the most lucid observation, but it brought him back again to what had started the evening's festivities. He'd suggested to Raffi that he hadn't taken a job because of the ghosts of past crews, and that was correct. It just wasn't *La Sirena*'s crews that needed exorcising.

Rios took a drink and rubbed the glass against his forehead. This bender was worse than usual, and he couldn't focus. He wanted to hear something, but his head ached and music didn't appeal. Instead, he went with something short and simple. "Play the log," he demanded.

"Specify," droned an impersonal voice from above. Rios had never set up any kind of custom computer voice, and it didn't look like anyone else had, either.

"Specify, my arse," he said, still in his act. "Play the captain's log, you miserable git!"

"Specify captain."

Rios's impulse was to swear—until he realized the problem. He'd never deleted anything from the ship's database because it didn't appear that the old owners had left anything digital. Metric tons of rubbish had been gift enough. But now he was curious. "I'm Captain Rios. Who is the other captain?"

"Captain Verengan."

Huh. "Play Verengan log entries."

"There is one Verengan log entry, protected. Do you wish to authorize playback?"

"What do you think we've been jawin' about?" he said, again in the voice. "Get to it!" Rios took a drink.

"Log entry Verengan One, recorded one hundred seventeen days ago."

Silence followed. Rios looked up. He'd expected to hear the computer's narration, even if Veren-whoosis didn't record his own voice. He was about to complain when he heard something behind him.

Wheezing.

Rios dropped the glass and looked back. There was a huge Klingon in his captain's chair.

"Greetings," the aged figure said. Then he clutched his chest and doubled over, coughing.

It took Rios a few moments in his state to realize he was looking at a holographic recording, projected in the exact place in which it was recorded. *When did the computer say? Four months ago?*

"This is a recording, right?" Rios asked. He'd had no reason to suspect otherwise—and the Klingon didn't respond. Rather, he recovered from his coughing jag and looked up.

Rios knew how long Klingons lived; this one seemed well past his date of obsolescence. The former captain looked up and spoke. *"HIq."* The concierge system in the recording responded, and a bottle of bloodwine appeared in his wrinkled hand.

"I am Verengan," he said, in gravelly Standard. *"My name is worth nothing, and never will be. I deal in things of value. I can judge."* He looked forward, dark eyes peering out through folds of skin. *"My words may have value, if you will listen."*

"Okay," Rios said, realizing only after he did how pointless answering was. He turned his chair to face the Klingon, who was now drinking from the bottle.

Finally, Verengan spoke again. *"I have traveled the spacelanes a hundred years. No merchant of my kind has matched that—nor would try. I am called as I am for a reason."*

He winced, and another coughing fit began. Rios's eyes narrowed as he thought back on the name. "Computer, mute entry."

"Muted."

"Access *tlhIngan Hol* dictionary. What does *verengan* mean?"

"Ferengi."

Rios gawked. It was a few moments before he realized the Klingon was speaking again—and seeming a lot more animated. He unmuted the recording.

"—and it doesn't matter how many times you trade for a better freighter, or how fancy the extras are. You believe me when I tell you this: the merchant life is a miserable stinking pile of targ *shit!"*

Rios raised an eyebrow. "You don't say?"

"I've been cheated by every species in two quadrants. They don't pay. They pay, but currency is no good. What they sell is phony. I get to buy what I want, but only if I take mountains of what I don't."

Verengan turned his head—and in that instant, he and Rios were both looking back at the junk piles aft. When the Klingon turned and spat, Rios wanted to do the same. United, in disgust, across time.

"Whoever gets this heap next," Verengan said, *"I warn you: if your father sired a child with a brain, do not take up this life. You will be cheated—and you will be alone. I am alone."* A tear glistened in his holographic eye. *"I have no son. I have no line!"*

Rios wanted to say something again, regardless of what he was looking at.

Verengan openly wept. *"I have no friends but the dead. Great Kahless, you—and Kor, and Kang. You have always accepted me!"*

He continued naming Klingons, his eyes darting back and forth in all directions. Some names Rios knew; others not. But he knew enough to understand that the odds of Verengan having met some of them were low. L'Rell—wasn't she the one right after the war? And Kahless was even centuries before that.

Verengan dropped the bottle, and it disappeared from view. He was wailing now, speaking to the air. *"Even you, Gorkon! Chancellor—my chancellor—who had no reason to speak to such a wretch. You said, 'Honor is everywhere to be seen, by those who know how to look.' How wise! How true!"*

Rios had no idea how to look for honor—but he could definitely see an old man in the middle of a meltdown. He waited and watched as Verengan began singing a mournful dirge in Klingon.

At last, all cried out, the merchant stared down at the deck. Drained by his fit, he appeared to be having trouble drawing breath. His eyes focused on a point off to his right. "I will tell you this," he said between gasping breaths. "I am done. I will not be Verengan anymore—and I will not continue trying to make money from that thing. *That dishonorable, shameful thing!*"

"What thing?" Rios could not stop himself from saying.

Verengan looked about to continue, perhaps even to provide something that would constitute an answer—

—when he clutched his chest and howled. Rios bolted to his feet and stepped toward the image of the Klingon. This wasn't another conniption, he quickly saw. The old man was in great pain.

"Help . . . help me!" Verengan called out. *"I suffer!"*

"Do you require medical aid?" Rios heard the computer's voice—but it didn't sound quite the same. The voice was coming from the recording. *"Emergency Hologram Installation Pack 5.0 has not been initialized. Do you wish to install it now?"*

"Typ—" Something gurgled in Verengan's throat, and he pitched forward. *"Typical!"* he managed, before falling from the chair.

Rios looked down—and up—and then at his feet again. The emitters were still projecting the message, though only part of it, the top of Verengan's motionless form, was visible. Rios stared at it, his sodden mind struggling to process everything. The Iotians hadn't killed the previous owner after all. And what was that about an EMH? He hadn't even looked to see that *La Sirena* had one.

A minute having passed, the computer spoke again. *"Entry ended due to inactivity."*

"No shit," Rios said as the remainder of the image winked out. He looked up. "No further entries?"

"All log entries by Captain Verengan have been played. Do you wish to play the log entry of Captain Rios?"

"Hell, no." He looked back to see his whisky glass on the deck, where he'd dropped it. He decided not to bother with it, and instead plopped down in the captain's chair Verengan had just—or rather, four months ago—vacated.

"Aguardiente," he said, and a fresh bottle appeared in his hand. He looked about at the empty chairs. "So this is the life, huh?"

9

LA SIRENA

DEEP SPACE

What the hell did I do last night?

Rios had asked it of himself a dozen times already. The first time was when he woke up, naked and inexplicably stretched across the massive cargo transporter pad. He asked the question again in the shower and then at breakfast, which was his first meal in a day and a half. He asked it another few times in between the bouts of regurgitation that followed, and once more during the second shower.

He started to get more of the picture when he saw the bottles strewn about the bridge. If it *was* a bridge: no bulkhead divided it from the main deck. *Is it a cockpit? A command well? What even is the difference?* Rios rubbed his temples in an attempt to dispel the vagrant thoughts.

His bleary eyes widened when he saw the captain's chair.

The Klingon. Right.

Rios wondered where the freighter had been when Verengan expired. The Iotians had seemed to suggest that he had been leasing it from them; obviously, they'd gotten the ship back somehow. Had *they* found him? He remembered the foul smell when he'd first boarded. The poor bastard could have been rotting on the deck for days. Given how quickly the Iotians seemed to turn the vessel around for sale, Rios decided to be happy that they'd removed the corpse. They could have just left it under a pile of junk.

Collecting the bottles, Rios vaguely remembered the Klingon's words of warning, and that they had struck home with him. Now, in what passed for the light of day on *La Sirena*, he wondered why the log entry had gotten under his skin. He already knew the profession he'd bought himself into was rough; it was part of why he'd been so slow to seek out any business. It was a lonely life—and death.

He wasn't that surprised that Verengan had died alone. Solitude was part of the merchant life; indeed, it was the whole selling point for Rios. Never having to depend on anyone ever again—and never letting anyone down.

Maybe the old guy just couldn't hack it. Got nothing to do with me.

Rios walked the starboard side of the railing that overlooked the galley deck until he arrived before the door. No longer the Mystery Door, it was now the Dear Merciful God Even More Crap Door. He worked the mechanism and was pleased to see that it opened automatically now; he was less enthused to see inside. There was maybe a square meter of free interior space in which he could stand.

He was in that so-called clearing when he started speaking. "Maybe I *am* going to need to just beam it all out into space." He wasn't in the habit of talking to himself, but it sounded like a plan when he heard it, and he couldn't find a flaw in the idea.

"That's it," he declared loudly, his voice barely echoing in the jam-packed chamber. "Cristóbal Rios, one of Starfleet's greatest rising stars, is going to litter. Did you hear that, universe?" He let loose with a diabolical laugh and smiled, a bushy eyebrow raised. He was sure his former colleagues had never heard him sound so . . . so . . . *what was the word?*

He snapped his fingers. "Arch!"

A flash of light—and the doorway behind him transformed. It still led to the rest of the ship, but it had changed from a simple metal frame to something sleek and copper colored, with control panels on either side.

Rios gawked at it—and then, eyes wide, looked back on the rest of the junk. "Computer," he said, making almost a question of it, "end program?"

A flash of light—and the room went black. Black, but not dark. The debris surrounding him vanished, to be replaced by pure, blessed nothing. Nothing but the telltale glowing gridlines of a holodeck.

Steady since his post-breakfast episode, Rios nearly fell down again. He reeled backward and caught himself against the jamb—no, the *arch*. Stabilized once more, he leaned out and looked at the rest of the vessel, and its clutter.

"Computer, end program!" he shouted at the upper deck. But nothing happened. It was all still there.

No such luck, he thought.

But inside it was still empty. "Computer, resume program," he said—and the mess reappeared. He reached out for one of the items in the pile.

It looked to be some kind of brass horn with Andorian characters on it. He turned to face the opening and threw the instrument. With a crackling sound, the horn lost cohesion and disintegrated the instant it crossed the threshold.

A holodeck—on a tramp freighter!

He smiled and reached for one thing after another. A big, greasy metal wheel? *Whoosh!* An easel made of some kind of bamboo? *Whoosh!* The exercise was needless, he knew, but it felt good.

At last, he ordered the deck to dispel everything at once, and he laughed aloud when it did.

Some of the odd readings he'd told Raffi about made sense now. There had always been a mysterious power drain he couldn't account for. The program must have been running all that time. The holographic junk didn't have true mass, but if Verengan had set it up to respond to the ship's movements, the holographic items inside and their attendant force fields would have pressured the door closed just as easily.

Or maybe the damn thing was just stuck. Who knows?

Rios walked fully into the room, studying the bulkheads and overhead as he did. It was certainly possible that the Kaplan series could have a holodeck option; the freighter was new enough, and such an install wasn't a big jump from having emitters placed shipwide for interfaces and comm usage—and, apparently, an EMH option. He just couldn't understand who would have footed the bill for all of it. Verengan didn't look like he was living the high life, and he couldn't imagine the Iotians springing for such luxuries, presuming they'd outfitted *La Sirena* to begin with at all.

He couldn't see an answer—but he did see *something*.

Rios walked to the far right-hand corner of the room. There, sitting apart from the gridwork, was something small and black, almost imperceptible against its surroundings. It had remained after the deactivation.

"It's real," Rios said, which caused him, a second later, to mutter, "Brilliant observation, Cris."

There was no way anyone walking into the room when the program was on would have seen it at all, much less gotten to it. Arriving at the corner, he knelt before it. It was a small black pouch, secured at the top with a drawstring. Through the velvety fabric he could tell there was something round inside. Round, and heavier than he expected.

The way life's been going, it's probably a grenade. But Rios felt for the drawstring anyway—

—only to be interrupted by a loud chime. Not from the bag, but from the ship itself. "What the hell?"

Pouch in hand, he rose and strode toward the exit. *Which klaxon was it?* he wondered. He'd never really heard any, and apparently the ship's systems weren't set up to give him any detail.

The answer became clear as soon as he took one step outside the holodeck—and saw motion far ahead through the main viewport.

It's a proximity alarm. Something's out there!

Confirmation came when *La Sirena* shook, causing him to lose his balance and more alarms to sound. Rios knew a low-power shot from a disruptor cannon when he felt one. So the something outside was not nice—yet also probably not interested in cracking the hull.

That meant one thing. *Pirates!*

Rios swiftly turned back to the arch. "Resume program," he ordered. If he was going to be boarded by brigands, he sure wasn't going to let them see what a prize the ship really was. *Let 'em see garbage.* The holographic material inside reappeared even as he closed the doors.

His cardiovascular system finding an occasion to respond to for the first time in weeks, he hurried forward and planted himself in the captain's chair. There, he looked directly into the bow of an advancing dreadnought, just like the Convincer vessels that had vied against him back in the Verex system. *Those guys!*

He had no idea how they'd found him, but it didn't matter. There was no way in hell Rios was going to let them get hold of him again. He called up the holographic flight controls, whereupon he immediately encountered one of the hazards of using a transparent interface: blinding light from the dreadnought flashed through it. He felt the disruptor fire in the next instant.

Forget shields, Rios thought. He wasn't entirely sure what kind of system *La Sirena* even had, if anything. It didn't matter. If the Convincers were firing to destroy the ship, they'd have done so. They didn't want to damage the merchandise—yet—and that gave him his chance. He swung the vessel around in an arc, in an attempt to find open space, and freedom—

—and found, instead, another approaching dreadnought. And then another. And another. Completing his three-sixty, he was uncertain how many he was looking at—and with no one at tactical, calling up the virtual station within his own interface required time he didn't have.

Fighting back was out; so was running. He could mess with trying to get shields going—or he could prepare for what was almost certainly inevitable now.

Rios chose without a second's hesitation. There was a rectangular panel on the deck just to the right of the navigator's chair; opening it, he found the phaser he kept there. Securing it, he spied the pouch from the holodeck near his chair where he'd dropped it. He shoved it into the hiding place in the weapon's stead; if it was by some chance a grenade, it might come in handy later.

He rose, a plan forming. His next stop needed to be engineering, where he might hole up and exercise a little leverage. If they were intent on killing him, he could threaten to scuttle *La Sirena*, ruining their prize and maybe taking a few dreadnoughts with him.

Rios started running aft, but he only got a few meters when he heard a transporter whine behind him. He heard an ominous click as he turned—and watched as his chair began to swivel.

He saw the barrel of the machine gun first, the woman's legs second. "How's it going, Ledger?"

"Better than it is for you," she said. "It's time to talk turkey."

10

LA SIRENA
DEEP SPACE

The Iotian obsession with anachronistic Earthly expressions, Rios decided, might actually be an evolutionary trait favored by natural selection. There was no doubt they got a tactical advantage from the reactions they inspired in others. Ledger's invitation to talk poultry, for example, had caused Rios to pause for a moment to work on what would have been a dry but witty response. That was time enough for more of her gunmen to materialize behind him.

I guess the jig is up. His phaser fell to the floor, and he surveyed the muscle she'd brought. From Verex III, he only recognized Stench. "New crew?"

"Let's just say your foofaraw prompted a housecleaning," she said, rising from the chair. Today, she looked almost fancy: gray high-necked blouse and long skirt, with brown gloves and belt matching her fedora. She passed off her weapon to one of the thugs. "I hitched a ride with our convoy to head out on a long-delayed and greatly deserved vacation. You can't *imagine* how much I didn't want to divert to chase after you."

"Terrible." Hands behind his head, Rios raised an eyebrow. "I wouldn't put up with it if I were you. I'd leave right now."

"Can't. Wouldn't be efficient," she said, strolling around him. "You were on the way—and we were checking your accounts. Strangely, no deposits."

Rios glanced toward the forward viewport. "Look where we are. I haven't been near any place where I could make one."

"That, I can believe. Our readings say you've been sitting here in this void for three months."

His eyes narrowed. "You put a tracker on my ship?"

"It's *our* ship, and thanks for again considering us absolute idiots."

"You're welcome?"

Hands clasped behind her, she sauntered around the command chair. "An investment this size requires monitoring."

"Still getting cleaned up."

"You must only work an hour a day." She looked back at the hold, her lips curving in disdain. "Burze told me there was a lot of junk on board. What have you been doing all this time? Indexing it for posterity?"

"The agreement was I'd have a month or two to get my feet under me."

"It's been three."

"That's enough to warrant all those?" he asked, eyes darting toward the dreadnoughts outside.

"That convoy is called the 'percentage pack.' It delivers the cut to the boss. It's always big. Like I said, we were in the neighborhood—and you did run off with the ship once. Having you do it again would rate as a personal embarrassment." She approached him. "Besides, that's not your only problem."

He rolled his eyes. "Can't wait to hear."

She stepped up to him and jabbed a gloved finger into his chest. "That sword of yours—the one you gave us to cover the damages you caused. Wolyx found out that the battle you talked about wasn't part of your Second World War at all. It was decades earlier!"

"That's right," Rios answered mildly. "I said it was during the War of the Pacific—and that's what they called the war between Chile and Peru. José Galvarino Riveros Cárdenas led a squadron that captured the ironclad *Huáscar*."

"*Pshaw!* You made us think it was from the big shindig!"

"It was big to us Chileans. That action knocked the Peruvian navy out of the conflict."

"That's not the same, and you—"

"Go ask Bolivia if the war was a big deal. They became landlocked because of it. You're going to be dismissive of landlocked Bolivians?"

She stared at him a moment, before saying, "I can't believe this." She looked to one of the goons. "Can you believe this?"

The tough started to respond. "I don't—"

"Shut up. Who asked you?"

Rios was still going. "And, you know, Earth was pretty much done giving out swords for victories by then. I mean, there was the Sword of Stalingrad, and I guess you can count—"

"You shut up too!" Her eyes flashed. "The point is, you kicked it in to sweeten the pot—and it's gone sour!" At that, her nose twitched. "And what is that *smell*?"

Hands still behind his head, Rios attempted to shrug. "I've been working on it. I think it's your dead Klingon."

"Dead Klingon?" She looked to her guards. "We have a dead Klingon?"

"It's the former owner," Rios said. "I think he may have died right where you were sitting."

"There?" She looked to the captain's chair—and then brushed the back of her skirt. "You could have told me that when I was sitting there."

"You could have told me that when I bought it." Rios grew irritated. "And how do you not know what happened to him, anyway?"

"I just sent someone to repossess the ship. Verengan was a deadbeat—he was going to leave feetfirst one way or another." She walked to the starboard viewport in the command area. "Which brings me back to you. You're about to be in breach of contract—but it does me no good to have this vessel making no money for two quarters in a row."

Rios watched her, cautious. "And?"

"The bank is taking over. I'm going to put a representative aboard this vessel, to ensure you make sensible business decisions."

Rios stepped forward. "Hey, wait! I don't—"

Stench moved as well, jabbing his pistol barrel into Rios's cheek. "Going somewhere, pally?"

Rios didn't respond. He was tired of this game—but there was nothing he could do. "A guest, you said?"

Ledger hummed. "Yes. I was thinking Burze."

"That asshole? I thought he was a salesman."

"He's whatever I tell him to be."

"Why not Wolyx?"

She laughed. "Nothing doing! You'd probably throw a book down the loading ramp and abandon him when he went after it."

Rios fumed, considering what life would be like with the shortish pissant wandering around playing tough guy all the time. It wasn't what he wanted—

—but then, he hadn't gotten what he wanted much at all lately.

"It's decided," Ledger said, producing a personal comm unit. "I'll send him over and that'll be—" She stopped when she saw Rios's face. He was looking at something out the portside viewport, even as another proximity alarm sounded. It was another new arrival, this one out of warp.

"Another dreadnought," Rios said. "How many were you going to send after me?"

"The unexpected is never good." Ledger, unnerved, stepped toward the portal in question. Her eyes widened with recognition. "It's *Velvet Glove*."

"It's *what*?"

Ledger's goons certainly understood what her words meant, because they suddenly hustled aft. The accountant appeared to swallow hard—before looking back to Stench, who had remained to watch Rios. "What are you waiting for?" she said to him. "Go!"

The gunman went into motion, prodding Rios along in pursuit of the others—while Ledger broke into a run, passing them both. Any thought Rios had of escape surrendered to his curiosity. Something had made the thugs up ahead split into two groups, assembling on either side of the cargo transport platform. They were at rapt attention, hats off, when Rios arrived.

"What gives?"

Ledger shushed him. He'd never seen her spooked before. But she seemed to be holding her breath as she took a position beside him not far from the platform. Even Stench stood upright, having holstered his weapon and removed his hat.

Light and sound, as something large began to materialize. Rios quickly made out the shape of a large, antique oaken desk—and a quartet of young adult males, two on each side of it. All four were blond and shirtless, their tanned physiques bulked up almost beyond belief.

Rios was working on a remark when Ledger clapped her hands twice. "Ready!" At her word, the four strapping individuals—also Iotian, he figured—lifted the hefty desk into the air by its corners.

They held it there for long seconds, during which Rios could not explain his bafflement. "You didn't think I had enough junk on board?"

"Quiet!" Ledger said as the air above the desktop began to sparkle and glow. *"It's the boss!"*

11

La Sirena
Deep Space

When Rios thought of teachers from his formative years, he always fondly recalled Dora Chen-Alvarez, who brought chemistry to life by leading her students through a weeklong Periodic Table of Death. If you wanted twelve-year-olds to pay attention, it was hard to beat a journey of words and images detailing all the various ways the building blocks of the universe could kill you. It instilled caution among kids beginning to experiment in the lab, but it also kept them awake. Air-breathers of many species left her classes wondering why they'd ever trusted oxygen at all.

One of the creepiest bits was on arsenic green, which was both a color and a killer. Also known as Scheele's Green, the highly toxic dye had been used in everything from toys to wallpaper—as well as the evening dress worn by the woman in one of the lesson's visual aids. Rios had never forgotten the color, so strange looking in the early Autochrome-method photograph—or the smiling expression of the woman in the gown, so unaware that her fashion sense was killing her.

A dress just like that was before him now, being worn by the reclining woman who materialized on the desk. It could have been the original dress, for all he knew—and while it couldn't have been the same woman, she looked as if she'd seen one century, and decided to stay for another. Her drawn skin and wrinkled hands gave him that impression—whereas her makeup and jet-black hair seemed to be trying to create another.

The idea she definitely conveyed, however, was that she was fully and totally in charge. "Let's go, boys," she said in a deep husky voice to the grown men. They lifted the desk higher in response, carting it with them as they stepped off the platform.

As her bearers carted along the woman—Cleopatra by way of Theda Bara—she kept her balance well, vamping about on the desktop. Emerald-painted lips smirked as they carried her into a clearing amid the debris. "*Love* what you've done with the place."

Ledger clapped again, and the carriers set the desk down gently, not jostling its rider at all. The accountant straightened. "Boss—"

"In a minute, honey," the older woman said. She slipped down from the desk with an agility that surprised Rios. Spying him, she approached. "Aren't *you* something? What's your story, Morning Glory?"

Rios didn't know what to say to that. He could only tell that she liked what she saw. She stepped right up to him and put her hand under his hairy chin, examining him like livestock at auction. "You know who I am, baby?"

He did now. "Boss Arkko—with the double *k*."

"Got it in one."

"That seems like one too many."

The statement surprised her. "One too many what?"

"One too many *k*'s. You don't see a lot of words with double *k*'s."

She smiled primly as Stench quickly deployed a blade and brought it to the side of Rios's neck. "*Jackknife!*"

Rios glanced at it without moving his head. "That's not a jackknife. That's a switchblade."

"What difference does it make?"

"A jackknife is an assisted-opening blade," Rios said, as cool as the metal touching his skin. "Switchblades are automatic. That's a knock-off of a Schrade Presto—see the side-mounted button with the safety?" He snorted. "You kind of missed out, kid. Your Great Book was too soon for the Italian stiletto. Now, *that* was a classic—favorite of little punks. You'd like it."

Flustered, Stench looked to Arkko. "What the hell is he babbling about?"

She regarded Rios. "He wants me to think he's a cool customer."

"I *am* a customer," Rios replied. "And I'm damned tired of explaining that. I've been around other beings twice in the last three months—and almost every minute of it I've been standing at gunpoint or knifepoint by your people."

"And you think complaining about it is going to get us to leave you alone."

"No, but I'm hoping it might get me a chair."

She locked eyes with Rios, apparently trying to decide what to make of him. "Should we give him the chair?" she asked, raising a painted eyebrow as she looked at the goons standing at attention. Getting the message, they all snickered. She faced Rios again. "You know, love, the humans used to have *special* chairs for people like us."

"We were done with that a long time ago," he said. "But when the Romulans were in business, they had a few chairs you would have found entertaining."

She stared at him—and laughed, a throaty sound he found both mesmerizing and a little frightening. "Get him *that*," she said, pointing to a broad-backed leather chair half-buried under Verengan's junk.

The hoods surprised Rios with how fast they cleared it off and brought it to him. *Maybe I should hire these guys*, he thought.

When they were finished, Stench reluctantly released Rios, who took a seat. He crossed his arms and legs and kicked back. "Your boys bring any cigars? Ones *not* from Iotia?"

"Don't push it, beautiful," Arkko said.

"Sorry." Rios flashed his best don't-blame-a-boy-for-asking smile.

"What's your name again, doll?"

"Cristóbal Rios," Ledger interjected. She'd been unusually mum until now. "Former Starfleet."

"Oh, really?" the boss asked, interest piqued. "I so seldom meet any of those. What's he to me?"

Ledger recited from memory the exact amount Rios owed the gang, denominated in gold-pressed latinum, Klingon darseks, and one other currency he'd never heard of.

"Ain't she quick on the button, Mister Rios?" The boss looked the accountant up and down. "Little Alys Ledjo here is about the age I was when *Enterprise* visited Iotia."

Rios's brow furrowed. "I didn't know they visited after the first time."

"I'm talking the first time, handsome. The big time."

"But that was—"

"*Unh-uh-uh*," Arkko said, waving her index finger. "Do the math if you have to, but it's unkind to bring up to a lady."

Rios couldn't help but do it. *Enterprise* had visited more than a hundred and twenty years earlier—but that was well within the life-spans of several other humanlike species. Why *wouldn't* the Iotians be like that?

"I'll admit I was just a kid then." Arkko gestured to her hunky bearers.

"When I was starting out, I wasn't much more than these guys—eye candy for Boss Oxmyx."

"I thought it was *Okmyx*."

"That was just on the signs he had printed."

Ledger piped up. "To be fair, it was still a new alphabet."

"I don't have to be fair," Arkko said, expression turning. "Everyone who worked for Bela was an imbecile. The Book told him not to trust anyone because they might be threats—but the better reason was that most of them were too stupid to operate a doorknob without supervision."

She sauntered past the desk, letting her fingers brush against it. "All the bosses had big desks, but nobody actually used them. You had to be literate to do that. They were just places for us to sit, and vamp. No office was complete without a tomato with a gat."

Rios figured it was better not to ask.

She paced back around toward him. "But the reason we stayed quiet wasn't because we had nothing to say. Oh, no. We were listening—*all of us*." She stepped behind him, running her fingers through his hair. "I was there when Kirk came along and he made his play. I saw through his act in a heartbeat. He had a little more shine than the ten-cent Casanovas that came around, but I knew a con when I saw one." She leaned in close and rasped in his ear. "You wouldn't con me, would you, Crissy?"

"Perish the thought."

Arkko glanced at Ledger before continuing to perambulate. "After *Enterprise* left, I got together with some of the other girls. We all knew each other. We'd been skimming for years, so we took that dough and started our own outfit." She stopped and crossed her arms, remembering. "I wasn't going to wear the red dress ever again."

Rios didn't understand. "Didn't Kirk's visit end the mob thing?"

"Oh, Bela's people mostly stayed put on Iotia, where your babysitters could come by every year to pat them on the head. But I wasn't gonna wear the dress for the Feds, either. We'd already put a century into acting like one kind of human—we weren't gonna let you shape us again. We left so we could be what we wanted to be."

"What you always were," Rios said. "Gangsters."

"Wrong, brown eyes. We're bigger than those lugs ever were—on our world or yours. And now that the Rommies have folded up, there's nothing but opportunity." She paused to put her hand on his face again, drawing his mouth into a pucker. "Oh, and if you interrupt me again, my people will separate you from your tongue."

Rios nodded.

"And I can see that would be a shame," she said, leering at him more lasciviously than anyone had in a long time.

At last, she released him and stepped away. "Former Starfleet. Mmm-mmm."

Rios scowled. He still wasn't clear on why she'd come. When she hopped back onto the desk and the bearers didn't carry it anywhere, he raised his hand. "Permission to speak."

"Ooh, how nice." She smiled at her companions. "Shoot." When several of them raised their tommy guns, she waved them off. "Not that, dimwits." She looked to Rios. "Ask away."

"Since I'm still breathing," Rios said, "I take it you're here to give me some kind of job." He'd always expected to field offers from those outside the law; he just wasn't expecting to get his first one from someone so highly placed in interstellar crime. "You need me to carry something somewhere, is that it?"

"No, Mister Rios, I've got professionals for that."

"You need something from me, then. Something from Starfleet." Surely, if Ledger had been able to find out that portion of his past, Arkko wouldn't have had any trouble doing the same. "Hate to tell you, but I can't help. Even if I wanted to sell secrets, I'd be useless. Any command or access codes I ever had are long deleted."

"I think it's *adorable* that you think this is about you."

"It isn't?"

"No." Arkko faced Ledger. "It's about *her*."

"Me?" Ledger bolted upright.

"That's right," the boss said mildly. "You see, I've been reading some more about Earth in the 1920s—just to see what we would have gotten had *Horizon* been carrying someone with different interests. Apparently there was a very interesting outfit in the huge country on the other side of the planet. Some gangster elements, to be sure—but under a zealous ideological hat."

Rios nodded. "A fur one."

"That's the bunch. We killed our troublemakers. They did their share of that—but they also sent others off to a *very cold place* to work and think it over. I don't know why the Chicago crews didn't come up with a spot like that."

"It was called Wisconsin," Rios volunteered. "But Capone decided he liked it so much he built a house. Well, more like a fort." He'd seen it once.

Arkko ignored him. "There's a certain bookkeeper of mine who's been getting too big for her britches—and she needs to go somewhere."

Ledger's jaw dropped. "She does? I mean, I do?"

"That's right. I've heard things about your operation—*from* your operation." She gestured toward Stench. "Kid?"

The skinny hoodlum hustled to her side and handed her a paper list from his jacket pocket. Ledger, her mouth still open, sputtered at him. "B-but you work for *me*!"

"And you all work for *me*," Arkko said, taking the list from Stench. "Good job, kid. Now go take a bath."

Stench skittered away. Rios leaned forward in his chair, hands clasped as he watched Ledger squirm.

"Boss," she said, "I don't know what he's told you—"

"Enough to put you behind the eight ball," Arkko replied. "Some pretty big side deals, off the books—and on my nickel."

Ledger's face sank. "You know about Coridan?"

"No, but I'll be sure to look into it." Arkko listed a number of other skims from the paper. "Oh, and also the bloodwine thing you've got going right there in Krellen's Keep. Did you really think you could do business in my own house and it wouldn't get back to me?"

Ledger moved from foot to foot. "Look, boss—it's just a little entrepreneurship on the side, like you did back in the day. You want us to always be thinking."

"Thinking about making *me* money. The only thing saving your fanny is that it doesn't look like you were actually ripping me off. But you're always dressed to the nines, and it sure isn't because of the Verex operations. The take is way down."

Ledger hemmed and hawed. "That's all because of things out of my control. We had some unexpected expenses—"

Rios waved his right hand. "*¡Hola!*"

"—and people who haven't paid on time."

Rios raised his left. "*¡Buenos dias!*"

"But I'm fixing that," Ledger said. "Right now, in fact, in Rios's case. I made a special trip!"

"While on your way to Risa—which you redirected my own treasure fleet to carry you to. Which brings us back to Earth—and Siberia." Arkko snapped her fingers, and one of her nearby bearers pushed a button on a comm unit. A second later, a small mountain of trunks, suitcases, and hat boxes appeared on a clear patch of the deck. "Your luggage, madame."

"*What?*" Ledger blurted.

Rios bolted to his feet—only to raise his hands when he attracted gun barrels in his direction. "Excuse me," he said. "*What?*"

"Mugs like these are a dime a dozen," Arkko explained, gesturing to her minions. "I can get them anywhere. Smart sisters are rare. I won't rub her out if I don't have to—but I will teach her a lesson." Arkko looked about the debris-strewn deck. "Making Mister Rios's enterprise—ooh, I said the word!—a success would be an appropriate test, don't you think?"

"No!" Ledger practically squealed. "You can't! I mean, you can, but you shouldn't!" She stepped near Rios. "This is as small-time as it gets. He's a loser, boss."

"Yeah." Rios checked himself. "I mean, no! I don't need her here. *La Sirena* is mine!"

Arkko shrugged. "If you mean this ship, it's mine, sweetie—until it's paid off. And *until* it's paid off, Ledger is here to protect my interests." She glared at the accountant. "And she'll do it, if she wants to protect her pretty little neck."

Ledger and Rios looked to each other, equally shocked and offended.

Arkko clapped her hands, and the sweaty bearers lifted the desk again. As they carried her to the cargo transporter platform, the old woman called back with a smile: "*Gulag La Sirena*. I do like the sound of that!"

12

PORT PELLIGRU
ALPHA CARINAE II

"You're a lifesaver, Captain Rios." Undeterred by the snow whirling about the spaceport, the white-haired Carinean woman shook the pilot's hand vigorously. "You can't believe the service you've done."

"Neither can I." He meant it. Rios had purchased *La Sirena* expecting to haul a lot of different kinds of cargo. Carrying a lovesick teenager to commune with an alien entity wasn't something he'd considered even once.

Alpha Carinae II had proved to be like a lot of other planets in the onetime Borderland: crawling with freighter pilots looking for payloads. Like a whirlpool, the area had drawn in countless independent transports in response to the Romulan diaspora—and many were still here. *Too many*, for what business there was. Rios hadn't found any interstellar jobs at all during a week in the system. He'd been reduced to renting time on his cargo transporter to shift goods around the globe.

The Carinean woman, Glern, appeared to have a role with one of the few thriving manufacturing concerns on the planet. She had contacted Rios the evening before, offering a job that took him within the same system—but any opportunity to raise ship was welcome, as far as he was concerned.

Or it had been, until their rendezvous at the port that morning revealed that the cargo was her oldest child, apparently the Carinean equivalent of a teenager. "Moon-eyed" fit Carineans as a description already, but young Glaal had doubled down on that, weeping and moaning incessantly over a lost first love.

"I *do* hope Glaal wasn't any bother," Glern said.

Unbearable, Rios thought to respond. But instead, he gestured for the youth to join his mother. "It was an experience. I've never seen anything that ate *angst* before."

"Oh, the drella is a wonder," she replied, putting her arm around her son. "Carineans live and love too much—and for our young, that first heartbreak is debilitating." She put her hands over Glaal's ears. "And it's also incredibly annoying. He's been *insufferable* around the house!"

That went double for *La Sirena*'s command well. Hopping from Alpha Carinae's second planet to its fifth was the definition of a milk run, but even that had been too long for Rios to listen to Glaal weeping about someone named Dynn and the true love that would never cease—until it did, when Dynn got smart and found a dockworker with more emotional control.

Yet, as advertised, the gaseous creature known as the drella had happily absorbed Glaal's lovesickness. Its feeding practices allowed it to revel in and amplify thoughts of love, making it popular with newlyweds—but it could also lessen the ache from unrequited attachments. It had left the young Carinean both quieter and wiser, if with depleted tear ducts.

"Big line to get to it," Rios said. "We waited for hours."

"Oh, yes. Thank you," Glern replied. Her attention was on her son—whose eyes had just locked onto some other youth he'd seen in the crowd. The instant she took her hand off Glaal's shoulder, he hared off after his new quarry. Glern sighed. "They're so resilient at that age."

Yeah, I nearly bounced his head against a support beam. Rios crossed his arms. "Are you going to pay me or not?"

"Oh, yes," she said, reaching for her satchel. "I completely forgot."

"Yes."

Glern fished in her pouch and found the payment. "It's all there," she said, passing it over. "Plus a sizable gratuity for a job well done."

Rios confirmed the fact. He thanked her and watched as she headed off into the crowd at the spaceport in pursuit of Glaal. He was additionally appreciative that this time, at least, he didn't have to get belligerent. He'd been forced into acting that way too often during the past weeks.

Nobody trusted anyone anymore. Not here, near the border of the former Romulan Neutral Zone. Many Federation worlds had acted ignobly in the years immediately before the Romulan supernova, refusing to take refugees—effectively thwarting then-Admiral Picard's rescue program, even before the Martian disaster. The resulting burden had fallen even harder on nonmember states in the region like Alpha Carinae II, and many planetary economies were still reeling with no help in sight.

It partially explained why the spaceport had more laborers looking for work than cargo moving through it. Glaal's mom was the exception with a job and means, but Rios really didn't relish the thought of running a shuttle service for the lovelorn.

Freshly paid, he headed for the spaceport's dilapidated restaurant row, hoping he might find something palatable that didn't come from a replicator. Instead, he found his unwanted Iotian guest emerging from one of the better-looking establishments while chatting away on the comm unit in her hand.

Ledger was in yet another outfit: slacks again, under a stylish tan overcoat. This hat was furry, perhaps following Arkko's Siberian theme. The accountant finished her call and noticed him. "What are *you* staring at?"

"Just wondering where you expected to find snow on Risa."

"I always pack for a getaway—even when *on* a getaway." She bulldozed past him. "I'm busy. Walk and talk."

Rios nodded to the café. "I'm going to eat."

"You can't afford to eat. Let's blouse."

One couldn't go through Starfleet Academy—or work as a cadet on a starship of any size—without being billeted with roommates not of one's choosing. The best thing about Ledger was that she had been a virtual nonentity after the hearing with Boss Arkko. She had claimed her own quarters aboard *La Sirena* and stayed out of sight, working on her next moves, he presumed. She'd seemingly dealt with her loss of stature a lot faster than he had, but he had decided not to take it personally. Adapting was what Iotians did—when they wanted to.

That morning, Ledger had skipped out on the short-hop journey to work on her own machinations planetside. She said nothing about them now. "Well, don't keep me waiting," she said. "How was the drella?"

"You should've gone," Rios said. "It feeds on love. You could have stood there looking at a bar of latinum and kept it fed for days."

"Crusty, are we? I was going to say you could've just looked in a mirror, but that chin shrubbery tells me you've never owned one."

It was the sort of medium-wattage hostility that had flowed between her and Rios ever since her exile began. It wasn't the sexually charged repartee he had experienced with other women; Ledger genuinely seemed to dislike him, when she wasn't indifferent to his existence. The drella would have starved to be around the two of them.

"I do have an urge to look at latinum, though." She stopped in the middle of the plaza and locked her eyes on his hand. "Fork it over, Chester."

"I've told you, you're not my business manager."

"And you're not much of a business. Get on with it."

Reluctantly, he passed her a fistful of small, etched, ruby-colored pentagons.

"What's this?"

"Carintals," Rios said. "Local currency."

"I know what they are. I want to know why you took them. I told you, slips of latinum or nothing!"

"I took what she was willing to pay." He pointed to the numbers on the coins. "Five thousand carintals is pretty good. I checked the exchange rate last night."

"That was then. The central bank devalued the currency this morning. That junk won't get you a fingernail's worth of latinum, if that!"

Rios's brow wrinkled. "Glern didn't tell me that. Wonder if she knew."

"Of course she knew. You took the kid for a ride—then she took you for one." Ledger flung the coins away and watched as they clinked across the icy pavement.

"Are you crazy?" Rios started to bolt toward the fallen currency—only to stop when he noticed all the hard-luck cases about. Several stepped right past the carintals, not moving to retrieve them at all.

"You see? They know it's worthless!" Ledger gestured toward him. "You're the only person on the planet who *doesn't*! You should have asked for some magic beans while you were at it."

"Magic beans?" He tilted his head. "How much was *in* that Book of yours?"

"I told you, I never read it. The beans thing was just some guff that Wolyx spouted. He was always nattering about something." She started walking toward the landing area. "The point is you need a manager, Captain. And that's your tough luck, because I've got better things to do."

"Since when?"

She waved her comm unit. "I'm working angles. Making calls." She scrolled through her messages. "The Convincers aren't the only game in town, you know."

Their loss is someone else's pain, Rios thought, but decided against adding fuel to the fire.

They rounded the corner to where he could see *La Sirena* parked, its massive form functioning as an umbrella shielding a section underneath from the falling snow.

He also saw something else. Rios pointed. "Look there!"

A bipedal figure dashed from an alley, pursued by someone nearly twice the size. The subject of the chase darted toward *La Sirena* in an apparent attempt to escape—only to lose footing. By the time Rios and Ledger got close enough to see better, the chase was over: the pursuer, a large Lurian, was looming over his prey just beside the parked freighter.

Ledger noted the victim's attire. "Argelian executive," she said. "They're pacifists. Tough luck for him."

Rios stepped up the pace.

"Hey!" he shouted to the assailant, who had the Argelian in the air. The smaller man was kicking futilely. "Hey, you! Stop!"

"What are you doing?" Ledger asked, hurrying after him.

"That guy's getting smacked around!"

"Maybe Fancypants hasn't paid his bookie. Leave it alone."

Not a chance. Rios charged forward, unwilling to let anyone get beaten to death next to his ship. "I told you to stop!"

The Argelian's collar clenched in his fist, the bully looked back to Rios. "Who the hell are you?"

"That's my ship!"

"It's *my* ship," Ledger called out from behind him.

"Ignore her," Rios said. "Why don't you let that guy down?"

The Lurian bared his teeth. "I don't think so. Get lost, human, or you're next."

"Everything's jake," Ledger said, arriving at Rios's side. "Sorry to interrupt your business transaction. Enjoy your day." She tugged at the pilot's jacket. "Once around the block, Murphy."

Rios jerked away from her and reached for his phaser—remembering only then that he hadn't brought one. There was obviously no need for it when escorting Glaal; indeed, it would have only tempted him to shoot the kid during the crying jags.

The Lurian dropped the Argelian and faced down Rios. "I told you to go."

Looking at the assailant—and then looking up—Rios decided to reach for something else: his comm unit.

"Calling for help." Ledger looked to the sky. "I didn't know you were a rat."

The Lurian laughed at the two of them. "You're wasting your time. The police won't bother with this."

"Thanks for the advice." Rios keyed the comm unit. "*La Sirena*, enter maintenance menu. Blow starboard aft hydraulic panel two."

Above the Lurian, explosive bolts on the ship's underside fired—and a bulky metal panel popped loose. It plummeted several meters before clanging against the bruiser's head. He hit the tarmac with a thud not far from the cowering Argelian.

Rios hustled up to examine him. Ledger hovered behind. "Did you kill him?"

"Just out cold. These guys have skulls of duranium. It's why no thoughts ever get through."

"Hmph." She pointed to the panel beside the fallen Lurian. "You're going to have to put that back, I hope you know. That's the outfit's property."

The Argelian got to his feet and brushed himself off. "He was going to rob me," he said between deep breaths. He smiled at Rios and Ledger. "I'm so happy you and your wife came by."

"Hah!" Ledger blurted. She looked up. "Drop another one of those panels on *me*, why don't you?"

"We're not related," Rios said. "She's a stowaway."

The flushed Argelian turned a little redder. "Sorry—it was the arguing. I just assumed." He looked up. "Did you say this was *your* freighter?"

Rios and Ledger responded at the same time. "Yes," he said again, shooting her a glare. Rios identified himself and gave the name of the ship.

"It's a fine vessel. I'm Melton Moyles—I procure raw materials for Massworks on Argelius II." The executive extended his hand, and Rios accepted it. "Port Pelligru used to be safer in the old days. I hope you won't be insulted if I offer you a reward?"

"Of course not," Ledger said, shoving in front of Rios. "Insult him all you want."

"I don't need a reward," Rios said, trying to reclaim his space.

"Go chase yourself!" She faced the Argelian. "Gold-pressed latinum or nothing. We're wise to the coin game around here."

"I meant what I said." Rios interposed himself between them. "I don't want a reward. But I will take a job."

The Argelian looked him over—and up at the ship. "What's the carrying capacity?"

Rios provided the numbers. "Cargo transporters are top rated. And it's fast."

"I can believe it." Moyles clasped his hands together. "Yes, I expect to have a shipment that needs carrying to Argelius later this week—it's why I'm here today, in fact. But there's some bulk to it. Even with the transporters you'll need personnel to handle it all. How big is your crew?"

"Just her—but she's got a strong back."

"*Hey!*" Ledger shouted.

Moyles grimaced. "It may be hard to do this without at least a *few* hires."

Rios ruminated. He didn't want any company at all—Ledger, least of all. *Then again, where did that get Verengan?* He kept his eyes on the exec. "If the price is right, I can find the crew."

"Excellent!" Looking delighted, Moyles stepped aside to place a call, not two meters from the fallen Lurian.

Ledger pulled Rios aside and whispered, "Don't talk price with this guy. That's my department."

Rios waved her off. "You said you had your own business. Go mind it. This is mine!"

13

PORT PELLIGRU

ALPHA CARINAE II

In the dire months between his service on *ibn Majid* and the acquisition of *La Sirena*, Rios had spent a lot of time in bars—probably more than many of their employees. Any place that offered both food and forgetfulness appealed to him, and he wasn't even that interested in the food part. He had done his best to avoid the temptation while looking for work at Port Pelligru, yet a tavern was just where he wound up. He really didn't see any other choice.

Having quickly wrapped his negotiations with Moyles out of earshot of Ledger—she had loved that—Rios had boarded *La Sirena* long enough to grab a quick snack and to transport the fallen Lurian to the spaceport constable's office. Thief or not, it was the right thing to do in case the brute was seriously injured—and if he wasn't, Rios definitely didn't want him waking up and camping out at the foot of the loading ramp. That achieved, he had stolen past Ledger back out into the streets in search of his new hires.

It helped his cause that Alpha Carinae II had a day considerably longer than Earth's; the employment offices he visited were still staffed and operating. But open doors didn't equal open arms. The local spacers' guild refused to help him unless he paid to become a member, and the employment agencies wanted a percentage not just of the salaries of the workers they suggested, but an up-front fee just for opening their files to him. "Nothing free about free enterprise these days," one of the reps had said.

So Rios had wound up at a spaceport watering hole, fully expecting it to be populated by dockyard types. Instead, everyone he encountered was just like him: they all had idle starships of their own. Nobody who had their own ship in drydock was going to sign on with him, of course. Worse, those he spoke with were overly interested in whom he'd gotten a job with; he swiftly realized how eager they were to undercut him and take his assignment away. Hiring was already new to Rios; having to do it without providing any details about the job made it all the more difficult.

Rios was looking fondly upon the bottles behind the bar when a twenty-ish Benzite sought him out. Reedy-voiced through his breathing appliance, Yerm seemed peppy and ready to work, but he looked far too scrawny to be a stevedore. Nonetheless, Rios had quizzed him, hoping to find any other role he could fill:

"Can you operate a cargo transporter?"

"No."

"How about flying? Pilot skills?"

"No, sorry."

"Navigation?"

"No again."

"Then what do you bring to the table?"

"I don't care what you pay me."

"You're hired."

Yerm, he expected, had some local problem that made sticking around unhealthy; it was a story as old as wooden ships. It didn't matter to Rios, who reasoned that seeing any warm bodies at all on the team might satisfy Moyles. He also knew he was also under no obligation to keep anyone on after the job. He'd further hoped that Yerm would have connections leading him to other potential hires.

Another round of fruitless questions and answers proved that hope unfounded, though Rios did find the kid's overeager desire to help a refreshing change compared to what he'd lately dealt with.

"There was a passenger on the transport I arrived in who was an engineer," Yerm had said. "At least, I think she was. She kept complaining about the smell, so I figured she knew something about circulation systems. I don't know who she is, but if I walked the city for a few hours I might see her again—"

"Thanks, I'll pass." After an hour of such conversation, Rios decided to pack it in, inviting Yerm to collect his gear and head over to *La Sirena*.

Night was beginning to fall at last when Rios, unhappy with the results of his efforts, started his lonely trek back to the freighter's parking stall. He was stone sober, at least—though he began to doubt that assessment as he walked. Crowd noise usually diminished after one departed a tavern; instead, low rumbles of conversation grew ever louder as he got closer to *La Sirena*.

What the hell? Maybe the Lurian had come back with friends, he thought—but this sounded like an army. Rios felt for the phaser inside his jacket as he stepped up his pace. He hurried around the retaining wall and spied the mob. Not one of Ledger's kind, but rather an immense, churning queue of vagabonds of many different species, all bundled against the elements and chattering amongst themselves as they waited.

Rios ran across the tarmac. "What's going on?"

An emaciated Romulan looked back at him. "If you do not know, you are in the wrong place."

Rios received similar answers as he orbited the group, trying to get to the landing ramp. It was in the down position, he could see, but reaching it was a challenge. He resorted to barging in between people, making light pleasantries as he did. "Excuse me." "*Perdóname.*" "How you doing?" "Nice night."

These elicited a glossary of expletives in a variety of languages, as well as several attempts to push him back. But he surged forward, finally reaching the ramp. He was most of the way up it when he collided with a living wall of flesh in the form of a towering Nausicaan.

"Out of the way," Rios ordered.

The roadblock smiled and seemed to bow. Rios, who did not recall having a Nausicaan butler, attempted to pass—only to realize, to his chagrin, that a bowing giant had a better chance of grabbing someone. Which the Nausicaan did, a precursor to slamming Rios against one of the ramp's hydraulic supports.

Rios tried to shrug off the assault and reach for his phaser—but he found locating it difficult when the Nausicaan yanked his fastened jacket upward, shrouding his head. After being spun around, Rios was treated to a reunion with the support beam.

It went that way for several seconds, less a melee than something Rios might have been party to when he was nine. He finally shouted through the fabric, "*Dammit, it's my ship!*"

"He thinks you're cutting in line," Ledger called out from afar. "Glake, let him go!"

The Nausicaan did just that, going so far as to help extricate Rios from his jacket. Glake bowed wordlessly again, an act that made the captain take a step back—but there was no violent sequel this time. Instead, the goliath clasped his hands together in front of him and stood at attention.

Pushing back his hair, Rios snarled three words loudly. "*Where . . . is . . . she!*"

No answer, until "Glake, send him up!" came from within the vessel.

The Nausicaan stepped aside, and Rios stormed onto the cargo deck, ready to kill. More people were here in a line that extended to a stairwell and continued up it. Rios looked around futilely until he heard Ledger again—her voice coming from above. "Up here. I don't have time to give you directions!"

Rios barged up a staircase. The fury in his eyes must have crossed interspecies boundaries, because nobody on the steps objected to him. Once topside, he saw where the line led: to the first starboard doorway aft from the command area. He charged through the portal—

—and nearly five hundred years into the past. Wood paneling, curtains, antique furniture: everything one might find in a high-priced Earthly executive's office space in the 1930s. Unlike the Convincers' facility on Verex III, there were no telltale vents, pipes, and sliding doors to give away that a modern space had been remade; this place had just been *made*, to order.

And with that, Rios's rage lifted enough for him to remember what this room was. *The holodeck.* And Ledger was at the center of it, sitting in a high-backed leather chair with her ankles propped on a broad desk just like the one Boss Arkko had ridden into Rios's life on. Hatless, her hair in a tight bun, Ledger studied information on a padd, reading through the eyeglasses she inexplicably wore.

Seated in chairs across the desk from her, Ledger had two guests. They turned to face Rios—and in so doing, gave him a start. The women had alabaster skin and what he could only define as "Dracula hair." They didn't look exactly alike, but their fretful glances at him did.

Only then did Ledger look up. "Ah, there you are. Finally." She slid her legs off the desk and rocked forward in the chair. "You've been holding out on me!"

Rios was too flustered to say anything other than "I have?"

"Why didn't you tell me there was a holodeck?" Ledger slammed the padd on the desk, an act that caused her two ghost-faced guests to hop a few centimeters out of their chairs. Ledger stood and gestured. "I just thought this was another roomful of garbage!"

"So did I, when I bought it." Rios tilted his head. "Your people sold it to me—how is it that *they* didn't know what was here?"

"We didn't install it. It must have been something the Klingon did."

That was what Rios had suspected too. "How'd you find it?"

"I knew we were going to need quarters for the crew, so I sent Glake in to clean it out. Imagine our surprise when the first thing he carted out dematerialized."

Rios was back on the first thing she said. "You're hiring a crew? Who told you to—"

"I did, and it's good for you I did." She gestured with her thumb. "After you skulked off, I checked out that egg."

"*Egg*?"

"Moyles. Turns out that outfit of his on Argelius is *rolling* in it. This job is definitely worth doing—and worth doing right."

"But I never said—"

"Just a sec." Before Rios could respond, Ledger stormed past him and shouted outside. "*Glake, cap the line!*"

A hideous growl emanated from below. Rios couldn't tell whether it had come from Glake, or the collected horde in line. As she turned back into the *faux* office, he reached for her arm. "What are you doing? What is this?"

She spun and addressed him, centimeters from his nose. "Single syllables: You have a job. You need a crew. Here it is." She yanked her arm away. "And if you put your mitts on me once more, I'll cut 'em off. And I don't mean your hands!" A whirl of skirts, and she was sitting back at her desk, speaking to the two women. "Sorry. It's always something."

"Of course, Captain Ledger," one of her listeners said in a tiny voice.

"Oh, I'm not the captain. I'm with the ownership group," Ledger corrected. "But it is hard to keep track. Captains come and go."

"Of course," said the other woman, even quieter.

Dumbfounded, Rios gawked at them—and then looked back out into the ship, where the disgruntled applicants were filing out. He felt dizzy. He had lost control of his life better than a year before; purchasing *La Sirena* was an attempt to get it back. He was no longer in control—only this time, he knew the reason why.

He turned, took a breath, and tried to assemble a sentence through gritted teeth. "You didn't need to do anything. I was hiring."

"You seem to have done a wonderful job." Ledger pushed her glasses past the bridge of her nose and looked at him over them. "Laborers with personal cloaking devices are always in demand."

"No, I did hire someone—"

"So did I—just now." She gestured to the women. "This is Ny-Var and Zo-Var. They're Miradorns."

Rios knew about Miradorns from his Starfleet days. They traveled in pairs, in many ways two halves of the same being. Working in tandem, they were highly efficient, but they tended to fall apart without their partners. These two looked glum, but he imagined that was just from having to deal with Ledger.

"They're a package deal," she said. "I figure them for pilot and navigator."

"*I'm* the pilot," Rios said.

"Not when you're asleep—and certainly not when you're tight."

"When I'm what?"

"You're zozzled every night. You're going to be the first person to wake up in both a black hole *and* a puddle of drool." She gestured to the Miradorns. "They're your relief."

"We fly ships," Ny-Var said, still quiet as a church mouse.

"Yes, ships," Zo-Var added, barely audible at all.

Rios looked from one of them to the other. Apart from the weird hairline favored by Miradorns, they didn't resemble each other much—but that didn't mean anything. The members of the species he had met were fraternal twins. "What have you flown before?"

"They know their onions," Ledger said. She lifted the padd from the desk long enough to glance at it. "Served on the *S.S. Somesuch*—"

"Ah, the famous *Somesuch*." Rios rolled his eyes.

"What do I care what it's called? Here!" She flung the padd toward him.

He caught it—and, righting it, studied the women's vitae. There were several cargo ships of varying classes mentioned. He shrugged. "Fine. I guess they're in."

"Of course they're in," Ledger said. "I just made the decision. Did you not see me send away the others?" Her eyes darting to the entrance, she noticed a commotion outside. "Glake, I said nobody else. I was only hiring for the flight crew."

Glake appeared in the accessway with a body slung over his massive shoulder.

Ledger chuckled. "What, did someone try to sneak past?"

"*Yeeesss.*" The Nausicaan's rumbling growl seemed to emanate from deep in his abdomen, and it made the three-letter word last three seconds.

"Spin around so I can see him," Ledger ordered.

Glake complied.

"Toss him back," she said after a quick look. "We don't need any small fry!"

"Wait!" Rios shouted, recognizing the trespasser's face and breathing apparatus. "That's Yerm!"

"What's a Yerm?"

"*He* is!" Rios pointed to the Benzite. "I've already hired him!"

"You did what?" Ledger sighed audibly. "Glake, down."

The Nausicaan dropped his burden to the deck with a thud.

Rios knelt and checked on the kid. "Sorry, Yerm. You okay?"

Yerm was shaken but conscious. "D-did I get the wrong ship?"

"This is the right ship—it's everything else that's wrong." Rios flashed defiance as he looked back up at Ledger. "I hired him an hour ago."

As Yerm sat up, Ledger looked the Benzite over. She clicked her tongue twice with disapproval. "It's a good thing you don't recruit muscle for the Convincers," she told Rios. "Our turf would be down to half a city block."

"I didn't hire him as muscle."

"What does he do, then?"

Rios didn't know the answer, of course—but only one response was in order. "I'm the captain. I don't owe *you* an explanation." He pointed at Glake. "Anyway, what does *he* do?"

Ledger pursed her lips. "I'm not sure—he keeps to himself. Don't you, Glake?"

"*Yeeesss.*"

Rios winced. "He sounds like his motor is stuck."

"We don't need him to give speeches," Ledger said. "You're looking to move cargo around. What do you care?"

He had no answer. Resigned, Rios helped Yerm to stand and pointed him toward the exit. "I'll get you all billeted." Then he looked at Glake. "Do you know how to raise the ramp?"

Once again, the elongated word of agreement.

"Do it. I can't deal with anyone else tonight."

Ledger clapped her hands and stood. "Right," she declared. "I'll have everyone's contracts in an hour."

The Miradorns filed out, making barely audible pleasantries to Rios as they passed. As the new hires departed, he sagged against the door, exhausted.

Seeing Ledger about to sit again, he said, "Computer, end program."

The office vanished, as well as the desk and chair; Ledger recovered before she fell. She shot him an icy glare. "Nice. You're a laugh riot."

"Honest mistake," he said. Then he looked out the door in wonder. "How'd you get all these people here so fast? I didn't get anywhere."

"I have my ways. What were *you* offering?"

"What we could afford."

She chuckled. "Well, there's your mistake. I shot the moon." Then, with a wink and a whisper: "By the way, if you see anyone actually *reading* their contract, beam them off in a hurry!"

14

La Sirena
Orbiting Alpha Carinae II

"So, are you designing uniforms?" Raffi asked. *"Something stylish for the Cristóbal Rios Merchant Marine?"*

"Not exactly," Rios said to the air, straightening his turtleneck while standing before the mirror in his quarters.

"You should replicate hats with feathers. And your feather should be bigger than everyone else's."

"You're in fine form for so early in the morning."

"Not morning here. And your feather should be all different colors. Forget the collar pips. Show some style!"

Rios had gone through his morning routine before crew reviews many times, and while he had no need to clean himself up on his own ship, something about the first real assignment had prompted him to trim his beard. It felt unexpectedly good to go through the motions of command, even if he wasn't in charge of much.

"I can't imagine what it must feel like to have a crew again," Raffi said, echoing his feelings. *"Four or four hundred."*

"Don't oversell it. There's not enough lipstick for this pig."

"So they're green. You've been on your own too long. This is good."

"I *wanted* to be alone." He put down the trimmers. *Good enough.*

He'd made no assignments the previous day, putting everyone instead on the task of consolidating Verengan's junk into portside storage. Everyone except Ledger, of course, who had a comm unit to her ear every time she emerged from the holodeck. She continued to use it as her office but hadn't yielded her original quarters, complicating the storage issues.

That they had cleared the main cargo deck in one day owed in part to the fact that Rios hadn't really been trying during his three months, and also to the sleepless energy of Glake and Yerm. He wasn't surprised that the Nausicaan seemed to have no limits, but the slender Yerm was something else.

However, every time Rios had been tempted to think the kid wasn't such a bad pick after all, something else suggested Yerm had never been in space before, much less served on a ship. "Can't we move this stuff by turning off the gravity?" was the sort of question that gave Rios little comfort.

"It's time," he said at last. "I have to go restrain my expectations."

"First ship's review. I love it."

"You've built this fantasy around my life here. You need to get out more."

"I'm way out," Raffi replied bouncily. *"Just promise me you're going to tell somebody to 'Make it so.'"*

"Good-bye, Raffi."

"See, before he pissed me off, that's a thing that—"

"I get the reference. Rios out."

He stepped out onto the upper deck, satisfied that, for once, he could look all the way aft without seeing junk piles. The stroll back was also novel: he'd cleaned every square of deck plating one at a time but had never seen them all uncovered at once.

The four workers—it wasn't yet reflex to consider them *his*—were assembled just as instructed, right in front of the cargo transport pad. They were neither fully in line nor at attention, and they all wore what they'd had on when he met them, but he wasn't going to be picky. "Good morning."

"Good morning, Captain!" Yerm yelped, saluting so hard he nearly slapped himself in the face. The women murmured something, while Glake issued another drawn-out affirmation.

I'll take what I can get, Rios thought. He began to pace, speaking as he did. "We'll be descending shortly to a manufacturing co-op on the dayside. There we'll transport up a large cargo of duranium-alloy ball bearings. We secure the containers and make for the client's factory on Argelius II."

There were no questions. He counted that as a win.

"The nature of the bearings makes them impossible to replicate locally, so this is a popular run. We do our jobs, we get paid. We land early, and they may—"

From behind, Rios heard Ledger prattling away in the distance. He turned to see her sauntering toward him and speaking into a comm unit, completely ignorant of the others' presence. "I told you to ship those cases to Ketorix," she said. "They're not doing anybody any good sitting on the dock!"

Rios gestured to the crew. "*Un momento*."

Ledger tapped her heel while the comm unit chattered. "Just stop talking," she finally said. "I don't care if you take a sample. Just refill the empties. Try tomato sauce in milk—color *and* consistency."

Rios cleared his throat. "Do you mind?"

"Never." Then, back to the comm, "I've got to go." She turned it off.

"We're having a briefing," he said. "You wouldn't know that, because I didn't ask you to attend."

"And I wouldn't have if you did. But pep talks are important." She stepped in front of him and faced the other four, accusatory finger in the air. "Do your jobs, and Moyles will give *La Sirena* this route for good."

Rios growled, exasperated. "I just was saying that."

"But if you guys make a botch of it," she continued, "they'll find all of you on a meat wagon."

Ny-Var looked spooked. "What . . . is a *meat wagon*?"

"Nothing," Rios said. "They don't exist."

"It sounds kind of nice," Yerm observed, hungrily patting his midsection. "I'd visit a meat wagon."

"*Yeeesss*," Glake contributed.

Rios put his hand over his face. "Ledge, I'm begging you."

"What?" she asked. "I'm just trying to tell these people this outfit doesn't tolerate failure!"

Zo-Var's eyes widened. "Is this some kind of crime ship?"

Rios looked up, baffled. "*Crime ship?*"

Ny-Var grew cautious. "Are these 'ball bearings' illegal?"

"So what if they were?" Ledger asked. "Your contracts specifically state—"

"Stop!" Rios stomped his boot on the deck. In the ensuing quiet, he walked down the line. "Glake and Yerm—we'll get you fed, *after* this. Flight crew—there are no illegal ball bearings. They may be the most boring cargo in the universe." At the end, he turned back to face Ledger. "You—stay quiet or stay in your rooms. You've got half the upper deck. It should be plenty."

Ledger smiled primly. "I seem to remember Arkko specifically putting me here to audit your operations."

"I seem to remember that all your calls route through the ship's subspace transmitter. I bet Arkko would love to hear who you've been talking to."

She froze for a moment, before shrugging. "Manage away." She strolled to the side and hopped on top of a console to sit. "Computer, iced tea."

"Sweetened, unsweetened, or Long Island?"

Ledger glanced at Rios. "Maybe it *is* your ship."

With the accountant sipping at her drink, Rios returned to the matter at hand. He stepped before the two Miradorns. "Okay. Who's my pilot and who's my navigator?"

Ny-Var and Zo-Var huddled closely and appeared to whisper to each other. The visual was the only clue Rios had. Considering their usual voices, he doubted any sound waves were in motion at all. At last, they broke the clinch.

"Navigator," Zo-Var said, raising her hand slightly.

Ny-Var raised her hand as well, only to ask meekly, "What did you say the other was?"

Rios let out a breath. They had to be putting him on—everyone else was. "Just go forward and settle in. We'll make a maneuver in ten minutes—I'll see you up there."

As the two hustled to comply, Rios stepped next in front of Glake. "I know you're good at moving things, big guy. You've worked cargo ships a lot?"

"*Yeeesss.*"

"By chance did they teach you to run a cargo transporter?"

"*Yeeesss.*"

"Wonderful." He gestured to the engineering chamber. "Get back there—you'll beam the stuff aboard. Coordinates are preprogrammed."

The Nausicaan uttered his catchword again and complied.

Relieved to have had one simple transaction, Rios moved on to Yerm. The young Benzite seemed jittery. "Did you sleep at all last night?"

"Oh, no. Too excited, sir." He stepped from foot to foot, rubbing his midsection again. "I've been learning all about the ship."

"See anything you'd be good at besides carrying stuff?"

Yerm looked away, bashful. "Well, I saw the clinic downstairs." He looked up. "I know how to use a hypospray."

Rios tilted his head. "We do need a medic."

"And if you give *him* the job," Ledger said, "you need a headshrinker." She hopped off the console. Leaving her drink behind, she stepped up to Yerm. "Come on, give."

Yerm looked at her, disconcerted. "What do you mean?"

She stepped aside and gestured to Rios. "Frisk him."

Rios looked at her as if she were daft—only to change his mind when he saw Yerm's expression. His heart sank a little. He gestured. "Come on."

Yerm cringed. "What?"

"Captain's orders. Let's have it."

Shrinking, Yerm finally gave in. He pulled up his shirttail and produced a hypospray from within his waistband.

Rios took it and examined it. "That's a downer," he said—and not just because it was a narcotic.

"Oh, he's not done," Ledger said. "Let's go, sport."

Yerm pulled out another hypospray. "That's an upper," Rios said.

Ledger walked around the kid. "I expect you'll find more of the pharmacy around back." She watched, satisfied, as Yerm pulled even more of the high-tech syringes from his waistband. "He may not be able to keep his trousers up after this."

Rios needed two hands for all the implements. He glared at Yerm. "Are you selling or using?"

The Benzite tried to look Rios in the eye—but his fast breathing outpaced what his respirator could handle, and he sat down on the floor to keep from hyperventilating.

"The gangs never messed with drugs on Sigma Iotia," Ledger said, "but I'll wager the experience your 'medic' has is purely recreational."

"Is this the only reason you wanted the job?" Rios growled. "To get at my med supplies?"

"Oh, no, sir." Yerm looked down. "I mean, no, Captain!"

"Then what?"

"I also needed to get off the planet. *And* to get at your med supplies."

"Are you wanted by the law? In debt? Running from a deal gone bad?"

Yerm figured. "Two of those."

"Which two?" Ledger asked with interest.

Rios blinked. "I can't imagine it matters."

Yerm started to cry. "I wanted to do so well, this time." He rocked back and forth. "Please don't beam me off, sir. I'll work—you don't have to pay me."

Ledger looked up. "I do like that."

Whatever composure Rios had started the review with was long gone—as was his patience. "We'll see," he said, walking away with the hyposprays.

Ledger called out to him. "So what about a medic?"

"We'll just have to hope nobody gets hurt. And if anything else happens today, somebody *will*!"

15

La Sirena

Orbiting Alpha Carinae II

Rios had not been in charge of *ibn Majid*, but as the first officer he had sat in the captain's chair many times, whenever he had the conn. There was something satisfying about seeing workers who answered to you sitting between you and space. In ancient times, a pilot holding a tiller could look out over the rowers up ahead knowing that they would execute his orders, taking the ship wherever he wanted to go.

Sitting behind the Miradorns, however, had been less than inspiring. "Your reaction times are for shit," he said. "No offense."

After his review went haywire, he had been overjoyed to get back onto the bridge. But he'd soon seen that the simple matter of bringing *La Sirena* into a geosynchronous orbit over the duranium forge was well beyond his flight crew's capacities. Again and again they overshot or undershot where the freighter was supposed to be—and when it did hit the mark, it soon slipped off station.

Rios desperately didn't want to seize control of the vessel through his own interface; that was the equivalent of leaning over the shoulder of whoever was at the helm. A Starfleet captain who did that would quickly become the bane of service. But he'd felt the inertial dampers kick in a dozen or more times in a five-minute period—and he wasn't the only one who noticed.

"What the devil is going on?" Ledger appeared at his side, empty glass in hand. "You spilled my drink."

"I'm not the one flying," Rios said.

"It feels like the ship has the DTs, so naturally I assumed."

Rios looked from Ny-Var to Zo-Var, not understanding what was wrong with them. A helm operator and a navigator needed to act in concert, acting on information supplied not just through shared telemetry, but each other's words, body language, and facial expressions. But the women were completely silent, and if they were reading each other's signals in any other way, the results weren't showing it.

Rios finally broke down and said something. "I don't get it." He searched for the right words. "I don't wanna be insensitive, but you're Miradorns, right?"

"Yes," said Zo-Var, looking back.

"Oh, yes," added Ny-Var.

"Aren't Miradorn pairs supposed to be hyperefficient?"

"Yes, oh, yes," Zo-Var said.

Rios stopped Ny-Var before she could add her agreement. "So what am I missing here? You're Miradorns."

"Yes."

"You're sisters."

"*No*," Zo-Var said.

"Oh, no," Ny-Var added.

"You're not?"

"Oh, we are sisters," Ny-Var said, looking to her companion.

"Yes, we certainly are," Zo-Var said. "We're just not *each other's* sisters."

At painful length—interrupted by several awkward pauses in which the two teetered on the verge of tears—Rios came to understand that they each had siblings who died as children during the Dominion War. Severed and adrift, Ny-Var and Zo-Var found each other and banded together for companionship.

"But your surnames?" Rios asked, scratching his beard.

"Very common where we are from."

"Yes, very common. The Miradorn vice president is a Var."

"And the leading talk show host."

Ledger barely stifled a laugh. Rios shot her an acid look and plowed on. "Okay, I'll make this simple. You can fly, can't you?"

"Oh, yes!" Ny-Var said.

"Yes," Zo-Var added. "But not land."

"No, oh, no. Not land."

Rios did the hated thing: he took back control and brought *La Sirena* to its proper orbital station. For good measure, he programmed their course. "When the cargo is fully aboard, you'll get an alert up here. Ny-Var, activate program number one and we'll go to impulse. Got it?"

She assured him that she did.

Number one is the skinny line that goes up and down, he wanted to say—but he decided it was better left alone. As he rose, he watched as they put on the oversized headsets they favored. Satisfied they could not hear him, he made his way aft, giving Ledger a piece of his mind along the way. "Great hires."

"You could have interviewed the flight crew, if you weren't off barhopping."

"That's not what I was doing." He glared at her. "And what's funny about this? If I fail, you fail—and Arkko gets us both."

"You were always just a longshot. I have plenty of outs. And now," she said as she reached the top of the staircase, "I'm out to lunch."

"You're not going to help? Or oversee?"

He could hear her laughing all the way down to the galley.

Rios walked quickly aft, unwilling to let her perturb him any further. The solution to everything would be a job well done. He could make sure of that. The factory had sent him a detailed scan of the cargo awaiting them: many huge barrels of ball bearings, each immensely heavy.

Verengan had left several antigrav pushcarts; Rios brought them out. He didn't think it wise to beam the cargo directly to the starboard stowage area. That would require a bit of precision, especially if any of the other junk back there had shifted. It would be an easy matter to transfer the material from the pad to the carts, and thence to a safe spot for the flight to Argelius II.

Arriving aft, he saw Glake through the transparent barrier that separated the warp core and engineering from the rest of the ship. The Nausicaan seemed to be in position, poring over the console. That just left Yerm, who arrived and took station beside one of the carts.

Rios powered it up for him. "You okay now, kid?"

"I am, sir." The Benzite looked tired but aware; if he was on something, it appeared to have worn off. "Ready to work."

"That's what I want to hear." Rios brought out his comm unit. "*La Sirena* to factory loading dock."

"Dock here."

"We're on station and ready to transport."

"It's in position, La Sirena. *It's in your hands. Safe trip."*

"Acknowledged." He looked back to engineering and called out. "Glake, are you locked on?"

Audible through the open door: "*Yeeesss.*"

Don't mind hearing it this time, Rios thought. They were on their way. "Glake, *energize!*"

In the Federation, Rios had never had to worry about anything having to do with money—and yet the sight of many large pillars of energy on the transporter pad thrilled him. They weren't going to be big barrels of treasure, not really. But they would be a start.

As the transporter whined, they began to resolve into clearer view. The cargo was exactly as described: shiny, duranium-alloy ball bearings of all sizes—

—but his next immediate thought was that he should not be able to see them. Rios's heart leaped into his throat as a third thought burned into his mind:

The ball bearings beamed up—but the containers didn't!

The transporter effect ended, leaving an eight-pack of colossal cylinders of metal balls, a meter and a half high. Without the barrels to constrain them, they held position momentarily atop the pad, shuddering as if possessed by a ghost. Then *La Sirena*'s artificial gravity had its say, causing the bearings to collapse to the deck in a thunderous waterfall.

"Look out!" Rios shouted—but it was already too late, as a tidal wave of tiny metal balls surged underfoot. The avalanche threw him off his feet and onto the bed of the antigrav cart, which spun forward with him, riding the newly moving surface.

There was no up, no down—no handhold that he could find. He could only hear a scream somewhere inside the bouncing tumult—and he could only see, as the dizzying rotations slowed, another batch of the unbound cargo materializing.

Glake, no!

Rios managed to tip the cart onto its side, jamming it into the deck and positioning it as a shield against the coming tsunami. It struck the cart hard, a thousand hammers pounding as one—and Rios flipped over, his back against the shield and his heels digging futilely at the rolling deck.

It was then that he saw Yerm, the source of the earlier scream, tumbling on his side in a haphazard surf that rocketed him past Rios—and toward the well leading to the deck below.

From the galley, another yelp: this one from Ledger, as ball bearings shot over the side. Yerm went with them, sliding neatly under the railing and disappearing.

Headed for a similar fate, Rios rolled over, redirecting the cart so that it slammed into the rails, blocking his progress. His head and arms hung momentarily over the pit, where he briefly saw a torrent of silver balls—and Ledger, cowering under the mess table and screaming her head off. He didn't see Yerm, but there was no time to look.

As the tidal wave subsided just a little, its force spent, he grabbed onto the railing and tried to pull himself up.

It was that moment, when all cargo was aboard, that the Miradorns executed their orders as directed, firing the thrusters on a buildup to going to impulse. No inertial dampers in existence could have prevented the sequel: a counterwave heading aft, both on the upper deck and below—and beneath Rios's feet. "Stop!" he yelled—understanding in that moment what had happened. The not-each-other's-sisters had evidently missed the excitement while wearing their bulky headsets, and they definitely weren't going to hear him.

The deck continued to act like a living thing for the long seconds it took him to crawl forward along the railing toward the bridge. Then it was the turn of Ny-Var and Zo-Var to squeal in horror, when they turned to see the fright that their captain had become. Rios staggered to his command chair and shut down the ship's thrusters.

He turned to see Glake on the move, gingerly trying to find a path from engineering. Rios couldn't wait for him. Fortunately, the forward staircase down was on the bridge side, and thus suffered from less of the moving cargo. Still, ball bearings continued to rain down as he descended.

He found Yerm's crumpled form first: battered and bleeding—and choking. Rios realized what was happening. His breathing unit was gone, but that wasn't the only problem. He lifted the Benzite up; there was no time to worry about broken bones or internal injuries. Rios turned Yerm around and applied pressure to his midsection, causing the ball bearings to spew from the kid's mouth.

Ledger emerged from beneath the table. Rios thought she looked shell-shocked—yes, that would have been the right word in the Iotian vocab—and her hair and clothing were a mess. Her wide eyes fell onto Rios and Yerm for a few seconds before she realized what she was looking at.

"Help," Rios said, clutching at Yerm.

"Right."

Together, they dragged the Benzite aft, stepping as carefully as they could; ironically, the rolling floor here made Yerm a lighter burden. Sickbay had its own cascades of ball bearings coming down the aft stairwell, and several of the movable supply carts had overturned during the Miradorns' herky-jerky flight adjustments. Clinic gear was strewn across the deck, coursing here and there as more pellets entered from above.

Glake appeared, having descended a rear stairway; to his credit, he immediately helped them get Yerm up onto the biobed. Assisting the Benzite was job one, but Rios couldn't stop himself from unleashing on his would-be engineer. "Dammit, Glake! Who beams up cargo without the containers?"

The Nausicaan did not respond. Ledger, perhaps having seen the look in Rios's eyes, offered measured words for a change. "Maybe when you gave your orders . . . you should have been *more specific*."

16

LA SIRENA
ORBITING ALPHA CARINAE II

Rios and his companions knelt on the deck, sorting through therapeutic tools that had been tossed around during the mayhem. "Anybody see a medical tricorder?" he asked.

The Nausicaan was about to answer when Rios jabbed a finger in his direction. "Don't answer 'yes' if you don't mean it!"

Looking glum, Glake said nothing.

"You see?" Rios looked over at Ledger. "He's your hire. And the only word he can say is *yes*!"

"To be fair," she said, "on my world, that makes him the perfect employee."

Rios understood there was no time to further litigate what had happened, not with the shape Yerm was in. The immediate issue was that Rios didn't know for sure what that shape *was*. He'd already tried to get the ship's concierge system to give him a tricorder, to no avail. Maybe it was too complex a task; maybe there was an authorization matter he didn't understand.

There was one thing he did know: the only care Yerm was likely to get was on *La Sirena*. Even if the freighter were in a condition to turn about and land, none of the overtaxed facilities on Alpha Carinae II were accepting walk-in patients, emergency or otherwise. He'd learned that from a couple of spacers in the same bar where he'd met the kid; it was another consequence of the Romulan diaspora. For good or ill, the burden fell on Rios—and here he was, scrabbling around on the deck.

"This looks like a tricorder," Ledger said, holding up a gray device.

"Yes!" Rios took it and hurried back to the biobed.

Every Starfleet officer went through basic medical training. It had only taken a single pass with the tricorder for Rios to see that Yerm's injuries were well beyond anything he had ever been taught to handle. There was the impact from the fall, but also his respiratory distress to worry about. Would just any replicated Benzite breather assembly do? he wondered. And what if he'd swallowed some of the damn pellets?

He finished scanning. "His blood's got elevated levels of—" He blanched when he read the results. "A whole lot of stuff."

"I knew he was on something," Ledger said. "I didn't even tell you: I saw him sneaking out of your quarters last night, when you were passed out on the bridge. That's why I was onto him."

The comments barely had time to register with Rios before several of the biobed sensors sounded their alarms. As if in response, Yerm quaked, the beginnings of a convulsion.

Or worse. "Cardiac arrest," Rios said. He gestured to Ledger. "There's a hypospray for this."

She glanced around. "What's it look like? I'm an accountant, not a—"

Rios tuned her out. There wasn't time to help her, or to find it himself. He put his knee on the biobed and hoisted himself up until he was straddling Yerm. He clasped his hands together for cardiopulmonary resuscitation, a method he had applied just once on a test patient on a holodeck.

Holodeck! Rios's memory jogged as he put pressure on Yerm's chest. "Computer, initialize EMH!"

"Unable to comply."

"Bullshit!" The feature existed, he knew. It had come up in Verengan's death message. "Computer, initialize the Emergency Medical Hologram package!"

"Unable to comply."

There were inopportune times to get into a debate with a starship; listening for a heartbeat with his head against Yerm's chest was one of them. "Explain initialization failure!"

"The package has already been initialized by Captain Rios. Do you wish to activate it?"

"The hell?" Rios looked up and shouted, "Activate EMH!"

Behind him, he finally heard the words he was expecting: "Good afternoon! Please state the nature of your medical emergency."

The fact that the words were in a perfectly pronounced English accent did not surprise him. The sound of the voice, however, did. Rios looked up into the gawping face of Ledger—and then followed her gaze as he turned his head.

Rios looked into his own eyes—and again heard it: his own voice. "How may I assist, Captain?"

He stared at the hologram for a couple of seconds before he remembered why he'd summoned it. He gestured to Yerm. "Help him!"

"Certainly." The EMH stepped around the table, neatly navigating around the stray ball bearings on the deck. "Curious flooring choice."

"Just shut up and look at him!"

The EMH complied.

Rios looked too—at the hologram. It was another Cristóbal Rios, only with better-manicured hair. He wore a white-collared shirt with no tie under a suave black suit. Rios had seen a lot of suits on the Iotians, but this style was different, more modern. The EMH combined the casual appearance of someone who'd stopped off at a party after work with the focused concentration of someone who'd left before the first toast.

Ledger, just as stunned as Rios was, blurted, "You made it look like you! Are you kidding me?"

Rios wasn't listening. He kept pumping, even as the EMH set to work.

"Benzite, approximately twenty years old," the hologram said. A medical tricorder materialized in his hand, and he went to work. "Malnutrition. Fractured left tibia. Broken right femur. Five broken ribs. Internal bleeding. Concussion." Yerm shuddered on the table, and the hologram kept on, matter-of-factly naming maladies. "Blood chemistry consistent with chronic use of barbiturates and painkillers."

"Told ya." Ledger crossed her arms and nodded, vindicated.

"Hypoxia due to atmospheric rejection, the beginnings of duranium poisoning—and gout." The EMH looked back at Rios. "Are you certain this is a real patient? Because it quite resembles one of my system's diagnostic tests."

"He's real," Rios said. "Do what you can!"

"I am so doing. You may stop pumping now." The EMH had already summoned a hypospray from the concierge system and was applying it to Yerm's neck. He then moved swiftly around the table, calling for a tool, using it, and dispelling it almost faster than Rios could see.

Hypnotized at watching himself work, Rios rose and stepped carefully back onto the deck. "Will . . . he survive?"

"Too many variables to calculate with any precision," the EMH responded. "This will take some time."

"Do you need my help?"

"Not with the patient. I will be quite busy and need the space. But if you are not committed to having these metal spheres as part of the décor, I'd prefer not to work around them."

"Got it." Rios looked down at the mess, wondering what to do.

Ledger snapped her fingers at the Nausicaan, who had been standing, spellbound, mesmerized by the two Rioses. "Glake, broom."

"Forget that." Rios surveyed the deck. "Computer, target clinic surface debris and activate transporter. Store in the pattern buffer."

Ledger watched as the pellets surrounding her vanished. "It'll only hold so much—and you can't keep it there long before it decays. We've tried smuggling that way before."

Rios couldn't care less. The EMH was working hard; the system wouldn't have mentioned the floor if it weren't impeding his work. "We'll get out of the way," he told the hologram. "I'll want a status update on him."

"I shall keep you apprised."

Rios wondered if he heard a little bit of lip in the EMH's tone. But that took a back seat to the greater mystery: *Where the hell did this guy come from?*

17

La Sirena
Deep Space

There had been times, when Rios was going through Verengan's garbage, that he had wanted to take a shovel to all of it. Having just spent four hours with a replicated shovel in hand, he had to admit the feeling wasn't as satisfying as he'd imagined.

Earlier, when he had arrived back on the bridge, the Miradorns had alerted him to a hail from Carinae Control, demanding that *La Sirena* get out of the patch of orbital space it had been loitering in. He had chosen again to ignore the sensitivities of his flight crew by taking the conn himself. Rios had over a million good reasons to, all strewn across his decks.

Modern starship design sought to eliminate any sensation of movement passengers might experience as a result of the forces applied during flight. Perfection at that usually required the helping hand of the helm operator, massaging the inertial dampers as needed. It was why few vessels needed to worry about harnesses and seatbelts—and why, during battle, so many officers wound up wishing for them. Whoever was at the helm usually had other things to worry about.

If ever anything was a test of a starship's inertial dampers—and the helm's management of them—a sea of metal balls rolling around on the decks qualified. Rios had only just touched the thrusters when he regretted the oaths he'd sworn at Ny-Var and Zo-Var earlier. Forces he'd usually consider negligible could be heard behind him in a low rolling rumble—and the not-so-low objections of Ledger. But he had seen it through, and the fact that he was able not only to go to impulse, but warp, without causing another avalanche was a testament to *La Sirena*'s systems.

He'd gone to warp more or less without thinking: there really wasn't anything else to do. Rios had a cargo, a destination, and a deadline. He didn't expect Moyles was going to give him a do-over on the grounds that someone he had met two days ago couldn't operate a sophisticated transporter properly. It was Rios's fault for not doing it himself; for not understanding Glake's limitations; for letting Ledger railroad him into hiring the guy at all.

Yet in a perverse way, those things were still better than what had happened aboard *ibn Majid.* Rios had taken all the blame for that but deserved none of it. At least this time, he thought as he drove the front edge of a scoop shovel underneath another mass of pellets, some of the fault was his. That made the manual labor a little easier to take.

He'd been forced to it in part because even after the previous day's cleaning, there was too much bric-a-brac scattered about to simply use the transporter for everything. Getting the pellets from the clinic out of the pattern buffer had told him just how much dust and other material they'd picked up. Better to get it all binned up by hand, and then see if the transporter could remove some of the impurities.

The fact that he had little idea how to do that was an issue he hadn't concerned himself with. If there wasn't time to find a method, chances were the whole mission was unsalvageable anyway. How much, he wondered, did a million or so custom-made ball bearings cost?

Behind him, Rios heard a rumble of a kind that didn't set him shivering. It was another just-replicated cylindrical container being rolled up to him—but this time it wasn't Glake delivering it.

"Fill 'er up," Ledger said, looking handy in a khaki pantsuit and a utilitarian scarf.

He didn't fault her for another clothes change. The chaos had done a number on his outfit, and he'd long since chucked the turtleneck to work bare chested. "*Gracias,*" he said, sweat shining as he dumped the contents of his shovel into the barrel. "Surprised you're doing this. I thought you were planning your escape."

"Heaven forfend! You're suggesting I would abandon this crew in its hour of need?"

"Couldn't reach anyone, could you?"

"Not a one. There must be a regional holiday."

He'd seen her furtively talking on her comm unit, trying to find any contact who would rendezvous with the freighter. *Maybe she doesn't have as many "friends" as she thinks she has,* he thought. *Or maybe she's just pissed them all off.*

"Besides," she said, her eyes following him as he worked, "now I want to unlock the mystery of Sawclones down there."

"Who?"

"You know—Cris the Croaker. The Rx Rios."

"I never know what you're talking about." He kept shoveling.

She walked in front of him. "I'm talking about your twin brother downstairs. He's you, but sober." Ledger chuckled. "I've seen some ego cases before, but you take the cake."

"I didn't make him that way," Rios said. *At least, I don't remember doing it!*

"He's almost charming. That's not much like you, I'll admit—whoever programmed him hadn't met you. But they certainly got the voice right. And," she added, looking sideways at him as she watched him dig, "a few other things."

Before starting his labors, Rios had taken a look at the records. The emergency holographic package had indeed been initialized the night he played the Klingon's message, and it was his command codes that did it. He had no recollection of any of that, but then, he remembered nothing from that night beyond Verengan's face and words.

Another barrel filled with the pellets, Rios tossed the shovel to the deck and ordered up a glass of water. Downing it, he glanced over to see that Glake was aft, still cleaning. At least he could do that right. Rios put down his glass, wiped his face with the back of his arm, and considered the time.

Top of the hour. Guess I've got to do this.

He looked up and spoke. "Summon EMH, if available."

A flash of light, and the EMH appeared next to Rios. He bowed his head slightly and said, "O Captain, my captain."

Ledger, who had been looking at her comm unit, smiled. "Oh, good," she said, jamming it in her pocket. "Show's on again!"

Rios walked over to the shovel, which now sat before the shiny black shoes of the hologram. He leaned over to pick it up, prompting the EMH to take a step back and say, "Normally patients don't disrobe until I ask them to."

"I'm not your patient," Rios growled, picking the shovel up.

"Are you certain? Because at a glimpse I can tell your electrolytes are out of balance."

"Don't diagnose me." Rios rose to his full height and waved the blade of the shovel in the hologram's face. "I'll send you right back to where you came from."

"Here, there, it's all the same to me," the EMH said, tapping his foot on the deck. "Did you want something, or did you just want to show me your tool?"

"*Murder!*" Ledger exclaimed, clapping her hands together as she looked between the two. "You boys could sell tickets."

The EMH looked at her. "What is she talking about?"

Rios responded drily. "She's insane. It's inoperable. Ignore her." He pointed to the hologram. "You didn't give me your hourly report on time."

"I didn't want to leave the patient." The EMH looked grave. "Your crewmate's condition is poor, I'm afraid. He's breathing on a respirator. I've placed him into a coma while I attempt a number of therapies."

"Is he stable now?"

"Not at a level we should like, but yes. His body has several systems that require time to heal; a watchful patience is the prescribed component."

Ledger smirked. "You sound like my uncle Emil. He was like Wolyx—a dictionary fell on him at birth. Always the ten-dollar words."

"Pardon me?"

"She means 'encyclopedic,'" Rios said.

"Ah. I speak as I was programmed to."

"We'll come back to that," Rios said. "We'll be at Argelius II in fifty-six hours. Does Yerm need a hospital?"

The EMH's eyes glowed for a moment. "There are no Argelian facilities specializing in Benzites. And one of the substances he appears to have been taking without authorization—recreationally, you might say—would upon detection result in his arrest under their legal codes."

Ledger's face displayed wonderment. "You certainly came up with that in a hurry."

"He knows what the ship's computer knows," Rios said. "And speaking of—you want to explain the look?"

"Look? What look?" the EMH asked.

"*His* look," Ledger said, pointing to Rios.

"Ah. You programmed me that way."

Rios's shovel clanged to the deck. "I did not."

"You very much did." The EMH turned and gestured toward the cargo transporter. "You initialized the emergency hologram package—and when given the option, activated the self-scan feature."

Rios frowned. "What's that?"

"The latest thing in personalization—at least, it was when the system was created." The holographic doctor began walking aft, leading the others. "When we were being initialized, you followed the system's instruction and stepped into the transporter. The system energized long enough to duplicate your appearance. Your chosen customizations were added later."

Rios stared at the transporter. "But my voice."

"Ah. The transporter, of course, models you entirely—even getting a peek at your brain."

The captain balked. "*It read my mind?*"

"Just a rudimentary engram, enough to better understand what you wanted from us."

Ledger stepped up beside the hologram, mesmerized as if looking at a magical being. "Wait. You just said *us*."

"He didn't," Rios said.

"He did so. He said it twice!"

The EMH nodded. "You were inebriated in the extreme when I first encountered you—but I can confirm that you initialized the entire first-level complement of emergency crewmembers."

Ledger gushed with delight. "Let's see 'em!"

"Hell, no!" Rios shouted, taking the EMH by the lapels. "Nobody else. Captain's orders. You understand?"

"Captain's orders."

Ledger sulked. "You're no fun."

The EMH waited for Rios to release him. Once free, the hologram stepped back. "And now, if you'll both excuse me, I would like to be present in the event my patient needs resuscitation."

"I swear he took vocab lessons from Uncle Emil." Ledger called out to him, "Should I call you Emil, Mister Hologram?"

"The prospect has nothing to recommend it."

She crossed her arms and tapped her foot. "Well, you're what Boss Arkko would call a real *hotsy-totsy*. Should we call you that instead?"

"Emil it is." The doctor bowed and disappeared.

Rios collapsed in the captain's chair, completely spent. Since purchasing *La Sirena*, he had put the vast majority of his working hours into cleaning it. But the most recent effort had been the most urgent, with the light-years before Argelius II, and his deadline, ticking away.

He'd tried. Damn it, he'd tried. The Miradorns had pitched in, taking brushes and pans to sweep up some of the smaller stuff; that's where they were now, skipping their dinner break. And while Glake had expressed no comprehensible regret over his role in what had happened, the Nausicaan had forgone sleep for the cleanup project. With the carts damaged, he'd lugged away every container the others filled, each one immensely heavy. He seemed at peace while doing it too: while certainly no engineer, neither did he seem like one of Ledger's usual dunderheaded enforcers.

Rios expelled a deep breath. "Aguardiente."

When it appeared, he just stared at the bottle. He was too tired. He'd thought about calling Emil—it aggravated him that he was already using Ledger's name for the EMH—and asking for a stimulant instead, so he could keep working. But he'd reconsidered. It was clear that Yerm had overused a drug or three before his hiring, and the hologram had remarked several times on it. Rios had no desire to get into a debate with his doppelganger.

Moments of Emil's creation had slowly crept back into Rios's conscious mind. It had been a true jag, a bender to end all benders after seeing the Klingon's valedictory message. He'd looked into the face of solitude and balked—that was all he could think to explain it.

Well, that and something else. He held up the bottle. "Take it away," he said, and it vanished. Zo-Var would be taking the night conn in a few moments; he didn't feel he could relax here anyway.

He began to get up when another thought hit him, jarred loose by the memory of Verengan. Rios opened the deck panel and brought out the black pouch. It had been there ever since his encounter with the Convincer dreadnoughts; he'd completely forgotten about it. He pulled at the strings to open the bag.

It was a child's toy. A golden apple, on whose metallic surface were set an intricate series of interlocking wheels with symbols etched into them. Rios had worked such puzzles as a child; one rotated the wheels to unlock a prize, usually a candy.

Of course, he had also played with the little puzzles with tiny ball bearings rolling around; after the day's events he wondered what amusement he had ever seen in those.

He brought the apple closer to his face. He'd never seen one so intricate, with so many different symbols and dials. When he shook it, he heard no reward within. A gift from some sadistic parents, for sure. *Verengan, your miseries started right here!*

But he thought again about that. It surely wasn't a Klingon toy. It was probably something the merchant had picked up along the way, like every other piece of detritus aboard *La Sirena*. Only—it wasn't like everything else. It was the only thing Verengan had hidden, if that was his intention. Did that mean anything?

There wasn't time to worry about that now, not with Argelius II looming in the morning. The control interface showed *La Sirena* would arrive with only minutes to spare. Rios shoved the toy back into the pouch and thought to return it to the spot beneath the chair—

—only to remember what Ledger had said about Yerm sneaking into the captain's quarters. He didn't trust her, either—she'd happily tell anyone she met the apple held a slip of latinum if she thought she could sell it. It was the perfect scam for an Iotian; by the time the tiny safe was cracked, the seller could be long gone.

No, Rios thought, *I think I'll put this someplace else*. And then he would go to bed.

18

NELPHIA PREFECTURE
ARGELIUS II

"In thirty years at Massworks," the Argelian woman behind the desk said, "I've never seen such a shoddy performance from a carrier. Indeed, it may be the worst ever!"

I guess that's one way of saying I did an exceptional job. Rios kept that thought to himself—and many others—as he sat in Director Sevastian's office. He'd met the silver-haired executive five minutes earlier; she'd been tearing him apart for four and a half of them.

"You only delivered ninety-eight point one percent of the bearings," Sevastian said, jabbing at a padd on her desk. "Captain, did you *really* think you could short us without us finding out?"

Actually, that number sounded a lot better to Rios than he'd expected. He was sure he'd be finding the damned bearings around the freighter for years to come. He was formulating a response when his uninvited guest beat him to it.

"Captain Rios is many things, but he's no chiseler," Ledger said from the other chair. "I'm offended you'd even make such an accusation. This business is obviously a clerical error on your people's behalf!"

"You're accusing Moyles?" Sevastian's eyebrows flared upward. "He's been with the company for decades as well. He could never make a mistake like that."

"Then maybe it wasn't a mistake. People skim all the time—and Alpha Carinae's a rough place. Maybe he's in hock. Gambling debts, blackmail."

Incensed, Sevastian stood. "My good woman, Melton Moyles is my sister's spouse!"

"Then you know all about him," Ledger said, charging ahead. "In-laws are the worst. You start by asking for a job—next you're selling sacks of tiny duranium balls by the spaceport."

Sevastian sputtered—and evidently forgot what she was going to say next.

That was Ledger's effect on people. Rios hadn't wanted her to come along, but she'd insisted when some deal she had planned for herself on Argelius II fell through before *La Sirena* arrived. Now he wasn't sure if he minded her presence. He would've told the customer off minutes earlier, but Ledger lived for this kind of wrangling.

The executive found her train of thought. "It's not just the missing material. We've discovered that nearly every single pellet is damaged. Scuffed, from contact with an outside surface. These things are intended for highly sensitive manufactures. They'll have to be in the polisher for a week."

Rios looked out the skyscraper's window. "Argelius isn't a bad place to have to wait, all things considered."

"This is a business, Captain. None of us are on shore leave!" Sevastian picked up the padd. "Moyles says that when you transported the shipment up, you left the containers behind. We assumed you beamed them into tanks of your own." She put down the device. "What did you do, carry them around in your pockets?"

"Of course not."

"Yeah," Ledger added. "There were far too many for that."

Sevastian slapped her hand on the desk. "I have a good mind to report you to the regional shipping guild for sanctioning!"

"Report away," Ledger said. "We don't belong to it!"

"How about the prefecture's constable, for reckless damage to property? For attempted fraud, in covering up whatever happened?"

Rios had to turn down the temperature. "Director," he said, keeping to even tones, "we're just starting out. Our system has had some bugs—"

"I'll say. Bacteria have been detected!"

"—but we did make the run in less time than your average shipper, based on what Moyles told me up front—"

"They'll all have to go under the disinfectant rays. That's another week!"

"—and we're sure the next run we do for you will be smoother."

"*Next run?*" The antique desk quaked under Sevastian's palms. She nearly shrieked. "You have gall, young man! Utter gall!"

Well, you can't blame us for trying, he thought. He already knew it was going to come to this. There was only the one question left. "We'll get out of your hair. We just need the payment for this run."

Sevastian gawked at him—and then broke down laughing. "You think you're going to get paid?"

"We made our delivery," he said. "Prorate for the missing one percent, if you have to."

"It's one point nine percent, and that doesn't approach our other expenses. If the prefecture courts weren't so tied up with all the refugee troubles, I'd launch a civil action and claim your ship!"

Ledger waved dismissively. "The joke would be on you. He doesn't own it. And the real owners eat swells like you for breakfast."

"Swells?" Sevastian looked to Rios. "What is she talking about?"

He shrugged. "I never know."

"Well, I do know," Ledger said. She stood and brought out her communicator.

The move alarmed Rios. "What are you doing?"

"Never you mind. This is my department." She pushed a control on it and spoke. "Glake, do you remember the address I gave you? Good. Come on over, and bring one of those big shovels."

"Shovels?" Sevastian gawked. "What are you talking about?"

Ledger looked up from the comm. "The Glake to whom I refer is a two-meter-tall Nausicaan. The shovel is just simple efficiency. He can brain you and bury you all with the same tool."

"*Ledge!*" Rios got up and reached for her wrist. "I told you not to do this."

"And I told you not to touch me. You're getting the shaft. This is my kind of problem!"

Sevastian, having stood in horror since the shovel comment, opened a drawer on the desk and took out a small device. "Good luck getting work at all at any ports on Argelius!"

Ledger glared at her. "What are you doing, calling security?"

"No. Good-bye."

Seconds later, she and Rios found themselves transported to the fountain plaza outside the Massworks headquarters. Ledger put the communicator away. "Well, that beats a trapdoor to the basement."

Rios put his hands on his head, fearful it might explode. His temper did instead. "You blew it! I could have talked her into giving us something!"

"*They* blew it, by messing with me. That contract was clean—I reviewed it myself."

"I agree. They owe us."

"And I'm still a Convincer." She looked back up at the tall building, her hands on her hips. "Yes, I damned well will *not* take it!" Seeing others wandering the sunny plaza, she went into motion.

"Wait! What are you doing?"

Ledger began shouting to the passersby. "Anybody good at cracking heads? There's a slip of latinum in it for you!"

There were no takers. Just some very bewildered looks.

"We're in the wrong neighborhood." She picked an avenue that looked shabbier than the others and started walking. "Come on."

Rios had no intention of following. But the sight of several armed security officers arriving on the plaza—attracted either by her nonsense or a summons from Director Sevastian—sent him after her.

Long overshadowed by Risa as a vacation spot, Argelius II had suffered as an alternative due to its proximity to Romulan space. First, because it was a dozen light-years from the Neutral Zone; more recently, due to the fact it was one of the stops for the displaced, and those the refugees had dislodged. The prefecture had done its best to keep Argelius II unsullied, but there was only so much a pacifist society could do. That the guards he'd seen wore phasers said something about how things had changed.

Still, it remained a civil society—not that he could convince the rage-walking Ledger of that. "This is a normal planet," he told her. "The Chicago way isn't going to work here."

"The Chicago way works everywhere. You just *think* you've moved past it." She stopped and pointed at him. "But when reality pops you in the beezer, you wise up. It's why all Starfleet's precious exploration vessels are armed to the teeth—and it's why the Feds gave the Romulans the high hat. You know what's what." She turned and continued walking.

He gave chase. "Where are you going?"

"I don't know."

"Then let me try it my way. There are people who follow up on bad debts. If you think our contract means we're owed something, we can put somebody on it."

"And die of old age. You seem to forget you're on a deadline."

We both are, he wanted to say, but that had never cut any ice with her. "We're going to need the funds sooner or later, so we might as well put somebody on it now."

She stopped in her tracks and frowned as she mulled it over. "Long-term investment."

"Why not try?" Rios looked to the side, where one of the Argelians' holographic hospitality stations stood. He approached it. "I need information," he said.

A happy holographic Argelian in a shimmering golden gown appeared. "Greetings, sir," she said. "How may I be of assistance?"

"Blonde, too," Ledger muttered. "Oh, brother."

"Do you have anything like a collection agent here in town?" Rios asked.

"Why, you're just a couple of blocks away from one of the biggest names there is!" The holographic model gestured to the right—and signal lights up a side thoroughfare blinked in sequence. "Cynosure Recovery Associates. You can't miss it."

It even appeared to be in a better neighborhood. "Thanks," Rios said.

As the pair walked to the facility, Ledger laid out exactly the sort of fee a collector should be able to obtain in her own world. Corporations didn't have knuckles to smash, but her expectation was the same.

But she revised her opinion about what the service might cost when they saw their destination. If the Massworks building towered, this one stretched, a chain of connected modules sprawling almost out of sight down the block. A variety of flying vehicles were coming and going from the complex's hangar bays.

"What a spread!" she said, nearly drowned out by the aerial traffic. "That's a lot of office space. I never imagined this many people were behind on their rent."

For the apparent scope of the operation, the lobby itself was small: a tastefully appointed area in which only a single receptionist stood at a podium. The Orion woman smiled as they entered. "Welcome to Cynosure. How may I assist you?"

Ledger strode up to the stand. "We're here to see the boss."

"Excuse me?"

"The top dog. We've got a business proposition!" She drummed her fingers on the stand.

The receptionist smiled sweetly and shook her head. "I'm afraid he sees no one without an appointment."

Rios stepped forward and turned on the charm. "I'm Captain Rios of the *La Sirena*—our freighter came in this morning. We've come a long way. Our business depends on your help."

"Yes, but new business is scheduled through our Intake Division specialists. You would have to go through—" The Orion woman stopped in midsentence, alerted to something on her display. "Oh," she said, startled. Then she gestured to the double doors behind her. "He's transporting to the reception gallery. You may enter."

Ledger and Rios looked at one another, each convinced their approach had worked. The doors swung wide, revealing a long, narrow, glassed-in gallery.

They entered to the howling strains of Klingon opera. There, between rows of displays, stood a black-haired man in a regal red lounging suit and cap. Freckles dotted the sides of his face, which had seen some years; Rios figured the hair was dyed. His eyes closed, the fingers of both his hands followed along with the music in the fashion of a conductor.

"What kind of caterwauling is this?" Ledger said over the din.

"Isn't it grand?" His eyes popped open—and they were alive with excitement. "It's the only known recording sung by the wife of Korrd."

Rios shielded his ears. "Korrd should've told her she couldn't sing."

"Yes, but it's the *only known recording*! It's a sonic etching on an analog Klingon device—that's what's playing now." He swung about, weaving with the cacophony. "Never duplicated digitally once. That would ruin it."

"Oh, yeah, that'd be terrible," Ledger said.

The music came to a welcome end, and Rios introduced himself. "I'm the captain of a freighter, *La Sirena*, that arrived this morning—"

"Would that be the Kaplan over at the main port?" the opera fan asked. When Rios nodded, he remarked, "That's a fine model. None of the other merchants here fly one."

"We're new—and we have a problem getting payment from Massworks. We need a collection agent. We're told you're the best."

The man looked confused. "Oh, but I'm . . ." He pointed here and there, seeming to do the math with his fingers. Then he chuckled. "Ah, that's rich. I see it now!"

Ledger frowned. "Clue us in."

"I'm sorry—I think there's been a bit of confusion. I don't do that kind of work." He gestured broadly to the objects lined up along the gallery. "I'm a collection *disposition* agent. I identify rarities—and find buyers for them." He extended his hand to Rios. "My name is Kivas Fajo."

☿ ♃ ♂ ♄ ♀

—2391—

THE FLIGHT FROM THE FOREST

*In which **Cristóbal Rios** finds the garden—*
and gets pinched

19

Cynosure Recoveries
Argelius II

Kivas Fajo was an oddball. If the opera hadn't tipped Rios off to that, he probably would have figured it out when he finally looked at the items on display in the long hall. And he definitely would have gotten it once Fajo insisted on telling Rios and Ledger about every last damned one of them.

There was the Denobulan gravy flute, possibly the most impractical food delivery system ever used at a table anywhere. Preferred by snobs who liked gaudy displays but not their gravy served in any kind of convenient manner, the meter-tall crystal tube was symbolic of the excesses of the Denobulan upper crust hundreds of years earlier.

Representing Earth was the publisher's file copy of *Queen Arachnia Stellar Special* #1, a comic book that was pulled from distribution and pulped because of an accidentally printed obscenity. It had later been encased in solid plastic, presumably to prevent anyone from seeing the offending word. Rios felt that was an extreme solution.

And there were Romulan items galore. Some were wholesome and appealing, like the collage of small figurines handcrafted for one of the praetors' children. Other items were wholly appalling, such as the blood-encrusted shoehorn that a servant used to slay an important politician. Rios hoped for the children's sake that the items had not come from the same household.

On it went, all the way down the atrium. None of the display pieces were especially dear, except perhaps to those who liked their space villains foulmouthed and their gravy served by someone standing on a ladder. They were pure conversation pieces, and Rios got the sense that was exactly what Fajo liked about them.

It was not what Rios had come for, and he expressed it when he finally got a word in edgewise. "Sorry to have wasted your time, Mister Fajo. We'll be on our way."

"You haven't wasted anything," Fajo said, "and there's no need to hurry off. So many are in financial need these days. You have a problem. I may not be able to dun people for money, but Cynosure may be able to help in other ways."

"I'm not sure how." Rios tried to turn, but Ledger grabbed his sleeve.

"Wait," she said to Fajo. "You buy old stuff like this, right? That's your racket."

"I wouldn't use that description—and it's more involved than that," Fajo said. "But perhaps you'd like to see for yourself." He gestured toward the exit in the rear. "It's no trouble. I was going to have lunch with the prefect, but she's been called away."

The prefect? Rios and Ledger looked at each other. That title was reserved for the top governmental leaders of Argelius II.

"He's connected," Ledger whispered as Fajo started to walk away. "Come on!"

Deciding it couldn't hurt, Rios followed them. He had a question for Fajo anyway. "You said you keep tabs on trading ships. Why is that?"

"Cynosure has a lot of traffic in and out, of course. But I'll always have an eye for freighters. I'm Zibalian—it's in the blood."

Rios had thought initially that Fajo might be Trill, given his facial spots—but Zibalian made sense to him. While nowhere as omnipresent or successful as Ferengi, the Zibalians were formidable traders in their own right.

"I live to tell people about what I do," Fajo said, waving his hands before the double doors at the end of the gallery. "But I have so little time these days. I have to seize any opportunity that arises." The doors parted, revealing a vast warehouse space beyond.

"*Murder!*" Ledger shouted, causing Fajo to take a step back.

Startled, Fajo asked, "What do you mean, 'murder'?"

"She's Iotian," Rios said. "Weird sayings are in *her* blood."

"*Oh,*" Fajo said, relieved. "Then I won't take the 'racket' comment personally."

"I find that not listening works."

Ledger ignored them—and stepped past Fajo into the broad space. "Would you look at this? It's *aces*!"

Rios understood what she was excited about. It was the Convincers' counting room on Verex III writ large. *Very* large—and new and beautiful. Rows of antiseptic-looking tables stretched on and on, each one attended by workers in white gowns and gloves. No offworlder might be able to get into a hospital on Argelius II, but bright lights, scanners, and microscopes were present in great number, each one employed in the study of—of what? Rios couldn't say, because it wasn't any one particular thing.

He got a better look when Fajo led them into one of the aisles. Here there were ceramics under examination. There, musical instruments. Another place, furniture. Clothing, sporting goods, basketry—if there was an order to what was where, he couldn't perceive what it was. Yet some kind of system was clearly in place, with blue-clad supervisors armed with padds stepping from counter to counter and observing the work. Every so often, an item under examination would vanish in a transporter glow, only to be replaced by something else a few seconds later.

"These are my assayers," Fajo said. "Your friend was correct: we do buy old things. But it's so much more. Cynosure is a service organization. We help refugees and anyone else impacted by the Romulan disaster to finance their survival—no, to *better their lives*—by finding markets for the only things they bring with them: their keepsakes from home."

Fajo led his visitors near where one of the white-clad workers was gingerly examining an orange jar. On the table across from her was a screen depicting an old Romulan couple. "They're at one of our intake facilities at a spaceport on the nightside," Fajo whispered. "Let's listen."

"It's held the ashes of the founder of our family line for centuries," the elderly man onscreen said. *"We brought it all the way from Romulus—and have carried it safely all this time, even when we had nothing else."*

"It's a lovely piece," the expert at the table replied. She directed her automated turntable to rotate it, revealing to the others a gilded design of some kind of avian creature. "I've identified the period and the markings already; it's genuine."

"Of course it is!"

"I meant no offense." The assayer looked back and noticed Fajo watching. Wordlessly, Fajo flashed the fingers of one hand three times. The assayer touched a control and turned back to the display. "A number should be appearing on your screen. You will note that I am increasing the offer we initially discussed by fifteen percent in respect of your honored ancestor."

The couple stared in wonder—and abruptly, both began to cry. *"Is all that really for us?"*

"Indeed."

They hugged each other. *"And you say you'll replicate us an identical one?"*

"The jar will say it is a replica, using the microtag authentication technique developed by our founder years ago. But that fact will be invisible to the eye."

"And we'll get the ashes back?" the old woman asked.

The expert chuckled. "Of course!" She quickly added: "The *real* ashes." She turned back to Fajo, who winked at her and gave a thumbs-up. On the screen, the couple reached for something—and the light above the table went green. The transmission ended.

"Well done," Fajo told his assayer, who thanked him and went back to work.

As Fajo began strolling again, Ledger frowned. "You got rooked back there. You opened too high—they didn't even make a counteroffer!"

"We don't haggle here," Fajo said. "People tend to see parting with their keepsakes as a violation of a promise to the past. It's admirable, but it prevents them from using some of the assets they have when they're in desperate straits. We try to help people through these moments, by recognizing their feelings in the matter."

"Maybe. But I can't see all this *stuff* being worth much. Where's the real sugar? The jewelry, the precious metals?"

"When whole families are forced to move, those are the first things to go. They're usually traded for essentials long before people get this far. It's the mementos they keep."

"I saw the air traffic outside," Rios said. "Are all the people you're dealing with on Argelius?"

"No, we have some satellite intake centers," Fajo said. "That's what's flying in. But we try to interview everyone, wherever they happen to be. Often, a piece's value comes from historical context—from the stories families pass down."

He gestured to another table where the Romulan onscreen clearly looked glum. "It's not pleasant for all—people's relatives embellish when it comes to heirlooms. Someone who was at an ancient battle may indeed have owned a particular helmet, but it might not have been used in the event."

"Sounds familiar," Ledger said. "The captain here gave me a sword and a tall tale. My people should have brought it to *you*."

"We'd certainly look at it. As long as there are veterans anywhere, there'll always be a market for militaria. I've even had a few . . . *exotic weapons* in my personal collection."

"So is that what happens with it all?" Rios asked. "You keep it?"

Fajo laughed. "Oh, no. I'm interested in the rare piece, it's true—but mostly we connect with traders where the economies are healthier. Taking a percentage to fund our efforts, of course."

Rios raised an eyebrow. "That's kind of an old game, isn't it? Colonial powers trading in native artifacts."

The Zibalian didn't take offense; rather, the comment energized him. "We're about more than that, Captain. Come along."

As they walked, Rios couldn't help but be impressed by what he was seeing. Earth had once had a vibrant tradition of turning old things into commodities; venues ranged from street bazaars, flea markets, and swap meets to professional pawn shops and antiques dealers. It had been a business for many and a hobby for others—until the ability to replicate matter had devastated those markets. Yet Fajo seemed to have figured out a way to make it work, somehow.

He led them out of the appraisal area and into another attached building. This place was quieter, carpeted, and with muted lighting. Many things were on display, but unlike his oddities beyond the reception area, these were conventional *objets d'art*: paintings, tapestries, sculptures, and more. And all had one thing in common.

"This is our development collection for a traveling museum of Romulan culture," Fajo said, his tone low and respectful. "It's the third one we've created, in fact. The Romulan people have brought their history to us; we, in turn, will bring it to them."

In one alcove, Rios saw several Cynosure experts working to restore a painting; in another, several were polishing a sculpture.

"I figured you had *something* worth the real scratch," Ledger said. "I do hope you're planning to charge admission."

Before Rios could even consider a retort, he heard a feral yelp from behind a door in one alcove. "What the hell is that?"

Fajo smiled broadly. "You'll love this." He opened the door, allowing Rios and Ledger to peer past him.

There, in a brightly lit room, Cynosure workers groomed a lanky, black-fur-covered creature. A half-dozen smaller versions sat in a pen nearby, mewling. To Rios, they looked like hyenas crossed with housecats.

"Romulan *woohgrahs*," Fajo said, leading the way inside. "They were nearly extinct even before the disaster." He stepped over to the pen. "We're always surprised at the number of living things that refugees bring us. Not just pets. People left their homes with livestock and even exotic animals, like these—"

"But the big blowup was four years ago," Ledger said.

"And some were on the move well before that. I don't know how they survived, honestly. But if they could get them to us, the least we can do is find a place for them." Fajo picked up one of the *woohgrah* kits and cooed at it. It responded with a trilling gurgle that sounded like its name.

"Are you also starting a zoo?" Rios asked.

"Oh, no. We'll be talking with the Sylvus Project—you've heard of them?—about reintroducing them into forested places, once they're ready."

"Once the *woohgrahs* are ready?" Ledger asked.

"No, the forests," Fajo said, putting the creature down. "Sylvus is constructing them. Everybody's doing their part."

Rios had to admit he was impressed by the whole operation—and by Fajo. "I'm sorry," he said. "I thought for a minute these guys would be just another exhibit."

"No apologies necessary." Fajo looked back at him. "But on that score, there is someone you should meet." He led them back into the museum area—and toward a doorway. "Indeed, it turns out there was something in the Romulan Star Empire that nobody knew existed. Or rather, some*one*."

Rios reached Fajo's side in the aperture—and gawked at what he saw inside. "What the hell?"

Fajo smiled broadly. "My new friends, I have the high honor of introducing to you one of the greatest figures of Vulcan history. *I give you the High Priestess T'Pau!*"

20

Cynosure Recoveries
Argelius II

The aged logician sat, cross-legged, on the temple floor before the altar, chanting words no one could hear. But the smoke from the censer before her listened, its wisps dancing as she spoke. She was the oldest person Rios had ever seen—and yet her face showed no indication that the years had been a burden. Her hands moved with the grace of a magician, tracing patterns in the air.

And when her eyes opened, Rios could swear that for a second he could see stars inside.

This was a place for Romulan things, yet he immediately knew he was looking at a Vulcan setting, and at a Vulcan ritual. And though he had only seen the person Fajo had named once, in a history class, he was certain of her identity.

"It *is* T'Pau," he said, taking a knee not out of reverence, but of wonder at the image. She wasn't reacting to him; she couldn't possibly be real. But as he looked at the woman more closely, time seemed to slow down.

And as he stood again, it seemed to roll backward.

The stone floor appeared to extend for two meters around the priestess, terminating at the carpet of Fajo's facility. Rios walked around the display, staring as if at a conundrum. "This has to be a hologram, right?"

"It's called an *actuality*," Fajo said, stepping closer. "That's the Earth term for it, but it's something that's to be found in many cultures at the dawn of videography. The Museum of Modern Art in New York City had a collection of them—somebody got them out before Earth's last world war. There's no sound—they just capture vignettes."

"But it's in three dimensions," Rios said. "It *is* a hologram."

"Oh, it's much more than that," announced a female voice. Rios looked to the far side of the room, where a human woman in a white lab coat entered. "Shame on you, Kivas—you didn't tell me we'd be having guests today."

Fajo turned and bowed to her. "A thousand pardons, Doctor." He seemed unsurprised by her arrival. "You're in the presence of academic greatness, my friends. Professor Xandra Quimby holds the seat in antiquities that Cynosure funds at the University of Oneamisu—my old alma mater." He turned to his guests. "May I introduce—"

"Rios. Cristóbal Rios." He had already stood and crossed the room to her. "*Captain* Rios."

Quimby's mien was that of a demure academic; her brunette, silver-streaked hair was tight in a bun. But her blue eyes lit up when she shook his hand. "Charmed, Captain." She turned to the Iotian and smiled politely. "And you are?"

"An admiral," Ledger said, arms crossed.

Fajo stepped to Quimby's side. "She makes the trip here from Iraatan V several times a year when something especially intriguing is discovered."

"And *this* is supposed to be intriguing?" Ledger asked, gesturing to the tableau.

"It's a Parch," Quimby said.

"A what?"

"Not a what, but a whom." The professor walked around the display. "Parch was the nom de plume of the greatest master of the actuality form in the twenty-third century. Nobody else did such rich, detailed work—and no one else got invited to depict the subjects Parch did. Luminaries who were media-shy like T'Pau."

"I was taught there were few images of her," Rios said, "and nothing where she's this . . . distinguished. How did Parch get to make this?"

"Partially on reputation. Many important people appreciated Parch's works. But mystery surrounds the artist's identity. He—or she, or they—were as reclusive as some of the subjects."

"I don't see what you're blowing your wigs about," Ledger said. "Rios was right. It's just a hologram."

Fajo's eyes widened. "Oh, no! No, no, no!" He hastened to Ledger's side. "Look more carefully."

"At what?"

"At T'Pau's eyes when she closes them," Quimby said, offering a jeweler's loupe from her pocket. "I mean, *really* up close."

Giving a shrug, Ledger took the implement and barged into the image area. Rios grasped for her. "No, wait!"

"It's not a problem," Quimby said. "She won't step on the emitter. Go ahead—get as close as you want."

The accountant got right up to T'Pau's knees, looming over the Vulcan. Then she knelt, almost nose to nose with the high priestess, and looked through the loupe. Within moments, her skepticism turned to shock. Ledger looked back. "Her eyelashes. *They're words!*"

"Vulcan words," Fajo said. "Do you know them?"

"No!" Ledger glared back. "Do *you*?"

Quimby did. "They are from a very old Vulcan prayer."

"And they match what she appears to be saying," Fajo added. "You'll notice the words cycle as she speaks."

Ledger did see it. "Well, it's a neat trick. I sure can't do it." She batted her eyes several times and stepped out of the display.

"It was the first thing we found," Quimby said. "But there are deleted words from the written prayer, and those sent us looking for more."

"More?" Rios asked. "More what?"

Fajo grinned. "It's your turn, Captain."

Quimby stepped beside Rios and crooked an arm. "Let's go for a walk, shall we?"

"My pleasure." He could tell she was a good deal older than he was—and that mattered to him not in the slightest. "Where are we going?"

"Not far." The professor pointed at the priestess. "First we're going to watch for T'Pau to say the first of the missing words."

Rios didn't speak the language and he couldn't read lips. But Quimby joined right in, speaking the Vulcan's words in perfect time. "Now," she said, shifting to Standard. "Where is T'Pau's left hand pointing?"

"Over there." Rios pointed to a spot on T'Pau's right, outside the display.

"Let's go, then." Quimby walked him over to it. "Now we're going to repeat the process as the actuality cycles—and this time you're going to tell me where her right hand is pointing when she hits the same missing word."

Rios watched closely as Quimby went through the chant again, up until she signaled a stop. "Over there," he said, tracing where T'Pau's gesture had indicated. "But she's not really pointing. She's just making her motions for her meditation."

"In real life, sure. But you're in Parch's world. Now we're ready. When the actuality cycles this time, we're going to start walking to where she's pointing, and I'm going to continue the chant. We'll stop when we get there—but in between, I want you to keep an eye on the stonework of the altar. Okay?"

Rios felt silly—but he didn't mind walking arm in arm with the professor. Quimby's chant started again, and on cue they started walking. And as he rounded the circle, he saw several of the stones in the altar behind T'Pau blink in and out of existence. He hadn't noticed it when looking from any other direction, at any other time. But they were doing so now.

"There," she said, stopping at the appointed spot. She released him and gestured to the altar. "Did you see it?"

"Yeah." Rios scratched his head. "There were missing parts of the stonework—they formed letters. But they kept changing, almost like a glitch. I don't imagine that was present in the actual altar."

"Not any more than T'Pau's eyelashes were made of letters. This is all Parch. Did you recognize any of the letters?"

"One was like a lowercase *i*." He looked to Quimby. "Does it stand for something?"

"It does. But would a Vulcan necessarily refer to a word?"

Rios was stumped. "I'm not following you."

"You saw characters from fourteen different languages, and they all meant the same thing. But it's not a sound—it's a symbol. In all the languages—as in Standard—you saw the mathematical notation for the square root of negative one. An imaginary number."

"Which is given shape in this image," Fajo said, "not by its presence, but by the *absence* of stones. The symbols are literally formed from nothing."

"Whereas stone is permanent," Quimby added. "Stone means something exists." She put her hands on her hips and studied Rios. "Can you put it together?"

He admitted he couldn't.

"*Nothing unreal exists*. It's the First Law of Metaphysics from Kiri-kin-tha, a student of Surak. A major element of Vulcan teachings."

"Afraid I didn't take philosophy," Rios said.

Ledger hooted. "I bought the other one, but this is baloney. This thing has you hopping around—and jumping to conclusions."

Fajo chuckled. "Tell her the omitted words from the prayer—where your walk began and ended."

"Certainly." The older woman stared pleasantly but firmly at Ledger. "The missing words are *first* and *law*."

"Holy shit!" Rios blurted.

"The Vulcans would have agreed about the holy part," Quimby said, amused by him. "It's another moment of Parch genius. You would only see the symbols if you're looking directly while in motion in that one specific manner. The reality of the image is just paper for the artist, parchment for visual poetry worked in after the fact. There are no glitches, no mistakes. Every seeming error, the saying goes, is Parch-*meant*."

Fajo gushed with enthusiasm. "We've found references to a dozen Vulcan laws in this one actuality—and we've barely scratched the surface." He clasped his hands together. "It works on so many levels. To own a Parch is a journey in appreciation that never ends. There's always something more to be found."

He clapped his hands five times. The image disappeared, leaving a small device where the altar had been. Fajo approached it and took it in his hands. "The actuality's effects are tied to this unit—and for something more than a century old, the technical skill behind it is astonishing."

"Have you cracked it open to see how it works?" Ledger asked.

Fajo and Quimby looked to her in horror. "Of course not," the professor said, her patience sounding a little strained. "It's one of a kind. Kivas's people here were fortunate to find it!"

"A refugee sold this to you?" Rios asked.

"Mmm. Indeed," Fajo said. "We got it from one of the Romulan adherents to Ambassador Spock's reunification movement, in fact. I have no idea how they acquired it, but it was used to help inspire others—while their movement lasted. That added bit of context makes it all the more interesting."

"I'm surprised they'd sell it."

"Desperate times, Captain Rios. But as you can see, as part of this collection, the public will not be denied the chance to appreciate it. Vulcans *or* Romulans."

Quimby shook Rios's hand again. "It was a pleasure meeting you—but I have more research to do. Perhaps we'll meet another time."

"I'm looking forward to it."

In his peripheral vision, Rios could see Ledger rolling her eyes; he knew it was from boredom and not jealousy. Indeed, as Fajo led them into another room, she quickly got to business. "Thanks for the nickel tour," she said as they walked. "But if you were willing to take a look at Rios's sword, maybe you'd be in the market for something else."

"What do you have?" Fajo asked.

"What *don't* we have is a better question. *La Sirena* is stuffed with antiques of every persuasion. I would call it a treasure trove."

Rios knew it wasn't that—but he also wanted to be rid of it. "It's all the possessions of the former owner. I'm guessing he must have shifted it from one ship to another for years, because it's a lifetime of stuff. A Klingon lifetime," he added.

"A Klingon trader?" Fajo seemed intrigued. "Not many of those. They seldom stay in the game long. Who was he?"

"Verengan. He's dead now."

Fajo thought for a moment. "No, I can't place him. But with the Khitomer Accords anniversary coming up, Klingoniana prices are spiking. Did he leave you with much of interest?"

"I'm no judge—but you are. I can say there's a lot of it. Enough I'd hesitate to try to beam it all here. Would you be interested in sending one of your people to the ship to take a look?"

"My boy, if it's a Kaplan F17 you're flying, I'd be interested in visiting myself."

"Great!" Ledger said. "How about dinner? Business always goes better over food."

"*Dinner?*" Rios looked back at her. That wasn't what he had in mind at all—

—but Fajo reacted before he could say anything. "I like the way you think, my Iotian friend. My meal with the prefect has been rescheduled to this evening, but tomorrow works. Shall we say dinner at eight?"

Rios sagged a little. "How could we refuse?"

"Excellent. I'll see you out. There's a shortcut through paper collectibles."

Rios and Ledger whispered to each other as they walked. "Dinner? All we've got is a replicator!"

"Eats make for better business deals. That's *our* first law."

"Yeah, from that Book you say you've never read." He growled in aggravation.

Rios was not surprised that Fajo had an entire room devoted just to evaluating and restoring old books, scrolls, and other biodegradable recording media. What did startle him, however, was an interaction Fajo had with one of the seated assayers when they were almost to the exit.

"What did you just do, there?" Fajo asked, confronting a Tellarite worker. "I just saw you hide something!"

Rios had seen it, too. As the trio had approached, the assayer had shoved a book off his table and into his lap. Ledger chortled. "You've got to keep an eye on everyone," she said. "What you need are some guys with gats keeping watch!"

"Our security measures are quite sufficient," Fajo said, glowering at the nervous Tellarite. "Now show me what you have, before I have you thrown out!"

Reluctantly, the assayer pulled a book out from beneath the table's surface and offered it to Fajo. The Zibalian ripped it from his hand, furious—

—only to throw it to the floor in disgust after a single glance at its cover. "*Ugh!*"

Rios looked to his feet, where the book had landed. A face stared up at him. It was one he knew, though he had never met the man. Overwhelmed by curiosity, he knelt for it—and flipped it over to reveal the title. "*All Our Lives*, by Jean-Luc Picard."

"Pseudointellectual celebrity claptrap," Fajo said. He faced the assayer. "How did that even get in here?"

Mouth dry, the frightened Tellarite choked out an answer. "It was autographed. The seller said Picard signed it on one of his Romulan mercy missions."

"Interstellar busybody takes time from failure to hustle overly wordy books." He patted the Tellarite on the shoulder. "You acted correctly, my friend. That's not the kind of thing I like to see here."

Relieved, the employee went back to work.

Rios read the inscription inside the book. "*May all your journeys find the light.*"

Fajo sneered. "Yeah, the light of a supernova!"

"You're really throwing it away?"

"This is a place for the classics, for the uncommon. That's neither."

Rios closed the book. "What should I do with it?"

"I don't care. Keep it, if you want, but it's a pretty lousy souvenir of your visit." Fajo started walking, only to call over his shoulder, "Just keep it out of my sight tomorrow night, hmmm? The man's face has been known to ruin appetites!"

All Our Lives

Jean-Luc Picard

Éditions Frontiére, 2371

(Excerpt from the introduction)

We are all driven. Some, by a thirst for knowledge; others, by possessions or power. Still others, by vindication, justice, revenge, or survival. Drives—and the ability to respond to them—might in the broad sense be common to all life-forms, sentient or not. Intelligence gives us the ability to recognize when drives are contradictory, or should be limited; wisdom allows us to do something about it. And while there is more to a living being than a record of these decisions, our choices do serve as the underlying sketch on which the pictures of our lives are painted.

I was driven, for example, to begin this monograph on philosophy while I await the commissioning of my new starship, colloquially called the *U.S.S. Enterprise*-E. My work is taking place mostly in seclusion, reflecting a response to yet another drive, for privacy.

In spite of the latter, colleagues who do know of my efforts have asked why I would use time otherwise suited for leisure in this manner. I assure you, I am not immune to the appeals of the beach chair and umbrella—and furthermore, I do not take lightly the job I have undertaken. George Sand, a woman of letters who lived just a few hundred kilometers from my home on Earth, said that the trade of authorship is a violent and indestructible obsession. As someone who already has more than his share of obsessions, I consider myself duly warned.

Think of how easily, how cavalierly we admit to many of our obsessions—almost as a mark of personality, of individuality. At the same time, destruction follows obsession often enough that one would think it might give us pause. Just weeks ago, I encountered a refugee so bent on reuniting with his lost loved ones that he was willing to defy the laws of reality to do it, even though success would have caused the deaths of millions of others. I have seen fellow officers dash their careers to pieces, trying to prove themselves over matters that were important to them—

only to realize, too late, that strength of commitment does not always mean strength of argument. (I will not share their names—while this work does draw on my experiences, there is little here to thrill the reader seeking gossip.)

Even the lighter pursuits we call hobbies can endanger us. Consider Kivas Fajo, a collector of rarities whose desires led him across the invisible border between harmless fancy and criminality. My able crew brought him to justice, and he is currently paying his debt to society. But we might well ask: Where would his life have gone had he found his possessions a trifle less captivating? And where might all our lives go, if we regularly rethought how we were distributing our hours and energies?

Whereas such introspection on my homeworld was rare—the province of the mythical mountaintop sage—people in other societies have been more adept. Gul Orzat of Cardassia was said to have divided his days into discrete units that he parceled out in rigid ratios, never giving any matter a minute more than he felt it deserved. The Vulcan philosopher Surak put it more simply in his famous analects: "To a thing, its time."

But while Surak's line is often quoted by those seeking a more regimented life, they ignore his interest in the arts—the appreciation of which seldom can be forced to fit a schedule. And Gul Orzat's steadfast refusal to overcommit to any cause or activity was, in its own way, a life-ruling obsession—and one that caused his downfall when his vessel faced that of an enemy with different priorities. The captain who made his crew practice gunnery skills to excess won that day. Sometimes, a little obsession can be a good thing.

While the phrase "Moderation is best in all things" was likely coined by the Greek poet Hesiod, the saying "Moderation in all things, including moderation" has variously been ascribed to Mark Twain, Oscar Wilde, and Zefram Cochrane—and that's just the humans. It reminds us that while we now have the philosophical libraries of dozens of worlds to draw upon, there are no easy answers when it comes to questions of obsession and morality—or much else, for that matter.

The human cleric John Wesley warned, "Beware you be not swallowed up in books; an ounce of love is worth a pound of knowledge." I believe there is truth in that. There is a light residing inside us all, and while it may not show us the road to be taken, it assures us there *is* a road.

Returning, appropriately, to George Sand, "*Le vrai est trop simple, il faut y arriver toujours par le compliqué*. The truth is too simple: one must always get there by a complicated route." I have traveled far in life, measured in light-years and experiences; it is my humble hope that this text helps you find your road.

—Jean-Luc Picard
Utopia Planitia Shipyards
Mars

21

La Sirena

Argelius II

According to the vita she had provided Ledger, Zo-Var was an accomplished hobby culinarian, having gotten her start working in galleys in the Miradorn merchant fleet. Rios had considered putting the menu in her hands a reasonable act, given that no actual cooking was involved. She was merely to program the replicator, drawing on her own experiences and judgment.

She created dishes that would have made the captain of any Miradorn vessel proud. However, unknown to Rios, the Miradorn palate was not one of adventure. The main dish appeared to consist of some variety of bran flakes, lightly dusted with the suggestion of salt. They were served upon a bed of grain squares of so little color contrast they were perhaps a full angstrom away from the bran on the visible spectrum. Boldly completing the first course was a tree milk soup topped with herbs cut so thin they were indistinguishable from cellophane. But it was all delightfully presented, and he could not fault Zo-Var for her efforts.

Rios was asking what wine went with cereal when Emil, coming forward to make a report on Yerm, offered a suggestion. "You *do* know there's an emergency hospitality program."

"I *don't* know that," Rios responded.

"You do."

"Go back to your patient, or I'll make *you* play host."

"But that's the idea. You don't have to be the one to—"

"That's it. Doctor gets a time-out." Emil disappeared. Rios looked to his crew. "If anybody hears Yerm flatlining back there, get the doctor back."

The Miradorns passing out of earshot, Ledger looked down at the table and sighed. "Emil's right, you know."

"One hologram is already one too many."

"You should've bit the bullet. At least it would taste like something!"

"Dinner was your idea," he said, buttoning his jacket. "Besides, if we give all the jobs to holograms, you might try to replace me next."

"Don't tease me with your sound suggestions." She shushed him. "Here he comes!"

Dressed grandly in regal blue, Fajo strolled into the canteen area. His bodyguard and driver had deposited him outside; Glake had escorted him up the ramp. "Thank you, my colossal friend." Fajo carried a bundle that looked a little weighty. "For you, Captain."

Rios unwrapped the gift—and looked into a pair of graven eyes.

"A mermaid," he said, holding the statue aloft. "You shouldn't have."

"I couldn't let that awful book be your memento—and I knew the name of your ship. Now you can start a collection."

Fajo's eyes turned to Ledger. Hosting a dinner in a freighter mess hall might have tested some people's wardrobes, but her ensemble combined elegance and utilitarianism in equal proportion. Rios wasn't aware they had evening gowns in Soviet Leningrad.

The Zibalian took her hand and bowed. "You look lovely, my dear." Looking up, he glanced at Rios. "I can say that without giving offense because gender roles are baked into Iotian cultural programming."

"Yes, we're all data-fed machines," Ledger said, acid to her tone as she drew her hand back. "Just remember those synths that went nuts and killed everyone."

Rios noted Fajo's double take and grinned. *You talked yourself into that one, pal.*

Fajo's gaze next fell on the table, and the dishes thereupon. "Ah, I see we're eating Miradorn tonight." He produced a data card from somewhere in his caftan. "I should've warned you—I'm on a restricted diet. I hope you don't mind that I brought my own replicator file."

"Not at all," Rios said, showing Fajo to the device. He couldn't imagine Miradorn cuisine harming anyone's gastrointestinal system, but it took all kinds.

Only after Fajo inserted the card and ordered up his dinner did Rios realize what he really had up his sleeve. A repast worthy of the bistros of Risa appeared at Fajo's place setting—as well as a bottle of wine, which he offered to the others as they sat.

"That's some good stuff," Ledger said after the first sip.

"I prefer my wines real, but even a replicated Bajoran merlot has its charms."

Rios didn't understand. "Isn't it just the same thing?"

"Not if I know it isn't." Fajo raised his glass. "We're all as common as the things we surround ourselves with. Don't be common."

"I'll drink to that." Ledger toasted with him.

Rios did the same. "I guess we're a step down from what you're used to."

"There's no insult intended," Fajo said. "I worked freighters myself. But I realized it mattered *what* I carried. Anyone can move raw materials around. If you're going to spend all that time between the stars, it's better to share your space with something interesting."

"Your operation is what's interesting," Ledger said. She spent the entire dinner prodding Fajo for information on Cynosure's total revenue and bottom line. He neatly sidestepped those questions, noting that every category his company dealt with had its ups and downs.

"I'll bet," she said. "I was surprised you'd waste the space on all those books."

"And I'm surprised to hear you say that. Are you sure you're Iotian?"

"No doubt about it," Rios said.

Fajo pushed his plate away and stretched. "It's a mistake to underestimate the book," he said. "Every civilized culture in its infancy finds *some* way of recording thoughts portably. You can't very well go around carrying sections of wall with glyphs on them—unless you're a Gorn, in which case they double as light afternoon snacks."

He ticked off a list of ancient media, from scrolls and parchment to the webworks of the Kyvalians—all mechanisms for doing the same thing. "And no matter what technologies rise and fall, you can still see what's on them without having to dig up old equipment. A book is a loyal ally."

"I hear they say that in prisons," Ledger said. "A good-sized one can clock somebody in the head."

Fajo didn't seem amused; in any event, he changed the subject. "Is this your whole crew, Captain?"

"We've got one laid up in sickbay. I'd been hoping to get him into a hospital here."

"Alas, he's probably better off where he is. Post-supernova Argelius is like a lot of its resort houses—pretty on the outside, messy on the inside."

Sounds like this ship. Rios rose to the occasion. "Do you want to have a look at our goods?"

"Let's."

Their tour of Verengan's cargo lasted more than two hours, long enough for Rios to realize that the Klingon probably never had actual buyers in mind when he accumulated anything.

"It happens all the time." Fajo tut-tutted over a small box he'd found amid the gear. "Merchants who don't educate themselves can't tell the treasures from the dross."

"What's that you have there?" Ledger asked.

Fajo held the box to the light. "A pedicure set—I don't recognize the markings, but we can assume it's for a species that has toenails. I doubt it has value, but I'd want my category experts to weigh in."

"You have pedicure set experts?"

"You've seen my place. Someone will know."

Rios's eyes narrowed. "Would they know about toys?"

"You'd better believe it." Fajo laughed. "It's part of where I started. As my friends outgrew the things that shaped them, they gave what they had to me. Later, when they grew nostalgic, I was able to sell them their own things—at a handsome profit."

"I'm wondering about a specific toy," Rios said. "It's kind of an apple, with a lot of dials on it. A puzzle game."

Fajo listened closely. "I think I know what you're talking about." He looked around him. "Are you buying or selling? I didn't see one here."

"Oh, it's not," Rios said, "and it's not important. I was just curious if they're worth anything."

"I would have to see it. If you have one, certainly send it along with everything else. I can assure you I would give it personal attention." Fajo stepped back. "Now if that's all, I've seen enough. Nothing leaps out, but there are interesting pieces. I'll send you an authorization code and you can transport as much as you want to us. We'll make an offer on the whole thing."

"That's swell!" Ledger said.

"Yeah, take it all." Rios was glad to be rid of it; getting something for it would be amazing.

Fajo stopped in his tracks. "I hate to ask this, but this Verengan—you're sure he died?"

"Absolutely."

"No heirs? Friends? Close associates?"

"He was completely alone," Rios said. "That explains the mess I found here—and I think it explains why he died."

Fajo's eyes narrowed. "You *know* how he died?"

"Yeah, he just keeled over. He was old."

That seemed to satisfy Fajo. "Sorry to have pelted you with questions, but I have to know I'm not accepting stolen property." He glanced at Ledger. "As fascinating as I find Iotians, my position on Argelius requires me to act with care. I'm not a fencing operation."

Rios and Ledger walked him to the bottom of the landing ramp. There, under the flickering light of the spaceport, Fajo paused. "Oh, Captain, I nearly forgot."

"What's that?"

"I detected a trace of Santiago in your voice earlier. I thought you'd like another little gift from an island nearby." He reached into his voluminous sleeve and brought forth a cigar.

Rios took it and brought it to his nose. He couldn't say much for Fajo's geography, but he certainly knew how to endear himself. "Almost smells real."

"It is. Oh, allow me," Fajo said, offering him a light.

Ledger watched Rios inhale—and spoke. "You know, Captain, maybe there's a way you could visit here more often."

Cigar clenched in his teeth, Rios looked back at her. "Did you just call me *Captain*?" He knew what Ledger had wanted to ask about; he was astonished she had waited this long.

"I wanted to know if you had any jobs for us," she said. "Running freight."

Fajo crossed his arms and looked off to the side. "Of course, we do have runs that have to be made to our satellite centers—and also to the markets that we sell into. Those are usually happier places to visit. I don't have to tell you that there's a shipping surplus."

No, you don't, Rios thought.

Fajo looked up at *La Sirena*. "Still, she's a beautiful ship—or will be when she's cleared out. Yes, you might fit in very well. And there are benefits, of course."

"More cigars," Ledger said over Rios's shoulder.

"There is that," Fajo allowed with a chuckle. "But also you'd have one of the nicer dedicated bays at the spaceport. We get our dilithium in bulk—and as you'd have a Cynosure charter, you wouldn't pay port fees."

Rios puffed. "That sounds great, Mister Fajo—but I'm just getting the ship broken in." He looked up. "Happy to do business on the cargo up there, but I'm not looking for a regular run yet."

"Are you sure?" Fajo sounded truly surprised. "It's a good offer."

Ledger grabbed at Rios's shoulder. "Just a sec," she said to Fajo, before yanking the pilot behind the ramp.

She spoke quietly, but urgently. "Are you crazy? This is what we've been waiting for!"

"This is what *you've* been waiting for. We've known this guy for a day and a half."

"What do you have to know? This gets you paid off—and me out of the soup with Arkko!"

"What do you care? I thought you weren't going to stick around." Over his shoulder, he heard the whine of an approaching hovercraft.

Fajo peeked past the ramp. "My ride's here. Think about it."

Rios stepped forward to shake the Zibalian's hand. "Thanks for the smoke—and the mermaid."

"And for a lovely evening." Fajo kissed Ledger's hand, bowed, and departed.

Her smile broke—and she smacked Rios on the back of the head, causing the cigar to tumble to the tarmac. "You idiot!"

"What did I do?"

"I just told you!" She stepped forward and blocked him from retrieving the stogie. "You heard what he said about the cargo—it's probably chump change. The job is the real deal."

"Yeah? Well, you buy a ship and work for him." He crossed his arms. "I was sitting on the bridge last night, about to have a drink—and I decided instead to take a look at that book he gave me. The one by Admiral Picard."

"What about it?"

"I was curious about the way Fajo reacted to seeing it, so I checked the index. Turns out he was mentioned in the introduction. Our guest there has done time—and it was Picard's crew that arrested him."

"*So?*"

"What do you mean, 'so'?"

"So what does that have to do with working for him? He's on the straight and narrow now. And he hasn't asked you to do anything illegal."

"Yet." He gestured with his thumb. "Do you really think a guy like that, running a big business, has time to give the grand tour to every tramp freighter operator that comes along? Much less drop by the next night for bran flakes and dry toast?"

"What's your point?"

"Point is, I looked him up. He's been away—*put away*. First in a hellhole called Thionoga, then at a minimum-security Federation lockup. I still can't find out what he actually did, and Picard's book didn't say."

"Once again: So what? He's out—and out in the open. He must not have escaped. He's done his time."

"Nobody does *that* much time on a customs violation."

"*Who cares?*" Ledger railed at him. "You're going to get all high-and-mighty about it? *You?* Are you aware of how many bodies Boss Arkko has left lying around? You know, the owner of your ship?"

"But I'm not doing anything illegal for her—or you. And it's not just because you haven't thought of anything yet. You're not as persuasive as you think you are."

"And you're not as smart." As he knelt to retrieve the cigar, she spoke again, her voice frostier. "Among my calls, I've made a few about *you*—about this Starfleet record you said you had. I found a couple of people who served with you on your last command. You know what they said?"

Rios just stared at the ground before him.

"They wish you were *dead*, pal. They say you destroyed their lives."

As Rios stood, he wondered for a moment who it was that she'd spoken to—until he remembered it could have been anyone who'd served aboard *ibn Majid*.

They all felt that way.

"I don't know what you did," she said. "Whether you made time with the admiral's daughter or bumped her off. But I'll bet that it's worse than anything a little old guy who knows about *pedicure sets* could have done!"

She yanked the cigar from his hand and threw it to the tarmac. "Think about that—or next time, I'll do *this* to your head!" She ground the stogie under her heel and charged up the ramp.

Rios stayed in the shadows long after she left. He put his fingers on his temples for a minute and simply breathed, wondering what he had done to deserve his fate.

At last, he knelt to retrieve the cigar again, knowing it was probably unsalvageable this time.

"*Don't move, or I'll blow your head off!*"

Feeling a weapon at the back of his head, Rios froze. "That's awful fast for you to have hired someone, Ledger."

"I'm not Ledger—and you're not captain of this freighter," said the nasal voice behind him. "*What have you done with Verengan?*"

22

La Sirena
Argelius II

An old joke on first-contact vessels went that Starfleet, which awarded medals for a wide variety of things, needed to come up with one for "Most Times Taken Prisoner." Rios had been held at gunpoint so often lately that he felt he was a lock for any civilian equivalent.

The quality of his assailant this time showed he had come down in the world. No nattily dressed wiseguys with gats; instead, the disruptor aimed at Rios quaked in the hand of an old Ferengi with a terrible head cold.

"Can I get you a handkerchief or something?" Rios asked from a chair in *La Sirena*'s canteen.

"Shud up and keep your hands on the dable where I can see them."

The Ferengi gave a wet sniff and brought the back of his wrist to his crinkled nose in order to wipe. But that was his disruptor-bearing hand, such that when he suddenly sneezed, he jerked so wildly that Rios slammed flat against the table for fear of accidental fire.

"Sorry," the red-eyed gunman said. "I mean, I'm not sorry! Keep your hands where—"

"I know the drill." Rios looked up. The Ferengi's sneezes had echoed all around, but the hour was late enough that Rios assumed everyone else had turned in, upstairs. "What do you want?"

"I dold you, I wand to see Verengan. Da Klingon who owns this—" The Ferengi blinked multiple times, fighting to suppress another sneeze. Winning this round, he muttered, "Musd be allergies. Whad did you do to this ship?"

"You've been here before?"

"Of course. Smelled differend then, bud now—"

"That'd be three months of disinfectant." Many Starfleet vessels had the capacity to cleanse with rays; the freighter's options were more limited. Rios named some of the chemicals he'd used.

"Thad's the answer," the Ferengi said, before sneezing again. He hung his head in misery. "No good."

"I'm going to call the medical hologram, okay? Don't shoot him—at least not until after he helps you. All right?"

The Ferengi wheezed deeply. "Okay."

Sickbay was just at the far end of the canteen, but Rios summoned the hologram to appear directly. Emil materialized nearby, initially facing the captain. "If you're asking about Yerm," he began, "there's been no change since—" Emil stopped when he spied the Ferengi. "Ah. Good evening."

Glancing from one Rios to another, the Ferengi looked as if a headache was coming on. "You look alike."

"And you look unhappy." Emil's gaze went to the disruptor. "*Very* unhappy."

"I hab allergies."

"I see." A tricorder materialized in the EMH's hand. "What's your name?"

"Hain." The second after he said it, the gunman blanched. "I was going to keep thad do myself."

Emil smiled pleasantly. "Your privacy is safe with me. A fast-acting antihistamine, I should think." The tricorder went away, and a hypospray replaced it. "With your kind permission."

Hain looked about to drop. "Yeah, whadever."

The EMH applied the medication—and followed it up by drawing a handkerchief from his jacket in a magician's flourish. "There." Then his eyes went to the weapon again—and over to Rios. "By chance is there anyone I should call, or—?"

"Get lost," Rios said, and it was just him and Hain again.

Hain rubbed his eyes. "That helped," he said, blinking. "Don't know why Verengan never turned the holograms on before."

"He had good sense," Rios said. "I take it you're his friend. You need to know: I didn't do anything to him."

"He loved this ship," Hain said, already looking a lot better. "He never would've sold it." He pointed the disruptor at Rios with reinvigorated menace. "Now, tell me exactly what happened to him, or you'll—"

Rios glanced behind Hain and went slack-jawed at what he saw. Dressed in a robe and soft house shoes, Ledger had tiptoed down the stairs from the flight deck—and now stood behind the Ferengi with something in her hand. Intellectually, Rios knew it was not *really* a Colt 1908 Model Vest Pocket pistol, but rather an Iotian knockoff—but it made no difference when she fired it into the air.

Hain yelped at the sound—and Rios dove, knowing that, while the space over the canteen area was open to above, the upper deck's overhead was quite capable of deflecting the round. It did so. The mess table then displayed that it, too, was made of stern stuff.

Rios did not see any of the ricochets after the first, but he did hear them—and a scream. When the sounds abated, he shouted out from beneath the table. "Ledge, what the hell are you doing?"

"Saving your keister!"

Crawling out, Rios saw her padding across the deck in her slippers. She looked down, gun in hand. "Who's this?"

Hearing an anguished moan from her side of the table, Rios scrambled around. He saw the disruptor first, on the deck—and then Hain in a fetal position, clutching his bloody shin. The Ferengi howled. "My leg! Oh, my leg!"

"You shot him!" Rios yelled at Ledger. "What is wrong with you?"

"There's gratitude for you. He was going to shoot *you*." She pocketed the pistol and cinched up her robe. As near as he could tell from her expression, she hadn't balked at all when the bullet was flying. "You never told me who he was."

"His name's Hain. He knew Verengan." Rios picked up the fallen disruptor and called for the EMH.

Emil appeared. "How can I—"

"The Ferengi again," Rios said.

The hologram raised an eyebrow. "Problem with the hypospray?"

Rios pointed to the floor behind the table. "Bullet wound."

"Not a side effect the serologists warned us about."

"Just get to it."

Emil complied, approaching the Ferengi, who was now wailing frantically.

"What did you do, what did you do?" Hain asked, tears in his eyes. "I wasn't going to shoot anybody. I'm a *rancher*, dammit!"

"A what?" Rios asked.

"A rancher. I raise livestock!"

"Then what are you doing here?"

"I told you, looking for Verengan!"

Ledger harrumphed. "Joke's on you, pal. The Klingon's dead."

Hain's face drained of color. "Dead?"

She faced Rios. "You didn't tell him?"

Rios shrugged. "I wanted to get to that when there wasn't a disruptor pointed at my head, thanks."

"You're lying!" Hain, already crying from pain, verged on a full bawl. "Verengan's lived through everything. Everything, I tell you. The big guy wouldn't let a couple of nobodies like you get the drop on him!"

"He's a stiff," Ledger said. "My people carted off the body."

"*The body?*" The Ferengi yowled. He clawed at Emil as he tried to get to Rios. "Why did you do it? Why did you do it?"

His ministrations stopped, Emil struggled to restrain his patient. "Perhaps now is not the time for these conversations."

Rios glared at her. "Ledge, you are not helping."

"That's it, gang up on me," she said. She looked back to Hain. "Rios didn't even know Verengan. The old coot just dropped dead one day."

"Ridiculous." Hain wiped his nose. "I've known him for years. He could drink a case of bloodwine and do warp nine in the morning. I refuse to believe he just died!"

"Well," Rios said with some reluctance, "there is kind of a recording."

"Of what?"

"Of his death."

Hain went apoplectic. "You recorded it? What kind of monsters are you?"

"I didn't record it. Verengan recorded it. He died while making a ship's log."

"He didn't keep logs!"

"Then you know more about him than I did."

Emil intervened. "This patient requires sickbay. I really must insist you take these matters up again there."

That made sense to Rios, who took steps to arrange an intraship transporter beam for Hain. The move did little to assuage Ledger, who'd recommended beaming the Ferengi off *La Sirena* entirely. "Have it your way," she said at last.

Nothing's been my way in two years, he wanted to respond. Instead, he cast his eyes onto his twice-cleaned deck and noticed the pool of Ferengi blood all over it. "It's never going to end," he grumbled as he slouched off to sickbay.

Rios woke Glake, asking him to join them in the clinic in case Hain got loose. But it turned out not to be a problem, as the intruder wasn't going anywhere. The biobed in use with a motionless Yerm, Hain sat on a bench as Emil tended to him. Emil looked to the others. "This will be more difficult to address than sniffles, I'm afraid."

Leaning against a wall, Ledger kept her eyes on her coffee mug. "It was just a .25. Use your medical magic."

"The angle of entry was vertical," Emil replied, "straight through the kneecap and shin for maximal damage. I can repair it, but it will take time."

Rios knew offworlders had little chance of being admitted to an Argelian hospital, but wondered if Hain had other options. "Do you live here?"

"No," the rancher said, calmer since being sedated. "My spread is back on Irtok."

That was in Ferengi space, Rios knew. "Why are you here?"

"Verengan used to stop here a lot, so I made this my base while looking for his ship. And *you're* only here because I brought you here."

Rios blinked. "You did?"

Hain looked down and recounted his efforts. "Verengan did—*was doing*—a lot of business for me. When he vanished, I searched everywhere for him—and paid Ider, a Lurian who does some work for my family, to watch for him over at another of his haunts on Alpha Carinae. When he saw this freighter come in at the spaceport, he contacted me and said Verengan wasn't aboard. I was afraid you'd leave before I got there, so instead I figured out a way to bring you to me."

"What do you mean?"

"*Melton Moyles* is what I mean. He owed Ider a favor for some guild-busting he'd done for Massworks—so he agreed to give you a job that'd bring you here. After a little show to get your attention, that is."

"Wait," Ledger said. "That scuffle outside the ship. That was a setup?"

"It was. We were afraid whoever had Verengan's ship wouldn't believe Moyles would give a big contract to a stranger. It worked, obviously—but I'm worried about Ider. I haven't heard from him lately."

"That's because he's in the hospital," Rios said. "I—uh—dropped a metal door on his head."

Hain winced. "Poor Ider. He's going to want a bonus for that."

"If you're lucky, he got amnesia," Ledger said. "Why were you looking for Verengan?"

"He's my friend—but also, we were in business together." Hain looked up. "I had a deal to deliver ten loads of agro goods to the Sylvus Project."

Rios and Ledger looked at each other. "Sylvus? The tree people?" he asked.

"Trees and more. Verengan and I ran nine shipments to them—and I had just gone back to Irtok to get the last one ready. But he never showed up to take the final delivery." Hain beat his fist on the bench. "And Sylvus won't pay until the contract's completed!"

"Why couldn't you just get another freighter to carry the rest?" Rios asked. "This region's wallowing in them."

"Verengan had run all the other legs. I couldn't do that to him." Hain shook his head. "This was a *big* payday. The fare was his."

"Correction: *ours*," Ledger said.

Rios looked to her. "What?"

She put down her mug on a counter and paced. "Don't you get it? The only reason the Klingon defaulted to the Convincers was because he died before finishing the contract. That money was supposed to be his—meaning, *ours*. Finish the run, and it will be."

Beaten by the day's activities, it took Rios a second to process her statement. When he did, he put up his hands. "No, no. I owe you what I owe you—not what Verengan owed too." He gestured to Hain. "I'll finish the contract—but I want Verengan's share."

"You didn't make all the runs!" Ledger said, stopping in front of him. "One-tenth is yours. The rest belongs to the gang."

"I thought you were about to strike out on your own."

"So what if I do? I want what the Convincers are owed, either way."

"It's Verengan's money!" Hain shouted, reasserting his presence. The action pained him, and he babied his leg. "I don't recall offering to hire you people."

That much was true. Rios and Ledger looked at each other—and then at Hain, who still seemed to be considering his options.

At last, the Ferengi shrugged, defeated. "I guess there's no other way.

Sylvus is expecting this freighter. They'd given Verengan a clearance code to approach their project area. Take me to Irtok for the cargo."

Rios consented. He could beam Fajo his stuff first thing in the morning, and then get underway. A weary smile crossed his face—until it dawned on him that he'd never introduced himself to Hain. He did so. "Anything we can get for you?" *Besides the new tibia, I mean?*

"Yeah." Hain looked longingly to where Yerm was resting. "Is there any way you can kick that guy off the biobed over there? I *really* want to go to sleep."

23

La Sirena
Irtok

Rios covered his nose and mouth. "It's godawful," he muttered.

"Putrid is more like it," Ledger said, holding her beret over most of her face.

"It's wonderful," Hain declared, inhaling deeply. Cane in hand, he hobbled through the doors of his massive storehouse.

Rios looked past the Ferengi at the veritable mountain range of jet-black manure inside the structure. He could get no closer; his eyes began watering, and he had to step back. "Cleaning solutions get you, but you love this."

"What you're smelling, Captain, is *profit*." Not discomfited in the least, Hain waved his hand before his face, soaking in the fragrance. "Wonderful, wonderful profit. It's the most beautiful smell in the galaxy!"

"It'd strip the hull off a warbird." Rios coughed several times. "When you said 'agro products,' I didn't think you meant—"

"*Byproducts?*" Hain turned back and flashed a toothy smile. "That's why it's so perfect. *Yashivoo* aren't much to look at, but they're money machines from birth to the slaughterhouse."

Rios had seen field after field of the gangly creatures during *La Sirena*'s approach: meter-tall spider-legged ungulates who lived, entirely, to procreate and defecate—turning, along the way, Irtok's already fortified grasses into a still-richer fertilizer. Those who owned the herds were the richest of all—most of them, anyway. Rios had already gotten the sense that Hain was an exception.

"Some of the biggest fortunes in the Ferengi Alliance have their beginnings in this stuff," Hain said, limping out to join his guests. "If you're in the dung cartel, you're made for life. The farmers on Ferenginar eat this stuff up."

"A portrait I did not need," Ledger said. She'd retreated to a position twenty meters from the storehouse, Rios saw, where she knelt behind a tree and breathed into her cupped hands.

Hain triggered the massive doors to close. "I'm not in the cartel, so those markets are closed to me—which is why I sell my manure outside the Alliance."

"Having dealt with Ferengi before," she said, "I'm not surprised it's an export."

"Laugh if you want," Hain said. "The thing about the Borderland is the region hasn't had many supernovae—which is where you get a lot of your naturally occurring boron compounds. They strengthen plant cell walls and serve as organic insecticides."

"But due to a supernova somewhere else," Rios said, "the place suddenly has a lot of new residents."

"Ironic, isn't it? The Sylvus Project has been retrofitting planets since before the Federation abandoned the Romulans to their fate—and it hasn't gotten to a fraction of the worlds in need. And many of the species that Sylvus plants *love yashivoo* dung."

"Why don't they just replicate it?" Ledger stood up shakily, holding on to the tree for support. "And while they're at it, they could make a perfumed version."

"Sylvus is a mobile operation," Hain said. "They travel light. They don't want to haul massive industrial replicators around. That's where I come in." He pointed to a gravel path. "Follow me."

As tumultuous as their introduction had been, Rios was glad he'd met Hain. From the way the rancher had spoken, even part of what Sylvus owed Verengan would help him make his looming payment to Arkko. A bonus was that it delayed the inevitable problem Rios would have with Glake and the Miradorns. He'd only taken them on for the Massworks deal, with no intention of having them aboard any longer—but even as badly as everyone had performed on that mission, Rios couldn't see cutting them loose without pay. He hoped that between Fajo's offer on the junk and the Sylvus deal, he'd earn enough to send them on their way.

Hain led them around back of the storehouse to where a dome adjoined the facility. "That's where we compress the product into cubic-meter blocks for shipping."

"Is that a good idea?" Rios asked. "Making them more . . . *intense*?"

"It makes them go farther, which makes them more valuable. Don't worry—they're wrapped in duranium-foil shrouds. Though given how Verengan's freighter smells now, I may rip a few open out of self-defense."

"Don't you dare," Ledger said.

The Ferengi looked up at the sun. "Time's wasting. I have to place a call from my office. My workers will set out a payload for—what did you call the ship?"

"*La Sirena*," Rios answered.

"The *La Sirena*."

"No, just *La Sirena*. The *La* is already a *the*."

Hain shuddered, confused. "It was easier when Verengan had it. He'd survived so many ships he didn't bother naming them." The Ferengi hobbled off.

Crossing the lawn back to the starship, Ledger and Rios found there was finally something they could agree on. "That door back there was open for thirty seconds and it's still clinging," she said. She brought the sleeve of her blouse to her face long enough to regret it. "I'm going to see if Emil can surgically remove my nose."

"Captains have priority," Rios said. "And we'd thought Verengan was carrying around a lot of shit before!"

She growled. "That is not funny." But then he saw her come within the same quadrant as a smile. "Okay, maybe it is."

He looked ahead at the ship, and his brow furrowed. "I wonder if that's where the smell came from."

"Manure, dead Klingon, what's the difference?" She glanced back at the dome and gestured. "And I don't buy the whole 'rancher from Ferenginar' act for an instant."

"Why am I not surprised?" Rios chuckled. "You shoot first and trust never."

"Trust is just a word in the name of a bank." She poked him in the shoulder. "Remember when Yerm broke into your quarters? Well, last night, our dear Hain made a visit to my office—*without an appointment*."

"The holodeck? How do you know?"

"I set my program to record all activities there—I haven't exactly had time to generate a team of secretaries to document my business. And there was our admirable agrarian, hobbling around and putting his big shnozz into everything he could find."

That baffled Rios. "What *did* he find?"

"Nothing. But you should know he's into more than hustling boring compounds."

"Boron."

"Same difference." Having reached the ramp, she looked up into the maw of *La Sirena.* "I'm going to program a bathtub on the holodeck and spend the next hundred years in it. Alert me when we lift off, so I can have these clothes beamed into space."

Rios had considered setting his on fire, but determined they were probably combustible enough as it was. Cognizant of his schedule, he settled for an inadequate shower and a quick change before heading back to engineering. He found Glake there, just where he'd been for days.

Back on Argelius II, the titan had stood alongside him for hours, watching carefully as he transported Verengan's collection to Fajo's offices. Somewhere in the Nausicaan's woeful stare Rios had inferred an interest to make right, and that was something his personal shields had never been able to deflect. On *ibn Majid* he'd been a sucker for all the career reclamation projects, and Vandemeer had made sure he got them all. His results had varied widely—for every Zinnell or T'kasa that made good, there was a Claggett or a Junipah who didn't—but he'd kept on trying. Maybe that was what made him take an interest in Raffi; maybe it was the other way around. He didn't know.

Rios hadn't thought Glake had any ambitions, until he saw him paging through the transporter's tutorial files. Verbal, he wasn't—but he could read, and the makers of the Kaplan-series ships, anticipating that many workers in shipping were relatively unskilled, had made things as easy as possible. They'd even provided an animated series of vids with peppy jingles, and since leaving Argelius, Rios had sworn he'd heard Glake singing along late at night. He still had no intention of ever letting him operate the machine alone again, but he got points for trying.

After a quick check on Glake, Rios got a hail from the flight deck. He had it piped into the overhead. *"Hain here. I've located the Sylvus operation that hired us. They've moved on since our last delivery, but not far. They're in the Bassen Rift."*

Rios knew of it, but hadn't visited. "Got coordinates?"

"Sending. We'll be ready to transport the goods in ten minutes. I hope those hovercarts are repaired."

"Taken care of. Rios out." Fixing them had occupied him for most of the trip from Argelius, but he'd finished just in time. He was getting the first one out of storage when Emil appeared. "I didn't call for you."

"No, but the situation calls for you. Yerm is awake."

"Good," Rios said. "Great," he swiftly added. *Truly good news.* It felt like things were finally working out. "How is he?"

Emil clasped his hands together, as if searching for a place to start. Where he did begin surprised Rios. "I heard a call that said we were bound for the Bassen Rift."

"Since when do holograms listen in on personal communications?"

"When they're played overhead when I'm on the stairs. Would Benzar be on the way?"

"It's not far off the route. Why?"

"I expect the Benzites are better able to take care of their own kind—and what Yerm is going to need is a long-term chemical rehabilitation regimen. I have healed his bones, but his cells still crave the substances he was abusing. I can retard those needs temporarily, but an ongoing solution is required."

"Will they take him? He'd said he didn't have any family or friends."

"There's an Interspecies Medical Exchange facility there; it will accept him if no one else will." Emil watched as Rios powered up the cart. "But I would like you to speak with him, if you could."

"Why? What's wrong?"

"He already feels himself a failure—and a burden. I expect the knowledge that he is leaving your service after so short a time may be a psychological setback for him."

"What are you, the Emergency Counselor Hologram now?"

"I'm no counselor, and that is exactly why this matter falls to you. As I understand it, in the absence of skilled personnel, it is the role of the captain to advise their crewmembers. Traditionally."

Rios stared off to the side, where the stairwell to sickbay stood. Helping Glake was one thing, but Yerm was something else: he'd *already* washed out. Rios had never found the words before for those he'd failed, for those he'd let go.

Nobody had said a damn thing to *him* as he'd hit the pavement.

Receiving no response, Emil said, "The decision is yours." He started to walk away, before pausing. "If you *do* choose to counsel Yerm, I would advise not involving alcohol, synthetic or otherwise."

The comment startled Rios. "What kind of guy do you think I am?"

Emil gave him a look—and disappeared.

In anyone else, Rios would have classified it as a knowing look. It was an expression any hologram could mimic—but this particular hologram had seen into his mind at least once, and that pissed him off.

He walked toward the stairwell—and kept going, right back to engineering. "All right, Glake," he said, cracking his knuckles. "Today we're going to transport aboard tons of manure. And this time, we're damn well going to bring over the containers too!"

24

LA SIRENA
ORBITING BENZAR

"It has often been said there are no answers to be found in books," the author wrote. "Those words provide a convenient refuge for those of us who write philosophy; our readers may consider them a condemnation of the whole endeavor. I tell you in closing that I hope you will consider my meager efforts in this work an earnest attempt, because I believe that *some* answers lie in books. Occasionally, they may even point us to the right questions. I wish you all speed in your journey toward the light."

Rios stared at the book he'd been reading. "Is that *it*?"

He flipped twice through the acknowledgments and index before slamming it shut. Jean-Luc Picard's face looked out at him from the back cover. A pleasant, gentle smile, as if the Starfleet legend understood that he'd just carried his readers for two hundred eighty densely footnoted pages only to leave them on the dock with a wave and an "all speed."

Rios looked again at the publication date on the book. It was just after the destruction of the *Enterprise*-D; the Romulan resettlement debacle was still years away. Picard would learn a lot about valiant but futile attempts then. Rios wondered if the book was in some sense one long prequel: a case of the legendary officer biting off more than he could chew. Picard had referenced every philosopher under a dozen suns, and had brought Rios no closer to understanding what it was all about.

It was amazing how much effort literary people put into overcomplicating existence. People had day-to-day problems. Rios didn't see how wallowing in words made any of them any better.

He had finished the volume while sitting in sickbay during the flight to Benzar. He'd grown uncomfortable spending his evenings drinking on the flight deck; between Hain, Ledger, and his crew, there were just too damn many people around. The solution had come, of all places, from Emil's earlier plea. Sitting vigil with Yerm guaranteed Rios solitude: the medical hologram vanished while he was present, and the Benzite slept almost all the time. The idea amused Rios, who knew that Emil would certainly not approve of him drinking in the sickbay. He didn't care what the hologram thought—if he thought at all—but defiance always made him feel better.

He hadn't read Picard's book aloud to Yerm; hearing deep thoughts on philosophy might have put the patient back into a coma. Rios had certainly yawned enough. "*Adios*, Admiral," he muttered, before idly pitching the book to the deck. It was a much less violent trip than Fajo had given it.

On the biobed, Yerm stirred. "Did something fall?"

"Nothing." Rios perked up. "You know where you are, kid?"

"Sickbay." The kid sat up. "On *La Sirena*. Same as yesterday."

"Both right. But you're home. We're orbiting Benzar."

"Oh." Yerm sounded disappointed.

"Not glad to be back?"

"Oh, no, I mean—I've never been there. But I've always wanted to go."

Rios berated himself for assuming. "Then what's the problem?"

"No problem. I mean, I hate to leave, but I know I can't stay." Yerm looked down. "I really am sorry for all the trouble, Captain. I only worked a day for you."

"Some Starfleet cadets don't last that long." Rios stood up. "We're waiting for clearance to beam you to the IME clinic. Your gear's already by the transporter pad. You want to walk?"

"Yeah."

Rios gestured to the deck. "Watch out for the empty bottles."

In no hurry, they headed aft to the cargo lift. Rios rarely used it to get upstairs, but it had turned into a substitute turbolift while Hain and Yerm recovered from their injuries. Seeing the Ferengi around had made Yerm visibly uneasy, but he'd never explained why. The kid had his secrets, Rios thought, and it wasn't his job to pry them out of him.

Even so, the sight of the symbol of his imminent departure, the transporter pad, turned Yerm talkative—and as they waited for the hospital's go-ahead, he spilled his guts. During his youth, his family had lived on one of the worlds inundated by those fleeing from the impending supernova; they had taken flight themselves, only to find they had nowhere to go. By the time Yerm reached adulthood, he was alone and detached from any support systems. When he got injured, self-medication was the only relief. The medicating continued long after he'd healed—only to be compounded by stimulants when he needed to work.

In another time, Rios would have expressed hope that the benevolent medicos of the IME—caretakers of last resort whom he'd heard nothing but good things about—could set the young man right. Then he would have advised emigrating to Federation space, where a better life—perhaps even Starfleet—awaited. But those entities had already let Yerm down, and they'd done Rios no better. It was better to keep to reachable horizons.

"Maybe it'll be a place to relax," he said. "Get some reading done."

"I'm not much of a reader," Yerm replied. "I'm hands-on."

Hands on other people's stuff, Rios could imagine Ledger saying. Fortunately, she'd kept out of sight since Hain's shipment came aboard. The big foil-wrapped cubes had generally been odorless, as advertised, but sometimes when moving them around, Rios could swear he caught a whiff. Even a micrometer-wide tear in the shrouds would be noticeable. The fact that Verengan had carried nine identical payloads answered every question Rios had ever had about *La Sirena*'s state when he came aboard.

With no hail yet from the planet, he snapped his fingers. "You know, I've got one of those puzzle games. Verengan left it—it's the only thing that didn't go to Fajo. You want that?"

The offer surprised the Benzite. "You mean, like, a toy?"

"Yeah, but it looks complicated. It'll kill some hours for sure."

Yerm seemed lost in thought. "Okay. I mean, sure. It'll be good to have."

"Come along." Rios led the slow-walking Yerm forward toward his quarters.

They were right outside the door when it unexpectedly opened, revealing a very startled Hain. "You scared me!"

"I'll do more than that," Rios growled. "What the hell are you doing in my room?"

"Looking for you," the rancher said, shrinking under Rios's wrath. "We're wasting time just orbiting here. When can we leave?"

"When I say so." Rios had known Hain objected to the side trip—but he was more concerned about something else. "My door was locked!"

Hain slunk past Rios and into the open. "I told Ny-Var to trigger the override from the bridge console." He crossed his arms. "I'm bankrolling this flight!"

"You're just another passenger to me—and don't bother my flight crew again." Rios pointed back across the deck. "And knock off the sneaking around. You break in on Ledger, she's liable to shoot your other leg!"

Hain barged past Yerm, who stepped back flat against the bulkhead to let him pass. The rancher then disappeared into another room—his own quarters, this time.

"Captain," an unnerved Yerm said, "let's just forget about the toy. I don't want to be any trouble."

"There's no trouble." Rios turned again to his doorway—only to see Emil approaching up the stairs. "Now what?"

"Zo-Var has just communicated that we have word from the facility planetside. They're ready to accept Yerm now."

Rios's cabin was just behind the flight deck; Zo-Var was within earshot. "Is that right?" he called out.

"Yes," she said in what he assumed was her loudest voice. He barely heard it. No wonder she'd sent a message.

Rios looked to the kid. "I guess that's it."

"I've sent your charts ahead," Emil said to Yerm. "Listen to your doctors, and I know you'll thrive. It has been a pleasure serving you."

"Thank you, Mister Emil." When the hologram walked away, Yerm grinned. "Captain, I think it's great that you hired your twin brother to work here."

"Whatever." Yerm had never seen Emil disappear, and Rios wasn't about to explain now.

Yerm got cordial—and audible—good-byes from the Miradorns. Glake, visible through the window to engineering, silently bowed. Ledger didn't emerge at all. So it was that Rios was the only one remaining at the transporter pad to see his first hire off. He was never good with these moments, and he rushed to finish this one. "Nice knowing you—brief as it was. Sorry I don't have anything to pay you with."

"Bringing me here was enough. Others would've kicked me down the ramp at the first stop."

"Well, that ramp sticks sometimes." Rios offered his hand. "Good luck."

He was about to unclasp and step away when Yerm suddenly pulled him closer. Hugs weren't for Starfleet sendoffs and they weren't for Rios either, who started to object. "Okay, now—"

The Benzite spoke into Rios's ear in an urgent whisper. "I didn't meet you by accident that night in the tavern. I was hired to approach you for work."

Hired? "By who?" Rios tried to pull away—

—only to have Yerm pull him back. "If I tell you, I'm dead. And if you get in the way, you'll die too."

"In the way? In the way of what?"

"I don't know. But I think you could be in danger too. Trust no one." Yerm released him and stepped back onto the transporter pad. A second later, he and his bag dematerialized.

Rios's head swam. So *two* of his meetings on Alpha Carinae II were set-ups. Hain had explained one. But this sounded like something else entirely. Why would anybody care about him and what he was up to?

Rios could only wonder—and shake his head at the warning. He'd joked about Ledger's lack of trust back on Irtok, but the truth was he would never trust anyone ever again.

Captain Alonzo Vandemeer had made sure of that.

25

La Sirena
Over Ruji Baroda

Not all political borders were created equal. The historic demarcation between Federation space and the Klingon Empire was less a legal construct than an expression of where the armed forces had stopped at various times. The worlds on either side of the lines tended to be not only populated, but militarized.

The Romulan Neutral Zone, by contrast, was at its creation both more formalized—and less real. More formal, because it had been negotiated by subspace after the Earth-Romulan War in 2160, delineating the precise regions it bounded and specifically establishing the zone's one-light-year width. And less real, because it was drawn upon a galactic map that had seen little exploration. Worlds existed on the Romulan side that no warbird had visited; Federation protection had been expanded to places no one had pointed more than a telescope at.

It was just as well, Rios thought, that the twenty-second-century negotiators apparently chose not to complicate matters by considering planets like Ruji Baroda. The Bassen Rift lay entirely on the Federation side of the Neutral Zone, but it had hosted several Romulan colonies. Fortunately for the diplomats—though not for the residents—they were already failing when the war ended. Too far from home and nestled in a nebular mass that was hard to navigate using then-current technology, the settlements were just the sort to be abandoned by the Romulan Empire. The writ came, calling everyone home—and ordering them to ruin whatever they left behind.

However it began, the Ruji Baroda that appeared in *La Sirena*'s records was a useless mudball. Targeted blasts had ignited the continents' forests; their ashes had triggered a century-long winter. What remained were lands that, while no longer radioactive, grew nothing. They had been the Romulan Empire's last, spiteful shots at the Federation over planets the latter had never coveted—and in the end, they had burned their own descendants when they needed refuge.

It sounded poetic—but what Rios saw outside the forward viewport was a new chapter to the story. It didn't look like the planet in his ship's files. "It's green!"

"The Sylvus Project," Hain said from his seat on the flight deck. "Show them a mess, they'll clean it up."

La Sirena's approach to Ruji Baroda had taken the ship to the planet's nightside first, obscuring the changes that had been made. It wasn't like any of the terraforming Rios had ever seen, which usually brought in heavy machinery to alter the entire planet. He saw long rectangular strips of foliage thousands of kilometers wide stretching across the surface, even as some of the ruined landscape around it remained.

Rios took control from the Miradorns and guided *La Sirena* downward toward the sunlit half. A formation of massive slab-like vehicles could be seen, glinting in the sun as they hovered in the troposphere. Only as he approached did he realize how truly large the platforms were: each one a mini-Manhattan, a kilometer and a half long. And just as that Earthly feature had for many years boasted a large green area, these craft all sported what appeared to be enormous rooftop gardens, open to the air.

"You're in for a show," Hain said, pointing. "Watch the ground under that one!"

Rios banked *La Sirena* so he could do as the rancher suggested. Below, the frontier between green and gray was stark—except in one location, where part of it was glowing. Rios focused on it. Several seconds later, a swath that had borne nothing appeared to have been replaced by a forest of young trees.

"What did I just see?"

"Amazing, isn't it?" The Ferengi's voice bounced with excitement. "Forget what you know about planetary engineering—it's too slow for the need. The Sylvus teams literally beam out the dead land a hectare at a time, down to a few meters deep. Then they transport in whatever they've prepared. Soil, brush, trees—even crops." He pointed to the nearest flying slab. "Sylvus calls it transporter-assisted horticulture—which is why everyone calls the ships *hortiporters*."

"I would call a new ad agency," Ledger said. "That sounds terrible."

Rios was about to call it a brute-force method—but that seemed too harsh for what he was seeing. This wasn't phasers or force fields turning over land, kicking up clouds of dust that could drift back into the planted area. It appeared clean and pure: instant biosphere.

"It's a neat trick," he said. "Where does the stuff go?"

"Depends on what it is. The useful elements are reclaimed," Hain replied. "I don't know about the bad parts."

Rios couldn't believe it. "That's crazy. It'd take a whole processor farm to handle that many gigaquads of transporter data."

"That's what's beneath the decks of the platforms. The mechanics below, the growers above." Hain directed their attention to the terraria atop the hortiporters. "They dome over the greenery for space travel and fly in from all over the place—bringing whatever species they think the biome needs. They introduce the local atmosphere a little at a time until finally they're ready to transplant."

"But even with all these ships, it'd take forever to make a dent in a whole planet."

"They've *got* forever. Duke Javen started the effort in response to the destruction of Praxis, nearly a century ago. The methods have improved a bit since!"

Rios banked the ship between one hortiporter and another, seeing as he did the range of activities on their surfaces. Large species, like old-growth trees, were the exception; some of the vehicles carried massive racks of grasses, herbs, and other small life-forms. He even thought he saw some hives and cages.

Standing by the forward port, Ledger looked back at him. "I'm surprised your Federation approves of this. Or doesn't your Prime Directive cover plants?"

"It's not Federation space," Rios said. There were definitely policies and procedures that governed colonial activities, but as an outside nongovernmental actor, Sylvus was free to do what it wanted.

Hain seemed proud to be tangential to the organization. "Genuine Irtok Brothers *Yashivoo* Dung is in many of the soils they introduce. Sometimes as little as a part per million, just to get the microbes going." He sighed. "I guess they've had to make do without since Verengan died. The poor bastard—"

One of the alerts sounded. Ny-Var, covering tactical from the helm, looked back to Rios. "Ten contacts approaching."

Rios stopped rubbernecking and paid some mind to his situation. Small contacts, moving speedily. "Interceptors." He turned to Hain. "You told them we were coming, right?"

Hain tugged at his collar uneasily. "There—uh—really wasn't a chance. You see, *I didn't talk to them at all.*"

"What?" Ledger said what Rios wanted to say. "You told us you called. They told you where to find them."

The rancher pointed in the air. "To be exact, I did place a call—just not to Sylvus. It was to an associate who knew where they could be found." He rubbed the back of his scalp. "I was afraid if I contacted them, they'd renege. Say this last shipment was too late. It's harder to do if we're here, unloading."

Ledger appeared to be calculating. "You know, that's not bad thinking."

The aerial vehicles, small and sleek, appeared on the horizon. "We're being hailed," Zo-Var reported. "Audio only."

"Go ahead," Rios said.

"Attention, freighter," said a female voice that was firm, but not unfriendly. *"You are not cleared for travel in our operational area. Repeat: you are not cleared."*

"This is Captain Cristóbal Rios of *La Sirena*. I'm delivering supplies for the Sylvus Project."

"You're not on the list for today, La Sirena.*"*

"We're on an *old* list," Rios said, adding with a wince, "and we were supposed to meet you on a different planet. But we're carrying goods you ordered."

A pair of fighters rose toward *La Sirena* so quickly that Rios responded without thinking, veering to starboard and touching his thrusters. The freighter fought a bit against the atmosphere, just as he'd noted on Verex III—but the greater noticeable effect was on the aircraft that had been holding back. Six interceptors tore away from the advancing chevron and rocketed to follow.

"Sorry," he called out, sensing his reflex action had ruffled feathers. "I'm not going anywhere. Just tell me where to put down."

"I told you, no unscheduled visitors. I want you out of here. If you have legitimate business, park at the edge of the system and make an appointment."

A pair of the bogeys trailed *La Sirena*, and on the aft cam feed Rios saw something that startled him on the fighters. "Those are disruptor cannons." He looked to Hain. "You sure these guys are gardeners?"

The cam lit up—and ahead, he could see a pair of disruptor shots sizzling overhead. *"Get the picture,* La Sirena. *We keep gardens, but we also keep safe. Now move before—"*

The squadron leader paused abruptly. Rios got ready to head for space.

But first, *"What did you say your name was?"*

"Cristóbal Rios. I'm here with Hain, delivering agro supplies from Irtok. That *you* ordered," he repeated for good measure.

Ledger clutched her fists. "Come on, Sylvus. Find the damn invoice."

For a moment, Rios thought his problems were over. The moment ended, when he detected fighters traveling along on either side of the freighter, their wingtips just meters from his nacelles.

"Listen closely, Captain Rios. We have the necessary arms to defend this space—and a superior who wants to see your ass in person. We're going to make for Sylvus Bestri*—and if you make any more sudden moves we'll be adding to our cleanup work. Do you copy?"*

"Affirmative." At least it got them where they wanted to go, he thought. Then he thought of something else. "Wait. Did you say someone wanted to see *me*? You meant Hain, right?"

"No, Commander. You."

Ledger looked to him. "Did she just give you a demotion too?"

Rios wondered about that as well. But he did as he was told.

26

Sylvus Bestri
Over Ruji Baroda

He towered, golden-haired and imperious—his immaculate white uniform festooned with golden epaulets and other signifiers of station. Six officers stood at attention on the lawn, ready to enforce his command. His right hand clutched a black swagger stick, which he kept tucked under his arm at a perfect right angle to his body. And, while scars beneath both eyes communicated rough experiences past, his face betrayed no emotion as he surveyed his domain: a pastoral campus situated atop a platform hovering a kilometer off the ground. He was the lord of the flying landing field, and all was his.

"Cristóbal Rios," he said, deep voice dripping with still deeper scorn. "I don't believe it."

"Royce Claggett," Rios responded from the bottom of *La Sirena*'s landing ramp. He didn't believe it either—and he didn't want to.

"*Chief* Claggett to you." He stepped forward and looked down on Rios. "That should have a familiar sound—Commander."

"It does." Rios set his jaw as he looked up at the taller man. "And it's *Captain*."

"*Captain—?*" Claggett stared at him—and then looked up at *La Sirena*. The uniformed man burst out in laughter, loud and booming. "You're hauling manure?"

And you're receiving it. Right on the head, if I had the choice!

Claggett's vanguard broke silence to join in his hilarity. "I take it you've met," Hain murmured to Rios.

"You could say that. We were in Starfleet together."

"To know you is to love you," Ledger said.

Rios had been directed to land on *Sylvus Bestri*, in a clearing amidst the gardens and groves that ran its rooftop length. While *La Sirena* had parked on the stern of the enormous vessel, the squadron leader had referred to it as "south," a convention that apparently held no matter what direction the ship was pointing. The interceptors had put in at a vine-covered hangar decorated to look like a floral grotto; Claggett had arrived minutes later from another Sylvus ship in his own fighter, a golden-tinted variant decorated with various marks of rank.

Claggett's uniform emblems glistened in the sun as he strutted past. He stopped in front of Ledger. "Who's this you're traveling with these days, Cris?" He studied her outfit and hat—and glanced at Rios. "Iotian? *Really?*"

"She's my business associate," he replied.

"Is that right?" Claggett leered at Ledger. "And what kind of *business* does he have you doing?"

Rios feared she would explode. Instead, she stared coolly at Claggett. "I don't smack dumb palookas," she said. "I have people for that. You're lucky they're not here."

He seemed amused. "Then I'm the lucky one."

"For the moment. I keep a ledger."

Claggett's expression froze. He no longer seemed as entertained.

Hain appealed for attention. "Chief, we've met before. I've made deliveries—"

"Not now." Claggett was more interested in Rios, whom he paced around. "I just heard you tell your friends we were in Starfleet together. But you didn't tell them for how long, did you?"

Rios knew it by heart. "Ten days."

"Ten days. What a memory." He clicked his tongue and shook his head—before turning to face Rios again. "You remember how we met, I'm sure."

"You were security chief when I came aboard *ibn Majid* as first officer."

"A post I was in line for, until Vandemeer balked."

"He balked because you're an asshole—and because you were one long before I got there."

Hain put up his hands. "Wait, now, gentlebeings, there's no need—"

"I think there is." Rios saw no reason to hold back. "I was barely there two days when he beat the hell out of an ensign."

Claggett quickly interposed himself between his guards and Rios, so they could not hear. In close quarters, he growled, "That was an unruly prisoner and you know it!"

"She was a kid in the brig for pulling a prank. You decided to take your shit with me out on her." Rios's muscles coiled, expecting violence at any instant. "And then there was that Vulcan down in engineering. You were a holy terror that week."

Claggett waved the tip of his baton under Rios's nose. "You threw me off the ship."

"Vandemeer did that."

"Because you told him to."

"You're damned right. I'd have thrown you out of Starfleet if I could."

"That's exactly what happened!" He shoved Rios, who stumbled back a meter. The rooftop lawn was real, and the moist grass caused his boots to slip, propelling him down against the edge of the landing ramp.

Claggett loomed over him, stick in hand like a club. After a threatening moment, he turned to his troopers and used it to direct them on board. "Make sure the scans were right."

"Three more people on board," Rios said, sitting up as the guards tromped past him. "They're not armed. They're no threat to you."

"I'll decide that. I'm chief of security for the whole project—and that's a bigger deal than our old ship even was." Reflecting on the words he'd just spoken, Claggett began to grin. "The *ship*. That reminds me."

Rios got to his feet. "What are you babbling about?"

"I hear from the old crew. They all got cashiered—every last one of them. I can't even find the damn ship in the records anymore. But they all tell me the same thing: it was your fault. What the hell did you do?"

"Nothing." Rios heard motion on the ramp, and stepped back. He watched as Claggett's guards directed his other companions off the ship. Glake was behaving, as he'd been ordered to; Ny-Var and Zo-Var looked terrified. "It's okay, everybody," Rios said. "This is nothing."

"You just said whatever happened to *ibn Majid* was nothing," Claggett said. "Are you going to screw this team over too?"

Rios took a step toward Claggett, an act that the chief's forces took as aggression. Disruptors appeared. And then—

—so did someone else. "What's going on here?" asked a silken voice.

The troopers stepped back and snapped to attention, much faster than Rios had seen them act for Claggett. He, too, stood board straight as a human-looking woman in her thirties approached from a small building across the plaza.

"I'm Liselle," she said. Dark skinned and dark eyed, she wore an executive ensemble that made everything in Ledger's voluminous wardrobe look cheap and replicated. Her black hair was bound beneath a tiara. She approached the visitors. "I'm the administrator of this project. What's going on here?"

Ledger saw someone she could deal with. "This is *La Sirena*—we have the tenth and final part of a delivery Sylvus contracted for."

"I recognize the ship, but not the name," Liselle said, looking up at the vessel while strolling past. "You said there was a contract?"

"It's with me," Hain said. "I don't know if we ever met—I only did business with your uncle."

"Great-uncle," she corrected. "That explains it. The duke doesn't tell me everything."

Ledger looked impressed. "A duke. What does that make you?"

"A marchioness—but I never liked the sound of it."

"*Marquesa*," Rios said, speaking up. Liselle's eyes went to him, and he smiled. "That sounds better."

Liselle seemed to try it on, and did not object. "And you are?"

"Nobody," Claggett said. "They arrived with no notice, claiming they're expected—it's a perfect setup for terrorists."

The word caught her attention. "And you let them land?"

"We did remote scans as they approached—and I've got people aboard checking out the cargo. No explosives." He glowered at Rios. "But you never know with these types." He clapped his baton in his other hand. "That's what I'm here for."

"Terrorists?" Rios didn't like the direction things were going. "What are you talking about?"

Liselle explained, though her voice was a tad chillier. "Our practices are environmentally sound, and our work is deeply appreciated by desperate people. But there are those who disagree with our methods, who would rather destroy than debate."

Hain appealed to her. "This is all a misunderstanding. Captain Rios works for me. I've got a payload of *yashivoo* pure up there, just as Duke Javen asked. I'm sure he could tell you."

"He's not on *Sylvus Bestri* today—he's touring one of the other vessels."

"Well, get him here," Ledger said, "so we can get this sorted out." Her patience was running thin. "We're not some rubes you can push around, you know. I'm connected!"

Rios saw several of Claggett's troopers gawk—and Liselle indeed seemed mortified to be spoken to in such a manner. She looked to Claggett, astonished.

"She's an Iotian," the chief said. "They're a whole race that the Federation turned into cosmic criminals." He nodded to Rios. "He could be one, too, for all we know—it just takes a change of clothes."

Liselle clasped her hands behind her back. "I don't want them here."

That seemed to be more of a reaction than Claggett was expecting. "Just let me lock them up. We can—"

Rios threw up his hands. "All right, this is enough. I've been held and detained enough lately for one lifetime!"

"You see?" Claggett said. "Iotian."

"You know damn well I'm not an Iotian, Royce. Starfleet frowns on wearing hats!"

Liselle's eyes darted to Rios. "You were in Starfleet?"

"And so was he," Rios said, pointing at Claggett. "And if you'd only asked for references, *Marquesa*, I could have told you stories that would—"

From the side, someone called out, "*Wing to starboard!*"

Liselle's eyes bugged—and she looked in the direction of the call. "Everyone, out of the way!"

Rios had no idea what was going on—but all the Sylvus personnel on the lawn fled in different directions, seeking cover. He stood, startled, only to be grabbed by, of all people, Liselle herself. She yanked him toward the shelter of the landing ramp. "Come on!"

Baffled, he went—and gestured for his companions to do the same as a low screech from the sky grew ever louder. It sounded as though an incoming rocket was bound for *Sylvus Bestri*. *The terrorists?* Rios wondered.

A flat chevron, fifteen meters from wingtip to wingtip, bore down on the aerial park, headed for a crash landing a fair distance from *La Sirena*. The sound grew deafening—and the metal mammoth slammed against the surface, bouncing several times as it began a spinning skid across the turf. This time it was Rios's turn to pull Liselle away as the projectile came right up to *La Sirena*'s ramp, spraying dirt and grass as it did.

Rios emerged to see a cloud of dust—and to hear a sound from within: a howling cackle. The particles settled, revealing a figure sitting behind controls atop the open-air flying wing. "Woo-hoo!" the flier shouted, whipping off his aviator's mask, revealing a chin and head covered with white. "Ayup-ayup-hey! And away!"

"Uncle!" Liselle shouted. She pointed to Claggett. "See to him!"

"It's the duke," Hain cried. Still hobbled from his earlier injury, he nonetheless made good time across to the crash. "Javen! It's Hain!"

"Hain!" The old man—for he was old, more than a hundred for sure—stood up in his passenger cage and slapped his hip with the mask. "Haroop-hey for Hain!"

Liselle was beside herself as Javen clambered out of the wreckage. "Uncle, I've told you time and again not to take the flier out. It'll be the death of you!"

"I'll let you run corporate operations, Lissie, but you won't run me." Javen walked past her, making instead for the Ferengi. "Hain, my boy! I'd thought you'd gone to the Great Checker!"

"Exchequer," Hain said, smiling broadly as they embraced. "But you can call it whatever you want."

They cheered together. "Haroop-haroop-hey!"

Claggett clutched at the back of his head, dumbstruck by the scene. Rios caught his eye—and made sure he saw when he turned to Liselle. "Captain Cristóbal Rios," he said, taking her hand and bowing. "If you didn't have plans for dinner, *Marquesa*, I just found a place. High in the clouds, nice view . . ."

27

Sylvus Bestri

Over Ruji Baroda

Inviting himself to dinner had been bold, but he'd felt it a safe bet: Liselle had surrendered to her uncle's enthusiasm for seeing Hain, and her word overruled any objections Claggett had. And Javen's word seemed to trump hers. He expanded the invitation to Rios's entire party. One quick change later, and the *Sirenas* were ready for their second formal dinner in a month's time.

But this was no mess-hall meal with Fajo. The table was rectangular and rounded at the ends, with Liselle and Javen sitting at one of the long sides, at once grand and intimate, allowing close conversations. Rios and Ledger were on the rounded end by Liselle, such that he was adjacent to his host; this appeared to irritate Claggett, who sat across from her. The *marquesa* had included him for some reason—but he rarely got her attention.

Raucous laughter was the rule at the far end, where Hain celebrated alongside the duke—and Ny-Var and Zo-Var appeared completely dazzled. Rios was glad to have given them a night out, and just as happy that Glake had elected to stay aboard, studying. He'd gotten a little more verbal but wasn't anyone's idea of a sparkling conversationalist.

The food and wine were, as he expected, exquisite, but the setting was something else. He'd been joking about the nice view, but he had turned out to be right. The dining hall sat in a cupola that hung beneath *Sylvus Bestri*, its transparent construction permitting a view of the project's handiwork in every direction—including down. It was an unnerving experience to look beside one's armrest down onto a newly transplanted jungle a kilometer below—but Rios had no problem with it whatsoever. He only had eyes for the *marquesa*.

Liselle and her uncle were Valtese, descendants of a people that had once ruled a great empire. Rios knew some of the story, but as the sun began to set outside, he enjoyed hearing Liselle recount it. The realm had been riven in two over the love of a woman—only in this interstellar Trojan War, both sides had fallen prey to the Klingons. A couple of decades earlier, both the Valtese and their Kriosian opponents had made peace through the intervention of—who else?—Jean-Luc Picard.

"That name seems to be following me around," he said.

"I know it sounds like a fairy tale," Liselle noted, "but it's true. The conflict began over a woman and ended with a marriage."

"Sounds like a happy ending," Rios said, raising his glass.

He wasn't the only one drinking. "More wine, to honor the passage of poor Verengan!" Javen shouted. The Klingon had apparently met the duke at some point in time, Rios understood, in the course of his deliveries. "Hain, you must try the latest from the vineyards. That's where I flew in from—the *Sylvus Beraldak*." He displayed a bottle. "We're cultivating some of the species rescued from a Romulan wine region."

"Good thing you did," Hain said, offering his glass for filling. "And good thing the bottle didn't break!"

"My uncle's lucky *he* didn't break," Liselle said, casting a sweetly reproachful eye at the other end of the table. She seemed tolerant of, but a little impatient with, her older relation. "A hundred forty and he just won't slow down."

"What's the Valtese life-span?"

"Not a hundred forty."

Rios smiled. He liked the old man. But he was curious: "What is it with your uncle and Hain? He's just a rancher."

"The duke has never turned a shovel in his life, but he's always felt a kinship to those who work the soil. Particularly if he finds someone who shares his other interests."

"Like what?"

"Hain and his brother will let him talk for hours about his various collections. It's practically an obsession." Liselle rolled her eyes. "Have you ever known someone like that?"

Rios grinned. "Had dinner with one just recently." He nodded to the table. "But this is a lot better."

"I'll say," Ledger piped in. "This is some real swank. You really put on the Ritz."

"What's that, dear?" the *marquesa* asked.

The Iotian seemed unusually fumble mouthed before the slightly older woman. "You know, you really know how to spread it around."

Seeing a blank expression on Liselle's face, Claggett chuckled. "She's giving you a compliment."

Liselle brightened. "Thank you. I'm glad you're enjoying yourself."

The *marquesa* was, bar none, the most charming and elegant person Rios had ever met. The latter wasn't a quality he'd run into often in Starfleet—and certainly not since his departure. In his younger days, he'd encountered a variety of people; he knew class didn't come from wealth and breeding. But he got the sense that Liselle would be an aristocrat, rich or poor.

He further noted that Claggett, frustrated at being unable to dominate Liselle's attention, had spent a lot of time talking to his seatmate instead. At a serving break, Rios leaned in toward Ledger and whispered, "You two finally make up?"

"He's a lout," she said, napkin shielding her words from the others. "Keeps bragging about that spiffy patrol craft of his—like I'd care. I deal with brunos every day. They don't change when you give them a badge."

Rios started to respond to that, but knowing Claggett, he probably *did* have a badge somewhere.

"And something else," Ledger added, her expression sour. "You Starfleet joes are all 'treat everyone the same'—but you'll condescend to Iotians without a thought. Explain *that one* to me."

"We just have a different idea of what your society is modeled after. We know what it really was." He added, with a little embarrassment, "You're what we left behind."

"Well, isn't that a delight, to always know you're superior? That's some cheek, brother." She dropped her fork to her plate, and the clatter attracted Liselle's attention. Ledger took advantage of it. "We still have a load of manure to talk about."

Rios put up his hand. "I'm sorry." He looked urgently at Ledger. *Come on, maybe wait for dessert!*

"Don't shush me." Ledger bore down. "Verengan made nine runs from Irtok for Hain; we made the tenth. The Klingon's rights descend to us. When are you paying Hain?"

Liselle patiently folded her napkin. "I've told you, that's a bargain my uncle made."

"Aren't *you* in charge? Don't you have petty cash?"

"Sylvus is a nonprofit operation. Most of the nonreplicable goods we require are provided to us through charitable donations." She clasped her hands. "The Ferengi, of course, do not respect or recognize charity—so in those cases we make other agreements. Including," she said, "barter."

"*Barter?*" Ledger spurted.

At the word, Rios nearly choked on what he was chewing. After swallowing, he asked, "Ours isn't a case of barter, is it?"

"The duke doesn't go doling out the project's latinum," Liselle said. "I don't know what he offered Hain. You'll have to ask them."

Rios and Ledger turned to face the far end of the table, where Duke Javen was amid some story that had the Miradorns rapt with attention. Hain, glass in hand, didn't look so well.

Before Rios could stop her, Ledger called out. "Hain! What's the deal?"

The Ferengi's half-empty glass started to tip. "What do you mean?" he asked woozily.

"What are you trading for?" Her words caused Javen to stop in midconversation to look her way—but what happened in the next second caused him to turn back to the Ferengi. Hain fell face-first into his plate, losing his glass to the floor.

"Hain!" Javen yelled.

Liselle leaped up. "Medic to dining room!" she shouted. Claggett and Rios rose too. They arrived at the end of the table in seconds.

There, the two humans had trouble prying Hain's unconscious form out of Javen's clutching hands. The frenetic duke appeared truly horrified. "Hain, my boy, what's wrong?"

"He's going into some kind of shock," Claggett said. He seemed surprised by what had happened. "Does he have health issues?"

"Not since we shot him," Rios said.

"What?"

"Nothing." Rios thought to call for Emil—but, of course, that only worked on *La Sirena*. "Come on, let's get him some air."

Heaving, he and Claggett pulled Hain and the chair back from the table; part of the tablecloth shifted as well, dumping the Ferengi's dishes onto the floor.

Everything melted into a whirl. Javen weeping openly; Liselle consoling him. Claggett supervising the just-arrived medics. And Ledger, kneeling on the floor near the overwrought Miradorns as they tended to each other.

"He's alive," one of the medics said, tapping a communicator. "Transport to sickbay!"

"Me as well," Javen said.

Liselle nodded to Claggett. "Us too." She cast a glance at Rios. "We'll help him. I promise."

A transporter effect glowed—and Rios was alone with his crew, standing on a window to a dark forest now stained with wine. He stepped between Ny-Var and Zo-Var and offered a supportive arm to each. "Ledger? Where are you?"

He turned to see her sitting in the duke's chair, his wineglass in her hand. He shook his head at her. "I can't believe what just happened."

"Me neither." She looked a little frazzled. "Tell me one thing, Cris."

"What?"

"*Who in this goddamn clip joint is going to pay us?*"

28

SYLVUS BESTRI

OVER RUJI BARODA

Rios had considered himself snakebitten since leaving *ibn Majid*—and now he was beginning to think *La Sirena* was cursed too. Verengan had died on it; the first crewmember Rios had hired had nearly done the same. Hain, his first paying passenger, had been shot on it, and now was gravely ill. While Liselle's skilled medics did not think Hain was at death's door, neither had they been able to figure out what was wrong with him, a full day after he collapsed. Rios had been visiting in *Sylvus Bestri*'s sickbay when the Ferengi awoke long enough to go into a seizure of some kind. There was nothing to do but stand back and allow the medical team to work.

While he waited, Rios had preemptively transported much of his cargo to one of the hortiporter's receiving stations. It was in line with the tactic Hain had suggested: making the delivery a *fait accompli*. It also got the damn stuff off his ship. He'd have sent it all, had he not received an order from Claggett to stop.

He hadn't gotten anywhere with Liselle over the matter of payment, though she had given him a walking tour of the vessel's facilities. The *marquesa*'s domain, he saw from the command center, was larger than he'd imagined, coordinating dozens of ships on Ruji Baroda—with duplicate efforts of varying sizes transpiring on seven other planets in the Bassen Rift. Fajo's operations, reclaiming the relics of ruined lives, paled in comparison both in scope and importance to Liselle's efforts. She was salvaging whole worlds.

There was only one way to get payment, she'd said—and by the third evening, he finally bit the bullet, to use Ledger's phrase. Eccentric or not, Duke Javen had to be dealt with. A mercurial figure, he delighted in the company of those he liked; everyone else was a nonentity. And the way to be liked, Liselle had said, was to like Javen's hobbies.

It was hard to call the duke a history buff when he was older than a lot of it, but Rios had gotten on the same wavelength with him at dinner discussing various conflicts from centuries past. Ledger, just by being Iotian, had fascinated Javen—and a turn in the conversation toward ancient philosophers had given Rios a chance to use some trivia he remembered from Picard's book.

That had led to something Liselle had suggested Rios would not be able to get: an invitation to the duke's conservatory, a pagoda-like structure nestled in the woods on *Sylvus Bestri*'s campus. He and Ledger had followed Javen as he showed off his library of printed media, including a sizable section on philosophy. He didn't turn to it often anymore, he'd said. "When you're my age, children, you don't go to the sages for the meaning of life. They come to you!"

There were also objects on display, although it wasn't quite the same as Fajo's showplace. No item was placed more than a meter off the ground, and none of it was protected. These were things he enjoyed, and he enjoyed making his infrequent visitors guess about them.

Take the sculpture Rios and Ledger stood before, a life-sized statue of an ancient Vulcan astronomer gesturing to the sky. Javen chuckled. "You don't know the secret, do you?"

Rios and Ledger looked at each other. "Secret?" he asked.

Ledger nudged him. "Sure we know it. We were just talking about it, right?"

"Yeah, the secret." Rios frowned. "Maybe we should discuss it." He looked to the duke. "You start."

Javen stared at them for a moment, before laughing loudly. "I can see why Hain hired you. You're pips, both of you." He directed them to circle the statue, looking up. "Notice anything?"

"She's got two left hands," Ledger said.

"Isn't that delicious?" The statue was damaged at some time, Javen explained—and whoever owned it tried to replicate and affix a replacement hand, never noticing that the one they'd copied was the mirror image of what was required. They'd have been better off leaving well enough alone.

He had some Earth artifacts to show as well. He pointed into an alcove. "Try over there."

Ledger peered at the paper envelope, sitting openly on a stand. Her eye went to a couple of stickers affixed to it. "Postage stamps. We had them back home."

"Look more closely."

"It's a steamship—and an airplane. And they're upside down."

"Or were printed that way," Javen said. "Oops!" He rocked back and forth on his heels. "They're all just like the planets I find. Imperfect in some way—made so, by the acts of the so-called intelligent."

Something else caught his attention, and he took both their arms and led them to it. "This, my friends, is a wonder I received many years ago." It was an oversized tome, with medieval printing on it. "You know of William Shakespeare?"

"Who doesn't?" Rios said.

"Who indeed? What you see there is an original copy of a First Folio, containing several of his greatest plays."

"If it's so great," Ledger said, rolling her eyes, "why did someone spill a drink on it?"

Rios advanced to her side of the display. The book in the stand was open to a particular page. It was a scene in *Macbeth*, but he could only just tell that—because much of it was illegible due to a ginormous purple-black splotch. It had clearly soaked through to the rest of the folio, but the paper did not appear to have rotted.

"A wine stain," Javen said. "It appears to have been relatively recent in the book's life."

"So much for that," Ledger said. "It's junk now."

"Oh, no, no! To me it's priceless. Imagine anyone treating something like it with such callous disregard. It wasn't damaged by a fire, or long years of neglect. I envision a single day, a single blunder. It was the worst day in someone's life."

"And you've got it out here like it's important."

"It tells me people are fallible, even with things that they should take the most care with—and it says that under all the scars, there is still beauty."

Rios contemplated Javen's words. Ledger, predictably, was only interested in valuations. "I wonder what Fajo would make of these."

Javen seemed startled. "You know Kivas Fajo?"

Rios nodded. "He's evaluating some goods of ours on Argelius now."

"Curious fellow." He scratched his voluminous beard. "A checkered past—but my whole project is about second chances. I don't begrudge him that. We don't do business, though. He would find some of my books valuable, but has little use for some of the peculiarities I prize. Collectors like Fajo see uniqueness created by errors in production as of legitimate interest; damaged goods they find worse than useless."

Ledger gestured to the envelope in the alcove. "But weren't those stamps over there an error of production?"

"Take another look." He encouraged her not only to approach it, but to take it in her hands. "What do you notice?"

Ledger thought for a moment. "They're on a letter?"

Javen hooted with glee. "Someone mailed it—an act that damaged the stamps' value."

"*There's* your 'oops.' He destroyed it."

"That's what Fajo would say—but here, he is certainly wrong." Javen pointed to the markings on the envelope in her hand. "It was sent to something called a video club, enclosing payment for receipt of a copy of an entertainment in which a spendthrift mails an 'inverted Jenny'—that's the airplane stamp—purposefully to destroy its value." Javen grinned. "So this letter's sender knew *exactly* what he was doing. He even went it one better: because the Jenny was one currency unit shy of the delivery rate, he added the inverted steamship, another valued rarity produced for the Pan-American Exposition, years earlier."

"That's crazy," Rios said.

"That's what you say." Javen nearly danced around the room. "I say Harold Winslow of Truth or Consequences, New Mexico, was a character after my own heart—and perhaps the greatest philosopher of his age. The act of mailing was art itself, a statement of independence and belief. He knew we only hold possessions for a time—and we must find a way to use them that makes us whole!" He gestured to his skylight. "It is the same way with planets."

At that, he darted off to the next room, causing Ledger and Rios to have to hurry to follow. "He's a nut," she whispered.

Rios didn't fully agree. *Conversation pieces*: that was just what Fajo wanted from the gallery behind his reception area. They were something to talk about. The pieces' value was there.

Which brought him, finally, to broach the subject he'd been waiting for the right moment to address. "The *marquesa*—your niece, I mean—told us that you and Hain had a bargain for the fertilizer shipments. Some kind of trade."

"Eh?" Javen said, flipping through a pile of what appeared to be unframed oil paintings. "Ah, yes. We did have an arrangement. He did want something." He looked up, his eyes cloudy. "He and I were going to discuss that after dinner. Poor old Hain!"

"If you can hold the waterworks," Ledger said, "tell us this. This thing he wanted—was it valuable?"

"Oh, indubitably," the duke said. He looked up. "Indeed, I was going to have to tell him that I'd changed my mind about our arrangement."

"Changed your mind?" Rios asked in alarm. "Changed *how*?"

"It's far too dear to me to surrender for *yashivoo* dung, no matter how many hectares it might fertilize. Why, it wouldn't be my library without it."

Ledger's eyebrows met. "But you've already used the other nine shipments, right?"

"Oh, yes. But I'm certain I could have talked good old Hain into accepting something of lesser personal value to me. We just needed to talk. To—"

With that, Javen began to weep.

Rios put his arm on the duke, trying to console him. "Look, Hain will get better. But we're with him. We can negotiate for him."

Javen rubbed the moisture from his mustache. "Dear me, no. No, no. You're fine beings, for sure—but it was a handshake with Hain, and I shall deal only with him—or his brother, perhaps. To do otherwise would be to betray a true friend."

"Phonus balonus!" Ledger spouted. "You're already expecting your 'true friend' to accept less."

Rios put up his hand, desperate that she not cause offense. "You said 'his brother.' Is he back on Irtok? Can we get him on the comm?"

"Oh, no. He hasn't been part of the family ranch business in decades—and I haven't seen him in a couple of years. I don't know how to find him."

Ledger swore. "I don't believe this."

"And I don't like your tone, young person." Javen fluttered his hands in the direction of the exit. "Shoo now. We will all talk to Hain when he awakens."

Then a sniffle—and more crying.

"Of course," Rios said, urging a recalcitrant Ledger toward the door.

Outside, under a lamp by the building, there was more swearing in the warm night air. "The month's almost out," she told him. "We do not have time to go find Hain's brother. We don't even know who he is!"

"Agreed." He didn't know she was this emotionally invested in the matter—but he did know she hated to lose. "Maybe Hain will come out of it. Maybe the *marquesa* can talk sense into the duke."

"If you can squeeze it in while you're drooling after her. This is no way to run a business!"

"I've already delivered most of the final load. What leverage do we have?"

"Oh, we've got something." Ledger reached into her pocket and pulled something out. "We've got this!"

Rios took the paper rectangle from her and held it up to the light. "*Home Video Club*," he read, before confronting her. "You stole his inverted Jenny!"

"He told me to take it and look at it. He never told me to put it back."

Rios faced the door of the pagoda, fearful it might pop open at any second. "What were you thinking?"

"He said it wasn't worth as much as it is—but it's worth something to *him*, I bet."

"But he'll know you stole it!" Disgusted, Rios put the letter carefully inside his vest pocket. "I'm going to make sure he gets this back, or we'll ruin the deal for sure."

"It's already ruined."

"What's ruined?" came a voice from the darkness, giving both of them a start. Liselle stepped toward them on the path. "It can't be the night that's ruined—we always navigate to where there's good weather."

"Nothing's ruined." Rios gestured to the padd in her hand. "Working late?"

"As always." She looked out at the path. "But I'm very glad to see you, Captain. Care for a walk?"

29

SYLVUS BESTRI

OVER RUJI BARODA

"It'd be my pleasure to walk with you, *Marquesa*." Rios turned to Ledger. "See you back at the ship."

Ledger stared at the two of them, then curled her fingers at the sky before storming off.

"Is your friend all right?" Liselle asked.

Rios shrugged. "She's just upset over a math problem."

"I'm sorry—I suppose I should have invited her as well." Liselle smiled gently. "Unless *that* was the math problem."

He smiled back. After spending a couple of hours exposed to the gale-force wind that was Duke Javen, he was delighted to be in calm waters.

The park in the sky was sublimely beautiful at night; just enough lamp-posts where they needed to be, with the moons to light the rest. The Sylvus crew had already restored the terrain damaged by the duke's crash—probably, Rios thought, using the same techniques it was using on the landscape far below.

"No matter how he seems today, my uncle is a great man," Liselle explained. "He and his sisters inherited a major industrial house. He could have continued spending all his time in high society—but after the Praxis disaster, he transformed the firm to do something important. I'm pleased he took an interest in you."

She had taken an interest in Rios, too, and while he didn't know why, it didn't seem to be because she wanted something from him. He liked that. She was responsible for the employment of tens of thousands, and her work helped millions. Perhaps she sensed, somehow, that he, too, had once been responsible for hundreds, and that was why she took him seriously.

She had more than hinted at it. "You're different, Cristóbal. I see freighter captains all the time. I do not make a habit of inviting them to dinner, much less three nights in a row."

"Does Chief Claggett usually come to dinner?"

"He insisted. He's here to protect Sylvus's assets—and that includes us. Assembling the patrol squadron was his idea; that golden interceptor of his is his pride and joy. He does his job adequately. But that is the extent of my interest in him—regardless of what he may think."

Good, Rios thought.

As they strolled, Liselle talked of the pressures she was under. Finding financing for the effort was a never-ending task, and the project was never far from ruin. She had been equal to that challenge, but there were others she struggled with. "When you're related to the project founder, nobody ever thinks you deserve your job. I've been administrator for a dozen years, and I still fight that. I have to give my all."

"Do you mind it?"

"I'll put it this way. There are empathic metamorphs among my people, able to shape themselves to whatever a potential companion requires. That war I told you about was fought over one, and resolved by another."

"Perfect mates," Rios mused aloud. Liselle seemed pretty perfect to him.

"I joke that the Sylvus Project is *my* perfect mate—it fills every minute of my day, and most of my thoughts at night. It gives me what I want, we rarely argue, and it's always here for me."

"I envy that." He nodded back in the direction of *La Sirena*, a shadow much farther across the lawn. "I bought that ship looking for something to do, something I could count on." He stared. "Hasn't really worked out yet."

"I'm sure it will. I don't know you well, but you seem like someone who is driven to succeed." Approaching a bench, she invited him to sit with her. "Success for me is every planet repaired—or prepared. Since the Romulan crisis, it's been nonstop."

"Important work," he said. "It must get lonely."

"I get what I need," she said, looking away. "There are particular visitors. Dinners, like tonight." She looked up through the leaves at the moons. "Nights like tonight."

Rios took her hand. She did not object; instead, the look she gave him was of quiet bemusement. "Won't . . . your friend mind?" she asked.

"Friend?" Rios's mind went blank for a moment. "Oh, Ledger?" He chuckled. "No. She's just a business associate. Employee, kind of on work release." He shrugged. "I'm her parole officer."

"I don't believe you at all," Liselle said, amused.

"Believe this," he said, drawing her in for a kiss.

And he began to believe, for the first time in over a year, that existence might actually be an okay thing.

Rios woke feeling confirmed in that belief—and in the most comfortable bed he had slept in his entire life. He also awoke alone, although that was not much to his surprise. The *marquesa* was an incredibly busy woman; he had no expectation that she would give her day over to him. The night had been gift enough.

They had both entered into it knowing precisely what it was, and what they expected. He didn't believe he was the only person she'd made time for; he made sure she understood he didn't come with strings attached. He wasn't looking for a job, a relationship, or even help getting payment from her great-uncle. It was just a night, and it was great—and with luck, there might be more.

He found his clothes neatly folded outside her bedroom, the work of a discreet servant; a hot breakfast was waiting as well. That, and the fact that no one he passed leaving her quarters interacted with him at all, suggested that as administrator, Liselle's life was her own business. Rios liked that too. He'd had his fill of people sneaking into his quarters and minding where he drank at night.

Learning that the *marquesa* was in meetings, Rios made his way aft in the guts of the hortiporter to sickbay, where for the past three mornings he'd checked on Hain first thing.

There had been no change in the rancher's condition, he saw; and the medics were no closer to determining what was wrong with him. The first night had seen a few bouts of waking delirium, but nothing since. Rios sat alone with him for a few minutes, trying to draw Hain out.

He was about to leave when he succeeded. "*Rios . . . ?*"

"You're awake?" Rios stood and approached the biobed. "Let me call someone."

"Don't." Hain spoke in a guttural dry voice. "They just think . . . I'm asleep. Did you . . . see Javen?"

That wasn't a question Rios was expecting. "I did. He said he was supposed to give you something from his collection. Why not latinum, or—"

"Worth . . . more. *Much* more." Hain sounded convinced of it. "It's in his library. Did he give it to you?"

"No. He reneged." Rios looked to the side—and noted as the biobed's telemetry indicated Hain's quickening pulse. "He wants us to take something else."

"No . . . good." Hain seemed to be struggling. "Original deal!"

"What is this thing?"

Hain wrenched in the bed, his head rolling from side to side. Rios feared another convulsion was starting. "Captain . . . get me out of here. Someone got to me."

"What do you mean?"

"Poisoned. To stop me."

"Who? From what?"

Rios heard footsteps in the hall, almost certainly personnel responding to Hain's blood-pressure spikes. Before he could turn, however, the Ferengi lifted himself from the biobed enough to clutch at Rios's collar with both hands. "Get me out!" he implored.

The Sylvus medics entered the room—and Hain fainted dead away, releasing Rios as he collapsed back onto the platform.

He watched, silently, as the doctors conducted scans—and wondered whether he should say anything about Hain's condition. But only for a moment. Then he looked from one monitor to another, trying to remember everything he saw. At last, Rios worked his way out of the room.

Using his visitor ID to gain access to one of the louder portions of *Sylvus Bestri*'s innards—near the churning machinery that digested and separated materials beamed up from the surface—Rios went to a corner and triggered his communicator. "Ledger!"

"Miss Ledjo's office."

"Who's this?"

"This is Myra." The woman sounded as if she were chewing gum. *"I'm one of the secretaries, sweetie. Who shall I say is calling?"*

Rios rolled his eyes. Ledger had added the character to her holographic office after Hain's break-in. Where Arkko surrounded herself with male eye candy, Ledger had programmed Iotians who seemed competent. "This is Captain Rios. I need to speak to Ledger, now!"

"Oh, I'm sorry. Miss Ledjo is not taking calls."

"Put her on, or I'll send a shutdown command for the whole damned holodeck!"

A beat. *"One moment."*

Ledger finally answered, her voice full of disgust. *"What now? Did she leave you naked on the planet's surface?"*

"Ledge, listen. Hain's awake—but he thinks he was poisoned!"

"Welcome to the party, flatfoot. I've been working that angle already."

Rios stared at the comm unit. "What? Working how?"

"The other night at dinner. I lifted the glass he was drinking from."

"What, did you think it was worth something?"

"I thought it might be worth something for your friends to croak our client. I didn't do anything with it until last night, after Javen stiffed us."

Rios caught up with her. "What does Emil say about it?"

"That it was a Romulan wine, just like the duke claimed. It's got a unique composition—but there was nothing in it that should have hurt a Ferengi."

He was glad to hear that much, at least. "So it's not the wine."

"Sorry, I didn't steal his dinner plate. My purse was only so big."

Rios explained that Hain had confirmed that his payment was somewhere in the duke's library. "I was going to go back over and try to talk to him, later today."

"For all the good that will do."

"I've got to try. Besides, I need to—"

Rios turned to see that he wasn't alone: a quartet of security officers had appeared behind him. He muted the call and turned, showing his badge as he did. "I've got clearance."

"Sir, the administrator would like to see you immediately."

"Sure, I'd been planning to—"

"*Now*, sir." The woman's body language made it clear it was not a suggestion.

"Got it." Rios began walking, flanked by the guards at a far enough distance that he did not, for a change, feel as if he was in custody. They had not frisked him, of course; he had not been armed once outside of the freighter, and was not now.

But he did keep his comm active, its channel to *La Sirena* open.

30

Sylvus Bestri
Over Ruji Baroda

Given the spectacular views of the outside world that *Sylvus Bestri*'s lofty perch offered, Rios might have expected the administrator's office to have had the best one of all. But as the *marquesa* had told him on his tour two days before, her attention needed to be on what the hortiporter was about to do, not what it had already done.

So instead, her work area sat deep inside the mighty vessel—and the landscape it overlooked was virtual. Her office was a balcony above the command center, close to the efforts her people were engaged in.

Over the railing behind her desk she could see the colossal holographic floor display showing the topography, geology, and hydrology of the area the vessel was transforming. Heavy cables attached to the ceiling hung over the map like metal stalactites, supporting indicator lights and other information for workers laboring at consoles below. Timers ticked down the minutes between each prospective transport, after which it was on to the next simulated hectare.

Liselle had been so proud of it all, showing him every step of the operation—somehow without interrupting her busy day. He could tell from her curt reception that *this* visit was going to be a lot less cordial.

"I had considered having you transported directly here," she said as she paced behind her desk. Flickering light from the command area behind and below her gave her an eerie aspect. "Our personnel transporters are down for maintenance—and it's just as well. I wanted to take some time to think more about what I've heard."

"Reflection is good," Rios said. She hadn't offered him a chair, but at least the guards had exited. "What have you heard?" The better question, *from whom did she hear it*, he left unasked.

She pivoted and looked back at him. "Have you heard of the Celarius Front?"

"No."

"It's an extremist organization that opposes the introduction of foreign species to planetary ecospheres. It's wrongheaded in times like these, when so many people need supporting." She waved broadly to the work going on behind her. "And our practices are sound—we supplement native life-forms. We don't harm them!"

"Of course not." Rios knew it was something she was passionate about; he just didn't know why she was telling him about it.

He found out. "The Miradorns you're traveling with. How much do you know about them?"

"Ny-Var and Zo-Var? They're my flight crew."

"Royce says that one of the ships they served aboard belonged to the Celarius Front."

Royce. As if I had any doubt.

"That ship opposed our efforts on one world," she said, "delaying by days the help we were there to provide." She studied his face. "Were you aware of that?"

"No." Rios couldn't honestly say whether it was true or not; he'd only glanced at their résumés. "Are you sure they were even aboard then?"

"Are you sure they weren't?"

He breathed out, a little relieved that this was all this was. "They're sweet, harmless people, *Marquesa*. I've never heard them speak a word in anger. Hell, I've barely heard them speak."

"Sometimes silence is deceiving." She crossed her arms. "But that's not all. Your 'business associate'—Ledger, as you call her? She's Iotian."

"That's no secret—and no crime."

"Of course not. But Claggett ran her image against one of his intel data-sets. Apparently she's a ranking member of a roving criminal band known as the Convincers." She scowled. "Don't try to tell me you weren't aware of that. You joked about her."

Rios hedged. "She's been traveling with me for the better part of a month. Perfectly law-abiding." Then, he added, "Yesterday's not my department."

"Well, I care about it." Liselle grew agitated. "Iotian gangs have hit Sylvus transports all across the region—the Convincers among them." She turned to face the facsimile of the world below, a beautiful goddess raging from the sky. "Stealing from a charity, Cristóbal! Can you *imagine* anything worse?"

At the moment, Rios couldn't. When Liselle turned, he took a step toward her and put up his hands to appeal for calm. "I didn't know these things. But that doesn't have to cause a problem for us."

"There is no 'us,'" she said icily. "Royce told me the rest." She spoke to the air. "Come."

The door across from the desk whisked open, and Claggett stepped inside, baton in hand. Two guards entered behind him. He strode up and thumped Rios's chest with the club. "Open your jacket."

"What, you think I'm armed?" Rios unfastened the garment and held it partially open. "Satisfied?"

"I am now." Claggett reached inside Rios's pocket and pulled out what was hiding inside. He displayed it to Liselle. "The stamps."

Rios blanched. He had forgotten about the envelope with the inverted postage. He scrambled to think of a dodge—and settled on one. "Nice trick. Did you plant it there?"

He could tell immediately from Claggett's shit-eating grin that he'd taken the wrong tack. "*I* found it," Liselle said. "This morning."

Rios remembered finding his clothes folded outside her room; that had to be when it happened. She said nothing more about how she happened to come across it in front of Claggett. Instead, she imprisoned Rios in a cold stare.

"Okay," he said. "I had it—I won't bother to explain how. But I was going to give it back. Today, when I saw Duke Javen later."

"You won't be seeing my uncle again." She turned to face the command center, where another countdown had just started. "The duke knows what you did—and wants nothing to do with you."

He looked at the carpet. "I know it's bad, but—"

She kept her back to him. There was no salvaging this.

But Claggett was still there, clapping his baton against his palm and looking like he had cards yet to play. "Is that it?" Rios asked him.

"You're not getting off that easy—*Commander*. I told her the rest."

"The rest?" Rios had never seen a smarmier expression—and had never hated anyone more. He waved his hand in the air. "Well, you've been busy, I'll give you that. I can't wait to hear this."

Liselle turned quickly and answered for Claggett. "He said you were punished by Starfleet for physically abusing prisoners."

Rios gawked. "That wasn't me. That was *him*!"

"He also thinks you had something to do with the death of your captain—what was his name?"

"Alonzo Vandemeer," Claggett said. "That's why you're here now—you're on the run. For killing him."

The accusation astonished Rios. "I didn't do that. I would never do that!"

"Then Vandemeer lives?" Liselle asked.

"No," he started—only to halt. He didn't know how much to share. "Vandemeer killed himself."

"I told her you might say that," Claggett said. "We know two things: there was a death, and a cover-up. You know, to protect the service from getting a bad name—from a bad actor."

Liselle seemed wrenched. "Tell me it isn't true, Cristóbal. Tell me there was no crime. No cover-up."

Rios couldn't. There *was* a crime. There *was* a cover-up. But he had nothing to do with his captain's desperate act. But to say more might jeopardize the careers—and maybe even the lives—of his fellow crewmembers, all of whom hated him today.

There was no salvaging her trust—and he knew it was no time to introduce his suspicions about Hain, not when the Ferengi was helpless. "All I want," he said carefully, "is to offload the rest of the cargo. It's no good to anyone else but you. Transfer Hain to us—my medic can look after him. Then pay me whatever you think is fair."

Claggett had something else in mind. He faced Liselle. "As director of security, I recommend you authorize me to lock them up and confiscate the ship."

"What?" Rios shouted. "On what grounds? All this crap you've been shoveling?" He waved to Liselle's desk. "You've got your stamp back."

For several moments, Claggett seemed to be searching for something. Then he found it. "*Piracy!* I remember now. There's a Klingon that owns this ship."

"That was then," Rios replied. "He's dead now."

"Under what circumstances?"

"He drank himself to death!"

"Likely story. Maybe you and your little Iotian killed him and took his ship."

"That's crazy. It belonged to her people to begin with."

Liselle spoke up. "The Convincers own *La Sirena*?"

Rios had spoken too fast, said too much. He clammed up now, too late.

Claggett looked to his superior. "Give the word and I can send people to the freighter. And if it tries to lift off, it won't get far. A Kaplan's gonna handle like a hog in this thick atmosphere—and I can have interceptors out of the hangar in a heartbeat."

"I'm sorry," Liselle said, looking at Rios. She nodded her consent to Claggett.

"I hear you," Rios said, hanging his head. "I hear you." Then—just as Claggett gestured for his guards, he added: "Did *you* hear them?"

"Every word." It was Ledger's voice, coming from his comm.

"Good," he shouted—and grabbed the end of Claggett's swagger stick with one hand. The security chief held on, refusing to let go—only to receive a kick in the groin from Rios for his efforts.

The office door opened, revealing more sentries beyond; one of the other guards rushed to Liselle's side. Rios leaped atop the desk—and from there to the ledge overlooking the command center.

He looked back long enough to blow a kiss. "*Chao, Marquesa.*"

He jumped from the ledge. One of the device-festooned cables hung over the holographic terrain nearby. Rios grabbed hold of it, arresting his plummet. Scrambling to right himself, he sized up another hanging target two meters away. He threw himself toward it. And then another: metal vines across a virtual jungle. Physical training at the Academy was never like this—but it served him as he made his way across the room without ever touching the deck.

Finally, he reached a ledge, where he tapped his communicator. "Ledger, get ready to take off!"

"The gals are already powering up. Where are you?"

"Nowhere I can get to you." He wiped sweat from his brow. The command center was one of the farthest "northern" portions of the vessel; *La Sirena* was parked far to the south and dozens of meters above.

"I'll have Glake transport you."

"*No!*" he shouted, momentarily flashing on what might happen if the Nausicaan transported him without an integumentary system to contain his innards. Instead, he looked back at the terrain displayed behind him, and the associated timers. "There's another way. Just don't get boarded—and I'll find you!"

31

Sylvus Bestri
Over Ruji Baroda

Muddy soil, wild grasses, some big stones, and a few clumps of trees. It would win no awards for aesthetic appeal; as starship arboretums went, the only thing special about it was its colossal size. No art had gone into the design; only science. That, and elements reclaimed from elsewhere on the surface and the atmosphere—or forged from the replicator, with plant life added from greenhouses and labs.

One day it would be a place, a place that children—perhaps Romulan or not—might race across, chasing a pet. A place where housing could be erected, where fruit could be harvested, where a sunset could be enjoyed. It might be none of those things, remaining wild and pristine. But at the moment, it was Implant RB77-24-15N14-22-09E/20, and it was sitting in one of twenty identical transporter domes housed beneath *Sylvus Bestri*'s top deck.

Rios had seen the implant number in the command center beside a timer; he was glad now he'd listened when Liselle had told him on their tour that the last two digits referred to which chamber it was assigned to. That was all he had needed to know. He'd reached the vast room without any opposition, a fact he attributed entirely to the transporter maintenance Liselle had mentioned. *Sylvus Bestri* might be able to beam a thicket, but today its bipedal occupants were taking the hoverlifts.

With one exception. "Coming through!" Rios yelled, dashing past mask-wearing scientists in lab coats. The timer outside the chamber told him he'd made it just in time; that, and the fact that the miracle forest ahead of him was still there. He charged into it, boots hitting mud as he heard confusion erupt behind him.

For a moment, he worried that the countdown had been stopped—but he then felt the expected tingling as he and his surroundings were whisked away.

Rios noticed the light immediately when he arrived at his destination; that, and the warm, heavy air. For several seconds he was blinded, having gone from a dark interior to a summer day, with Ruji Baroda's sun beating down on him. As his eyes adjusted, he saw blue skies above—and several hortiporters, including one directly overhead. *That's mine*, he thought.

He took a deep breath and confronted his next problem. Even if his flight crew could get *La Sirena* past Claggett's beloved interceptors, Rios didn't think they were capable of reaching him. Landing lessons weren't for today. Fortunately, he had something else in mind; unfortunately, he realized, he wasn't sure how to get there.

The patches the hortiporters laid down, he'd learned, had only looked square from a distance: they were actually hexagonal, allowing for both a better accommodation of existing water flows and a more natural look for the streams it introduced. He'd known from the timers that the next hexagonal hectare of native soil would be brought up from Rudi Baroda's surface ninety seconds after the adjacent implant went in; he just had to find it—and reach it.

He climbed one of the flat rocks and looked about. Beyond the sizable patch that he was in, gray desert stretched across half the horizon; grasses and trees, the other half. Logic combined with *Sylvus Bestri*'s heading above told him the leftmost part of the gray zone would be the one replaced next.

He ran as fast as he could manage through the sodden soil, wondering how much, if any, of Hain's *yashivoo* poo was under his feet—and how long it would have taken the sleepy-looking crew he'd seen manning Transport Chamber 20 to alert the command center that he'd stowed away with their forest.

Huffing and puffing, he approached the border with the rough, original terrain—and realized he had a new problem. The prospective area to be removed was more than two meters higher than the just-transported land on which he stood. Sylvus did not move mountains; it conformed as much as it could to local landforms. But it was carving out and doing away with toxic pollutants, and using some more matter as raw materials.

Rios reached the wall, where a single attempt convinced him not to bother clambering over the hard way. Time was too short—and so was he. The tree a dozen meters to his right, however, was not. It sat near the edge, and looked too young and insubstantial to hold his weight for more than a few seconds. But that was all he wanted. He quickly began scaling, taxing a root system that had sat in different soil entirely an hour before. With a nasty creak, the trunk began to give way—but in the right direction. He released it like a pole vaulter and dropped, gracelessly, onto the dusty plain above.

He lay on his back for several moments, gasping. "*Mierda*," he said. "I've been sitting around on the ship too damned—"

Another transporter effect interrupted him. When his pupils refocused, he was in the dark again—and in imminent danger.

Rios sat up. He'd been in the twentieth chamber; symbols on the walls told him he was now in the first. By running across a freshly created field and climbing a tree, he'd just moved from the end of *Sylvus Bestri* farthest from *La Sirena* to the complete other side. Now he just needed to avoid getting digested.

He'd seen the process: the lights above and rumbling below told him it was about to start. Detailed scans were already underway for the transporter to pick and choose between the native elements for processing or disposal. Rios didn't need to see it up close. He rose and bolted for the control area, where he again startled several workers.

"You're doing a great job. *Adios!*"

They chattered at him; so, too, did one of the consoles he passed, loudly conveying an order to shut down all transport activity. Rios had made it—but only just.

Stairs, ladders—anything leading up. It would have taken him a month to see all of *Sylvus Bestri*, but he had come to understand one thing about the place: Claggett's security personnel seldom appeared belowdecks. He was in sight of a hatch leading to daylight when the first one spied him—and that woman went for her communicator rather than her weapon. Rios dove for the ladder and climbed.

He stepped into sunlight again, this time from behind one of the surface buildings. He worked his way forward in the direction of *La Sirena*'s parking spot. Breathless, he emerged from the trees and looked upon it—

—but not the freighter.

Damn you, Cristóbal—you beamed back onto the wrong ship!

He knew immediately that wasn't the case; sirens were blaring across the aerial park. Still, it was hard not to fret. The ship was gone. He went for the communicator. "I'm topside! Where the hell are you?"

He didn't have to wonder long, as an infernal clamor came from the stand of trees off to one side. Branches shattered as the hovering freighter yawed across the deck, taking down anything that was more than ten meters tall. More sentries appeared on the scene, aiming their weapons—only to drop them in panicked flight as *La Sirena* twirled and swerved sideways in their direction, threatening to sweep the flying park clean. Rios had made use of the freighter's long protrusions in frustrating attackers on foot back on Verex III; here, they combined with the erratic guidance of his flight crew to scare the wits out of anybody below.

That included Rios—but he had no choice. Waiting until *La Sirena* pivoted in a direction where he could be seen, he charged into the open, heedless of the guards. The freighter dipped and turned, exposing its open landing ramp. Rios took a deep breath and bolted for it, heedless of disruptor fire around him.

This vault was without a helpful tree—and he didn't entirely make it, his chest slamming against the edge of the ramp. But he couldn't cling there for long, not with the ship veering and threatening to gouge the ground with the ramp's edge. Rios pulled himself up and began to crawl—only to tumble in as *La Sirena* bobbed.

"I'm in," he called into the communicator as he ran. But there was no indication anyone was listening as the freighter continued to pitch and roll. The bridge needed him, he knew—but it couldn't be his first stop. He dashed to the stairs heading for the back of the upper deck—and the transporter he knew he was going to need.

What he wasn't expecting, however, was to find it in use. In use—with the transporter platform surrounded by heaps of books of all shapes and sizes.

"Hurry!" Ledger called out, shovel in hand. She was not alone: Zo-Var and Emil were both there, shoveling and carting tomes to get the platform clear. The instant it was, more books materialized.

Rios gawked. "What the hell is going on?"

"Finally. Grab a shovel!" Ledger shouted. "We didn't know which book Javen was going to give Hain—so we're grabbing them all!"

"*The whole library?*" Rios was stunned. "And none of the shelves?"

Through the window to engineering, Rios could see Glake behind the transporter controls. The Nausicaan gave a proud and silent salute.

Well, at least he's consistent, Rios thought.

Emil approached him. "Thank goodness you're here. This is not my duty, and—"

"Stay there!" Rios said, helping to shove off the latest mountain of volumes. They were everywhere; he guessed that Ledger would have had to have started as soon as his meeting with Liselle began to go wrong. But he had to get the transporter clear.

When he was finished, Ledger called out to Glake, "Next batch!"

"No!" Rios shouted. He scrambled over the fallen books to enter engineering, where he took over at the transport panel.

Sylvus Bestri's sickbay located, he locked onto Hain. Moments later, the Ferengi appeared, biobed and all, on the pad.

Hain's eyes opened—and he beheld the exploded library all around. "I must be delirious," he said.

"I'm sending him downstairs," Rios called out, starting another transport. He looked to Emil. "Go!"

"Right away." The EMH vanished.

"No more books," he ordered Glake. He looked up to see a fretful Zo-Var waiting. "What?"

"Sorry for the intrusion, Captain, but Ny-Var says Chief Claggett is hailing you."

"Why hasn't—?" It dawned on him that *La Sirena* was still swinging about over *Sylvus Bestri*; he had never given the order to depart. He looked around, flustered. "Put him through," he shouted to the overhead.

"Quite the exercise, Commander. But too little, too late." Rios could hear an engine revving—and it wasn't *La Sirena*'s. *"My interceptor squadron is in the hangar, powering up and ready to go. Your ship might be fast in space, but the skies are ours."*

"You don't say."

"I do. And oh, if you see a golden interceptor firing on you, that's me." He laughed. *"The bell is ringing, Cris. The court-martial is about to begin!"*

Rios had to get to the command area. He stepped out of engineering and was poised to break into a run through the book-laden obstacle course when something caught his eye off to the right.

He spun and headed back in, much to Ledger's alarm. She followed him in. "We've got to scram, Charlie!"

"The job's not done yet!" Rios worked the transporter controls frenetically—punching up one set of coordinates and then another. At last, he breathed easy. "That's it."

She stared at him as he relaxed. "What do you mean, 'That's it'?"

He led Ledger and Glake out of engineering and into the starboard cargo area. "I just delivered the last of the manure," he said with a smile.

"What? Where?"

"To the hangar, one meter above the interceptors. Oh, and Glake—I followed your lead." He gestured to a crumpled mass of deflated, stinking foul coverings on the deck. "I sent it all without the packaging."

Glake and Ledger looked at him, both astonished.

"Beam the wrappings over now, with my apologies to Chief Claggett for the mistake. I'm getting us out of here." As he started forward, he called over his shoulder, "Oh, and tell Hain his delivery is finally complete!"

32

La Sirena
Over Verex III

Claggett had been right about one thing: once *La Sirena* reached space, there was no stopping it. The only problem came when it stopped again.

With the next payment to Arkko due soon, Ledger had suggested returning to Verex III, where she'd assured Rios she had a solution for them both. It was the last place he wanted to revisit, but messages he'd received while departing the Bassen Rift convinced him lawless space made sense.

Liselle's message was to the point: he was *persona non grata*, and anything good that had happened between them had been erased from her mind. The message from Claggett, meanwhile, contained more obscenities than Liselle's missive had contained words. No one had been injured by Rios's parting gift, but the chief's prized interceptor was forever tainted. Between that and the theft of much of the duke's library, the Sylvus Project had declared war on Cristóbal Rios, the terrorist and thief.

As mortal enemies went, benevolent environmental projects rarely ranked among the more bloodthirsty. But Claggett announced that he'd hired freelance security operatives to comb the neutral regions for *La Sirena*. The threat was a foolhardy act, surrendering surprise for the chance to strike fear—but that tracked with the kind of Starfleet security officer he'd been.

Both on the way to and at Verex III, Rios and his companions had spent hours sorting and boxing the duke's library. He had no idea what Hain had wanted—and he hadn't been able to ask the Ferengi. The magical moment back at Ruji Baroda when Hain opened his eyes to a mountain of books had sadly turned out to be his last lucid one. And while Rios had taken to reading in sickbay with Hain just as he had with Yerm, Emil had not been able to work magic of his own.

Ledger saw it in Rios's eyes when she stepped off the transporter pad. "He's gone, then?"

"Died this morning. Emil tried. Hain's systems just failed, one after another." Rios shook his head. "Poor guy never had a chance."

Dressed in light-colored business wear for the Verexian surface, Ledger took off her fedora and looked down. Then, coolly: "They whacked him."

"We don't know that."

"Of course you don't." She charged forward. "The duke, Claggett, your *marquesa*—one of them did it. Maybe all three."

Rios walked quickly to keep up with her. "Emil can't identify a poison. He's on with the Interspecies Medical Exchange now, trying to find out more."

"Well, I'm sold, brother." She approached her office—only to pause outside the door. She appeared thoughtful as she turned to Rios. "You know, except for the sneaking around and the bartering, he was an okay joe. I'm sorry I shot him."

"That makes three of us."

Rios followed her into her office. She tossed her hat at the holographic coatrack, which miraculously grew several centimeters taller to catch the throw. A bun-haired middle-aged woman wearing horn-rimmed glasses on a chain sat by an old-fashioned switchboard. "Oh, hi, Mister Captain!"

"Cheese it, Myra," Ledger said, and the hologram vanished, leaving the two of them alone.

He sat across from the desk, feeling drained. "I need to find that brother of his, but Irtok is the first place Claggett's people will look."

"Find the brother?" Ledger fished around in her purse. "Whatever for?"

"This was Hain's deal. He's owed something."

"Hah!" She checked herself in her compact mirror. "You're a sap if you give him anything. You don't even know his name." She frowned at her reflection. "When I'm boss, I'm going to make sure all the planets we're on have air-conditioning."

Rios was going to interject that the Iotians could have it now, if they believed in it—but settled for returning to his quandary. "At a minimum, Emil has Hain's corpse in stasis. He'll keep testing it, but we can't hold it forever. I don't know what the Ferengi traditions are, or what the brother will want to do."

"Well, if your concerns ever return to making money, I have news."

She'd gone down to the countinghouse she ran, to check in with her successor. Rios had expected it to be a galling trip, and for her to return in a worse mood. Instead, she seemed buoyed. "I told Arkko's stooge you had a sure thing here and I got the go-ahead to pursue it." She put her purse away and looked up at him. "I've reached out to Kivas Fajo."

That caught Rios off guard. He leaned forward. "What, did he finally give an estimate for Verengan's stuff?"

She snorted. "I get the impression he'd pay us to take it back. Our Klingon pal was not a fellow of taste and refinement."

He hated to hear that, but it didn't surprise him. "I guess I'm glad I didn't send him the stuffed *targ*."

"No," she said, "what we talked about were the books. We've come into a large collection; he's in a position to buy."

Rios's eyes went wide. "But they're Javen's books!"

"Tomato, *to-mah-to*. Javen owed Hain. Hain owed you and Verengan. Both of you owe the Convincers. We're going to be made whole somehow."

"But we told Javen we knew Fajo. Claggett's sure to have put out word the books were stolen."

She shrugged her shoulders. "You said Fajo had gone up the river for something. Maybe he doesn't care."

"Fajo asked us whether Verengan was alive, remember? He seems to have gone fully legit."

"We'll see. The point is, he wants to talk." There was a rap on the door. "Come in, boys."

The holodeck opened, and Rios turned to see the very first people he'd met aboard *La Sirena*. The squat gangster Burze, looking as dyspeptic as ever, and his well-read partner, Wolyx.

"Love what you've done with the place," Burze said, before laying eyes on Rios. "Oh, it's *you*."

"It is indeed!" Wolyx stepped past Burze to shake Rios's hand. "May I say how delighted I am to see you again—and how thankful I am for this wonderful opportunity you've given me?"

Rios accepted the handshake and nodded graciously. Then to Ledger: "What opportunity?"

"The way Arkko sees it," she replied, "those books are nine-tenths hers. And what's yours, you owe her. The boys and I have been ordered to carry the stash to Argelius and babysit it, no matter how long it takes to get an offer. If Fajo deals."

Rios knew she'd been looking for her chance to leave, but he was surprised this was it. "You sure about this? Fajo could call in Claggett and have him waiting for you."

"Not if he knows I'm speaking for Arkko. He'll think twice about that. He's got a nice, big operation there in the open. Be a shame if something happened to it."

More diplomacy from old Chicago.

Rios stood. "I guess that's it." He jabbed Wolyx, whom he'd always liked, in the arm. "Don't be reading everything when you're supposed to be sorting."

"There's a solution for that," Burze said in annoyance. "Never learn to read."

Rios met Ledger at the transporter pad after Burze and Wolyx—her former henchmen, now her coworkers—departed with the last shipment of books. She'd already sent ahead most of the trunks she had aboard, leaving her only with an oversized satchel and a small suitcase. With her quick good-byes to the others made, she looked ready for her next challenge—and life with different companions.

"It's a good thing I rarely gamble," she told him. "I never would've bet that Wolyx could carry all those books out of here without wetting himself."

"He's happy. Good for him," Rios said. He glanced at the suitcase. "I guess you think this is going to pay off. You don't look like you're coming back."

"The math works." She offered her gloved hand for him to shake.

"Good luck."

She picked up the suitcase—and thought for a moment. "Still," she said, looking over his shoulder, "maybe you should save my office program."

"Because you never know?"

"Because if this bunch gets too quiet for you, you can go see Myra. She's an okay secretary, but she'll talk your ear off. So long."

Rios stood for several moments after she dematerialized, wondering what he would do now—and whether he would keep his "crew" on. His contemplation was broken when Zo-Var rounded the corner, holding a box.

"Oh, Captain, I completely forgot," she said. "There were a few cases of books we stored behind the stairwell."

He didn't remember seeing those. "I guess they didn't get them all."

She nodded as she passed the box to him. He looked at the books inside.

Sartre. T'Plana-Hath. Camus. Ving Kuda. Even the precepts of Kahless. Volumes of thought, from thinkers of many worlds. "You say there are more?"

"All on the same subject, yes."

It must have been from Javen's philosophy collection, he realized.

"Should we tell them?" she asked.

A faraway look crossed Rios's face before he responded. "Not right now."

He retired to his quarters, box in his arms.

☿ ♃ ♂ ♄ ♀

–2392–

THE TRAITOR IN THE FLAMES

In which ***Cristóbal Rios*** *sees a ghost—and gets the kiss-off*

33

LA SIRENA
DEEP SPACE

"I don't know what it is with you," Raffi said over the comm in Rios's cabin. *"Whenever I call you, you're bleeding. What's today's special? Knife slashes or puncture wounds?"*

"Dragged across a gravel road," he said, wiping the side of his torso with a towel as he sat on the edge of his bed. "A Gorn working for Claggett tried to haul me back to his ship, but I pelted him with rocks until he got so pissed he let go."

"At which point I hope you found your phaser."

"No, Glake found *him*. It helps to have Frankenstein's monster on the payroll. He still doesn't say much, but he doesn't seem to want me pummeled."

"I'm surprised you kept the others on," Raffi said.

"It was a rough start, but the women are coming along—we've almost come to an understanding on landing gear." He winced as he raised his arm and applied the hypospray Emil had dropped off. "And Glake is handy for moving things."

There had been many things to move in recent months. Since before the new year, he had committed less time to the bottle and more to building a business. The cargoes had been small and not very lucrative, and with Claggett's people hounding him, he hadn't been able to do repeat business. But he had earned enough to keep *La Sirena* in dilithium and his crew from bolting.

He still hadn't found Hain's brother, and Emil hadn't learned much more about what killed the rancher. Then again, Rios rarely kept the EMH active. *Did holograms think while they were offline?* He assumed they didn't but had never been interested enough to study the matter.

Instead, he'd been making his way through Javen's philosophy collection, much of which now sat on his shelves. To the extent that he used to drink to get to sleep, several of the Vulcan thinkers were a worthy substitute.

He'd also spent his evenings alone. Raffi didn't call as often as she once did to listen to his adventures, but there was a subject she always returned to. *"You haven't mentioned any lady friends in weeks. Miss* Marquesa *still haunting you?"*

"There's this thing called 'work.' "

"What about you and that mob bookkeeper?" She laughed. *"Now, that would have been an interesting pairing. Two rogue elements, mashed together—"*

"Yeah, like in a bomb. Civilizations would fall."

Donning his undershirt, Rios explained that Claggett's hired guns had been watching Fajo's place, forcing Ledger to slow-roll the valuation process. According to her infrequent messages, she'd been forced to send Wolyx and Burze as her mules into the Argelius facility with only a couple of books at a time. The fact that Wolyx always wanted to jaw with the assayers about every single tome had only drawn the process out further.

He got a coffee from the wall replicator. It was something he could ask the concierge system for, but it was a short step from there to asking for aguardiente. The sense memory of walking to the replicator helped him pretend that the room was a dry zone. "What are we drinking?"

"Oh, we're not drinking." Then, more drawn out: *"Ooh, not at all."*

Rios knew this sound from her. She was using snakeleaf again. Their sobriety over the last year had seemed to cycle in opposite directions, and that appeared to be the case this evening. She'd lost her husband and son at some point, and she used to tell him when it was a birthday or an anniversary. These days she hadn't volunteered anything.

He hadn't known what to say to Yerm about his addictions, and the only reason Rios could think of for his own small improvement was preoccupation. So he talked about that. He didn't expect to turn Raffi into a philosophy reader—he couldn't believe *he* was doing it—but there was something else.

"I've got the craziest thing here," he said, wandering over to the side of the cabin near the shuttered exterior port. There sat Verengan's stuffed *targ*, feral and glassy-eyed—and it held something in its mouth. Babying his still painful side, Rios leaned down carefully and drew from the *targ*'s teeth the golden apple toy its master had left.

"I'd forgotten I had this. I don't even know why I hid it—it was after one of the break-ins." He described the puzzle to Raffi as he settled gingerly on the bed. "I'll get somewhere with it—and then it locks up again. I mean, I keep getting the outer rings with the Romulan and Klingon characters in alignment, but doing the smaller inner rings causes it all to snap back the way it was."

"You're entering your second childhood."

"I only liked parts of the first one." He turned the wheels that had the Greek signs—*or were they Byzantine?*—for the Sol system's planets, trying to align them. He explained what he was doing—and swore when it snapped tight again.

"You want to send me a holo? I can research it."

"And ruin my fun?" He already knew she spent too much time trolling data networks for support for her conspiracy theories. Snakeleaf only made it worse. Odds were she'd find some way to tie the child's toy into an interstellar Illuminati within a day, and he sure didn't want to hear about that. He put the puzzle on his nightstand and sipped his coffee. Not hearing her for several seconds, he asked, "You still there, Raf?"

"Cris," she said, her slurring worse, *"can I ask you something?"*

"Sure."

"These old books you're reading. Are they giving you any answers?"

"What, about the puzzle?"

"No. About your life."

Maybe she is interested after all, he thought. But he didn't know exactly what to say. "I mean, all these dead people babbling for pages and pages on everything imaginable—law of averages says they'd land on something relevant, right?"

"Yeah," she said, sounding a little pained. *"But has anything related to what happened to* you *pacifically?"* A beat. *"I mean, specifically."*

Rios exhaled. When Raffi was in a different state, he'd have recognized the question as another attempt to draw him out. This seemed different, and he responded as honestly as he could without going too near his older, deeper wounds. "Yeah, actually. There are dilemmas that recur, that kind of jump out at you."

He looked at the books on the shelf—and thought about the incident aboard *ibn Majid.* He wasn't ready to think about it: not sober, not tonight, not with Raffi on the comm. But it had involved someone he cared about doing something he had been ordered to do—despite its being antithetical to his being.

He picked up a book. "Do you know the story of Abraham and Isaac?"

"Refresh my memory."

"God asks his most devoted disciple to prove his loyalty by taking his son out and sacrificing him."

"Like, with a knife?"

"Yep. Turns out there are parallel variants in the lore of other planets, but the general idea is usually the same. And in some tellings, when the kid asks what's going to happen, the dad says, 'Nothing.' "

"That's cold. The killing—and the lying."

"That's what Kierkegaard thinks." He glanced at the book. "He's saying, 'What kind of deity would ask such a thing? And what kind of follower would take it seriously?' This poor guy is being asked to prove his devotion to a set of ideals—only to be asked by the Big G to do something that is completely against them."

"I'd say the hell with that," Raffi replied.

"So would I. So would Kierkegaard." He picked up another book—and held it up next to the first one. "Then along comes Jacques Derrida. You'd like him—he invented deconstruction. All about our words having multiple meanings—there's no such thing as subtext because they mean many things simultaneously."

"That sounds complicated."

"Interdimensional calculus was clearer. I'm probably even wrong about what I just said. But where he goes is here: When Abraham said he wasn't going to kill Isaac, that *was* a lie. But it was also a hope. It was also a prayer." Rios spoke with reverence. "In that one word, *nothing*, it's a father telling his son things are going to be all right, not because they will be, but because he desperately, fervently hopes that they will be. That he's doing the right thing. That his faith isn't misplaced. That he's . . ."

He looked at the trunk across the room—the one he'd brought with him from *ibn Majid*—and stopped talking. He felt the pain in his side again.

"You there, Cris?"

He shook his head from left to right and blinked. "Yeah." He put the book on the table. "I need to go."

"Just like that?"

"Lying down hurts. I need to walk around." He sat up. "I get to pretend I'm on security patrol. Not like I could take on Glake if he decided to get out of hand."

Rios downed the last of the coffee—and as an afterthought, picked up the apple. He walked with it toward the door. "Take care, Raffi."

"Wait," she said. *"The guy."*

"Who, Glake?"

"No. The guy in the story. Did he kill his son?"

"No," Rios replied, glancing back at the chest. "No, he did not."

34

La Sirena
Deep Space

The problem with strolling *La Sirena* was there wasn't a lot of variety to it. Rios could walk from behind the cockpit down to the galley deck, and then back up the stairs behind the sickbay. Or he could go in the opposite direction. That was about it.

Maybe, he determined after the fifth circuit and countercircuit, *this is why Verengan put in the holodeck.* It wouldn't be hard to put a scenic walking trail in there—or at least an exercise room. Hell, he could even ask Myra the secretary to join him if company, real or otherwise, was what he wanted. Of course, company was the one thing he *hadn't* wanted.

It was on one of his passes through sickbay that he summoned Emil to look at his wound. Rather than dispelling the hologram immediately, Rios asked the thing he'd wondered about. "I know how Starfleet's holograms work, but this ship may be different. Your program—what else on the ship can you see?"

The EMH straightened. "I value our passengers' privacy."

"That's not what I mean. You're part of *La Sirena*'s mainframe. Could you tell me our heading?"

"There's a different hologram for that, as you well know."

"I'm not activating it, so don't bring it up." Rios scratched his bearded cheek in thought. "But it's in there, right? Do you all talk to each other?"

"I don't understand the question. The spanner and the screwdriver do not have conversations in the toolbox."

"Hand tools don't make metaphors, either." Rios got to what he was really interested in. "I want to know about Verengan." He held up the puzzle he'd been working as he strolled. "I want to know about this too—why it was the only thing he hid away."

"Ah, the former captain." Emil shook his head. "As you know, I was not yet activated when he expired."

"Yeah, but *La Sirena*'s got sensors. The concierge system delivered him bloodwine. The computer recorded his last log. It had to have seen him, known something about him."

Emil put up his finger. "I understand now. Just a moment."

The EMH tilted his head, and a little spark appeared in each of his pupils for a split second. *That's new,* Rios thought.

"I have your answer," Emil said. He clasped his hands together. "I'm afraid it's no. The firewalls between the emergency hologram personalities bar us from certain other information outside our bailiwicks—including what you're requesting. Seeing what you're interested in would require a deep command-level survey using the main terminal."

"Already tried it. Couldn't find anything—wondered if you could."

"I fear there's not much else I can do." The EMH looked down at the deck in programmed solemnity. "The only marks we have of Verengan's life are those he left behind in his final message—and in his belongings, I should think."

Of which only the targ *remains,* Rios thought. He looked at the golden apple. *And this.*

Then he remembered there was someplace else he hadn't looked. "Follow me."

Rios wasn't in the habit of asking Emil to tag along anywhere, but it occurred to him that his perspective might come in handy. The two approached the door to Ledger's former office. "You can walk into the holodeck with another program running, right?" Rios asked. "Your program just hands off to the deck's emitters."

"Technically, I believe I'm a guest subroutine at that point. But again, there is a skilled engineering hologram who could answer you in much greater—"

"*Silencio.*" Rios opened the door.

Inside, Myra was sitting at Ledger's desk, filing her nails before an electric fan. She looked up. "Well, if it isn't Mister Captain. Long time no see!"

"No see now. Computer, end program." The office vanished—and almost as an afterthought, he added, "Save and protect office program."

He triggered the portal behind them to close and began working the panel inside the arch. Emil stood by patiently. "I don't understand why my presence is required."

"I'm seeing what else is here." After a moment, Rios brightened. "Yeah. Verengan's got another program, hidden away." He used the captain's command-code override. "Computer, launch program."

The instant after he gave the command, he had to step back, to avoid the massive body being hurled past. It was a burly Klingon—thrown by another.

Any impulse he had to help the victim up ended when the hairy-headed giant on the stone floor bared his teeth and snarled up at him. The assailant charged past, ignoring Rios and Emil to tussle anew.

It was the Klingon equivalent of an ancient mead hall, he saw—a dark room lit by braziers and torches. Several dozen Klingons were seated, milling about, or wrestling; a *bat'leth* duel was underway near the fireplace. And mugs were in almost every hand that didn't hold a weapon, supplied from a counter across the room where Myra's switchboard had been.

To his right, the individual who'd thrown the other Klingon had finally won his melee. Physically smaller, he was young and hale, with an old-fashioned mustache and an expression of absolute confidence. He knelt over the chest of the defeated, hand at the titan's throat. "Now get yourself a drink!" he declared with a laugh.

He stood—and turned to face Rios and Emil. His alarm was apparent. "This is *Sto-Vo-Kor*. It is not for the likes of you!"

"*Sto-Vo-Kor*?" Rios knew the name of the Klingon afterworld from his Academy classes; it had come up in several of Javen's philosophy books. As afterlives went, however, what he saw was pretty familiar. "It looks like a bar."

"And *you* look like someone who does not belong here!"

That the Klingon's words did not attract more attention attested to the commotion that already existed behind him. "Very sorry to disturb," Emil said. "We'll be on our way."

Rios knew the one thing he shouldn't do was shrink back. "We're staying," he declared. He slapped his own chest. "We're friends of Verengan."

The Klingon's eyes narrowed—then widened. "Why didn't you say so?" he asked effusively. All belligerence disappeared, and he clapped his hands on Rios's and Emil's shoulders. "Welcome, friends. I am Kor!"

Rios did a double take. "Did you say you were *Kor*?"

"Of course, you are astonished—my fame precedes me. Yes, I am he. Commander. Governor. *Dahar* Master. Ambassador. My titles are too many to name. Use any that you like, or none at all." He led them farther inside the room.

Rios *was* surprised, but that was because the Klingon in question had died more than a decade earlier in the Dominion War. This Kor was much younger. "I'm Cristóbal Rios."

Kor looked to the EMH. "And you, my fretful friend?"

"We call him Emil."

Kor turned to face the gathering. "Honored ones, hear me!" When the din dropped a few decibels, he spoke again. "These are allies of the great Verengan!"

A cheer went up at the Klingon's name. "*Verengan! Verengan!*"

"This is Cristóbal, son of Rios," Kor announced. "And this is Emil, son of—"

"*La Sirena*," Emil replied sheepishly.

It was the height of peculiarity, Rios thought: one artificial individual from part of the freighter's digital brain making a program from a different subsystem feel uncomfortable. But then, the setting around him was already bizarre: a rustic Klingon tavern populated entirely with figures he thought he recognized from his history classes.

Kor confirmed Rios's guesses as he introduced his new guests around. Kang. Biroq. L'Rell. Some warriors of legend; others, more recent figures. Most looked as they did when they carried out their greatest deeds—predictably, for an afterlife. Yet the presence of some others surprised him. "I'm not even sure some of these people are dead," Rios muttered.

"Of course," Kor said. "Kahless the Unforgettable runs *Sto-Vo-Kor*—but the tavern is open to whomever Verengan chooses to invite. Tell me, do you come alone? Is the great man with you?"

"Verengan? No, but he sent us."

"Out on a quest, I am certain. The others long to hear his adventures." Kor approached a standing woman. "There you are! Meet our guests."

Rios spoke her name before she did. "You're Azetbur."

"And you are the son of Rios," she said.

"Just Rios is fine."

"As you will. I am honored to meet you." She gestured to the man sitting at the table she stood near. "My father, Gorkon."

Rios hadn't immediately recognized the young man's face, but he certainly knew the name. Gorkon had been chancellor nearly a hundred years earlier when the Klingon moon Praxis exploded; it was he and his daughter who took the first steps toward a permanent peace with the Federation. Yet here they looked to be the same age, which fit with Kor's appearance. Apparently Verengan's invites only covered Klingons at certain times of their lives.

The real Gorkon was dead, assassinated in the conspiracy engineered in part by his underling General Chang. Rios did not see the eyepatch-wearing general around—nor other Klingons of mixed repute. There was no Kruge, no Duras, no Lursa and B'Etor. Not even T'Kuvma, the instigator of the Klingon War. Verengan had been choosy.

And as near as Rios could figure, the sad and lonely old Klingon had not simply created a bunch of digital companions; he'd created a legend for himself too. He looked to Emil and spoke out of the side of his mouth. "They don't know what happened to Verengan."

"It's as I told you. The holodeck is even further firewalled against knowledge of the outside world. They will not know his fate unless you choose to tell them."

Rios remembered something about that from the Academy. The Moriarty Protocols, they were called—strengthened protections instituted after a pair of incidents on Picard's *Enterprise*.

"Friend Rios, mighty Koloth would speak with you," Gorkon said.

At the mention of another of James T. Kirk's onetime opponents, Rios turned—and looked into a blade, which Koloth thrust before his face. "If you would stay here, you must become our brothers."

Rios looked down at the *d'k tahg*. "Blood brothers?"

"Of course!" Koloth laughed.

Emil whispered over Rios's shoulder. "I don't like the sound of that."

Rios decided not to argue. "It's just a holodeck." He offered his hand, palm upright. "When in Rome," he said.

The Klingon ran the *d'k tahg* over Rios's palm, drawing blood—and a reaction. "Jesus!"

Emil gawked. "The safety protocols are off."

"Safety?" Koloth bellowed with laughter. "What's this creature nattering about?"

Rios pulled back his hand, clutched tightly closed. He winced. "Your turn."

"My *what*?" Emil nodded graciously to the others. "Medical conference," he said, before whisking Rios aside. Near the wall, the EMH looked at the wound. "This is real."

"You're damned right it's real!" It smarted like hell.

"Until you reactivate the protocols, you are at risk here." Emil produced a handy dermal regenerator from his pocket and applied it, out of sight from the others.

"Why would Verengan have turned them off?" Rios wondered aloud.

Emil had no idea.

"I would not share the knowledge of Verengan's fate," the EMH cautioned. "You are vulnerable here, and the response might be unpredictable."

"Right." Rios rubbed his quickly healing hand. "But they couldn't injure you, surely."

"All the same, I should be glad to remain no one's brother, blood or otherwise." They heard Koloth, back in the crowd and calling out for Emil. "Must we stay?"

"I need to find out what they *do* know about Verengan. I can't pick it out of a database somewhere, can I?"

"Probably not. This much is in my knowledge base on the topic: holographic characters are crafted around heuristic algorithms that are in many ways like the living brain. The information pathways are complex. You may learn more by asking people than from brute force."

"Then I've got to stay."

Somewhere, he heard Koloth call out. "Son of *La Sirena*, where are you? We have business!"

"I'd better go on alone," Rios said. Before the EMH could argue, he ordered, "Dismissed."

If the Klingons on the main floor saw Emil vanish, no one said anything. The only comment came from the direction of the bar: "A time of wonders indeed."

Rios turned to see a Klingon with a kingly mane of hair and a towel in his hand wiping down the counter. "Are you—?"

"I am Kahless. If you have questions, I have answers."

In the Company of Giants: The Parch Actualities

Alexandra Quimby

University of Oneamisu Press, 2389

(Excerpt from the introduction)

Come away from your daily life, for a moment, on a journey. Imagine that you've been imbued with miraculous powers—the ability to traverse space and time, to see anyone anywhere. With all the discoveries in recent centuries, that's not such a difficult thing to picture. Miracles do happen. When your miracle happens, what would you do?

Odds are you would not travel to a time nobody ever discusses, to spend the day with someone you've never heard of. Few humans would visit a nameless herder on the African veldt or a European blacksmith in the fifteenth century; nor would they drop in on itinerant laborers a thousand years from now. Not when they could spend time in Queen Elizabeth I's court, locate Amelia Earhart, spar with Kahless the Unforgettable, or have a drink with Zefram Cochrane. Across cultures, species, and societies, it appears to be a universal trait that "great persons" have magnetic appeal—and even those with godlike powers find it difficult to resist them.

A recent Starfleet study of casual holodeck use found that a surprising number of characters depicted real people—and of those, the vast majority were historical figures from politics, science, and the arts. When people are given the pseudo-godlike ability to spend time with anyone, lost loves and departed relatives don't stand a chance. They need better publicists!

Great figures in few eras had publicists better than Parch, a cultural phenomenon active in the second half of the twenty-third century. A polymath who liberally drew upon many planets' histories at once, Parch used access to dozens of people of importance to create some of the most moving portraits ever made. Renderings in Parch's trademark medium, the holographic actuality, are masterpieces of both style and substance, surpassing any bust or painting in both detail and subtext. And in a Parch, the subtext is sometimes literal, with words and phrases built into the pieces.

Legend is replete with tales of Parch's working attire: a hood and full facial scarf concealed the artist's species and identity, while a voluminous cloak hid gender and other physical details. Yet it is almost certain that even in that era, many of the subjects involved would have been surrounded by the technological means to scan any individual. Whatever they suspected or knew about Parch, all chose to keep the artist's secrets—and many bestowed gifts in return. Wherever Parch's collection is, its value is likely beyond reckoning.

This five-volume set examines every one of the known Parch actualities. Attention is given to the individuals they depicted, naturally, and the contents of each recording, with exhaustive lists of embedded references (colloquially, "Parch-meants" or "Easter eggs"), ranging from the confirmed to the debunked. Specifics are provided on the technology and physical housings Parch utilized for each actuality, as well as the circumstances of their discovery. A section on forgeries is included. Finally, the work closes with the most tantalizing topic: reports of rumored actualities yet to be found.

A traveling companion once asked me the question I opened with, "If I had the ability to visit any place at any time, would I seek to discover who Parch really was?" My answer then, as now, is no: it is far more interesting to follow the clues that Parch placed. Reality is the canvas for this game, and it could well be Parch's greatest masterpiece of all.

Let the journey begin.

35

La Sirena
Deep Space

Rios asked Kahless: "Are you the emperor or the Unforgettable?"

"I am both." The bartender grinned. "I was emperor before I was unforgettable, of course."

"Sorry, I just didn't want to—"

"I know—and be it known I will hear no insult to the clone who later took my name, and sat as emperor. He has deeds worthy of song."

Rios saw an opening. "What can you tell me of Verengan's deeds?"

"You are his friend. You should know." He looked up from the mug he was drying and locked eyes with Rios. "I think, perhaps, we *both* know his deeds fairly well. Better than the others here."

Rios blinked. It sounded very much like the founder of the Klingon Empire bore some skepticism about the creator of his program. "I'm . . . surprised to hear you say that."

"You should not be. People tell things to their bartenders—and to their deities—that others would never hear."

Rios gestured to the counter. "I'm also surprised to see you back there."

"Any Klingon would find the idea enraging." Kahless looked about. "*Sto-Vo-Kor* is a place one knows with the heart, not the eyes. Anyone who thinks as a true Klingon would find this representation to be a sacrilege, an offense."

"I'd wondered about that. What do *you* think?"

Kahless spoke after some consideration. "I believe I came to be here because I was needed by an old man who had never done ill. This is the manner he chose, the place he imagined for me. And while it may not be as other Klingons imagine, it is my honor to serve." He gestured to a row of bottles. "Bloodwine?"

Rios laughed. "Trying to cut down." He leaned farther across the bar. "It sounds like you and Verengan spoke a lot."

"Only after he tired of the revelries here." Kahless looked up. "He would speak of his daily life. Not much of his past—though I think his thoughts went to those times quite often."

"Was any of *this* in his past?" Rios gestured behind him to the notables populating the tavern, discussing their accomplishments.

"Have you been in the company of great people, Cristóbal?"

"Occasionally."

"Then you would find imagining such meetings idle." He allowed that to be his answer.

Kahless looked down at Rios's hand—the unscarred one—and grew more reserved. He crossed his arms. "I see you have it."

"What?" Rios realized he was still clutching the golden apple. "Oh, this. You recognize it?"

"It was kept inside a black bag," Kahless said, more standoffish. "Verengan brought it to me to hold for him on his last visit." His hairy eyebrows went up. "It disturbs me that you have it."

Rios sought to avoid a confrontation. "He left it to me." That was at least not entirely a lie. "I have kept it safe."

"Hmm. He did not tell you anything about it?"

"No."

"Ah." The emperor relaxed his arms and nodded thoughtfully. "Yes, he would not have wanted to share his burden."

Now we're getting somewhere. "What burden?"

Kahless took the puzzle from Rios. "When last I saw him, Verengan was much upset. The item was an heirloom, he said. For years, he had been unable to unlock it—until at last he encountered someone who did."

"Who?"

"Brothers. Ferengi brothers."

Rios brightened. At last, something made sense. "Was one named Hain?"

"He did not say." Kahless evaluated the puzzle. "Verengan did not tell me how they opened it—but he did see what was inside."

"What was it?"

"He did not say that either. But I know that it troubled him." He placed the apple on the bar. "The Ferengi offered to buy it from him, but Verengan would not part with it."

"So he hid it here, with you."

"No, that came later. They offered him work. They told him there was an object that could make the value of the item incalculable—but it was in the hands of another. Verengan was hired to complete a number of labors, the reward for which would be something to unlock this secret, revealing wealth, in some manner, for all three to share in."

It all sounded fantastical to Rios. *Could the fertilizer flights to Duke Javen have really been connected to a child's toy?* He had to know more. "Why did he share this with you?"

"Verengan was on the verge of completing the quest when he came to me, much aggrieved." Kahless stared off into a dark corner. "He had come to believe there was no honor in what he was being asked to do—that whatever the relic was had a taint of shame on it that no riches would cleanse. He regretted ever having gone along with the idea to begin with." Kahless looked down at the toy. "*That* is when he gave it to me."

Rios saw it all. Verengan had given the apple to "Kahless"—which meant it remained on the holodeck when he ended the *Sto-Vo-Kor* program and activated in its place the camouflage of holographic junk. That had kept Rios and everyone else out of the room.

And then Verengan had died, apparently never telling Hain he had balked at their quest.

"Hear me, Cristóbal." Kahless placed the apple in Rios's still-healing hand. "If Verengan did not want the world to know what this trinket held, he surely had a good reason. Have you never carried a personal shame, my friend—a secret that you bore with honor, so as to protect others?"

The question startled Rios, and he did not respond.

Kahless knew the answer. "Yes, I can see that you have. In respect of your burden, I will not ask about it. Grant Verengan the same respect."

Rios bowed his head slightly, without knowing why he had. This Kahless was a holodeck creation; a historical profile filtered through Verengan's initial preferences and their later conversations together. And yet he seemed to care, and that caring affected him.

Artificial gravity was still gravity.

After excusing himself, Rios called for the arch and exited, leaving the program running behind him. So much more made sense now. After Verengan died, Hain had sought him out; finding Rios instead, the Ferengi had hired him in part as a means of getting back on the freighter. Hain's intrusion into the captain's cabin, he now understood, was in search of the puzzle.

But much still confused him. What was the item Javen would not trade away, and what was the treasure it could unlock? Had it gotten Hain killed?

And what of Verengan, dying alone sometime after the ninth fertilizer drop-off at Sylvus? Rios's breath caught as he considered something for the first time. Could whoever poisoned Hain—if that was what happened—have done the same to Verengan?

He called for Emil, who appeared beside him. The EMH looked relieved. "You escaped without injury, I hope?"

"Forget that. I need you to diagnose Verengan."

"I believe the clinical term is 'dead.' "

"No, smartass. I've got a holographic recording of his last moments. I want to know what you can see." He'd never had a hologram examine a hologram before, but it seemed possible. "What do you say?"

"I'd say it's taking holomedicine a bit far. But I will see what I can do."

36

La Sirena
Argelius System

Rios hadn't expected Emil to find anything conclusive from Verengan's last moments, and the EMH had not surprised him. The visual symptoms the Klingon presented during the log entry were consistent with a myocardial infarction, but Emil noted a range of other things that could explain them. It bothered Rios that Emil had most of his success as a first-aid kit; with Yerm, Hain, and Verengan he'd shown his limits. It appeared to disturb Emil too.

Rios had little time to worry over it during the weeks that followed, as at *La Sirena*'s next stop, he picked up a pursuer he could not shake. He hadn't even been able to meet his prospective cargo clients near Draken when a happy-go-lucky Orion woman named Seejee brought her five-ship flotilla down on him.

As names for roving mercenary bands went, "The Core Breaches" translated into Standard in a manner that undermined their fearsomeness; Rios had taken to calling them the Britches. They had certainly been riding up on him lately, arriving in one system after another soon after *La Sirena* did. Near Yadalla, they'd lobbed torpedoes so close that the Miradorns hid in their quarters for a week afterward.

Most recently, he'd warped to a distant nowhere before doubling back to Argelius in the hopes of losing them. There was no job at the destination. Rather, heading to the system where he'd met Fajo was an admission of defeat. As much as Rios had gotten into them, Javen's philosophy books were the last things he had to sell, and the time had come. He decided he might as well also throw in the puzzle. If the founder of the Klingon Empire said it was worth something, that was good enough for him.

But Seejee had other ideas, her light corvettes dropping out of warp at various places near the planet. Individually, each ship was an even match for *La Sirena*, though in space, the freighter was far faster. They just never seemed to be alone when he encountered them, and too often they'd challenged him while he was still in an atmosphere. Limitations he'd known about from his first flight had gone unaddressed too long—and he was paying for it now.

Seated behind Ny-Var and Zo-Var, Rios surveyed the situation. Seejee's partner vessels were some way off, but closing; they weren't the problem yet, but they would be. She had come out of warp closer to Argelius, and her emerald-colored flagship guarded the approach to the planet.

How the hell does she keep finding me?

He decided to open a channel and ask. "Well, if it isn't the Britches, tight on me again. My favorite pains in the ass."

The helmet-wearing beauty smiled toothily on his display. *"Rios, darling, I love you—but I never understand your jokes."*

"What's important is you know I have a sense of humor. That's important to a relationship."

"If only," she said, smacking her lips. *"But business intervenes."*

"You're in my business too much these days. Did your clients plant a tracking device when they did their walkthrough?"

"You're ruining the magic, love. I'm drawn to you by your pure animal magnetism."

Rios smirked. Seejee was easily a match for Boss Arkko in the innuendo department, but he knew not to tussle with the mercenary leader. When the two were on Lorillia, Seejee had gotten a shot off at him that he was sure had been set to kill. Whatever Liselle had authorized Claggett to do, the chief had clearly given his hoods more leeway.

"I'm curious," he said, buying time. "What are the working conditions over there?"

"You want to be a Core Breach?"

"I'd see more of *you* that way."

"Ooh, I like that. But you're worth a stack of latinum, and Seejee's got her own bills to pay."

"That's tragic." Rios muted his comm and looked to Zo-Var, who appeared nervous as ever. "Did you get them?"

"Um—yes. They're waiting on another channel."

Rios switched to it. *"Argelius Control,"* a male voice said.

Rios spoke frenetically, mimicking a high voice he'd once heard. "This is Melton Moyles! I need your help!"

The controller sounded startled. *"Did you say your name was Moyles?"*

"Yes! I'm aboard a freighter hauling goods for Massworks—and there are pirates after me! They just dropped out of warp. There's five of them!"

Seconds passed, during which he overheard commotion. *"We see them—and you. But we weren't expecting your arrival."*

"Damn it, it's because we've been running for our lives! And if my sister-in-law finds out you didn't help me, you'll be running for yours!"

Rios, of course, had not had dealings with Massworks since being chewed out by the aforementioned chief executive. But the CEO was important enough to warrant action by the planetary patrol cruisers, which rose from their low orbit to challenge Seejee's vessel. Rios took the opportunity to rocket past, waving at Seejee as he did.

He switched channels—and saw her face, less jovial than usual. *"That was a dirty trick,"* she said.

"I just thought you sounded lonely."

"Never, with you around. You know we'll just be waiting at the edge of the system, don't you?"

"I'll see you then."

"Promises, promises." She cut the transmission.

It was night over the Argelian capital as he descended, which he figured was just as well—his gambit might bring repercussions. He decided to put down in the wilderness, hoping that the local authorities had enough to worry about besides prank callers.

With trepidation, he'd given over control of the approach to Ny-Var; with exhilaration, he celebrated it. "A night landing, and you nailed it."

She thanked him, appearing surprised at the compliment. He'd been harder on everyone as his fortunes had worsened, but his flight crew was finally getting it together. *Probably too late to do any good, but there it is.*

He walked back to engineering, figuring what his next steps would be in order to see Fajo. But glowing figures appeared on the transporter pad, causing him to reach for his phaser instead.

"Now, that's not the greeting I expected," Fajo said. He was holding a bundle under his arm. To his left stood Ledger, oversized satchel at her side.

"Sorry," Rios said, pocketing the weapon. "I was just coming to see you!"

"Ledger shared your message—and when my people saw your approach, we thought I'd better come to you." Fajo offered the bundle. "Here you are."

Rios began to unwrap it. He looked up. "Another mermaid?"

"Like I told you: now you have a collection. Everyone needs one."

"He's charmed," Ledger said, stepping off the platform. She spoke as she passed Rios's ear. "This is where you say thanks—and tell us to take a load off."

Sorry that the present wasn't more cigars, Rios quickly asked the concierge system for comfortable chairs, which materialized nearby. "Have a seat. Are you here because of the books?"

"We've milked that for about all it's worth," Ledger said. "It's what's kept Arkko off your back so far this year. But we're on to new business."

New business? He looked to Fajo. "What's she talking about?"

Fajo sat back and put up his feet. He spoke matter-of-factly: "Your associate tells me you're aware of my past—and that it may have put you off before."

Rios was irritated but not surprised that she'd broken his confidence. "I didn't mean for—"

"It's quite all right." Fajo waved his hand dismissively. "The truth is it was a wrongful incarceration, over a trifling misunderstanding. I appealed to reason, and found none."

Rios nodded. Starfleet was certainly capable of doing things that didn't make sense.

"But I'm a firm believer in second chances—and that is all behind me now. I've gotten reestablished." Fajo rocked forward and clasped his hands together. "It's time to do something I haven't done in a long time—*entertain*!"

Animated, Fajo described the crowd he used to run with: cultured aesthetes, lovers of rarities, and academics specializing in antiques. "It's been *so* long since I could hold a showing." He gestured all around. "I'd like to bring the event to them, using *La Sirena* as both hotel and gallery. A flying festival!"

"Using *this* ship?" Rios looked about. "Why would you want to do that? You've got that big place in town."

"That's more a workplace than a showplace—and some of my friends don't like to be seen in public. Meanwhile, my compound on Theta Zibal III—my home, actually—is a bit too remote. But a cruise on a course that split the distance between my guests would be ideal. The Kaplan F17 is fast enough to bring people together, and it has ample room aboard for my displays."

La Sirena wasn't a showroom, either—it wasn't long ago that it was hauling manure. "You're sure *this* is what you want?"

Ledger rolled her eyes. "Still talking yourself out of jobs, after all this time. Did I teach you nothing?"

Evidently not. "I'm just saying this is a freighter, not a yacht."

Fajo hastened to explain. "Ledger tells me you have an excellent holodeck aboard. I can make use of it during the dinner—and of course, the auction."

"Auction?"

"Wait 'til you hear this," she said, beaming. "I negotiated this."

At that, Rios inhaled deeply, expecting the worst. But what Fajo then described sounded reasonable. "You'll do the flying and the feeding. Then on the final night, I'll stage an auction for many of my items on display. I've contracted with Ledger to give you a portion of the proceeds. The happier my passengers are, the looser with latinum they'll be."

"We'll put on a show," Ledger said. "Class, all the way. We'll be togged to the bricks."

Rios had to admit he missed hearing her weird expressions. But there was a problem he couldn't avoid mentioning. "I'm being pursued. Sylvus has mercenaries looking for me everywhere."

"A charity hiring mercenaries—how amusing!" Fajo chuckled. "Yes, I heard about your little trick. Very resourceful. I like that."

"There's some kind of tracking device aboard. I need to tear the ship apart, but there's never a good place or time."

"I have some experience in not wanting to be followed," Fajo said. "Ledger has Boss Arkko's permission for the project—and a dreadnought will protect *La Sirena* against any difficulties on your way to Starbase 234."

"Starbase 234?" Rios knew of the place. "Why there?"

"There's an independent hangar and workshop I do business with nearby. They'll take you in, no questions asked—and will make whatever modifications you want, charged to my account."

"That's . . . very generous."

"Not so fast. Hosting the event will require a few changes around here. Some serious deodorizing, for starters. And added accommodations for my guests." He nodded to Ledger, who had a padd in hand. "I've asked our Iotian friend here to be my liaison on this effort. Her attention to detail is quite impressive."

"We'll need to convert some of the cargo areas into staterooms," she said, "and subdivide some of the ones we've got." She offered Rios the padd. "It's all here."

He'd often wondered if anything could make Ledger want to set foot on the ship again. Whatever this opportunity was, she clearly thought it lucrative enough. He scratched his beard as he went down her list. "This isn't bad. And I do have some other things that need doing."

The answer satisfied Fajo. "Consult your wish list, Captain. Spare no expense." He rose. "I'll rejoin you when it's time."

Rios walked him to the transporter and saw him off, hardly believing how quickly his luck had changed. He turned to say something about it to Ledger, only to find her walking quickly forward, bag in hand.

"Wait!" He hurried to catch up with her. "Does this mean you're back?"

"The dreadnought isn't staying with us after the starbase." She opened the door to her old room and placed her bag inside. "Where else am I going to live?"

She headed back outside, barreling past him as she headed farther forward. Rios again moved to catch up. "There have been some changes I probably need to tell you about."

"Pishposh. I've got work to do," she said, arriving at the next door and opening it. After one look inside, she shut it immediately and glared at him. "Why, pray tell, did you open a Klingon bar in my office?"

37

LA SIRENA
THETA ZIBAL III

The reason so few visited the Zibalian homeworld, some said, was that the natives were rarely, if ever, home. They were always somewhere else, doing business.

Part of that, Rios now suspected, had to do with how drab the planet itself was. It resembled the Atacama, not far from where he grew up—a desert so dry it had doubled for Mars in several of the early planetary lander tests. Canyons and widely separated peaks provided the only real contrast.

Mount Fajo was what geologists called an inselberg, an island mountain surrounded in all directions by a blasted plain—and various structures had been erected on and hewed into it to create the collector's compound. Towers on the peak and spaced along a several-kilometer perimeter around it generated a force field; it had to be deactivated long enough for *La Sirena* to be allowed within. Even so, he'd been commanded to land well away from the mountain.

"I don't want intruders while I'm away," Fajo had told him, *"and I don't want visitors when I'm here."* The Theta Zibal sanctum was for his most cherished possessions, those he would never put on display in any of his remote offices. The fact that Rios's cruise—Ledger had begun calling it "FajoFest"—would include some items from the compound made it a special event.

On the desert floor, Rios looked up at *La Sirena*, admiring the work the renovators had done. He'd been all over the ship, spanner in hand, double-checking—and hadn't found a single thing wrong. The technicians had succeeded in finding and removing the tracking device left by Sylvus; Rios hoped that meant he'd seen the last of Seejee and her ilk.

He'd learned there was another tracker aboard, placed by the Convincers, but Ledger had blocked its removal. "Still our ship," she'd said. But having stayed aboard during the work, she hadn't noticed that the freighter had changed outside as well—until now, when she walked down the landing ramp.

"What the hell are *those*?" she asked, looking out from beneath a floppy white hat. *La Sirena* had gained two new accessories: large, flat pontoon-like structures attached to the hull port and starboard.

Rios grinned. "You'll see. Or maybe you won't. Depends on what we run into."

He explained the outriggers functioned both as thrusters and aids to the impulse engines, adding to the large number of drive units already aboard the freighter.

"This class is already fast. You tried to make it *faster*?"

"They're the oomph I need for atmospheric travel. Nobody's catching me, ever again." Rios had no plans of going to another world where Sylvus was operating, but *La Sirena* would be more than a match for any of Claggett's interceptors. "Trouble never finds you at warp—only when you're in-system."

"And I assume you found some while I was away. Hired guns, pirates, angry spouses—"

"You forgot gangsters in funny outfits looking for payments. Whoever it is, I'm not going to get near enough to anyone to get tractored in."

She looked skeptically on that, but did not object. "Fajo's people are about finished. Back inside, flyboy."

Rios nodded to Glake and the Miradorns on the way in. *La Sirena*'s crew manifest was the one thing that hadn't changed. Fajo had forbidden Rios from making any temporary hires, for fear they might squawk about his ultraexclusive cruise. Having met Rios's existing crew, however, the collector seemed confident of their silence. That seemed to Rios to be a good read. There wasn't going to be room to billet anyone else.

Boarding the freighter, he and Ledger found Fajo and his people positioning the collectibles they'd transported over. Some were exceptionally delicate, like a Vulcan flute made of crystal so fine it looked as if it would shatter if anyone used it. Other items were macabre, like the shrunken head of one of the early Orion emperors.

But the biggest and most spectacular artifact now dominated the port cargo area on the upper deck: a maroon-colored limited-production automobile from the golden age of the combustion engine.

"Nice wheels," Ledger said.

"A little after your people's preferred time," Fajo replied, breathing warmly on an exterior mirror. "It's a Tucker 48. It's also known as the Torpedo, but that was never an official name."

It looked like a weapon, with its snout nose and sloping body. Ledger jabbed Rios in the ribs. "Now, see, why couldn't your people have made more cars like this?" She looked to Fajo. "You should see what they did. Cars were just fine, and they decided they didn't have enough plastic."

Rios could find no objection to the vehicle. It certainly looked a lot more fun to operate than the rare Betelguesian velocipede on the other side of the deck. He'd had to restrain himself from running his hand across the hood, something that Fajo had strenuously objected to when Ledger tried it.

"Your EMH appeared when my people started it up," Fajo said. "Nattering about carbon monoxide. All the items, whatever they are, have to be demonstrated."

"I'll tell Emil to put a holographic sock in it."

Fajo stepped away from the car and surveyed the deck. *La Sirena* had become part museum, with theater ropes and stretches of red carpet. Lighting had been set up to showcase the displays. During the refit, Rios had ensured that the inertial dampers worked perfectly; a little jolt could turn a priceless Romulan vase into junk.

"I think we're ready," Fajo said. Seeing off his workers, he took a package from one. He turned toward Ledger. "You've done a great job helping to set everything up." He presented her the package. "For your services."

She seemed surprised. "Should I open it?"

"Do. I'm certain you got tired of looking at books during our transactions—but this is something I had around the house that I expect you've never seen."

It was ruby red, with golden letters embossed on the cover. Ledger gawked. "*New York Mobs of the Thirties*?"

"It's the sequel to your infamous book," Fajo gushed. "Exceedingly hard to find."

"I didn't even know it existed," Rios said.

"Apparently no one did. Sadly, a case where something is rare because it wasn't popular." He stepped toward the transporter pad. "I'll be back with our baggage and course headings. Happy reading."

Rios watched as the Zibalian dematerialized—and then glanced at Ledger. "You said you never read the first one."

She seemed mesmerized. "A second one." She clutched it to her chest and began to walk toward her office. "This one, I might read."

Rios followed her. "Fajo is certainly making a push."

"What do you mean?"

"Just that you're getting drawn more and more into his world."

"And what's wrong with that? You know I was looking for options."

"I know. I just—"

She faced him. "It can't be that you think he's on the wrong side of your precious law, because look who you're talking to!"

"I am." Rios shrugged. "Just be careful."

"Power up the ship." She regarded his grease-stained clothing. "And change into something presentable. This isn't your flophouse anymore—it's a swanky joint. If the swells see you looking like that, they'll beam right back off!"

38

La Sirena
Iraatan System

They beamed aboard, one by one. All from different systems: some transported from planets, others across from shuttles that met *La Sirena* along its route. It was hard for Rios to understand how something could be secret and still attract the attention of people from such different places. It was almost as if the world of high-end collectors had a subspace network all of its own.

The first guests were demanding, but in ways that were both peculiar and highly specific. There was the Andorian legislator, whose cabin temperature could not be allowed to exceed ten degrees Celsius and whose monocle, almost certainly a cosmetic accessory, kept fogging over when he went in and out of the room. Rios doubted he would ever need to replicate silk monocle wipes in his future travels, but the program now existed in case he did.

The Cardassian gul, expected to arrive alone, had brought a guest—and a chore. Someone needed to walk her *glink*, a cross between a Chihuahua and a lizard, once every other hour. Rios had determined that the *glink*'s needs were medical in nature and had put Emil in charge of the matter.

And then there was the old Trill man who *had* arrived alone, but who insisted on being spoken to in the plural, with all communications being addressed first to him and then to his symbiont. This had puzzled Rios, who knew Trills, and had never heard any request that before. But as Fajo had quietly explained, this particular collector had never been joined anyway. The symbiont was all in his head—but as the latinum for any prospective auction purchases was already on deposit, everyone was expected to go along with it.

"The people who can afford to play at this level," Fajo had whispered, "don't like to share anything with others. That includes reality."

Rios blanched. Apparently, Duke Javen was just a warmup.

The first guests were odd enough that Rios was delighted to see the arrival of a familiar face, beamed over from a commercial shuttle on the edge of the

Iraatan system: Xandra Quimby, Fajo's itinerant professor. She was dressed plainly, with her hair pulled back—but her academic reserve melted when she caught sight of Rios. "We meet again!"

He didn't have to wonder at her presence; Fajo had brought her in to testify as to his relics' authenticity. "Welcome," Rios said, taking her hand to help her off the platform. "I read your book, you know."

She beamed. "Which one?"

"The Parch one." It was probably the newest book in Javen's collection. "I read part of it. I haven't gotten to volume two."

"I'm surprised *I* got to it. I had no idea how big that project would turn out to be."

They stood for a few seconds before Rios realized he was still holding her hand. Someone else noticed: Ledger, across the room, looked to the overhead and muttered, "Oh, brother."

Quimby glanced over. "Hello again!"

Ledger gave the faintest of nods before heading to Fajo's side to discuss the next arrival.

Seeing Glake heading out from engineering to tote Quimby's suitcase, Rios rushed to claim it first. The professor smiled gently at the Nausicaan. "It's taken care of. Thanks."

"Afraid the best compartments have gone to the VIPs," Rios said as he escorted her to her cabin. "You're sharing with the women who fly this thing. But they're quiet." He chuckled. "Beyond belief, in fact."

"That's fine. It's my first one of these events for Kivas. I'm not expecting to be in the room much."

"Guests will have the run of the place," he said. "But if you need a break, I know the captain very well."

She smirked. "I hear he's a fan of big books with small circulations."

"True, but he has discerning taste."

They arrived at the door—and as she reached for the suitcase, her hand touched his again. "See you around the ship, then," she said, before disappearing inside with the bag.

The door slid shut—and Rios turned to see Ledger leaning against a nearby bulkhead, reading a padd. As he walked by, she said without looking up, "Another one. You've got to be kidding me."

"What's your problem with Xandra?"

"It's *Xandra*, now?" Ledger gave a derisive laugh. "She dresses like a Mrs. Grundy—a canceled stamp. But I don't buy it." She jabbed her thumb in the direction of the door. "That Sheba's on the grift."

"You lost me three references ago." Rios looked back at the cabin. "The doc's a famous professor. She writes books."

"She also happens to be advising a guy who was in the cooler longer than you or I ever imagined. He brought her around a few times during the fence to evaluate books for him." She pointed at Rios. "Don't tell me she didn't know the goods were hot."

Rios shrugged—and winced in wonderment. "What is it with you and *canceled stamps*?"

She blew a razzberry. "Move. Next victim just arrived."

Another guest had flown on the commercial shuttle that had carried the professor: Palor Toff, whose extrication from first class had been delayed by the transport of a load of luggage that put Ledger's to shame. Fajo had told Rios to expect a grotesque dandy, and Toff had not disappointed. Rios didn't know whether the strange golden spiral curling from Toff's nose around his head was considered appealing to his species, but it certainly stood a good chance of getting caught in a closing door.

"Kivas, you old rogue," Toff said, arms in the air as he stepped off the platform.

"Palor, my good and oldest friend." Fajo returned the gesture. Both greetings dripped with insincerity. Rios had been warned that Toff was Fajo's biggest rival in the collecting world.

He'd also been told he was a handful. "I hesitated about boarding a freighter," Toff said, sniffing the air. "They're so beastly. But then I said to myself, 'Palor, your boon companion Fajo has been many years a captive—and if he has learned to make do with less, the least you can do is support him.' "

"It is indeed the least you could do," Fajo said, wearing a placid smile. "I would have you meet Captain Rios."

Rios nodded. "Mister Toff."

"It is *Baron* Toff, now." With a flourish, he flashed a signet ring beneath Fajo's face. "Would you believe it? I acquired the title from a Romulan in dire straits."

"Intriguing," Fajo said. "Especially as Romulan aristocracy has no barons."

"Of course *you* wouldn't know of them. It is quite an exclusive circle I travel in." Toff's eyes fell on Rios. "And speaking of travel, I should like your guarantee, Captain, that all my outfits will be cleaned and pressed before I rise each morning."

"I'm not sure that's something we—"

"And I have a bit of laundry from the cruiser. The two trunks over there. I knew you wouldn't mind taking care of it."

Rios was fighting the temptation to tell Toff where to stuff his trunks when rescue came in the form of Ny-Var's voice on the overhead. *"Captain to the bridge."*

"That's my cue." He pointed to Ledger. "This lady can help you, Baron."

She looked up from her padd. "Wait just a—" was all he heard; he bolted forward like the ship was under attack.

It was not under fire, for a change, though it was racing for the other side of Iraatan, where another pickup was expected. "Message incoming," Ny-Var said.

"Probably from the next guest. Thinks we're late." They all had complained, even though *La Sirena* had reached each rendezvous ahead of time.

Ny-Var shook her head. "The call is from Federation space."

Huh? Rios sat down and clicked open the channel. "Oh, hey, Raffi."

"Been a while, Cris."

"It'll be a while longer. The circus is in town."

"Is the bookkeeper back? That's something she'd say."

"Seriously, I have to go."

"Touch back when you can. Someone's trying to find you."

That's been my day, Rios thought as he closed the connection.

Whether Raffi's "someone" meant good or harm, he had no time to deal with it now. He picked out an incoming Ferengi vessel on the scanner. "That's the one."

He worked with Ny-Var to set the course. Rios's aid was needed, as her navigator and counterpart had already been drafted into galley detail. The Miradorns wouldn't be making any menu selections—Fajo had expressly prohibited that—but Rios didn't want the guests accessing the concierge system unsupervised.

The flight deck and the upper deck were the same thing, with no barrier between; the result was that the captain's chair, so often his place of solace, had lost that distinction for the duration. Not counting various Iotian incursions, there had never been this many people aboard *La Sirena*—and he could hear half of them somewhere behind him. And even more intraship pages popped up on the display before him, some messages likely coming from the same passengers. Everyone wanted something.

There's no getting out of this. He didn't have ensigns to handle things.

"I'm heading back into the fray," he told Ny-Var as he stood. "If I'm not back here in an hour, fly us into the nearest sun."

39

LA SIRENA
IRAATAN SYSTEM

Rios successfully deflected or diverted three different appeals before reaching the transporter platform. Fajo, at least, did not appear too alarmed at how things were going. "Our gatherings are always rambunctious. But we haven't destroyed a transport yet."

"Glad to hear it." He was also glad that the approaching Ferengi vessel represented the last pickup before a long warp jump to collect the final invitee. Rios actually found himself breathing a sigh of relief when the glow appeared on the platform.

If the short Ferengi who appeared on the pad was not a spy, he had missed his calling. Rios had never seen anyone so furtive with hand-clasping, so anxious to direct his narrow eyes away from others. If he'd had a trench coat, he'd have been hiding behind its collar. As it was, his garb seemed faded and worn compared to the finery of Fajo's other guests.

"Welcome," Fajo said, much more drily than his other greetings. He faced Rios. "Sovak is one of Ferenginar's foremost collectors of antiquities. Some of his discoveries are legendary."

Sovak. Rios recognized the name from, of all things, Picard's book. He'd turned up in a passage relating to some artifact the then-captain had chased while on Risa many years earlier; even then, Jean-Luc didn't appear to understand the proper use of vacation time. There'd been few specifics, as it was an aside in a longer philosophical discussion—but Picard had written that the Vulcan-sounding "Sovak" name seemed deliberately chosen to confuse people, and Rios had remembered it.

And now he would never forget what Sovak sounded like. "My expectations in coming here were high," he said in an angry whisper that sounded like he was trying to domineer, but not over too many people at once. "I will not be disappointed again."

Fajo launched into a discussion of his finds, ignoring the fact that Sovak was ignoring *him*. The Ferengi's eyes darted in all directions—and there was plenty to see, as every guest but one picked that moment to converge onto the upper deck.

The Cardassian gul shoved her pet into Rios's hands. "Are you aware, Captain, that this vessel is sorely lacking in urgles?"

"Lacking in *what*?"

"Only the staple food in every *glink*'s diet. Can't you see my little Froo-Zoo has the shakes?"

Rios did notice a slight trembling in the creature, but he had attributed that to its ongoing urination. He did not want to hang on to the thing an instant longer. "Zo-Var's going to be helping at the replicator later. I'm sure if you tell her you need gurgles—"

"Urgles!"

"—she'll be able to look it up."

He turned—and looked straight into the face of the aged Trill. "Sir, we need a different stateroom."

"Why's that?" Rios asked.

"In an earlier life, my symbiont was in a bad starship accident while staying on the starboard side of the ship."

"Then there's no problem, because you're staying on the port side of the ship."

"No, we're on the left side."

"That's what port means."

"I'm sure you're mistaken." The Trill looked to Fajo. "Where did you find such a poorly informed pilot?"

Fajo was too busy dealing with Sovak to respond—and there was nowhere else to turn. The Andorian legislator was in the door to engineering, ranting about something to Glake in what Rios was certain was a one-sided conversation. Even Ledger had been cornered, in her case by Toff.

The incontinent *glink* attempting to crawl up his shoulder, Rios glanced over and saw the only missing passenger. Quimby appeared in the hall, took one look at the company present, and turned right back around. He respected the professor's intelligence.

The Andorian gave up on Glake and stormed toward Rios. "I am certain this vessel's drive is emitting baryons. I told Fajo before I arrived, I am allergic to all subatomic particles with an odd number of valence quarks. You must attend to this matter, or I shall lodge a protest with—"

Enough! He'd hit his limit. With guests on all sides badgering him—and with Fajo giving him a look of urgent concern—Rios did the one thing he'd sworn he wouldn't do on this voyage, or any other. He looked to the overhead and shouted, "Activate Emergency Hospitality Hologram!"

In the only space in that part of the deck with room to stand, another Rios appeared. "Greetings!" he declared effusively. "Are any of you having a hospitality emergency? Tell me all about it, and I'll be sure to make everything beyond perfection."

Rios's eyes bulged. He'd known the hologram would be another version of himself, but not what it would look like. The EHH wore elegant, understated gray, with a sweater zipped up to his neck, and clutched a folio as if it had all the answers to the universe's questions. His voice was something else. Maybe it was because he'd just burst to life, but this Rios spoke like an American on a combination of affirmational hypnosis and amphetamines.

"Uh . . . *Mister Hospitality*, can you help these people?"

"It would be my absolute pleasure," the EHH said, effervescing. "Make your requests one at a time or all at once. Your wishes are my command. A problem is nothing but a divine solution waiting to happen."

"Here." Rios shoved the squirming critter into his hands.

"A *glink*! How even more delightful! I adore when passengers bring pets."

"Think again in about ten seconds." Rios looked for the clearest path out of there and made for it. "Let it rip."

Given how the day had gone, Rios had fully expected the evening to be miserable. That it was not he attributed to two factors.

The first was the hospitality hologram, which Rios steadfastly refused to choose a name for, lest Ledger or anyone else decide it was a permanent feature. Mr. Hospitality had been a blur, working in concert with the concierge system to obtain the guests' needs even before they finished their requests. Then he would vanish to attend some other guest's complaint.

In the hologram, the more eccentric passengers found their perfect matches. The *glink* got the exercise its owner wanted, without the EHH ever bringing the beast near Toff, who had revealed his visceral dislike for the creature. The hologram also treated the Trill's imaginary symbiont with all seriousness and respect, earnestly meeting the elderly collector on his own terms. Rios was baffled that anyone would ever program for that, but he was glad they did.

Mr. Hospitality also adroitly managed the food replicators, making certain that the guests enjoyed private dining on *his* schedule, while simultaneously convincing them that the timing was of their choice. Fajo had figured the banquets he had planned would be incendiary enough; the fewer group meals beyond that, the better. The hologram had made the impossible possible.

Rios was the exception to solo dining, and that was the other highlight of his evening—thanks to his company, Xandra Quimby. She was no stuffy academic; to hear her tell it, her research had taken her to all corners of creation, bringing her into contact with many important figures. She had set her own course in life and done so successfully. Just hearing that such a thing was possible improved his mood. The years between them seemed as nothing.

It was near ship's midnight when the two ascended the stairs, chatting away. Rios gave a checking-in glance at the command area—and was startled to see Ledger sitting in her nightgown, staring out the window at the stars. Hearing the chatter, she looked briefly back—and turned her head again.

Quimby noticed his curiosity. "It's been a long day. I'll see you tomorrow."

"Looking forward to it," he said, and he was.

The professor departed, and he approached Ledger. "Everything shipshape?"

"Don't bug me," she said, arms crossed and eyes fixed outside.

"Okay." He started to leave.

He'd gotten halfway to his quarters when she called out. "Got a minute?"

"Sure."

She rose, beckoning for him to follow.

He and Ledger had talked plenty about their respective experiences since their earlier parting, but in the last couple of days that had tapered off, and he'd sensed it might be about something more than the festival. Nonetheless, he was surprised when she led him to her quarters.

"Don't get too excited," she said as she opened the door. "You're not staying."

He'd seen into her room on her previous tenure on *La Sirena*. It was done up in early twentieth-century American; spare but homey. There was less in the cabin now, but she'd evidently spent some time replicating her old surroundings. She gestured to her dresser.

He saw what was on it. "The book Fajo gave you?"

"Be my guest."

She paced the room as Rios flipped through the edition. He'd only seen the Iotian's cherished volume, *Chicago Mobs*, in images from class, but this looked similar. Oversized, and with a purposefully archaic cover to evoke the period it covered.

"There was always talk that the Book—*Chicago Mobs*—was missing pages when it got to Sigma Iotia," Ledger said.

"Who would do that?"

"Either those who left it—or those who found it. Nobody knows. It was always just a legend—none of the replicas my people made from it ever had page numbers. You can't really tell anything is missing."

"I thought you never read it?"

"I read part, okay? Try being an Iotian and never seeing any of it." She was agitated. "This book covers everything that the previous one did—instead of Capone and Nitti, it's Lucky Luciano and Dutch Schultz." She paused. "But it's also got stuff the previous one didn't—or at least it was removed when we got to it. *Bad stuff.*"

Rios read some copy—and began to understand.

She looked away. "I'm not just talking about the drugs. Women were treated like chattel. Some of the stories about the molls—" She shook her head. "It was just a horrible, horrible life."

Indeed, the Second Book appeared to Rios to be a no-holds-barred account of a seamy lifestyle. Even so, her reaction surprised him. She seemed shaken when he looked back at her, and he didn't understand why.

"Iotians have been in the real world for a century plus," he said. "Somebody has to have seen other gangster stories by now. You know what it was all about."

"I did," she said. "But seeing it this way made me think: What if we'd gotten *this* book instead? What would my life, my mother's life, be like if *Enterprise* hadn't come around?"

Rios took her meaning. The phenomenon of people dressing up and play-acting roles from other times was by no means limited to Earth; civilizations across the cosmos had their versions of medieval fairs, of war re-enactments. But another thing was also universal: those pasts were almost always sanitized for people's enjoyment. Nobody ever play-acted at digging latrines or burying the dead. The Iotians that Captain Kirk found had been a violent people—but their lots could have been so much worse.

As long as he'd known her, Ledger had been all about control. The Second Book told the story of a world where that wouldn't have been possible for her.

But that wasn't the only thing on her mind.

"Here's what I really don't get," she said. "Arkko rebelled against the role the Book had for her—but she was pretty quick to make playthings of her own."

"Yeah." Rios remembered the bearers carrying her desk.

"It seems silly." Ledger stared at the book and shook her head. "I just don't see the percentage in it."

He didn't either—but neither did he know what to say.

"I'm beat. Shoo."

He stepped out onto the upper deck, more than ready to call it a night. As her cabin door closed behind him, he cast his eyes in the direction of his quarters—and put his hand over his face. "Oh, give me a break," he said aloud.

Sovak was kneeling before Rios's door, fiddling with the locking mechanism. He looked back to see Rios, said "Bah!" and went right back to fiddling.

"Hey!" Rios called out, hurrying over. "Ears not working? This is off-limits."

"Off-limits?" Sovak sneered. "Who are you to say?"

"Fajo told you. I'm the captain."

"Ridiculous. I know the captain of this ship, and you're not him."

Rios stopped his approach. "What are you talking about?"

"Oh, you've changed things, all right." Sovak gestured wildly. "Clamped engines to the sides, moved walls. And I never saw the deck without junk around. But one of my contacts in Fajo's operation told me the truth. This ship was Verengan's!"

I feel like I've been here before, Rios thought. He took another step toward Sovak. "Look, I know you're a guest, but you need to—"

"*You* need to stay where you are," Sovak said, pulling a disruptor pistol from his vest. He stood. "I want answers!"

Rios put his hand on his forehead and grimaced. "I can't believe this is happening again." He looked up. "Look, it didn't end well for the last Ferengi who pulled a gun on me."

"I know," Sovak said, voice full of disdain. "Hain told me you shot him in the leg!"

It was a big galaxy—but for Rios, it had suddenly gotten a lot smaller. "You're the brother!"

"Of course. Where is he? I want to know what you did with him, now!"

Rios took a deep breath. "Come with me . . ."

40

La Sirena
Deep Space

As brothers went, Sovak and Hain appeared to have little in common. As the sibling who stayed on the ranch, Hain had seemed affable to Rios, after the minor *faux pas* of the gunshot was forgotten. Sovak, meanwhile, had treated everyone he met aboard *La Sirena* as an enemy agent.

But they both cried the same way: a braying bawl that sounded like it came from some creature Hain might have raised.

"Why didn't you tell me?" Sovak said, looking down at his brother's refrigerated corpse in the sickbay drawer. "Why didn't you find me?"

"I tried," Rios said, standing next to Emil. "I couldn't find you."

"I keep a low profile." He was not keeping one any longer, as his voice echoed through the deck. "But you'd been to Irtok. Someone there could have reached me!"

"I was going to try—but Sylvus's people started chasing me. And, well, it kind of got away from me."

"Got away from you?" Sovak's sobbing turned to anger. "My brother's been here like a block of ice for months, and it *got away from you*?" He lifted his disruptor anew. "I should fry you on general principle!"

"And you shouldn't raise your voice like this," Rios said, unflinching. "I'm assuming Ledger still has that pistol of hers. She gets insomnia again, there's no telling what'll happen."

Sovak responded with a hellish glare—which soon melted into tears again. Emil stepped up with a tissue.

"Thanks." Sovak blew his nose with a honk. The Sovak that Picard had described was a threatening but ultimately hapless fortune hunter; he'd gotten a fleeting mention in a chapter on futility for repeatedly breaking into the hotel room of a rival, looking for something that wasn't there. That behavior seemed to run in the family, Rios thought. But the intervening quarter century appeared to have taken its toll on Sovak. On the right frontal lobe where Ferengi officers wore tattoos of rank, he had an old scar that suggested an emblem had been removed. He also appeared a lot more tired than his brother had.

Red-eyed, he looked up. "You say he was poisoned by someone at the Sylvus Project?"

"That is where he fell ill," Emil said. "I cannot confirm he was poisoned."

"You haven't found anything?"

"I've checked for all agents known to my programming." The hologram looked down at his clasped hands. "Of course, I *do* have certain blind spots."

This was new to Rios. "Blind spots?"

Emil seemed embarrassed. "I've begun to perceive there were a number of deletions after I was initialized—as if after running the self-scan option, you changed your mind."

That's it, blame me. Rios scowled. "Where are these blind spots?"

"I don't perceive any pattern. The side effect of a drug here, the behavior of a genetic marker there."

Sovak waved the weapon anew, this time at Emil. "Hear that? He admits his incompetence!"

"He's a hologram," Rios said. "You're going to shoot a hologram?"

The Ferengi hissed. "*It would give me satisfaction!*"

That was enough for Rios. He had wanted to punch someone for the better part of a year, and while it seemed disrespectful to deck someone in the throes of grief over a departed sibling, he decided to live with the shame.

The belt to Sovak's jaw sent the disruptor flying far across the room. Rios retrieved the weapon well before the Ferengi got back to his knees.

Emil noticed Sovak's bleeding. "That I can help you with."

Rios watched him work. "These blind spots. True for the other guy too?"

"You refer to the Emergency Hospitality Hologram? You would have to ask—but I suspect it applies to all."

Rios growled. As if he needed another reason never to activate the others.

Sovak stopped mewling long enough to ask, "Why'd you hit me? You said yourself, he's just a hologram!"

"I don't want you waking up my guests." He and Emil helped Sovak to sit on the examination table. "Will you listen now?"

Sovak snuffled. Rios took that as an answer.

"Here's the truth," he said. "Hain hired us to fulfill Verengan's contract—

to get the thing you wanted from Javen. The duke reneged—but after your brother got sick."

Sovak winced as Emil treated his fresh injury. "Did you get *anything* from Javen?"

"We got *everything*," Rios said. "Took almost his entire library."

Sovak sat up straight, excited. "Where is it? Show me!"

"We don't have it. Most all of the books we sold to Fajo."

"*Him!*" The Ferengi was nearly apoplectic. "You had the book—and you sold it! Why would you do that?"

"We didn't know which book Hain wanted. He never told us." Rios shrugged. "If you're looking for your share of the proceeds from the manure, I can take care of that—after the auction."

"This was never about the damn manure!" Sovak swore repeatedly for what felt like a minute. "My contact at Cynosure said there were rare books coming through, but never saw what we were looking for. Fajo must still have it!" He looked to the overhead. "Perhaps it is with the items he intends to auction."

Rios shook his head. "We didn't bring aboard any books."

More swearing.

"No matter," Sovak said, recovering. "I sought the invite for another reason entirely." He stood from the table and walked over to his brother's body. "I will say no more."

Rios had a good idea what Sovak's reason was. "I don't have time for more nonsense, so let's lay our cards on the table. You're here because you're looking for a child's toy. A puzzle."

The Ferengi's eyes went wide—only to narrow again. "A toy. Ludicrous."

"And this book is supposed to unlock some secret in the puzzle—leading you to some fortune. Am I warm?"

Sovak was, because beads of sweat developed on his lobes. Then he erupted into a rage—directed not at Rios, but at Hain's corpse. "Oh, you stupid bumpkin. You blasted fool. I should have known better than to bring a *rancher* into my plan!" Sovak spun back to Rios. "I only included him because he'd been Javen's supplier before—and because he always wanted to be in one of my ventures. And there he goes, telling you everything!"

"Actually, a holographic bartender told me."

"Bartender?" Spittle flew from Sovak's mouth. "What are you talking about?"

"Never mind."

Sovak took a breath. "You have the puzzle?"

"Maybe, maybe not. But let's pretend I did. I'll tell you this—breaking into my room won't get it for you." Rios opened his jacket to reveal Sovak's disruptor in the pocket inside. "Understand?"

"I see," Sovak grumbled. "So if you had it, you would expect me to buy it from you."

Rios scratched his beard. He hadn't really thought about it.

"Don't imagine that you can open it," the Ferengi said, the sneer returning. "It's far beyond a dolt like you. I have decades of experience with artifacts and even I had to study the works of several worlds after Verengan showed it to me. You would be lost trying to unlock it."

That's been the case, Rios thought. "Still, it seems worth something to you. Hypothetically."

"I won't make you a partner. I only dealt Verengan in because he owned it to start with. I'll pay you outright for it, but that's all." After that certain declaration, he shifted uncomfortably. "I just need to wait to pay until after I reach the final prize."

"I owe people now."

"So do I!" Sovak spouted. He lowered his voice. "While Hain's been flying around in your freezer, his employees have been robbing him blind. I had to raid the corporate account myself just to pay to attend this event. Fajo wouldn't let me come otherwise. But his junk on display is nothing compared to—"

Sovak clammed up again.

Rios figured he'd gotten all the information he was going to. Sovak's story rang true, moreover. His clothes looked more than shabby next to the other guests'.

"Let me think on it a day or two," Rios said. "I expect you want Hain's body too—and I can't take that anywhere until the event's over."

The Ferengi scowled, only to glance again at his brother. "I would rather eat nails than listen to Fajo's blather—but you make sense." He closed the drawer holding the body and bowed. "We will speak again."

Rios was sure they would, but he wasn't entirely sure what he'd do then. Both Kahless and Sovak had indicated the puzzle belonged to Verengan; the Ferengi brothers' only claim to it was that they knew what it was.

Maybe I'd better get busy solving it.

41

LA SIRENA
DEEP SPACE

The rendezvous point for Fajo's last expected guest was distant enough that Rios had indeed been able to devote much of the next morning and afternoon to kicking back in his room, relaxing as he worked the dials of the puzzle. Ledger liked pretending she was in charge of the freighter and Mr. Hospitality was handling all the little things, so he felt no guilt whatsoever about his absence. And nobody during the whole time he was in his quarters had attempted to break in.

His respite ended when an alert warned him he was expected to appear on deck in advance of the final pickup and the banquet. Reluctantly, he crawled from the unmade bed, knocking aside pages of crumpled notes about the puzzle. He'd sacrificed an entire sketchpad to the mystery; art had once been a hobby, but he hadn't felt much like drawing since *ibn Majid.*

Dressed in his cleanest outfit, he surveyed the messy state he'd left the room in. An old tunic hung over the snout of the stuffed *targ*, where he usually hid the golden apple. Figuring Sovak might try again, he wondered if he needed a new location.

An idea struck. He asked the concierge system for a storage box, adding dimensions. When the container appeared, he placed the puzzle inside. "Transport storage box to underdeck maintenance locker C," he commanded.

As installed, the concierge system did not transport much nonreplicated matter; a passenger could not ask to be beamed from deck to deck. But moving real tools and foodstuffs about was an expected task, and the box vanished promptly, spirited away to a place no one could reach. Satisfied, he exited.

Fajo's walking tour of his collection was supposed to have wrapped up, but instead, Rios found it had gone into overtime. He understood why within the first minute of joining the group and listening to their comments:

"There's no way this painting can be from the Vorat Dynasty. The Orions didn't even use oil-based pigments until the Huldavell."

"That can't be the weapon that killed Praetor T'Vahna. Everyone knows his assassin was left-handed!"

"Oh, but the turquoise-label version is *much* more valuable. You should see the one in my collection."

"Your display says 'Tucker '48,' but of course the 48 had no apostrophe. Any fool would know that!"

"Kivas, why did you ever *think* of including this? My last exhibit was *much* better . . ."

And on, and on. As Rios had done the previous evening, he found refuge with Quimby, who seemed to find the whole flying antiques show amusing. She didn't have much to do. The other collectors rarely turned to her for a second opinion, because all of them were convinced their own takes were correct. Fajo called on her to confirm authenticity only when he needed to protect an item's value in the upcoming auction—but he, also, was too full of himself to defer.

"How can you break ties," Rios asked her, "when the arguments never end?"

"I don't know how well it was *ever* going to work," she replied. "They all know Kivas funds my position. Any judgment of mine is already suspect."

"Then why are you here?"

"Change of pace." She smiled at him. "And company."

One guest had been absent: Sovak. When he finally did join, he appeared sullen and not a little inebriated. Quimby excused herself when he approached, an option Rios wished he had.

"This is a waste of time," the Ferengi grumbled to him. "We have our own business to discuss."

Rios had no intention of doing that, and was about to say so when Ny-Var called back with a proximity alert.

"Ah. My final guests," Fajo said.

"On it." Rios excused himself and dashed forward.

He did not recognize the sleek yacht cruising alongside *La Sirena*, but he certainly admired it. Professors and threadbare Ferengi aside, Fajo's guests traveled well.

With any luck, they'll be on and off soon and all these people will be out of my hair. After directing Ny-Var's close approach, he straightened his jacket and strolled aft.

On the way, he met Ledger coming out of her quarters. "Who's arriving?" he asked.

"Fajo never told me. A late addition." She rubbed the sides of her eyes.

Rios noticed. "You okay?"

"Lousy sleep. Worry about yourself."

He *was* a little worried about her, after the New York book episode—but forgot about it as they arrived beside Fajo in time for the transporter effect to begin.

And then, Rios forgot about everything else.

"Ah, the Marchioness Liselle," Fajo said, bowing to the Valtese woman on the platform.

Where his other guests' outlandish apparel was meant to shock, Liselle's green gown was set to stun: at once elegant and flattering. She wore an exotic flower in her hair, with another like it pinned above her breast. Her face betrayed no emotion at all. "Mister Fajo."

"Kivas, please." He turned to her uniformed companion. "And you are?"

"Royce Claggett, chief of security for the Sylvus Project." His eyes found Rios and Ledger. "You're carrying fugitives, Mister Fajo."

"I don't know any fugitives. There are only my guests—and the crew."

Fajo offered his hand to Liselle to help her off the platform. She politely declined it, instead stepping down on her own. She looked up at Rios—and the temperature on *La Sirena* seemed to him to drop by several degrees. "Cristóbal."

"*Marquesa*."

Ledger gestured for him to join her as she approached Fajo with a pad. "If I could cut in?"

"Business calls," Fajo said. "I won't be a moment." He joined her and Rios near the bulkhead.

Shielding her mouth, Ledger whispered, "You invited *them*?"

"Of course," Fajo replied. "Duke Javen is a longstanding member of the collecting community. Now, I mustn't keep them waiting." He returned to Liselle and Claggett.

While they spoke, Rios took the chance to confer with Ledger. "What is this?" he whispered. "I thought Fajo knew that the books came from Javen's library."

"No idea." Ledger looked over at the trio—and Claggett, who even in deep conversation with Fajo had never taken his eyes off Rios. "In my world, it's no-questions-asked—and that's fine with him. Everyone in his set owns something that's hot. It's part of the game. Nobody cares."

Liselle cared—as Rios discovered when she raised her voice so he could hear. "What my security chief was trying to say, Kivas, is that this ship is responsible for the theft of much of my great-uncle's library. We alerted your firm. You must be aware of this?"

Fajo tut-tutted. "I heard there was a theft—terrible, just terrible. But the details are news to me. Is there proof to this accusation?"

"Substantial, and conclusive."

He pursed his lips. "That *is* alarming news. But as our cruise is only in areas beyond any government's jurisdiction, Captain Rios would be the one aboard authorized to prosecute any crime."

"He *did* the crime," Claggett snarled. "He's guilty. They're all guilty!"

"So you say. But you agreed to abide by my conditions before I sent you our location." Fajo paced the deck, seemingly unconcerned. "Outside problems are left at the transporter pad. Once the event is over and I have disembarked, your matters are your own."

"Or else what? Who are you to—"

Liselle held up her hand. "Chief."

That was enough. At just a word from his superior, Claggett restrained himself.

She glided past Fajo. "When I learned of your event, I thought it was important to attend and make sure that none of my uncle's property was being sold. He's not traveling these days. He's been unwell since the . . . *incident.*"

That startled Rios. "Is he okay?"

She glowered at him. "He has given the galaxy much—and is at an age where things are being taken away from him. You have accelerated that."

Rios swallowed. It wasn't what he wanted. He searched for something to say, but Fajo spoke first. "I'm sorry to learn of the duke's troubles, of course—we're old acquaintances. But you'll see there's not a book for sale." He gestured to his displays, and the crowd of other guests who had gathered to gawk. "Certainly none of us here would want anything to do with the matter. Nothing is more personal than a prized collection, is it, my friends?"

Words of agreement came from them.

"We've all traveled so far," he added, facing Liselle again. "We'll have a fine banquet tonight—and then tomorrow, my auction. You'll see there's nothing untoward here—and perhaps you will find something worth investing in."

"I'm not here to—" she began to reply, only to pause when her gaze went from Fajo's guests to Rios. "I will attend your auction. To observe."

"Wonderful! I'm sure we'll make a buyer of you yet." Fajo hastened to introduce her to his other guests.

Rios marveled to see Fajo work. The slickest merchant had nothing on him.

He looked to Ledger and exhaled, glad to have averted the crisis—when another disaster loomed. Sovak, who had been off in the wings, beheld Liselle and Claggett.

"What are *they* doing here?" he said, starting to approach the gaggle.

Rios stepped in and grabbed his arm. "I didn't expect them."

"They killed Hain!"

"We don't know that." He yanked Sovak back toward the open door to engineering.

"Yack, yack, yack! My brother's life demands justice. No—retribution!"

Rios grabbed the shorter man by the collar and pulled him fully through the doorway. "Listen, I want to know what happened too. But you're not going to find out by accusing them."

"I'll find out by killing them! Give me back my disruptor!"

"That'll disrupt things, all right." He covered Sovak's mouth with his hand—and beckoned for Glake's help. The Nausicaan responded, easily restraining Sovak.

Outside, Ledger noticed the commotion. She hustled toward engineering, mindful that Liselle and Claggett were not far away. "What's going on in here?"

"I need your help," Rios said, feeling Sovak's jagged teeth against his hand. "He wants to kill the *marquesa*!"

"I'm not too keen on her myself. What's the problem?"

"I'm serious. He thinks they killed his brother." Rios looked imploringly at her. "You remember? *Hain?*"

"Hain's your *brother*?"

"I've tried to tell him to cool down," Rios said. "They don't know we think Hain was poisoned. We can use that."

Sovak pushed futilely against Glake's mighty hold. "Release me. Now or later, I will have vengeance!"

Ledger stepped in. "Buddy, listen. Remember the Rules of Acquisition!"

"Hah!" Sovak spat ineffectually in her direction. "What would *you* know of them?"

"Plenty." Ledger laughed. "If my people had adapted your list first, things would be a lot different." She put up her fingers. "Remember lucky Number Seven!"

Sovak stopped struggling—and his eyes narrowed. "*Keep your ears open*," he recited.

"And Forty-Eight?"

"*The bigger the smile, the sharper the knife.*" Sovak looked to his captors—and exhaled. "I guess I can wait."

"Now you're on the trolley, kid!"

Rios shot her a look acknowledging her feat. *Well done.*

He checked the time. "Dinner in an hour. Two jobs: we find out what we can—and keep him from Liselle and Claggett. Make sense?"

Ledger let out an exasperated sigh. "You just want an excuse to pitch woo with your princess again."

"Just information. Woo is optional."

42

La Sirena
Deep Space

If Kivas Fajo had been of a mind to kidnap all his other rivals in the collecting game, there would have been no question of anyone finding them. *La Sirena* had swiftly left Liselle's yacht far behind, embarking on a tour of the more colorful nebulae of the former Romulan Neutral Zone.

The viewports behind the bridge weren't large and the location Fajo had selected for the banquet had none at all. However, it was a holodeck, so it was possible to program the walls, overhead, and deck to depict the scenery from outside. *Sylvus Bestri*'s dining room had only been atop a transparent floor. *La Sirena*'s gave one the impression of dining in a bubble in space.

Mr. Hospitality had warned Fajo that the experience might be a little nauseating for his associates, but the collector had been indifferent. "We live to torture one another."

It was already that for Rios, whose previous formal dinners had not gone smoothly. This one had introduced a new complication: choreography. Three four-person tables had been set for the dozen diners, but Fajo's seating chart had already gone out the virtual window.

Rios had initially agreed to sit with Sovak, to keep an eye on him—but he also greatly wanted to talk to Liselle, seeking a chance to explain. He pawned the Ferengi off on Ledger, who sputtered as Rios hurried to a chair opposite the *marquesa*.

She did not speak to him, but neither did she bolt. Rios was about to launch into his apology when Professor Quimby appeared at his side. "May I join you? There's someone I don't want to get stuck with."

Rios imagined he knew who it was: Sovak, whose eyes were on the empty chair beside Liselle. The Ferengi rose from his table—only to have his seatmate, Ledger, scurry over to the other chair beside Rios. "Sorry," she said. "Business talk."

Sovak, frustrated, trudged back to his table, which was now populated by three of Fajo's other guests.

Rios leaned to Ledger and whispered, "What's the deal? I told you to stay with Sovak."

"You want to keep him away from Liselle and Claggett? This is the only way it works out!"

It meant something else. Rios was to spend the evening with three very different women: the professor, the princess, and the profiteer. Any one of them might have made for a pleasant companion; any combination of the two offered the potential for a volatile reaction. All three at once upset any game plan he might have had, unnerving him more than the scenery outside ever could.

He tried, anyway. "Liselle, I've been meaning to—"

"There's no need to explain," she said primly over her appetizer. "When a person tells you who they are, listen."

"*I* know who you are," Quimby said, snapping her fingers. "You run the Sylvus Project."

"The place cards gave it away," Ledger muttered.

Liselle paid her no mind. "I understand Mister Fajo funds your seat at the university, Doctor." She stared coolly at the professor. "How does the institution feel about the allegations?"

Looking over her tea, Quimby didn't blink. "Allegations? I don't know what you mean."

"That he trades in stolen property." Liselle nodded to Ledger. "What is the term in your world, dear—a *gate*?"

"A *fence*." Ledger rolled her eyes. "You've really got to be behind the grind not to know that word."

"I'm sorry—the grind?"

Rios put two fingers up. "Excuse me—"

Liselle ignored him. "Iotian talk is so colorful," she said in her regal way. She pressed Ledger. "So *is* he?"

"Is who what?" Ledger asked.

"Is Fajo a fence?"

Quimby gave a lilting laugh. "No one would think that on Argelius. He's quite respected—"

As Liselle turned to the professor to debate Fajo's honesty, Rios noticed with alarm that Ledger had her fork in her fist, motioning as if she wanted to stab Liselle in the back of the neck. Rios reached for her with his left hand and pulled her abruptly toward him, almost knocking over her wineglass. Into her ear, he rasped, "What are you doing?"

"Fitting your *marquesa* for a Chicago overcoat."

He didn't even try to guess at that. "Behave, or I'm sending you back to the Ferengi's table."

"Behave *yourself*, Romeo."

Rios felt a hand on his right wrist. He looked over to Quimby, who smiled sweetly. "Cris, is there a problem over there?"

"No," he said, releasing Ledger. "Just a question about the serving order."

"Ah," declared Mr. Hospitality, appearing behind Liselle. "That was the first course of nine. There is more heaven in store!"

Liselle stared at Rios through her wineglass. "Lovely."

Elbow on the table, Ledger leaned on her hand. "Swell."

Quimby squeezed Rios's wrist. "More time to talk!"

Ledger eyed the professor's hand. "I'm sure *you're* glad to get out, Doc. It must get dull in the egghead set."

"Oh, it was," Quimby replied pleasantly. "But then we found out that more than one book existed."

"That's no problem," Liselle said. "They could just *steal* a few more." She stared directly at him. "Perhaps *you* could help them with that, Cristóbal?"

Rios slid down in his seat—and wondered if *he* should have hidden in maintenance locker C instead.

Rios had not been able to convince Liselle of his remorse, and he had not learned a single thing that would explain how Hain had died. That said, she had grown a trifle less icy at moments during the meal, and he could tell around the second entrée that someone's foot was visiting his ankle. He at least knew it wasn't Ledger, the kick of whose pumps he'd felt whenever she became irritated. When Fajo in his speech had asked Rios to stand up for a bow, he nearly faltered due to the bruise on his left shin.

The Trill guest had given him an eighth-course reprieve by complaining that some ingredient in the baked Andoria had upset his symbiont's system. The episode mortified Mr. Hospitality, baffled Emil, and made Rios want to give the nonexistent being a kiss. It effected his escape, and he hid in sickbay until he was sure the event was over and all the tables had been cleared and dematerialized.

Defeated, he staggered up the stairs, jacket in hand, wondering how he'd ever survived the evening on nothing stronger than Fajo's wine of the moment. He looked just for a second onto the vacant bridge; *La Sirena* was parked and floating for a silent night. It was all he hoped for when he reached his door.

It was unlocked. He put his hand on his forehead. *Not again.*

The door opened, revealing a darkened room. "All right, whoever it is," he shouted inside. "Enough nonsense. Get out now."

"That could be a problem," replied a familiar voice from the direction of his bed.

Rios walked in, and the door sealed behind him. Broken by the slats of the blast shutters, the light from the stellar formation outside revealed a woman, sitting up amid his bedsheets and scratch paper. "Professor."

"Hello again." She smiled. "I just dropped by to see if you'd really read my book."

"It's on the table," Rios said. His eyes did not go to it. "You're not wearing anything."

"And you are," Quimby replied. "But no scientist would report results until the experiment is complete."

He dropped his jacket on the deck and approached. "Who let you in?"

"My roommates—Ny-Var and Zo-Var."

"They did that once before." Rios frowned. "I ordered them not to."

"Don't blame them. They knew I wanted to see you—and besides, I think they wanted their privacy." She arched an eyebrow.

It took Rios a few seconds to understand her. "You mean—?"

Quimby chuckled. "Are you telling me they've been on your crew all this time and you never knew they were a couple?"

"I had no idea. I can barely understand what they're saying!" He only knew that they weren't related—and they were as close as any two people he'd ever met. He had to grin. "Makes sense. Good for them."

"They respect you immensely—and they seemed to think my dropping in would be good for *you*."

"Remind me to give them a raise—if I ever pay them." He began to disrobe.

As he did, Quimby gestured to the papers strewn about. "What are all these? It looks like you're deciphering hieroglyphics."

"It's a puzzle."

"Puzzle?"

"Kind of a brainteaser. I unwind with it. I'm trying to put this matrix of symbols in the right order." He sat beside her and picked up a page. "Take these. They look like the astrological symbols for planets."

She recognized them. "And this batch are alchemical symbols. A lot of the same ones."

"The two lists should interlock in five places—and in a certain order." Rios had figured that out already from working the dials with Romulan and Klingon glyphs. It annoyed him that he'd solved those yet was still baffled by the ones with symbols from his own planet. He flipped idly through pages. "I've tried arranging them in the order of the planetary orbits—and also the order of the periodic table. Nothing works."

"Hmm." Quimby glanced over at her book. "You know, a line that's attributed to Parch is that we are wiser when we 'think interculturally.'"

"I read that chapter."

She squeezed his shoulder. "I'm glad. I'm just thinking—" She let go of him and took a page from his hands. "Yeah. Maybe the *Wuxing*."

"The woo what?"

"Wuxing. It's a scheme in ancient Chinese medicine that organizes a large number of things into phases—it ties into history, chemistry, pharmacology, you name it. The order depends on what process you're trying to describe, but the phases are wood, fire, earth, metal, and water."

"Elements?"

"That's what *Wuxing* means. The Five Elements." She pointed to the page. "But the phases—or seasons, as they're sometimes called—are also tied to planets. Wood is related to Jupiter, for example."

"Of course. Famous for its trees." Rios began to take it more seriously as he looked at the symbols. "Looks like the astrological character for Jupiter is the alchemical one for tin."

"Fire, Mars, iron," she added. "For earth, the planet is Saturn—"

"Why not Earth for earth?"

"Don't ask. And Saturn shares its symbol with lead."

"So the lists could interact through the order of the ancient elements?" Rios scratched his beard. "You say there are different orders?"

"There are," she said. She kissed his cheek. "But is this really what you want to be talking about now?"

Rios faced her. All through the past months, he had wanted to sort out his fraught relationship with Liselle—but that seemed farther away than ever now. Quimby was right here. They had a difference in age, it was true—but she had considered him an equal, and that had made him do the same in response.

And the way she looked at him in the light . . .

When I make any money, I am definitely giving the Miradorns a bonus.

•

The hours that followed were different from his night with the *marquesa*, but no less special—or needed. The setting was part of it: it was his own room, rather than a wealthy woman's boudoir. Another novel experience was that whenever they broke for a rest, they invariably returned to going over his notes. Scholarly research had not really been a part of his romantic regimen before.

But the most important difference was Quimby herself. Xandra seemed to want nothing from him more than a fun time, stimulating mind and body.

Or so he thought. A couple of hours before shipboard morning, he woke—only to find himself alone. He turned on his side and saw Quimby in silhouette, her back to him as she looked under the tunic to examine the *targ*'s empty mouth.

I give up. He rolled over and went back to sleep.

43

La Sirena
Deep Space

Rios rose alone, but he understood why. The big day had arrived: the great auction, at which Quimby was expected to assist Fajo. A river of gold-pressed latinum was expected to flow, with a small rivulet branching off to Rios in the process. Ledger had calculated that *La Sirena* might be completely paid off before the second session even began, freeing them both.

He'd encountered Ledger earlier; she'd apparently seen Quimby emerge from his quarters that morning. She hadn't even bothered to berate him for that. "Just focus, if you know how. Today's the whole ball of wax."

His focus *was* divided, but that was because his role was mundane, and he was needed only intermittently. Working with Glake, he'd transported the smaller items from their display locations to the holodeck, where the dining room from the night before had been replaced with a program for an elegant auction hall. Ledger signaled after each sale, whereupon he transported the sold items right back to where they'd been.

It had been a monotonous job, and he had spent most of the time in between scribbling on his papers and checking the ship's reference database about things Quimby had suggested the night before. There were several sequences in ancient Chinese medicine that might be adapted to the puzzle, which he left in its hiding place.

"*Sheng cycle: to strengthen or create*," he mumbled. "Wood feeds fire, fire creates earth, earth yields metal, metal collects water. But what if the cycle starts with a different phase?"

Every so often, Glake looked over at him, baffled.

He must think I've lost my mind.

At last, the session break approached. Jamming the papers in the pocket inside his jacket, he went forward to the holodeck.

The carpeted chamber was well lit, with the auctioneer's podium facing exactly the number of chairs necessary. The audience for the exclusive sale numbered seven: Fajo's four collecting rivals, plus Sovak, Liselle, and Claggett. Meeting Rios at the entrance, Ledger acknowledged she'd been working with Mr. Hospitality to keep the Ferengi from confronting the Sylvus contingent.

"Is it working?" Rios asked.

"Mister H has been a little too free with the giggle juice. It's been flowing since after breakfast." She frowned. "But that's not our only problem."

Rios looked ahead to where a holographic auctioneer stood at the podium beside a stand holding a Romulan lyre. The female Bajoran looked fashionable and sophisticated—and concerned.

"Once again, it's a five-stringer, gentlebeings—secretly crafted by the musician Ptonus just one year after instruments with more than four strings were declared a danger to the regime." A digital display on the wall indicated it had not received an opening bid. "Just two hundred bars of latinum. Don't miss this one."

She looked over to Fajo, who stood at the side with Quimby. "Come on, people," he said. "Don't make me reduce another starting price."

Toff called out, "You set the price. You might have thought of that then."

Rios turned to Ledger, who indicated it had been like this all session.

Ahead, the piece finally went at half the asking price, and Fajo called for the session break. As the audience rose, he charged toward the door, refusing to lock eyes with his rivals. He beckoned for Rios and Ledger to follow him outside.

On the main deck, he shared his distress. "I don't understand it. These are some of the greatest finds in years, and they're pooh-poohing all of it."

Ledger glanced back at the door, where the would-be bidders were emerging for the refreshments Mr. Hospitality had provided. Her brow furrowed. "They're freezing you out."

Fajo steamed. "You're right, of course. Not Liselle—she just thinks I'm shady. But the others have always envied me. They were delighted when I went away."

Rios didn't understand. "I don't see what their problem is. You came back in a big way with your salvage operations."

"*Too* big a way," Ledger corrected. "He scarfed up every collectible to come from the refugees. The others were totally shut out." She faced Fajo. "It's classic street stuff. They're sending a message here, both to one another and to you: they want you to flop."

"I can't *make* them bid," Fajo grumbled. He glowered at Rios. "This whole event is becoming a losing proposition."

Rios knew what that meant. *No sale means no percentage—and no freighter payment.* Something had to change. He snapped his fingers. "Open it up to *their* stuff in the next session—and take a piece."

"That's humiliating," the collector said. "And their goods aren't here."

"You told me they all had prized possessions that everyone knew about. They don't have to be here—they just have to sell them."

"So he's selling access to the audience." Ledger chewed her lip. "I don't see them going for it. Why would they help Kivas when they can do their own deals in the hall?"

"Side-dealing—during one of *my* events?" Fajo's eyes filled with anger. "That's unspeakable. It violates every community standard." He frowned. "I'll open it up, but I don't like it. I need something else."

Rios shrugged. "I guess we could go pick up some new customers—"

"*Will we do?*"

Rios spun to see several people materializing on the transporter platform. Iotians with machine guns, all—and at front, the first arrival, seated on a desk held aloft by bearers: Boss Arkko in a black dress. She winked at Rios. "Hope I'm not too late for the big show!"

Rios took a step in her direction, before raised guns prompted him to stop. A commotion rose behind him. Stench and Dinky were there, prodding a terrified Ny-Var and Zo-Var forward at gunpoint.

"I'm so sorry," a shaking Ny-Var said to Rios. "They dropped out of warp right next to us!"

The gunmen filtered into the crowd of panicked guests, prompting Claggett to step in front of Liselle.

"Now, see here!" he declared, chest out. "Keep away from her, you filthy—"

"Shaddup!" Dinky shouted, slamming the butt of his weapon into Claggett's chin. Rios's nemesis hit the deck like a bag of bricks.

"*Chief!*" Liselle called out.

She knelt beside him. Claggett appeared conscious, but dazed and bleeding profusely. The *marquesa* looked to Rios. "Cris, *do something*!"

With his hands already up, he didn't have many options. "Everybody calm down," he said. He looked at Arkko. "I'm going to summon my holographic doctor. Tell your people not to shoot him. I've seen what bullets do in this place. You won't like it."

Arkko raised no objection. "Have at it, flyboy."

Emil appeared on summoning—and didn't know what to make of what he saw. Before he could ask, Rios pointed to Claggett. Seeing the bleeding chief, the hologram knelt and got to work.

Rios noticed Ledger approaching, as yet unobstructed by any of the Convincers. She looked bewildered.

"What's going on here, Ledge?" he asked.

"That's what I'd like to know," Fajo said in anger. He glared at Ledger. "Did you bring these people here?"

"She didn't," Arkko said, hopping off the desk and onto the deck. She began to walk, surveying the captive guests as she swayed through the crowd. "We own this ship. It's got our tracker on it—and I'm tired of waiting. All accounts are due."

Ledger tilted her head. "You didn't come all the way out here for a ship payment. That's small potatoes for Boss Arkko."

Arkko smirked. "You've wised up in your time away." She gestured broadly with a many-braceleted arm. "You got me. I read your reports about this to-do—and decided I'd see how the upper crust lived. Been a long time since the Convincers have seen a fancy soirée."

At the names of the boss and her gang, Liselle stood up from where Emil was helping Claggett. "I manage the Sylvus Project," she said, unafraid as she stared down the elder Iotian. "Am I to understand you run one of the gangs that's been striking our operations?"

"So what if I do?"

"We're a relief effort!"

"It's like the book says, honey. I rob banks because that's where the money is."

"Wrong era," muttered Quimby, one of the captives a few meters away.

Arkko heard her—and shot an acid look in return. "There's more than one book, smart mouth."

Quimby elected not to respond.

When Arkko approached Fajo, he appeared to make a mental calculation. He took a step forward. "If you know enough to find me, you know who I am," he said, "and what this function is. There's nothing to steal here. All of the latinum they were bidding with is on electronic account—and the goods on this vessel are mostly valuable to the people on this ship."

"If even that," Palor Toff said.

"No hard currency?" Arkko tsk-tsked. "Spoilsports."

"And if you want to get paid by me," Rios said, "you need to let the auction proceed. I get my end, you get paid."

"I do like your end," she said, unembarrassed in the least as she checked him out. She brightened. "Sure. I've never been to an auction with society swells before."

Arkko clapped her hands together. "Somebody bring me a tiger milk. Let's get this wingding started!"

44

La Sirena
Deep Space

It had not been necessary to explain to Mr. Hospitality that Arkko was not actually expecting the milk of an Earthly jungle cat. He had, however, asked why Arkko expected him to be shirtless while attending to her. "A boss has gotta have standards," she said.

If the auction had gone poorly before, the second session was a disaster. It had begun in the cargo area with the vehicles; but even though Arkko had compelled them to stay, Fajo's guests were too unnerved to bid. Rios had thought Arkko might be interested in the Tucker sedan, but it was too far out of her preferred automotive timeframe for comfort, and the novel center-hood headlight gave her something called "the willies."

That left the final session, back in the auction hall, and even at the engineering station Rios could tell things weren't going well. Too many items were cycling through too quickly, their bidding going nowhere.

He'd already seen Arkko's starship *Velvet Glove* alongside *La Sirena* to port; fretful Zo-Var had whispered that two more Convincer dreadnoughts were astern. That was already enough to convince him not to use the transporter as a weapon against the boarders; Stench pointing a tommy gun at him and Glake was barely necessary.

With items closing fast and time running down, he had a thought. He drew his notes out of his jacket pocket, nearly getting shot by a jumpy Stench in the process. Placing the pages on the engineering console, he summoned a pen and went back to work.

He'd only gotten a few minutes in when time ran out. Ledger called back on her comm for the last item on the agenda. "We're getting killed up here," she said. She didn't mean it literally—but it was all the same to him.

After transporting the centerpiece of Fajo's festival—a gleaming crimson bauble that a philandering Romulan praetor had choked on after being force-fed it by his wife—Rios gathered up his scraps of paper and started for the door. He was halfway there when Stench threatened him with his gat. "What's the idea, pal?"

"That's the last item. I've got to go forward."

"Nobody said anything about that."

Rios saw his crewmate looming behind the punk—and nodded.

Glake reached around Stench in a partial bear hug, seizing the young Iotian's wrists so hard the machine gun slipped from his hands. Rios seized the weapon before it could go off. Before he could react, Stench was pinned on the deck, his hat forcibly jammed in his mouth by the Nausicaan.

"Just a second," Rios said, heading back to the transporter panel.

He changed his mind about using the transporter with Stench; something had to be done with him. After dealing with that, his next act was to retrieve the box from where he'd hidden it. He addressed Glake: "Send Emil a message. If he notices somebody stuck in the other morgue drawer, tell him not to let him out!"

Rios took the box under his arms and fled forward.

Gunmen stopped him at the door as he entered the holodeck. Inside, Palor Toff had just sprung a surprise on Fajo. The true so-called Ruby of Revenge was back in Toff's home collection; the one on the auction block was a replicated fake created for insurance purposes. When Quimby's handheld scanner located the microcode confirming the fact, Fajo accused Toff of having set him up. But nothing could conceal Fajo's look of degradation.

"I speak for all of us," Toff said, "when I say this has been a most disappointing event. Far below even *your* miserable standards, Kivas."

Arkko, being fanned by Mr. Hospitality, looked bored. "I've never seen such a bunch of stiffs. You call this fun?"

"I do *not*," replied a very drunk Sovak. "And if you ask me, you people are a bunch of conniving thieves and hypocrites!"

The Convincer boss noticed Rios being held at the door. "Looks like you're out of luck, dollface. No sale today." She smacked her lips. "Unless you'd like a job. If you're built like your hologram, you can carry my desk any time!"

"Just a second," Rios said. "The auction's not over. I have something to sell."

"Come on then," she replied, waving for her guards to release him.

Fajo, worthless ruby in hand, looked at him, startled. "What could *you* possibly have?"

I'm not entirely sure. I might not have anything. Rios set the box on the floor in the clearing by the podium and opened it.

In the front row, Toff chortled. "What is that—a toy?"

Sovak's big ears perked up. "Did you say *a toy*?"

Rios placed his papers next to the puzzle as he knelt. There were so many possible permutations of planetary and alchemical symbols, it would have taken a synth at top speed a decade to work through them manually. But he knew something now: which symbols mattered.

Five elements. Five seasons, of seventy-two days each. He'd memorized the earlier steps by now; was it just a matter of finishing the sequence? "Wood, fire, earth, metal, water," he said.

The puzzle snapped to its original state, resetting its dials.

"What are you doing?" Ledger called out. "Have you lost your mind?"

Rios caught his breath. *Maybe the sequence begins with a different season?*

He returned it to its nearly finished state and tried again, with a new element as the starter. "Fire, earth, metal, water, wood."

As it snapped tight again, Quimby stepped over from her observation post. "Is that—?"

He didn't hear her. "Earth, metal, water, wood, fire."

Snap! It reset again.

Sovak was on his feet—and trying to get Rios's attention. "Don't," he shouted. "Stop! Don't do this!"

Fajo watched, spellbound, as Rios tried again. "Metal, water, wood, fire, earth."

This time, the snap was followed by cries from two of the front-row spectators. Sovak crawled over the space between the chairs of the Cardassian and Toff, jostling them both as he tried to reach Rios. "*Rios, don't!*"

"Last try," Rios said. He looked up at Quimby. Eyes wide, she nodded. "Water, wood, fire, earth, *metal*!"

The puzzle left his hands entirely, flipping up in the air like a sprung mousetrap and tumbling onto the floor. Before he could retrieve the thing, the metallic petals that had just opened on it went back into motion, righting the device.

And then something appeared, floating in the air above it. Kneeling beside Rios now, Quimby spoke. "Holodeck, reduce lighting ninety percent." She looked to him as darkness fell. "*It's an actuality!*"

Rios's eyes had never left it. He saw the wisps begin to coalesce into a shape, with color. He and Quimby crawled back to give it space—and then the world changed.

A man, life-sized, sat before a table. His face remained obscured, even as the details surrounding him came more into view. The table held a wineglass and bottle—and a large book, which the man studied with great interest.

About him, more details resolved. Many more, for the display was much larger than the holographic diorama Rios had seen for T'Pau. A window appeared beside the man, with stars visible beyond. Was the setting a house, or a starship? The metal frame led Rios to conclude it was the latter, but it was dark enough that it was difficult to see—

—until it wasn't. From outside the portal a light flashed. A light so blinding that he and Quimby had to shield their eyes, even as it caused the others in the room to gasp aloud. The book reader, now but a silhouette bathed in brightness, stood. His sudden movement upset the wineglass, even as his hand instinctively reached for the dagger strapped to his chest. He looked directly into the light, weapon in hand—whereupon the whole image began to shake. The chair toppled, and the table shook—but the man was unmoved. He stared into the light, steadfast and resolute.

And as the light outside abated, the figure's face came fully into view. The bone-crested forehead. The mustache. The iron jaw. And as flames began rising all around, the final feature resolved: an eye patch, riveted into place.

Most present in the room knew at that instant not just his identity, but the moment at which the actuality had been recorded.

He was General Chang—and history had just found him. Praxis had just exploded!

45

La Sirena
Deep Space

In ninety-nine years of alliance, two words had united the Federation and the Klingon Empire in a way that no others had. "General Chang" stood for deception and dishonor, for shame and hate.

He was not the only one who had, in the wake of the Praxis disaster, conspired to keep the Federation and Klingons at odds. Romulan Ambassador Nanclus and Starfleet Admiral Cartwright, among others, had played roles in attempting to prevent a lasting peace. Deceit was rooted in Romulan political culture, and Starfleet officers had been known to defy authority for their own causes. Meanwhile, Chang was seen as having united the worst of all three societies.

He had presented a false face while violating the chain of command—and while challenging a leader for dominance wasn't uncommon in Klingon society, he had let someone else hold the blade and falsely prosecuted others for it. It was the greatest of ironies: had he simply slain Gorkon in combat, he might not have succeeded in revolution—but many Klingons would have accepted the act. Instead, Chang became a man without a people.

Disdain had not stopped countless individuals from being fascinated with him, nearly a century hence—including several audience members at the auction. They rose from their chairs and shouted his name as the actuality finished its cycle, freezing on the final image.

But another name was spoken next, by a dazzled Quimby. "*It's a Parch!*"

It was hard to tell which name caused more of a stir.

"No, no, no," the Trill called out. "Praxis was 2293. That's too late! Parch had left the scene."

"It's only a year after the last known actuality," Quimby replied. She'd written the book on it.

"This is nonsense," the Cardassian gul declared. "There's no record of

Chang having sat for Parch. He was a great warrior—why would he bother with an artist?"

"I don't know," Rios said. "But there it is!"

"It's a forgery, a fake," Toff said. "I'm not bidding on this!"

Sovak caught Rios's eye. The Ferengi had successfully opened it before when it was in Verengan's possession; now, he was agitating for the others to disregard what they had seen. "Yes, it's a fake for sure. Amusing." He looked to Fajo. "I will give ten bars of latinum for it—and that's too much."

Fajo had been silent, still spellbound by the display. Sovak's words broke through. "Why would you pay for a forgery?" Fajo asked.

"To get it out of circulation," the Ferengi said. "And I find fakes interesting."

"You weren't interested in the ruby." Fajo returned to studying the actuality.

Farther back, Arkko expressed her impatience. "What is this damned thing—and who even cares about it?"

Ledger did. She stepped forward, eyes locked on Chang's ephemeral table. She stood there for several seconds before declaring, "I'll be back." She ran out of the room.

They were all up and circling the actuality now, each bidder a silhouette in the low light. "It's Parch's technique," said one.

"But that's impossible," said another.

Looking past the image of Chang, Rios caught sight of Liselle. Her expression was different from the others. It was one of concern, verging on wariness.

Sovak spoke up. "It's a weak effort, I say. Ten bars is the offer."

Rios didn't like it. It was too little to accept in a direct transaction, much less in the current situation, where a portion went to Fajo as the auction organizer. "Xandra, is it real?"

Quimby was on all fours, examining the mechanism with her scanning tool. "It looks like Parch's handiwork—but it could take months to determine."

"You don't have months," Arkko piped in. "And ten bars is small change."

"The offer stands," Sovak said to Fajo. "Take it or leave it."

"Leave it!" Ledger shouted. She burst into the room, carrying the satchel he'd seen her arrive with when she boarded on Argelius II. She asked the holodeck for a table, which materialized next to the actuality. She pulled a large book from the bag and slapped it on the surface. "Lay your peepers on this!"

It took Rios no more than a second to recognize it, once he opened it. It was the wine-stained First Folio, the book of Shakespeare that Javen had showed them.

Liselle recognized it. "That's the duke's book!"

"It's more than that," Quimby said, breaking into the immaterial image from the actuality. She moved the just-created table over such that the real book was right beside the projection. "It's the book Chang is reading!"

Fajo moved, craning his neck. "The stains—they're a perfect match."

Rios saw it too. Chang was reading *Macbeth*—and that's where the stain was. The discolorations were different: the spill in the actuality was fresh, while the injury to the real book was dried and hardened. But their shapes matched.

He faced Ledger. "What are you doing with the book? I thought you were going to—" Remembering Claggett and Liselle were present, he thought better of finishing his sentence. "You didn't tell me," Rios said instead.

"A girl's got to put away something for a rainy day," Ledger replied. "Besides, you didn't tell me about the doodad there."

Toff dismissed even this new evidence. "This is nothing. The book could be fake too—just a prop used in creating the false actuality."

Sovak, who had been speechless since the arrival of the book, agreed. "Yeah. A fake and a fake. Twelve bars for the both of them, and that's too much."

Rios looked to Quimby—and spoke like a first officer. "Options?"

She nodded. "Get your EMH up here. I need to put in a call to my university."

Sovak had not welcomed the pause. But Arkko had endorsed it, and that was all it took to make it happen. While confused by it all, the Convincer boss was canny enough to understand that the wait might yield money.

Rios found the Ferengi between a panic attack and collapse when they conferred briefly away from the crowd still surrounding the actuality. "Why are you talking this thing down?" Rios asked. "You know it's real, don't you?"

Sovak growled. "I will say nothing."

"Don't bother. That book was it, wasn't it? That was the payment for the deliveries you were trying to get from Javen. That unlocks the puzzle's value."

"It's more than—" Sovak began to say, only to strike the side of his lobe with his hand. "I mustn't say." He glared at Rios. "Why didn't you tell me you had it, instead of putting it out in front of everyone?"

"What difference does it make?" To Rios, this seemed the way to realize the most for it. "It's more valuable if others know about it, right?"

"Oh, you fool. You don't understand. The value—"

An interruption, as Quimby called Rios over to the group. "We've got something."

The Wine-Stained Folio—the collectors had already decided on that appellation for it—and its table had been moved off to the side of the actuality, and the lights had been brought up. Emil leaned over it, examining it with a tricorder.

"Definitely fingerprints in the wine," he said. "And I've detected several cells—even what looks like a mustache hair—embedded in the stain," he said. "The Iotian traces are newer, from Ledger; the older Valtese ones, I expect, are from Duke Javen. But the other forensic remains are from contact with a Klingon, perhaps eighty to a hundred twenty years ago."

"I don't believe it," Toff said. "It must have degraded by now."

"There's formalin in bloodwine. It's a fixative for histology. We have some actionable strands here."

"Who has Chang's DNA and prints?" the Cardassian asked. "He was blown to bits over Khitomer. And the Klingons aren't big on keeping records."

"The Federation is," Quimby said. "Spock ordered a variety of items impounded aboard *Enterprise*-A during the murder investigation. Everything from the gravity boots used by Gorkon's assassins to the dishes on which his final meal was served. Starfleet hung on to the investigation records for seventy years, after which they were declassified and filed with Memory Alpha." She handed the padd to Emil. "It helps to have university access."

"Full marks for this," Emil said. He began comparing his sample to the information—and for a minute, no one said anything.

At last, he looked up and gestured to the folio. "General Chang held this book."

The room erupted. If Chang really had the book, chances were the scene in the actuality was authentic. Bidding for the device renewed with a fervor.

"A hundred bars of latinum," said the Trill.

"A hundred ten," Sovak said, his voice shaky.

"Two hundred," the gul responded.

"Five *bricks*," declared Toff, signaling the time for small denominations was past.

"Ten bricks!"

"Ten and a slip," Sovak declared.

"Twenty!"

Fajo had dispelled his holographic auctioneer earlier when the ruby debacle happened; this auction seemed to be running itself. Rios looked from collector to collector, stupefied by the quantities he was hearing. His mind raced to keep up. *What's my percentage again?* Once the bid level was above the outright purchase price of *La Sirena*, he stopped trying to count.

He feared Sovak would collapse from hyperventilation, so frenetically was he trying to outbid everyone. But the fact that he only offered a fraction more each time was a tell, and Arkko asked Ledger to confirm he had no such sum in his declared account. She had the answer in seconds—and the boss ruled. "You're out, jug-ears."

Sovak snarled at her. "What business is it of *yours*?"

Her armed escorts didn't like his tone, and Arkko thumbed to the exit. "Bum's rush, fellas."

Sovak kicked and screamed as the toughs dragged him toward the exit. "I worked for this! You'll regret this!"

Once he was off the holodeck, the bidding began anew. Now it was the Andorian legislator who bumped every offer, and not by fractions. Rios wondered what governmental corruptions could produce such a fortune—but only for a moment.

"Six hundred bricks!"

"Seven hundred!"

"A thousand!" Toff's offer set off a chorus of oohs.

Bewildered, Rios looked at Fajo. The Zibalian said nothing—but his expression suggested his mind was racing. *Whose wouldn't?*

Toff patted his chest. "I expect there will be no other—"

"*Five thousand bricks*," announced a new voice.

All eyes turned to see Liselle.

Rios gawked at her. "*You* want it?"

"*No!*" Outside the holodeck, Sovak—who could see from where he was being held in custody—screamed. "Not you! Not after what you did!"

Arkko's patience was up. She called back, "Pitch him over the railing if you have to—but shut him up!" Then she faced Liselle. "You were saying, Princess?"

"Five thousand." Liselle's face betrayed no emotion; Claggett, still medicated from his injury, looked at her in a daze. "That's my offer," she said. "It's firm—and final."

Toff couldn't believe it. "Who has that sitting around?"

The *marquesa* acknowledged the expense. "That's what we have budgeted for next quarter—enough to repair an entire planet. But Sylvus is good for it."

Ledger didn't get it. "You don't even collect this stuff!"

"I didn't ask your opinion." Liselle approached the actuality. When she lifted the contraption from the floor, the imagery disappeared. "I'll arrange payment as soon as—"

"*Ten thousand bricks!*"

The bid was incredible enough. The bidder was an even greater surprise.

"Fajo," Rios said, "why did you just bid in your own auction?"

"I've decided I want it," he replied.

Liselle had been unflappable—but now Rios saw her jaw drop. "*You* want it?"

"Along with full instructions for opening it." Fajo approached her. "And whatever you offer, my good lady, I will top. I'm willing to bet my enterprise is a little more liquid than yours."

She stared at him—and looked down at the puzzle. She did not stop him when he took it from her hand.

Rios couldn't believe his luck. "You're going to pay me ten thousand bricks—minus your cut for placing it in the auction?"

Fajo shifted his gaze from the puzzle to Rios—and his expression changed. "How do I know," he said slowly, "that this is yours to sell?"

Rios remembered this routine. "It's not stolen. I told you before. It came with the ship."

A wild hoot came from Arkko. "Rios, doll, you say the sweetest things."

"What?" Rios looked searchingly at her—and then glanced at Ledger. Her arms were at her sides—and her eyes told him he'd just made a terrible mistake.

Arkko's gunmen reentered, having disposed of Sovak somewhere. She snapped her fingers, and they flanked her as she strolled toward Fajo. "I'm afraid, Mister Collector, that this is one *hot* actuality."

Fajo studied her. "You don't say."

"This crate was owned by a Klingon. When he bought it, he was in debt to me—same as Rios. Either way, that thingie is mine."

Fajo did not object to her plucking it from his hand. "And what would you want with it?"

"To sell it, of course." Actuality in one hand, she pinched his cheek with the other. "That price—are you good for it?"

A trace of a smile appeared on his face. "We'll need to talk some things over—but I think we can do business."

Rios felt like Sovak, but sober. "Wait. What's happening here? I found the thing!"

"I've never believed in finder's fees," Fajo said.

Arkko smirked. "I'm going to like this guy. Rios, darling, he's shutting you out."

"But I solved the puzzle," Rios said. "You wouldn't even know what was inside without that."

"And I thank you." Fajo pointed to the pages Rios had left on the deck. "I'll pay you something for your notes—but if you don't deal, it doesn't matter. I'll just leave the actuality open. It should reactivate when I place it on the ground." He looked back to Quimby. "Will that work?"

She seemed astonished by all that had transpired. "It should," she said.

"Excellent." Fajo waved the back of his hand to his rivals. "It's been the usual pleasure seeing all of you. Thank you for a lovely weekend—*and get out!*"

46

La Sirena
Deep Space

Drama on the holodeck; chaos outside it.

None of the guests Fajo had so brazenly dismissed wanted to stay a second longer given the presence of the gun-toting Convincers, but *La Sirena* was nowhere near the planned drop-off points for most of the passengers. Worse, buzz from the collector's negotiations inside the auction room suggested that he intended to order the freighter directly back to his facility on Argelius II, dumping the transportation problem onto his guests. Claggett had recovered enough to put in a call to the Sylvus yacht, and Liselle was in the process of offering rides to the fretful passengers.

As captain, Rios knew he should care, but his mind was on other things. "What the hell is this?" he asked Ledger amid the angry throng. "What are we supposed to do now?"

"I don't know," she said, looking through the holodeck door at Arkko and Fajo as they conferred. "If the others here didn't have the money for the dingus, I can't imagine it being worth ten grand to anybody else."

None of it made sense. Neither did the sudden noise aft—a roar, reverberating across the upper deck. He and Ledger looked at each other and said the same words. "*The car!*"

In the next instant, they saw it: the Tucker 48, in gear, squealing into view from the port cargo area. Two of Arkko's gunmen clung desperately to the hood. One was holding on for dear life; the other, trying to raise a pistol. Neither remained on the vehicle for long, as its tires bumped over the raised transporter platform, sending the thugs flying across the deck.

And inside behind the wheel, its driver, visibly beaten and bruised, laughed maniacally as he gunned the engine.

"*Sovak!*" Rios began running aft, even as the automobile bounded off the platform and ground its way into the starboard cargo section. The vehicle made the turn, bouncing off support columns with horrific clangs as it entered the narrowing space.

Rios found he had company as he ran. More of Arkko's hoods behind him—and alongside, Claggett, his chin still swollen. Rios had just reached the spot where Arkko's desk had been left when automatic weapons fire rang out—with the predictable ricochets sending bullets flying wildly. He slid across the slick deck, ending behind the heavy furnishing even as bullets struck it, sending splinters everywhere.

Claggett arrived beside him and was ducking behind the desk when Rios heard the engine roar again—along with new sounds of plastic cracking and pottery shattering. Rios dared a peek over the barrier and witnessed the sedan plowing through Fajo's precious display items, crushing everything underneath.

From one side, automatic weapons fire rang out. What didn't strike the chassis obliterated the back-seat windows; what passed through struck bulkheads and ricocheted back, just as Rios expected they would. Sovak swerved, striking one gunman; a stray bullet struck another.

Hearing a pause in shots, Rios started to stand. "What the hell are you doing?" Claggett shouted. "The Iotians will get him."

"I don't *want* them to get him!"

Rios broke from behind the desk, racing past Convincer toughs hiding behind cover as he charged into the space. Sovak, having reached a cul-de-sac, slammed into the bulkhead—but did not stop, grinding into reverse gear and attempting to turn for another go.

When Sovak barreled forward again, Rios dove in from the side, grabbing hold where the driver-side back-seat window had been. He clambered halfway in—and was nearly brushed off in a close shave with another column.

A hail of bullets struck the vehicle, destroying the windshield and nearly taking Sovak's head off. Sickening thuds followed, ending the shooting—and another jarring impact came when the Tucker slammed into Arkko's replicated oak desk. It caromed forward, half broken, knocking Claggett for another loop.

The collision halted the car's progress, but did not disable it: unlike many vehicles of its day, the Tucker's engine was in the back.

Rios used the pause to pull out from the rear side window and reach into the open driver's window. Inside, Sovak, bloodied from the spray of glass—if not something else—struggled with the unfamiliar controls. Rios grabbed at his shirt. "Stop!"

"Never!"

Given the car's heavy structural damage and a couple of blown-out tires, Rios had hoped its journey was done—but the car had more life in it as Sovak found the right gear. He backed off the bulkhead long enough to reorient the vehicle. Then it was into drive and off again, with Rios hanging on outside.

Bullets scattered and so did *La Sirena*'s passengers, diving for cover wherever they could find it. Frightened faces went past as Rios hung on with one hand and clutched ineffectually through the window with the other. But there was only one person Sovak cared about.

"This is for you, Hain!" Rios heard Sovak shout. He looked forward to see Liselle standing in the vehicle's way, just meters ahead, trying to assist one of the terrified Miradorns. Rios sacrificed his hold on the doorframe to lay both hands on the wheel, swerving the vehicle away from the *marquesa* and toward the railing overlooking the galley deck.

He released and fell away just as the machine struck the barrier. The structure that had saved him during the ball-bearing storm surrendered immediately to the automotive attack. Rios hit the upper deck and rolled, his scrambled senses reorienting in time for him to see the vehicle vanish into the pit below. The impact felt like a photon torpedo had gone off.

In the galley.

Ledger reached him first. "You okay?" she asked—or so he thought. His ears were ringing too loud.

Eschewing help, he crawled to the ledge and looked down. The car had met its Waterloo in the form of the forward bulkhead in the canteen—and had slammed to the deck, demolishing the mess table in the process. It was not on fire, that he could tell, but plenty of smoke was coming from somewhere. And there was no sign of movement from Sovak.

Rios stood. As he staggered wobbly around, his eyes would land on a face, and someone would say something—and then he would see somebody else.

Arkko, berating her goons, even as they sought to look after those whom Sovak had injured. Baron Toff, tearfully describing the experience as being akin to fighting a war, despite all present knowing he'd seen no conflict that didn't involve a chef. Quimby, looking at Rios with concern even as she helped Ny-Var deal with Zo-Var's panic attack. Ledger, frantically trying to assuage a still-more frenetic Fajo as he assessed the destruction of his collection.

And Liselle, who simply walked up, nodded gently to him, and stepped back to assist others.

Rios's comm unit chirped, relaying an incoming call that no one was at the bridge to take. "Not now, Raffi," he said, cutting the call before his friend could say a word.

She'll never believe this one, he thought. And as he prepared to summon Emil, he knew the hologram would never believe it either.

47

La Sirena
Deep Space

In fact, Emil was already on the scene—the auto crash site being just forward from the lab. The medical hologram's emitters were among the few features undamaged by the fracas, and he was able to get in close enough to determine that Sovak could not be extracted from the wreck except by transporter. Rios had handled that operation, sending the Ferengi to the very sickbay where his late brother was interred.

The horrific nature of the crash had, ironically, saved Sovak's life, since Arkko's hoodlums had initially assumed him dead. Learning that he was only critically injured seemed to satisfy their need to retaliate, as it wasn't a targeted takeout of their boss. Indeed, the Convincers had no idea who he was or why he'd snapped. Arkko had simply figured it was in retribution for being manhandled by her people—in which case, Sovak's wild ride was deserving of some respect. "I like a guy who won't just take the bounce."

For Liselle, the *why* of the attack was a much more pressing question. While looking in on Emil as he ministered to an unconscious Sovak, she and Rios had their first civil conversation in months. The *marquesa* barely remembered Sovak, who had apparently visited *Sylvus Bestri* once with Hain before Verengan's fertilizer deliveries began.

"Sovak seriously believed we poisoned his brother?" She seemed wounded by the concept—and by her next question. "You thought this too?"

"I didn't want to," Rios said, "but we haven't found any other answers." Emil was too busy with Sovak to provide many details, so Rios opened the drawer containing Hain's preserved body.

He regretted doing so immediately. Momentarily in his mind he'd thought it would be a test, to provoke her reaction. But her gasp and expression of horror seemed completely normal, and her tears that followed made him feel like a heel. "I assure you, Cristóbal, we did nothing but try to help him."

He closed the drawer quickly. Rios wanted very much to believe her.

But, he explained, that wasn't Sovak's only trigger. He brought up again the bargain that Hain and Javen had made. "Their deal was for that book," he said, gesturing to the Shakespeare folio she had brought downstairs with her. "That's what the duke reneged on."

On this, Liselle fully agreed, explaining that she'd spoken with her uncle about the matter since *La Sirena*'s abrupt departure. "The book came into his possession years earlier—he'd changed his mind about parting with it. His moods are . . . unpredictable."

"I gathered. Do you know where he got the book? How did it get from General Chang to him?"

"Many things he has are castoffs—and a century is a long time." She handed Rios the volume. "The damage is done. The book is rightfully Sovak's. The duke may protest—but we pay our debts."

Rios took the book, a little surprised. "I'll let Sovak have it when he comes to, but it's clear he only wanted it to verify the actuality." He peered at her. "Why did *you* bid for it?"

"I expected my uncle would be interested, were he here."

It seemed to Rios she'd offered quite a price for an impulse buy. And there was something else: "It doesn't really fit into his Museum of Broken Things."

"If you'll recall, the destruction of Praxis is what set my uncle to create the Sylvus Project," the *marquesa* said, clasping her hands. "So, in a way, that device depicted the birth of our entire effort." She looked to the overhead. "Fajo's interest was quite surprising, to say the least."

"It sure shocked the hell out of me."

She studied him. "Do you know what he wants with it?"

"Having it all. With humiliating his rivals a close second." Rios looked down at the folio. "I'm afraid I can't get back all the other books we took." He exhaled. "I mean, stole."

"And that's between you and us," Liselle said. "But we can take that up at another time."

"Are you saying Claggett will call off his dogs?"

"I'm saying I will call off all your pursuers—understanding you cannot make it right at this time. The debt will not be forgiven," she added, "but I can get my uncle to wait."

Rios thanked her. It took a good diplomat to operate in all the places Sylvus did; he'd just seen that in action.

She checked the time; *La Sirena* was to reach her yacht early in the morning. She took another look at Emil, still working on the Ferengi. "Argelius is some ways off. If it makes a difference, we could take Sovak to a medical facility."

"He wouldn't want to go with you. And I don't think Fajo's guests would want Sovak sharing their ride—not now."

"You're probably correct." She straightened. "I should retire. It has been a long day." After a brief pause, she offered her hand.

Following some thought, he decided to shake it rather than kiss it. Some chivalries didn't feel right in a surgical setting.

Liselle was still holding his hand when she heard a pounding in the drawer below the one where Hain's corpse was kept. She nearly leaped. "What's that?"

It took Rios a moment to remember. "Oh, that's just one of Arkko's thugs. It's cool in there—he'll keep."

Before the transporter platform, Rios found that his temporary imprisonment of Stench and the injuries to several of her goons had not bothered Boss Arkko a bit. She'd beamed them all over to *Velvet Glove*, pausing only to lament over her destroyed desk.

But only for a moment. In what Rios imagined was a hundred fifty years or so of Arkko's life, the sale of *his* actuality had to be her biggest score—and in her good humor she spared him a little largesse.

Very little, Rios thought. "You're giving me an extra week to make my payment this month?"

"I know you've been busy." She patted him on the cheek. "Take two weeks. I'm in a good mood."

Her deal with Fajo was so immense it was going to take some time to unwind, she explained—and before it could even start, *La Sirena* had to get Fajo back to Argelius II.

"What about me?" called a voice from behind.

Arkko turned and saw Ledger standing, clutching a large bundle close to her chest. "What *about* you?" the boss snapped. "Your job was to manage Rios. He's still in hock."

"Yeah, but I thought with this score I could—I don't know, move back up."

"I don't see you having anything to do with it." Arkko pointed to Ledger with malice. "And don't think I forgot all your side deals, missy. You'll keep hoofing until I tell you to stop."

Rios braced for a trademark Ledger retort—but it didn't come. Instead, she looked down at the bundle in her hands.

Arkko followed her gaze. "What's that? Show me what you have."

Ledger unwrapped the copy of *New York Mobs of the Thirties*. "Have you seen one of these before?"

Arkko took it and laughed. "Found one, did you?"

"You knew it existed?"

"Came across one a few years after I cut loose from Oxmyx." Arkko casually flipped through the large volume. She caught Ledger's expression as she did. "Shook you up, huh?"

Ledger nodded. "Some."

"There was a legend among the molls—said it was a woman who razored the rough part of the Chicago book out, back at the start. She's kind of the patron saint." Arkko paused to read a passage to herself. "Yeah, I remember this stuff. Hard to forget. Rotten bums, the lot of them."

"If you know that," Rios said, "why do you keep on with the whole mobster act?" He looked over to her young men-in-waiting, standing at attention. "And it seems like you treat these guys in ways you didn't want to be treated."

Arkko turned to face him. "One answer for both, pretty boy. The other lessons from the Book that are still good, and still hold." She called over her shoulder to Ledger. "Tell me the first commandment."

She recited, "*Do unto them before they do to you.*"

"Bingo." The old woman planted a kiss on the side of Rios's cheek and stepped onto the platform. "Let's go, boys. I can't wait until the other gangs hear about this!"

Late that evening, Rios sat in his quarters finishing his instructions to open the puzzle. He'd been forced to do some of it using his old notes and from memory, as the device itself was in Fajo's chambers, and he expected it would remain there until *La Sirena* reached Argelius II. He'd avoided talking to Fajo, who was still unhappy about the fracas despite winning the actuality. Rios was no cheerier. Selling the instructions was a consolation prize, and he was in no hurry to finish.

When his door chimed, he called out, "I'm not done yet!"

A second chime got him up. *At least they're not breaking in,* he thought as he went to the door.

It was Quimby. Seeing his face, she hugged him—allowing the door to close behind her. "Hell of a day," Rios said as they broke.

She saw the notes he was working on. "I've come up with the name for the actuality," she said. "*Chang at the False Dawn*. What do you think?"

He glanced at his shelf. "You'll probably get a whole extra volume for your series out of it." He looked back to her. The discovery was a big thing for Quimby, he knew. "I'm guessing he'll keep you busy studying it."

A little shrug. "Sometimes people guess wrong."

His brow furrowed. "What?"

"No use putting it off," she said, pacing away from him. "I'm leaving in the morning on the Sylvus yacht."

Rios gawked. "Why? Fajo had you doing research at his place on Argelius. I thought you were staying aboard until he left."

She ran her fingers across his bookshelves. "I just had my own conversation with him. He's going to Argelius now to start the financing, but he doesn't think it's secure enough for the actuality. He plans to do the study of it on Theta Zibal III. But I don't like what I've heard of that place. Bonnalo, one of my academic rivals, says it's a fortress."

"I saw. But I can't imagine you'd give up a chance to study it—if it *is* the last Parch actuality."

She paused to contemplate. "It could be the study of a lifetime, I'll grant you. But mere mortals only have so much time." It was the first instance in which she'd come close to acknowledging her age.

"So you're going back to Iraatan? To the university?"

"Fajo covered that, as well. Since I'm not going—and since he owes Arkko enough latinum bricks to build a house—he's not going to be able to fund my chair anymore."

Rios scowled. "Bastard."

"Eh." She extended her hands in a show of indifference. "I was never in the office anyway."

He didn't understand her reaction—but didn't like the notion of her being cut off, just like he had been from Starfleet. "There might be a place for you—well, somewhere else."

Quimby chuckled. "You mean here?"

"I didn't say that."

She watched him. "No, you didn't." She shook her head. "I've traveled more than you can imagine, Cris. I'm done for a while."

"But if not the university—"

"I'll find someplace. I have a few ideas."

"You sure?"

"Cris—*mi amor*—of course I'm sure." She glanced again at his shelves. "Look at what you're reading. *The Concept of Dread. Fear and Trembling. Sickness unto Death.* And that's just the Kierkegaard." She turned to face him. "Cheery, it's not."

"It sure isn't."

"It's also not the shelf of someone who wants company every night."

Rios shrugged. "I could take or leave that stuff. The books were here, so I read them. It was a change from drinking myself to sleep."

"I don't want to be anyone's sobriety program either." She walked over to him. "Come on, Cris. It was fun—but we've both got important things to do."

"I look like I have important things to do?"

Her eyes went to the overhead. "I think you have a *lot* to do." But she did not clue him in. Instead, she gave him one last embrace.

"Do you want to stay—you know, just tonight?"

She didn't look into his eyes. "Cris, nothing against last night—it was wonderful. But do you really think it's a good idea?"

He stared at the Starfleet trunk behind her and exhaled. "I haven't known what to think in a long time."

"Then figure that out." She touched his cheek and smiled gently. "You see? You've found something important to do already."

The doors closed behind her as she left.

48

La Sirena
Argelius II

The freighter that landed on Argelius II was quieter, but hardly any cleaner. Verengan had strewn around the junk of a lifetime. In five intense minutes, a much higher class of garbage had been spread everywhere across the upper deck—and the galley still had a bludgeoned car leaking fluids everywhere. Rios and Glake had only gotten as far as draining the gasoline when the journey ended.

He'd then made a quick check on Sovak, whose body had been immobilized by Emil in order to facilitate healing. The pain medication had prevented him from having any conversations longer than a few seconds, but that was enough for the Ferengi to make clear that he had no intention of returning home. He had striven his whole career to escape the agrarian life Hain had embraced; the events of the festival had cost everything that had kept him independent, and then some.

Rios found Fajo upstairs, conferring with Ledger. His baggage had already been transported off *La Sirena*; only he and the actuality remained. The puzzle was a golden apple again; Rios had provided his full instructions, and Fajo had worked the solution several times.

Ledger stepped away when she saw Rios approach. The look she shot him was discomfiting; she appeared to know something he didn't. Rios didn't want to wait any longer in wonder. "Guess it's time to settle up," he said.

"If you insist," Fajo replied, ice in his voice.

Rios looked back to Ledger. "You have the bill?"

"Let me sidestep any awkwardness," Fajo said. "You were to receive a portion of my auction sales." He gestured to the debris. "But as you can see, all my merchandise was destroyed."

"By one of your guests," Rios countered.

"Due to *your* lax security." Fajo gestured to Ledger. "What does the contract say about indemnity?"

She looked to the overhead. "It's on us."

"It's on you."

Rios had mostly expected that.

Fajo held up the puzzle. "This item, as we've established, was offered by you, but really belonged to Arkko. And while you were to receive a percentage on items guests purchased in the auction, the contract specifically excluded any items I might buy myself. That leaves us with the instructions, which I have already committed to memory."

Rios frowned. "You're not saying—"

"Relax. You have saved me a certain amount of time, and it would be gauche to deny that." He placed the apple in his pocket and looked about. "In exchange for your information, I won't seek compensation for these collectibles. In fact, you can keep the debris—the car included."

"This junk? Everything's shredded. What use is it?"

"You didn't mind selling me useless garbage—for which, I should say, I paid you more than anyone would have." Fajo kicked at a broken piece of pottery. "Maybe you can go talk to Duke Javen. Damaged goods are his specialty."

"You know we can't do that."

Fajo laughed. "I wasn't serious. This dreck would even be beneath his ridiculous standards."

Disbelieving, Rios turned back to Ledger. Her expression said it all. It was a mess, for sure.

"What about other work?" Rios asked. "You'd talked about routes—"

Fajo laughed loudly. "Captain, when I said I believed in second chances—I meant for *me*." He fished in his other pocket. "Here," he said, pitching a handful of strips of gold-pressed latinum into the trash on the deck. "A tip, to encourage you to clean this place up."

Rios wanted to bash the Zibalian's face—but he held back.

Fajo glanced at the transporter platform. "I'll use the ramp, if you don't mind."

"I'll see you out," Ledger said, beginning to follow. She stopped by Rios first and spoke into his ear. "I'll think of something."

Rios watched her depart—and then stood for a moment, surveying the mess.

"Broom," he requested, and one appeared in his hand. He looked at it for a moment before casting it, too, onto the deck.

He was on his hands and knees, fishing for the latinum—a mix of strips and smaller slips—when he noticed the approach of his flight crew, luggage in hand. "Now what?" he said, looking up.

"I'm afraid we must go," Ny-Var responded.

"Go where?"

"We're going home," Zo-Var said, more audible than he'd ever heard from her. "We need to go home."

Rios stood up, latinum still cupped in his hands. "What is it?"

Ny-Var put a comforting hand on Zo-Var's arm. "You know we both suffered the loss of our siblings. For a Miradorn, such relationships can never be replaced." She looked to her partner. "We have come to rely on each other's company—and neither of us could bear another loss."

"Your life is just too dangerous," Zo-Var said.

He understood fully. From torpedo near misses to wayward automobiles, they'd seen too much. He passed them the handful of latinum strips. "Back pay," he said.

The women brightened, placing the currency in their bags.

"And I'll fly you to Miradorn. No need to go commercial."

Zo-Var smiled weakly at him. "You mustn't do that, Captain. It is far, and you have to earn. Do what is in your interests."

He believed she meant that—but he also sensed their fear of traveling with him was part of it as well.

As ever, exit interviews were not his forte. "You've been nice to have around—and you've gotten better at the job." He offered his hand. "Thanks for hanging in there."

They both put their hands on his. "Thank you," Ny-Var said. "We hope that you, too, find what makes you whole."

He watched as they beamed away—and stood for a moment afterward. He looked over his shoulder to Glake. "You're sticking around?"

"*Yeeessss.*"

Well, there's that. So often, Rios had wanted to be left alone—especially at times during Fajo's event. If he was going to be left with an empty house after a big party, however, it helped to have a strong back around to help with cleanup.

Rios walked forward and looked down over the nonexistent railing to the demolished car. Above, he could hear and see rain pounding the forward ports. Whatever Argelius's wet season was, he'd landed in it. Ledger underscored that when she returned upstairs, completely drenched. "You didn't go out in that?" he asked.

"This was just walking him from under the ship's canopy to his transport." She shook water from her hat. "Thirty seconds, and more than Verex III sees in a year."

Rios wondered why Fajo didn't just beam out—but then a guy who'd just offered ten thousand in bricks probably needed time to think over what to say to his stockholders, if any. He gestured to the vacant bridge. "Did they tell you?"

"Yeah, I spoke to them in my office." Ledger wrung droplets from her hair. "They were good eggs. Never caused any trouble, and the price was right."

"So it's just us and Glake." He looked back to the deck, shaking his head at the mess. "I don't know how we're going to do this."

"Chin up," Ledger replied. "Anything is possible—when you've got the right contact list." She thought of something. "But while we're talking cleanup . . ."

Rios watched her step forward. On the bridge, she picked up something from behind the captain's chair. "I found this little item this morning." She displayed an empty bottle. "You've been leaving these behind after night watch. I thought you were off the sauce."

"It's just been a bad week. Hell, you lived through it. There are times when reading philosophy doesn't answer."

An alert sounded, indicating a hail. "You want to answer something, answer that." She started walking to her quarters. She called over her shoulder, "If it's a job, take it."

"Fine. You dry off."

"You dry out!" The door closed behind her.

Rios stared. He thought he'd caught a glimpse of a grin from her when she called back—and he noticed he had one as well. Maybe they were turning a corner.

Again, the alert. He answered. "Rios."

"Don't you dare cut me off!"

He blinked. "Raffi?"

"I've been trying to reach you for days."

"Sorry about that. Fajo—the guy I've been telling you about, from Picard's book—screwed me over pretty badly."

"I'm sorry."

"Yeah, I wish I'd known more about him going in. What's the big crisis?"

"Someone's been trying to get in touch with you."

He vaguely remembered her mentioning that. "Who?"

Raffi wouldn't say. *"It would be good for you to meet."*

"What, is it business?" The job that Ledger had hoped for would come in handy about now, and he wouldn't argue about where it came from.

"It's better if I don't explain." Then, after a pause: *"Cris, it would . . . mean something to me if you went."*

"I don't get the mystery."

"You will. I told you I didn't want anything for the ship's down payment. I'd like it if you'd give me this." He could hear her voice quaking. *"Go."*

She must be having a bad time, he thought. "Okay, sure, Raffi. Just give me the when and where."

"You're wonderful."

"Yeah, well, I owe you." *And damn near everyone else.*

49

NELPHIA PREFECTURE
ARGELIUS II

With *La Sirena* in no shape to make a good first impression, Rios had suggested a quiet-looking bar he'd seen on the outskirts of Massworks' executive plaza. He'd transported himself over; he knew he'd probably be walking back in the rain, but at least it wouldn't be too far.

He waited at a corner table, no drink in hand in case it was someone official. Even in her reduced state, Raffi knew everybody, and while he doubted any miracle worker could straighten things out with him and Massworks or Cynosure, there were other prospective clients out there.

Rios stood when he saw a human woman enter, her back to him as she dried off.

Then she turned—and he nearly fell back down.

Marta?

"Cristóbal!" Marta Batanides crossed the room to him. "I can't believe it!"

He couldn't either. He straightened, snapping to attention—only to have the older woman laugh and offer a hug.

He didn't seem to know what to do with it. "Good to see you, Admiral."

"It's Marta to you," she said. "Where have you been? I've been looking everywhere!"

There was nobody in Starfleet that Commander Rios had looked up to more than Captain Vandemeer; there was nobody Vandemeer looked up to as much as Marta Batanides, his former captain and mentor. She had been a classmate of no less a figure than Jean-Luc Picard, and if her career had not encompassed as many adventures, it was far from undistinguished.

Seeing her in civilian dress was jarring for him; realizing that she was *talking* to him was something else.

"It's so amazing seeing you again." Seated across the table from him, she gestured broadly, her eyes alive with delight. "I never would have found you if I hadn't touched base with Raffi."

"Yeah, Raffi." He nodded. "She's something."

"She was a huge help. I couldn't find you in Starfleet's records at all." Marta lowered her voice. "Have you been doing something secret?"

Rios's mouth hung open. When he closed it, he raised his hand. "Waiter? Drinks for me and my friend."

The Argelian bowed. "What'll it be?"

"I really don't care."

Minutes passed, as Rios struggled from one part of an explanation to the next. Each one was an alphabet soup of words, but the gist was always simple:

No, I'm not doing something for Starfleet Intelligence.

Yes, I am a tramp freighter pilot.

No, it wasn't something I ever talked about doing.

Yes, it was an abrupt decision.

No, I haven't seen any of our old friends.

Yes, have you seen the waiter?

Drinks arrived—followed by another round, and another. He thought he had a reprieve when he got her chatting about her own life, but there was not much of interest there. She was on leave from a stint on the engineering vessel *U.S.S. Galadjian*, overseeing tests of new shield systems for nebular travel. But past talk of that, and of her family, she returned to a single north star: his life, and what had happened to it.

"You had so much promise, Cris. You could have made captain in Starfleet if you waited. Were you really in such a hurry?"

"I was in a hurry, yes." He took a drink. "My ship now is fast. Very fast."

Attempts to steer her elsewhere were never successful for long. He described his problems with Fajo; she sympathized, but admitted not knowing anything about the collector. If Fajo's time had been served, she said, it would be hard even for her to learn more about the act that put him away. He mentioned having gotten entangled with Iotians; she despaired of how Starfleet's posture in the area had ignored law and order.

He had even mentioned having read Picard's book. She said she hadn't read it, but added that Starfleet had made a mistake in letting him go. For that matter, Rios should be in Starfleet himself, and she really hoped there was no misunderstanding that had resulted in him living on the fringe.

Another hour, another round. Marta had stopped drinking, but not asking. Rios had stopped answering, but not drinking. She kept coming back to revisit one theory after another for his predicament. Intel work resurfaced again and again; *ibn Majid* had been erased from the records and no one spoke of it, including his former crewmates. Starfleet would never make a starship disappear from the records, she said—but clearly here it had.

She worked him as he'd worked the golden apple, trying to get the puzzle to open, to see the actuality. And Rios snapped back shut each time, resetting to his initial position.

"*I wanted to see the galaxy on my own terms.*"

As admiral, Marta had run several courts-martial. This was no interrogation under oath; she clearly asked her questions from care. But also from a wounded heart of her own; her protégé Vandemeer's reported suicide had shocked her to the core, and she wanted to put it straight in her mind.

And before long, he began putting into words in his own mind things he had locked away, tight in the trunk in his quarters on *La Sirena*.

"Cris, things were going so well for both of you in '89. What happened?"

The Vayt Sector happened. We got called in to do a first contact.

"Alonzo was skilled at so many things. You should have seen him light up when we discovered something new."

He did. We did. Two aliens came aboard. They looked human—but also amazing. Different, special.

"Nobody who met Alonzo forgot him. And I never knew anyone with a better memory for names."

Jana and Beautiful Flower. Strange names—I wondered if they were in some kind of holy order.

"Everybody loved Alonzo."

He talked to them for a while—fed them dinner.

Then he took out a phaser and shot them both.

On his own ship.

"I haven't shared this with anyone, but I was considering putting his name forward for a bump to admiral."

I never yelled at the old man like that before. I used to call him "Pops."

He knew it was wrong, but said there was a reason.

A "black flag directive."

"He would have made a great admiral. I could almost see him as C-in-C one day."

I said I'd never heard of a directive like that. That Starfleet would never give him such a command. He looked scared to death.

"Were you there when it happened?"

I was there when it happened.

He put the phaser in his mouth and fired.

I was there when it happened.

Hours and countless empty glasses in, he melted. He could not, of course, tell of how he had been ordered to cover it up, to beam the alien bodies into space. Nor could he explain that *ibn Majid*'s disappearance from all records was another part of that cover-up, and that his acceptance of discharge six months later under a diagnosis of post-traumatic dysphoria was the only way he could save the careers—and maybe the lives—of his fellow officers.

No, what came from him instead were tears and a smattering of unconnected words that only served to confuse the admiral more. She had suspended her questioning well before then, seeing its impact on him. The hour before closing time he spent with his head against the table, her hand resting gently on his hair.

The cold night rain was slackening as she walked him back to the landing pads, but it was some time before he could tell her which freighter was his. When they found *La Sirena*, Marta gazed up at it. "She's beautiful, Cris."

"Just . . . saying that," he mumbled. He'd staggered most of the way on her shoulder, drunker than he'd ever been in his life.

They stopped beneath the shelter of the dripping fuselage, and Rios somehow managed to trigger the landing ramp to descend. Exterior lights shone down on him, momentarily blinding him.

With thunder rolling outside, the admiral embraced him again—this time, more the hug of a mother than a friend. "Cris, I should never have come. I'm so sorry."

He opened his eyes—and saw Ledger at the top of the ramp looking down on the two of them. There was no trace of emotion on her face, and she quickly disappeared back inside.

"Who's that?" Marta asked.

"Nobody."

"Hopefully someone that can help." Marta released him. "I came here tonight because I missed Alonzo. I can tell you do, maybe more than me. I should have left well enough alone."

"Well enough," Rios muttered.

She helped him up the ramp until he began walking on his own. "If you need anything—*anything*—call me."

He didn't respond.

The admiral exited his world, as quickly as she had reentered it.

50

LA SIRENA

ARGELIUS II

It rained all night and into the next day and evening. More than a day could have passed without Rios knowing it; he spent the entire time in the captain's chair, except for occasional runs to hit the head—when he remembered in time.

He seemed to recall summoning something to eat, only to grow irate when Mr. Hospitality brought it to him. He didn't need some damned peppy clone around when the concierge system would serve him without giving him any lip.

Rios's only other interaction had been with another plague: the medical hologram. Emil had materialized on deck for a progress report about Sovak—or, rather, a lack-of-progress report. He'd repaired much of the damage to the Ferengi's body, but several of his systems had been slow to recover. It seemed like a familiar failure to Rios.

He had tolerated the exchange—a one-way exposition, really—until Emil said something about Sovak needing to recover the will to live. Rios had snapped then, snarling that a hologram had no conception of what a "will to live" even meant, and had demanded something for his headache. When the EMH expressed concern for Rios's well-being, he dispelled the hologram with orders not to return to the bridge.

Waking from a nap soon after nightfall, Rios called up a bottle of aguardiente—he had to say the name four times for the system to recognize it for some reason—and began to wander the deck. Exercise was an important part of shipboard existence, and he had been disregarding his regimen for a couple of years or so.

The stairs to the galley deck he saw as a dare, and he navigated about half of them successfully. The other ones he saw while tumbling. But he felt no impact and managed to hang on to the bottle, losing only half its contents, and that felt like an accomplishment.

A cool draft whirled past him, and he followed it. The landing ramp was down, and at the bottom of it Ledger was visible, standing in the spotlight beneath the shelter of the ship. She wore a wide-brimmed hat and a tan raincoat as she operated her comm unit—and at her side was a suitcase and umbrella.

He negotiated the ramp only barely, and with great care, to arrive beside her on the tarmac. He announced his presence with a belch.

"Going out again?" she asked, not looking at him. "I haven't seen your latest chippie, but if I do I'll let you know."

"That was just a friend."

"Sure she was. If they get any older, you might as well sign up with Arkko."

He decided to let that go by. "Are *you* going someplace?"

"As a matter of fact, I am." She put away the comm unit. "While you were blotto this afternoon, I talked with Fajo again. He needs an intermediary with the Convincers while he's paying for the actuality—and Arkko gave him the right to select one. He's offered me the job."

Lightning flashed beyond *La Sirena*, and thunder rang out.

"Arkko isn't thrilled about his choice," she continued, "but this is the biggest deal the gang has ever known, and if anyone can ride herd on the numbers, it's me."

Rios took a step back—only to be pelted by runoff from part of the fuselage. He retreated to cover.

His head hurt. He wiped his face and tried to focus. "Did you say you're leaving?"

"You don't miss anything. I've already transported over my other things."

"You can't leave me."

"This should be rich. Why not?"

"You're in love with me. It's why you came back." He staggered toward her. "It's why you brought back the book. You know, the Shakeshear Polio." He put his hand behind her back and tried to draw her to him. "I love you."

"Ugh!" she said, pulling away. "*Bank's closed, pal!*"

"What are you talking about?"

"You!" She dusted herself off, as if trying to dislodge mites. "The last thing I need is a drunken gigolo who goes for a hayride with every princess and professor that comes along."

"You're just saying that."

"The devil I am. Believe me, fancier gents than you have tried. Beaus with class, real class. You look like someone I'd scrape off my shoe."

Rios clenched his eyes closed. When he opened them, he looked at her anew. She was beautiful, he realized—a tower of competence and defiance, as she always had been. And now she had turned her guns on him.

He threw the bottle. It smashed against the pavement just as more thunder sounded. "It's Fajo, is that it? You and him." He glared at her. "Fajo screwed me over. And now you're going to be his girl on the desk, just like that boss of—"

Ledger slapped him.

He stared at her for a moment—before casting his eyes to his feet.

As he sagged, she straightened. "You just don't get it." She started putting on her gloves. "I'm not who I want to be yet—and I can't get there alone. But I'm only working with people I choose. *Successful* people, people I believe in. You don't even believe in yourself."

"Why should I?" He looked up at her, eyes red. "Ask anyone. I ruined their lives." He went through the litany. "Yerm's broken. Hain's dead. Now Sovak's a mess." He took a deep breath. "And my crew. My old crew . . ."

She stared at him. In the rain, a black hover vehicle with a Cynosure logo approached.

After a few moments, she spoke quietly. "I don't know what happened to you, Cris. I just know you can't fix what happened. You can only fix what's *going* to happen."

Rios chortled. "That's my Ledger. The mob fixer."

She opened the umbrella. "So long, Captain. You won't see me again." She took her suitcase and walked to the limo.

☿ ♃ ♂ ♄ ♀

—2392—

THE EARTH IN THE WINDOW

*In which **Cristóbal Rios** goes to ground—*
and hits paydirt

51

La Sirena
Deep Space

In the weeks that followed Fajo's disastrous festival, Rios began to understand that his status had changed yet again. The best example came on Draken when, after he completed a delivery, he ran into Seejee's Core Breaches outside a supply shop.

Words were exchanged, whereupon it became clear he had humiliated these particular "Britches" during an escape months before in a manner that they both remembered and minded. They had beaten him mercilessly in the brawl that erupted, leaving him bleeding in the street when their mistress intervened.

"There's no price on your head," Seejee had explained. "They're just pissed at you."

"You mean they're pummeling me in their spare time?"

"You got it, love. But that's it. Terrible thing when nobody cares enough about you to want to pay to kill you!"

It was the way of his life now. He was in demand by no one, again. No past clients had inquired after his cargo services—and leads were thin. He had even spoken to Raffi less.

That, however, was his choice, as he was still smarting over the Marta ambush. He had never said anything to Raffi about that night, just adding to the mountain of things she had no answers about. One more mystery wasn't going to matter. Eventually she stopped asking, and that suggested to him that the admiral had told her to lay off.

So Rios had kept their conversations short and about the laments of the day—along with sizable helpings of complaint over Fajo's betrayal and unease over Ledger's defection.

"I didn't think you and she were an item," Raffi had said. *"Or even friends."*

"She was just a good business manager."

"I didn't think she was with you that long."

That didn't matter. While she'd been around, he'd been a little more organized. Now, she was organizing for Fajo—and doing a monumental job of it. He'd heard that from Wolyx, whom the Convincers had retasked to keep tabs on their debtors. The gigantic cost of *Chang at the False Dawn* was such that Fajo had been forced to find ways to bring the Convincers into his own operations; now the criminal gang and the salvage firm functioned almost as partners. Fajo fenced for them, they stole for him. Rivers of latinum were flowing. Ledger had finally gotten the break she was looking for.

She had not contacted him since her departure. She was never coming back, and he needed a good manager now more than ever. The fact that he and Glake, his only remaining crewmember, had scraped enough trade together to make Arkko's payments to date was nothing short of a miracle.

Responsible for part of that result: since his setback on Argelius II, he'd mostly stayed out of bars. Then there was the reality that many of his off-hours had, by necessity, gone into getting the crushed automobile out of his galley.

Eschewing his philosophy books, Rios had obtained some ancient automotive manuals. With them as a guide and Glake's help on the heavier stuff, he'd nightly dissected the vehicle, one component at a time. Bit by bit, the wreckage had migrated to the aft lower hold, where he was piecing the vehicle back together, replicating replacement parts when necessary. In a way, it was a shaken fist at Fajo, who had left him nothing but garbage. Rios would make something out of it yet.

The auto model had never officially been called a Torpedo, but it often felt like he was working on one, connecting lines and tightening panels. This was more akin to his reading habits of old: learning to do something useful, even if the product itself had little purpose anymore. It was the reverse of reading philosophy, where much useless had been written about matters important.

Nothing aboard *La Sirena* had been of as little use, however, as Sovak. He had recovered from his injuries enough to allow him to wander around the freighter, muttering daftly to himself about Fajo, Duke Javen, Liselle, and cruel fate in general. He had nowhere to go, and no skills of use to a shipping concern.

And worse—he was sick. Emil had noticed several issues hindering Sovak's progress following his initial operations; the longer he stayed on *La*

Sirena, the weaker he seemed to get. This time when the hologram spoke about the will to live, Rios didn't argue.

"It is time to face facts," Emil said as Rios worked to dislodge a jammed hubcap. "Sovak is past my ability to heal."

Same old song, Rios thought. "What's wrong now?"

"His vital signs continue to decline. I think it is a matter of days—two, perhaps three—before he'll be bedridden again."

"And then he's in a bunk beneath his brother."

"I would not use that phrasing, but it seems likely." Emil shook his head. "I still have located no reason—"

Rios waved him off. He'd heard it before, and daily. With a heave, he freed the hubcap. Bent and scratched, it would have to be completely replaced. "What do you want to do?" he asked.

"We took Yerm to the IME center on Benzar because Benzite behavioral addiction was outside my capabilities to address. The organization has sent all the data on Ferengi biology I've requested, but I think their medical skills are what is needed most."

"That's fine." Rios put the hubcap down and wiped his hands with a rag. "We'll go now."

The quickness of his assent appeared to surprise Emil. "Just like that?"

"Just like that. I don't have anything better to do—and we owe the guy." It had the further benefit of being one debt Rios could actually make good on.

Hubcap again in hand, he ascended the finally cleared stairs to the bridge and set a course for Benzar. Glake, whom he'd been trying out at helm, had no objection to the course change; indeed, his monosyllabic response had a little more lilt than usual.

"Oh, I got the last one loose," Rios said, displaying the battered silver bowl. "Looks like we'll need to replicate a new one. No surprise there."

Rios didn't understand why, but Fajo had made a big deal out of vehicle collectors wanting "original equipment" when possible. Rios didn't think there was any chance of finding a market for a refurbished car any more than Sovak would find buyers for the Wine-Stained Folio. But if he was going to pretend to have a hobby, he might as well adhere to its conventions.

Rios walked aft, only to pause before the door to the holodeck. He opened it—and looked inside at nothing. Ledger had deactivated her office program when she left, and nothing had been done with the room since. He hadn't been a fan of Myra's voice, but disliked the silence more.

Oh, hell, why not? "Computer, run *Sto-Vo-Kor* program."

The Klingon tavern appeared. As before, the din was deafening—and also as then, he'd entered on the brawlers' end of the room. This time he knew to step carefully on the way in.

Kor met him with a wide smile. "Rios, friend and ally of the heroic Verengan! Is he here?"

"Just me."

A hearty laugh. "I will make do." He gestured to the item in Rios's hands. "You bring me tribute?"

"It's a hubcap from a Tucker 48."

"Is it from a great battle?"

"It is indeed." He handed it to the Klingon. "Go nuts."

Rios wandered the room—and as he did, a purpose other than company entered his mind. In recent days, he'd done his best not to think of the actuality; that wound would remain fresh for a long time, ripping open whenever he thought about his financial situation. But like the relic, this room had come from Verengan. And one person knew more about who the actuality depicted than anyone.

He found Gorkon sitting with a young Klingon. "Friend Rios," the chancellor said with a smile. "Have you met Torav?"

"I haven't."

The hairy-faced warrior rose and saluted Rios. "They say you know Verengan. It is an honor."

So I've heard.

Torav was an adult, but he looked younger than most present. After Rios sat, Gorkon explained that Torav had saved his commander from disintegration by taking a disruptor bolt himself—ending a promising career prematurely and qualifying him for greatness in *Sto-Vo-Kor*. "The others spin yarns from lives well lived," Torav said. "I have only a death well spent."

Guess things could be worse, Rios thought. *I only have the terminated career.*

"Torav, your honor exceeds my own," Gorkon replied. "Your greatness was assured from the start. Better an end of one's own choosing, than fall to treachery."

There it is. "Can I ask you about that?" Rios looked to Gorkon. "Do you mind?"

Torav snorted. "You see, Chancellor? Always they talk to the one of years." With a good-natured punch to Rios's shoulder, Torav stood and meandered off.

Gorkon watched as he departed. "Never undervalue the short career, Rios. That warrior's young son lived long—and was not one-tenth his father's worth."

Rios sat up. *Could that mean Verengan?* A new question jumped to the front of his agenda, and he phrased it carefully given the regard the characters held for their creator. "Is . . . Verengan's father here?"

"No, he would not be." Gorkon chuckled. "I should say *certainly* not."

Enticed by the answer, Rios kept nonetheless to his original line. "I need to know something—if you will forgive me—about General Chang."

"Ah." Gorkon took a sip of his drink. "As long as you do not want me to forgive *him*, ask your question."

"You're okay with this?" Rios had never asked someone about their murderer before, and didn't know the etiquette in any culture. "I hate to even say the name here."

"Some deeds are so foul even discommendation cannot prevent their names from being uttered. They must stand as examples." Gorkon templed his fingers on the table. "We all must die, Rios—and to be frank, I would have predicted Chang to be responsible for my end in one way or another. He simply lived down to my expectations."

Rios looked about. Azetbur was across the room, talking to Kahless at the bar. The chancellor might be willing to tut-tut his own murder, but Rios feared staying on the topic with Gorkon's daughter around. He quickly got to the point, explaining the artifact that had been in Verengan's possession, and whom it depicted. The first question was obvious.

"Do I think Chang could have posed for such a vignette?" Gorkon stroked his luxurious beard. "Certainly, yes. He was a great warrior, but also vain, and possessed of a drive to become as legendary as the characters of opera—of the tales he read."

"Characters from Shakespeare."

"I have been known to cite the Bard as well. But then I speak better than I sing."

It merited a hearty Klingon laugh, and Rios shared in it. It paved the way for his next question: how Verengan got the thing. On this, Gorkon only had a theory, and it surprised him.

"You asked if Verengan's father was here. He is not—and I know because I knew him." Looking around, Gorkon lowered his voice. "His name was Grokh—and *that* name is not spoken, because he was a lesser light, a footnote in Chang's tragedy."

"They worked together?"

"Another general. One of his confederates. Killed in the battle with *Enterprise* and *Excelsior.* Oh, how I should have loved to have seen that!" Gorkon wore an eerie grin. Then he raised his finger. "Verengan told me who his father was one night after much drink—it explained why he was always so fearful around me. Indeed, he never approached me again after that. So to answer your question: yes, if he had such a relic, I expect he would have gotten it from his father."

Rios's eyes widened. *A chain of custody.* "And the book Chang was reading—how would that have reached Javen? Did you know the duke?"

"I met him, of course. The Valtese were a subject species; he often agitated for freedom, but he never took up arms."

The holodeck wasn't making this fact up for his benefit, Rios decided: as with Grokh's identity and status, "Gorkon" was likely drawing upon some historical record of a known meeting with Javen.

But the character would speculate no further. "I have no idea how Javen would have found a book owned by Chang. But when a glass falls, the pieces scatter."

Rios looked down at the table, feeling he understood Verengan better. The trader's family dynamic was the opposite of Torav's. "Son of a fallen father. Discommendated, without a name." He looked up. "But he *had* a name."

"*Verengan* means *Ferengi,*" Gorkon said. "Do you think it was given in kindness?" He took his glass. "People meander about, named or not. You have to call them something."

The whole exchange amazed Rios. Emil had been right. The holodeck's characters knew something of what the historical figures knew—the known parts—but they also knew whatever Verengan had told them, overtly or otherwise.

For his part, the Gorkon character seemed to find the questions refreshing. "Most who ask me of that time wish to know how Chang could have done it—disregarding that he did not act alone."

Most people who ask. Rios had heard that holodeck manufacturers had a vast database of historical characters somewhere; portrayals were advised at least in part by live user responses.

"Humans will act unsurprised over the acts of Chang and the Romulans' involvement," Gorkon said, "as if treachery came naturally to us. But they are most horrified at Cartwright and his allies, as if the Federation and Starfleet should be above such behavior. I am gratified you have said nothing of the sort."

"And I wouldn't." Rios had been disappointed enough by his own people. He began to rise. "Thank you," he said to a man who had died ninety-nine years earlier. "I would like to have met you, had I—you know, lived back then."

Gorkon emptied his glass. "Are you going to leave without asking what you really wanted to know?"

Rios froze. "What do you mean?"

The chancellor put his fingers together and looked to the air, speaking in an antic tone. "*A man walks into a bar and meets a ghost—and asks him about the weather.*" Gorkon looked intently at Rios. "My lot here has been to assist Verengan with who he is. I see the same weariness in your face, Captain. You really only wanted to ask me about odd items of personal property?"

Rios stared at him—and slid back into his chair. There was something, and there was a way to phrase it. He began to speak, having no idea how the computer running the characters would react.

"Chang's conspirators," he began, "killed innocents. Killed *you*—to do what they thought was right. And then they expected others to keep their secrets."

Gorkon nodded. "It was wrong. They should have spoken."

"But what if they lied to protect other people from harm?"

The chancellor studied him. "You have been in such a place?"

Rios had asked his question. He let it stand.

Gorkon opened his palm—and then clapped his hand on Rios's wrist. "You speak of right and wrong as if there is some way to tabulate one's accounts and arrive at a balance. No such arithmetic exists, known to the living—or the dead."

Rios pulled away. "Then what am I supposed to do?"

"*A great deed!*"

Rios looked behind him. The booming voice belonged to Kahless, here to refill Gorkon's glass.

He did so—and looked down on Rios. "You should do a great deed, young Rios. Not because it will solve your problem or make right a wrong." Kahless showed his teeth. "You should do a great deed because *you should always do great deeds.*"

Rios stared. "What would this deed be?"

Gorkon leaned across the table and poked him in the chest. "*You tell us.*"

52

La Sirena

Deep Space

"I'm not thinking of this right."

Laboring over the automobile's transmission, Rios wondered whether he had attached the second torque converter correctly. Very little about the vehicle and its drive system was typical for its day, and much of the guidance he'd found in various databases simply didn't apply. He'd learned the manufacturer was an outsider from its beginning to its infamous end, and while he empathized, he'd begun to wish Fajo had brought a simpler car aboard.

"'A great deed,' Kahless said. If I get the engine to turn over, will that count?"

The car was, in some ways, like the Chang actuality: it came to life only when all its components were correctly oriented. The vehicle's precomputer-era subsystems did communicate *some* things to one another; telemetry was reported on analog displays, and the middle headlight turned when the steering wheel reached a certain point. But those connections were few. The windshield wipers did not bother to tell the brake system that it was raining.

"*Get the parts to talk.*" Rios stepped back and wiped his hands. He considered how much time lately he'd spent interacting with holograms. He knew that in doing so, he was really just talking to *La Sirena*—but as Emil had said about the holodeck's characters, some information was siloed. The ship actually might know quite a bit more than it was telling him.

He walked through sickbay. Emil was there, keeping watch over the biobed while Sovak slept. "No change," the EMH said on seeing Rios. "He has less and less time before he feels faint."

"We're going to Benzar as fast as we can."

Emil's expression suggested that might not be fast enough.

"Come with me," Rios said.

Finally, he had removed the last car parts from the galley; all that remained was the damage. The two found Mr. Hospitality using a very small cloth to buff a mess hall table with a very large dent. The hologram had only taken on the chore after some debate. Rios had convinced him the maintenance of a clean canteen was part of *La Sirena*'s hospitality mission—and thus, his problem.

He looked up from his work. "Captain! What can I get you today?"

"A seat. And get ones for yourselves. You two stand around way too much. It's exhausting to look at."

After some initial reluctance, Emil and Mr. Hospitality took chairs on opposite sides of the table. Rios found their interaction—or rather, the lack of it—remarkable. Living crewmembers summoned to a surprise staff meeting would sit at a table looking at one another, communicating their curiosity. But Rios knew the service holograms had no reason to interact.

It bothered him anyway. "Why is it you guys never talk to each other, but the Klingons on the holodeck do?"

"They do so for your benefit," Mr. Hospitality said. "Do you want us to talk?" He put on a big smile and looked to Emil. "It's a wonderful day, isn't it?"

"My patient would not agree," Emil said, his expression far less ebullient.

"That's a shame. If he needs anything, all he has to do is say my name."

Rios put up his hands. "I get it." Then he had another thought. "Mr. Hospitality—what's *your* diagnosis of Sovak?"

"He hasn't asked for anything today." A finger in the air. "He could be hungry!" The hologram started to stand.

"Halt!" Rios grabbed the hologram's shoulder and forced him back in his seat. "That's not what I mean. What's your *medical* diagnosis?"

Light flickered in the EHH's pupils. "I'm not really the one to ask, Captain."

Emil piped up. "As I mentioned before—"

"Shut it," Rios warned.

Emil sat back. "Shutting it, Captain."

"I don't care what your job is," Rios told the EHH. "I ask again: What's your medical diagnosis?"

More flickering. "It could be something he ate," Mr. Hospitality said. "Or drank. Passengers have physical needs that I help fulfill. When anything is wrong, they let me know."

"And when anything is *very* wrong, they let *you* know," Rios said, glancing at Emil. "You've accessed information on everything Sovak and Hain ate while aboard, correct?"

Emil nodded. "There's no sensor recording of such things—but my jurisdiction does extend to accessing the replicator history in cases of gastronomic distress or poisoning."

"And you didn't find anything."

"No."

Rios looked to Mr. Hospitality. "You weren't active when Hain was alive. But did you serve Sovak anything that wasn't from the replicator?"

The hologram brightened. "Ah, yes. He wanted a salad tossed by hand. I took care of that."

"Yeah, but the vegetables were replicated, right? I mean something off the menu entirely."

"Oh." He tried again. "There was a lovely vintage Romulan wine that Kivas Fajo asked to serve at table the night of the dinner."

Rios remembered it. Full and dark—he might have remarked on it had his table not been a free-fire zone. "I thought that was one of ours."

"Oh, no," Mr. Hospitality said. "Fajo told me he would never serve replicated wine at such an event."

Rios looked to Emil. "That mean anything to you? We all drank it. Could a wine have poisoned Sovak and nobody else? Just a Ferengi?"

The medical hologram processed the new information. "There is no known agent that could do that—not alone."

"What do you mean, not alone?"

"There is nargolosis." Emil clasped his hands on the table. "It involves nargolin, an additive to Ferengi food."

Mr. Hospitality's eyes widened. "Oh, yes. An old ingredient, used to extend the shelf life of some products." He smiled pleasantly. "Behavioral surveys show a high proportion of Ferengi passengers care about economic matters. I'm programmed to expect that."

"This nargolin is dangerous?" Rios asked the EMH.

"No," Emil replied. "It builds up in cells after long periods of consumption, but it is expelled in time. Acute nargolosis only ensues when triggered by cytocylic acid. It begins a chain reaction in which the Ferengi system converts nargolin into a toxin."

"Was there cytocylic acid in the Romulan wine?"

For the first time in minutes, the holograms looked at each other instead of Rios. Lights flashed in their eyes.

Mr. Hospitality spoke first. "The contents of Romulan wine vary by the vintner, and no database I consulted when I was given the bottles set off any alert about potential reactions. But the information was incomplete."

"Do any Romulan wines have cytocylic acid?" Rios asked.

More eye flashes. "Yes. But no warning flag was evidently set in my database." Mr. Hospitality looked glum for the first time since Rios had seen him. "I feel I've let someone down."

Rios slapped the table. "You sure haven't." He was glad to be getting somewhere. "Hain was served a Romulan wine aboard *Sylvus Bestri*—something from Javen's vineyard. Would Javen have known about the dangers to Ferengi?"

"I would doubt it," Mr. Hospitality said. "As I said, nargolin is a folk preservative—seldom used outside family dishes. Even if a server knew about the wine, there would be no reasonable expectation that a diner had consumed nargolin."

"But he did consume it." Rios pointed to the replicator. "Nargolin—it was in the Ferengi dishes both Hain and Sovak ate while aboard?"

"Oh, yes," both holograms answered at once.

"Didn't your programmers set *any* kind of warning flag about nargolin?"

Mr. Hospitality shook his head. "The Ferengi dishes in the replicator were not in *La Sirena*'s basic system. They were uploaded by a user more than a year earlier." He provided the stardate.

Rios glanced at the replicators—and then at the table. He remembered a meal long ago. "Kivas Fajo brought his own recipe file!"

It was the dinner aboard *La Sirena* when Fajo visited to inspect Verengan's junk. He had brought his own wine that time too. But it didn't make any sense. On further consulting the records, Mr. Hospitality confirmed that Fajo ordered no Ferengi dishes for himself either during that first visit, or the later festival. Was he just far thinking, looking out for guests on a ship he hoped to rent one day? Or was it something worse?

What kind of person is Fajo, anyway?

Emil looked antsy. Apparently, he'd been working while sitting there. "From what I've referenced, the effects of nargolosis could easily be responsible for his condition. With your leave, there are steps I can take to mitigate the—"

"Don't talk—and don't walk. Vanish!" Rios pushed back from the table. By the time he rose, Emil had dematerialized and re-formed in sickbay.

Mr. Hospitality watched Rios make for the stairs. "While you're here, Captain, did you need something? I put together a torte that's an absolute delight. Or perhaps you'd care for a lovely beverage?"

"Later. I need to make a call!"

The Letters of Jean-Luc Picard

(Excerpt from a 2392 personal correspondence to Admiral Marta Batanides)

My Dearest Marta—

It was a pleasure to learn you had called, and I'm only sorry I wasn't present to take it. I am committing much more time to my writing these days, and it is easier to create without a comm unit around.

I also apologize for writing rather than calling; again, something about life in France has me embracing the old ways. When one has the time, the need for immediacy fades. At any rate, your message was welcome, and I hope this missive finds you well. I am certain Starfleet has been keeping you busy.

I was amused that you said a friend of yours had read All Our Lives. *My deepest sympathies! That was a case of my having too much free time—and not the skills to match my ambition. The novice philosopher spends half of his manuscript preparing to say something, and the other half apologizing for not having said anything. It is certainly not a book I would have written now, if at all.*

Of substantially less amusement was your mention that your friend had gotten into difficulty with Kivas Fajo. I admit I had not known Fajo had been paroled, and would have advised against it had I been asked.

It was not something I would have said in my book, but Fajo is a frightful, devious little man—and a murderer. He kidnapped Data, looking upon him as a one-of-a-kind collectible. At the same time, Fajo planted evidence making the Enterprise *believe he was dead. Data might be imprisoned today had my crew not seen through the deception and had Data not rebelled against Fajo's coercions.*

You might wonder that Fajo was a match for Data at all. He was. Fajo protected himself with a novel personal energy shield—and by practicing blackmail of the most heinous kind. The trader threatened to kill Data—and when he did not submit, Fajo instead killed Varria, a woman in his employ. It was a cold-blooded execution using an illegal weapon of the most painful variety—a Varon-T disruptor—performed in full sight of Data.

After he gained the upper hand, Data saw that Fajo was fairly tried and prosecuted; I dare say I would have reacted more angrily. I encountered Fajo at the trial and shuddered to think of what other crimes he had committed that we didn't know about. When I needed an example of obsession in my book, I could think of no better—but I avoided the detail. Looking back, perhaps I should have been more explicit. Data's passing has only amplified the disdain I have for Fajo and his crimes.

I don't know who your friend is, but if he or she has any further dealings with Fajo, my advice is to watch out. *And if they have any confederates or loved ones in the collector's employ, I recommend getting them out in all haste. Varria was, by reports, a loyal longtime employee—and he disintegrated her without a thought. I give the word: beware.*

On that grisly note, I discordantly wish my best to you, wherever your travels take you. Please stay in touch—and stay well.

Warmest regards,
Jean-Luc

53

INTERSPECIES MEDICAL EXCHANGE FACILITY

BENZAR

Emil had never failed anyone, Rios realized; he had just lacked sufficient information. When he had it, he succeeded almost immediately.

In Sovak's case, the EMH had gotten the information just in time. Following his meeting with Rios, Emil had been called upon to stave off his patient's cardiac arrest. That done, he had started a regimen that stabilized Sovak until they reached the staff at the Interspecies Medical Exchange.

Further good fortune had ensued there, as one of the doctors on the staff had once interned at a Ferengi facility called the Home for the Aged and Insolvent. Having seen nargolosis before, the doctor quickly confirmed the diagnosis, and a simple biopsy confirmed it as the cause of Hain's death. Steps were already underway to bring Sovak back to health.

If he didn't give himself another heart attack, first.

"*Fajo!*" Sovak snarled while sitting up in his hospital bed. "What a filthy sack of dung!"

"I'd be happy to drop one on his head," Rios replied, "but we didn't save any."

As Rios sat with Sovak in the hospital room, they'd put together a possible timeline of what Fajo had done. When Verengan told Hain of the actuality in his possession—the only piece of junk the Klingon had a hope of profiting from—the rancher had contacted his fortune-hunter brother for guidance. Sovak had then made quiet research inquiries while trying to confirm its authenticity.

Those inquiries must not have been quiet enough, Sovak admitted. "People have been chasing Parch actualities for years. It's a madness—everyone's always on high alert. Somehow it got back to Fajo that we'd found it, and that it was probably still on your freighter."

Rios had come across a missing piece of the story literally on the way into the building. He rose and looked out into the hall. "Come on in."

Sovak looked up in alarm as Rios invited a young medic into their private conversation. "Who's this guy?"

"His name's Yerm." Rios greeted the young Benzite, who looked much better than he'd ever seen him. "He's an orderly here now—but first, he signed up to work for me on *La Sirena*. He showed up when I put the word out on Alpha Carinae II—the same place where Hain discovered Verengan's ship was back in circulation." He nodded to Yerm. "Tell him what you told me."

Yerm looked nervously at Rios before speaking. "I joined the captain's crew because someone offered to pay me if I did."

"Who?" Sovak demanded.

"Someone I'd never seen before—or since. I don't know who he worked for." But Yerm had been given a mission on the freighter, he explained. He was to look out for three things: an old Klingon, any Ferengi who boarded, and any kind of small trinket that might be hidden away.

The junk-ridden state of the ship had thwarted Yerm immediately; Rios wasn't surprised. The other relic hunters didn't know what the actuality looked like. So even after breaking into Rios's chambers, the Benzite came away empty-handed.

Yerm's injury prevented him from doing anything else, so it fell to Fajo to infiltrate, Rios said. Evaluating Verengan's junk in person gave him not just the chance to check through what was on *La Sirena*, but to have it transported to his facility for further analysis.

And for good measure came Fajo's other step: salting the ship's recipe files with something targeting Ferengi passengers, should Hain or Sovak come aboard.

"My guess is Fajo knew Hain was on Argelius," Rios said, "and he fully expected he'd find us and take a ride to see Duke Javen. If he knew Hain and Javen were tight, he might have expected the wine from Javen's vineyard to flow—activating the nargolin from *La Sirena*."

"And Fajo served something similar to me," Sovak said. "Bastard!"

The conversation flummoxed Yerm, from whom Rios had spared the details about the actuality. "I'd only been told someone would kill for whatever was on the ship," the youth said. "But this poisoning stuff sounds crazy. Who would do something like that?"

"Kivas Fajo." Rios described the jarring message that Marta Batanides had forwarded him that morning. The admiral had been astonished to hear from him, but there was no one else he could turn to; Raffi's feelings about Picard were too raw, and probably always would be. Rios figured Marta was someone whom Picard might respond to quickly, and he had. "Picard says Fajo is diabolical—and a murderer. I expect we can believe it."

Sovak pounded the biobed with his fist. "Picard! I hate that name." He glared at Rios. "A friend of yours?"

"Never met him—but he apparently tangled with Fajo before. Our collector is a killer."

Yerm looked to Rios. "Didn't you tell me earlier that Ledger was working with him? Maybe you should warn her."

"Can't reach her. Nobody at Cynosure will talk to me."

Rios exhaled. It was exhausting recounting all the various machinations—but it felt good to actually know something.

"I forgot," he told Sovak. "We still have the Wine-Stained Folio. It's yours—I can beam it over if you'd like."

"Bah!" Sovak dismissed the idea. "It's of no use now—and I'll be damned if I spend another hour of my life worrying over ancient garbage. I'm going back to Irtok, to see what I can salvage of the ranch. At least in the manure business, you know what you're getting yourself into!"

Rios stepped into the hallway, Yerm alongside him. "You look good," the captain said.

"Thanks to you, for bringing me here. Nobody cared about me before."

"And I see they hired you." His brow furrowed. "They're okay with you? You know, given—"

"Given my past?" Yerm wore a crumpled smile. "The people here know everything about me—and have done everything to help me. I'm working for them—and they're helping me work on me." He chuckled. "That sounds silly to say out loud."

"Not so much." The IME sounded like it really was trying to fill in some part of the gap left by the Federation's abdication of the Romulan-facing outer territories. It bothered him to think of the latter, but he was glad to see there was no monopoly on benevolence.

Outside the building entrance, Rios shook the orderly's hand. "Good luck."

"Thanks, Captain. I'm sorry I didn't get to talk to Glake again—he's a good listener! But I guess he's on his way."

Rios tilted his head. "What do you mean?"

"I saw him earlier by the spaceport. My flat's just past it."

Rios was puzzled. "Are you sure it was him?"

He smiled. "Oh, yeah. I called out his name and he turned—but I was in a crowd. I guess all Benzites look alike to him." He pointed to a sign on the horizon. "He was outside the booking office for the Zaghama line. Glake was waiting for it to open."

That sounded crazy. In more than a year, the Nausicaan had rarely, if ever, left *La Sirena* on his own. Indeed, he appeared to have no friends, no family, no outside life at all.

It was peculiar—but Rios decided not to involve Yerm in any more mysteries. Finishing his good-bye, he headed into a courtyard and messaged *La Sirena*.

Glake could normally be counted on to send at least a text response, but this time there was nothing—and a direct call to the ship didn't yield so much as a "*yeeessss.*" Rios made tracks for the spaceport, and the Zaghama pads.

Contrary to expectation, shuttle traffic to passenger liners in orbit had not uniformly declined in the transporter age; something left Benzar's spaceport every other minute. Rios took a turbolift to an elevated automatic walkway. Several of Zaghama's pads branched off from either side.

Too many to search, Rios thought. *Maybe the kid got it wrong.*

He was about to give up when he glanced down at a lower walkway crossing beneath his perpendicularly, seven or eight meters below. The presence of a Nausicaan amid so many shorter Benzites was something nobody could miss; the giant tan duffel the figure carried was something he'd seen aboard ship. He hurried forward and called over the side. "*Glake!*"

The Nausicaan below looked up at him, startled. But rather than going back to his business, he responded by pushing ahead of the others on his conveyor, rushing to get out of sight beneath Rios's walkway.

Rios ran backward on the belt to avoid being carried away. "Glake, stop! It's me!"

Certain he was being deliberately ignored, Rios turned and cut across traffic on his own level, dashing toward the other side. When he reached the railing, he saw there was only one Zaghama launchpad in that direction; a shuttle was parked there, its ramp down. *"Now boarding for Nel Bato, Lya IV, and the Giles Belt,"* an announcement declared.

Rios climbed onto the railing—and over it. A Benzite constable called out to him. "You there! What are you doing?"

Something I'm going to be awfully embarrassed about if I've got the wrong Nausicaan. Hands clinging to the railing behind him, he looked down below.

Glake emerged on the lower moving walkway and glanced up—in time to see his commanding officer's feet, hurtling his way. Rios's boots struck Glake's shoulders, and the force of the impact knocked the titan down. His fall further broken by panicked pedestrians, Rios tumbled haphazardly onto the conveyor.

Also falling: Glake's duffel, which opened at the top when it hit the surface. Various contents spilled from it—including a shining item that rolled forward in an arc. It wobbled between Rios's splayed legs on the ground, spinning to a stop very nearly in his lap.

His eyes went wide. *A golden apple!*

"What is this?" Rios asked, holding it up. "Is this it? Is this *it*?"

Several tourists had gathered around Glake, seeing to the assault victim. On his hands and knees in their midst, the dazed giant finally saw what had happened. He opened his mouth. "*Giiive that baaaack.*"

Rios had heard Glake use other parts of his vocabulary—but he had only ever been good for a word at a time. Three at once was unprecedented.

And then came more. "*I wooorked for that. A whole yeeear. Giiive.*"

"I've paid you when I could," Rios said, standing up on the still-moving walkway. "I'm asking again, what is this? Did you swipe this from Fajo?"

If Glake had more to say, a Bajoran traveler interrupted. "Security, stop that human! Assault and robbery, in broad daylight!"

Rios looked up at the walkway above, where several officers had appeared, attracted by the jumper. He only had time to give Glake three words of his own before he took off running, sped along by the conveyor.

"*You're fired!*"

54

La Sirena
Leaving Benzar

Escaping his pursuers had been easier than Rios had expected. As he'd seen on looking back, Glake had hurled several of the tourists trying to help him out of his way, creating a much more visible menace in the process. With frustration amplifying into rage, he'd drawn security officers to him like a magnet, allowing Rios to slip from one launchpad area to another until he'd made his way back to his ship.

He was free—but the fracas had put an end to any thought of remaining on Benzar to question Glake. And he had so many questions. He had solved and opened the actuality; it appeared to be the genuine *Chang at the False Dawn*. How Glake had come by it was another question. Rios also didn't know why he'd been bound for a destination inside Federation space, far on the other side of Earth.

No, if Rios wanted the truth about his erstwhile would-be engineer, there would only be one way to get it. And that meant sacrificing the one thing he'd just gotten back: solitude.

I really don't want to do this. But as Rios looked around the empty engineering section, he saw no other way. "Activate Emergency Engineering Hologram."

"Hello! Please state the nature of your engineering emergency!"

Rios had expected the engineer would be another version of himself. He had not predicted, however, that it would appear as a longshoreman, with a bushy beard and fuzzy cap. Nor was the hologram's thick Scottish brogue something he'd been prepared to hear.

"Let me guess," Rios said drily. "You're Scottish because of Montgomery Scott."

"I am as my good creator made me, sir. And ye'd best not judge someone by the way he talks."

If he calls me "laddie," Rios thought, *I'm going to delete the entire system.*

All three of the holograms he'd activated so far had speech patterns and behavioral attributes that were antic and unreal: Emil was English, but English-by-way-of-Rios, and apt to use politeness as a weapon. Rios could only wonder what lunatic at Kaplan had thought the self-scan option for the holograms was worth installing, and how he could ever have been drunk enough to use it himself.

"I need information," he said, "and I don't have time to search for it."

"Ooh, an emergency." Spanner in hand, the hologram tapped it lightly against the side of his hat. "Are we going to red alert?"

"There are no alerts. This is a freighter." Rios paused. "I would want an engineer to know that."

The EEH stared at him blankly. Then: "*Gotcha!*" The EEH smiled toothily. "Just a wee bit of humor. It makes for a good introduction, I find."

"You have literally never met anyone before."

This was how it was going to be, Rios supposed. Dissatisfied with how the EEH's acronym sounded out, Rios went with something close. "Look, I'm going to call you Ian."

"Barry!"

"You want to be called *Barry*?"

"No, it's a barry name. That means good." A concerned look. "Is that *I-A-N* or *I-A-I-N*?"

"It couldn't possibly matter." Rios blinked, wondering already if it was all worth it. "Look, I need to know what Glake, your—uh—predecessor was doing. Every interaction with the systems." He paused, calculating. "For the last year or more."

"A quality check. Last fellow something of a dobber, was he?"

"Just give me a report."

Ian went to the engineering control panels—an action Rios took to mean he simply couldn't call up all the data using his innate access to the ship's systems. *Silos, again*. Before long, the EEH had an answer.

"I don't know what you're on about, Cap'n. Your boy Glake appears to have been a class engineer."

"Do I have to turn down your sarcasm settings?"

"It's true. The Kaplan interface adapts to the knowledge levels of the user as it senses 'em. Glake may not have used the systems much, but he was proficient from the start."

That didn't make sense to Rios at all. "He transported a shipment of ball bearings without the containers!"

"Oh, that was deliberate." Ian called up the records from the Alpha Carinae II visit and walked Rios through the displays. "Y'see here, he has the containers locked on, goods an' all—then he redefines the parameters to target just the pellets."

Rios couldn't believe it—and didn't know what to make of it. "Sabotage?"

"Or a practical joke. Engineers like those, y'know."

It was no joke; it had nearly prevented him from going to Argelius at all, where encounters with both Fajo and Hain awaited. "Tell me about his replicator use." Rios gave a start time of a few months earlier, around the beginning of Fajo's festival.

Once again, Ian located the data in short order. A trip to a different display brought up the records. "Here, see—you've tapped the concierge system to move a thingie to maintenance storage."

Rios remembered. "And?"

"And here, Glake sees that you've done it—he accessed the record. So he transported it back here, to engineering."

He did what? Rios looked at the time code. "He did it while the banquet was going on. Everybody but him and the Miradorns were there."

"You might've done better to invite him—because he kept busy." Ian pointed. "See this? He's using the transporter to analyze the contents of the what-have-you—"

"The actuality."

"—and to create a duplicate using the replicator. But it's a mean little beastie he's fooling with. It took the replicator most of a day to cook up something close."

Rios stared at the records. "He sent the original back to its hiding place. So the one I displayed at the auction was real."

"But two days later, he locks onto it again—this time it's in a box in a stateroom."

"Fajo's quarters." Rios remembered the timeline. "I'd taught him how to close and open the actuality by then."

"And Glake beams out the true thing—and puts back its mate."

Rios looked at the apple. "So this is real—and Fajo left with the fake?"

"Aye."

He was tempted to rejoice, but there were a couple of things wrong with what he'd heard. The dinner was the day before Rios had revealed he had the actuality—and Glake wasn't in the auction room to see it.

And there was a much more vexing question. "If Glake had the real thing, why didn't he just leave right away? Why stay aboard until now?"

Ian stared at nothing for a few moments. The questions were well out of an engineer's domain, and Rios figured the hologram probably had nothing to say. But literal inspiration appeared in his pupils, and he moved to a different console. "Haw, take a look at this!"

"What?" Rios joined him.

"Every day from when Fajo left to now, Glake's been trying it again. Trying to make another clone of your widget there."

Isn't having the real one enough? "Go on."

"But he's hit a wall here, you ken?" Ian pointed. "What he's synthesizing doesn't work." He looked to the apple. "Let's have a scan."

Rios handed him the actuality—and watched as Ian swept a tricorder past it.

"Oh, that's pure dead brilliant!" Ian looked up. "Whoever made this installed copy protection, replicator style."

"What do you mean?"

"The transporter functions by scanning all the component particles into the pattern buffer—then extracting them. This little creation's not of new manufacture at all, but some of its workings are magic."

"Another expression, I hope."

"Aye, but it's about near." Ian walked him through the dynamics. When opened, *Chang at the False Dawn* had a hidden switch that allowed it to be transported. If that wasn't set—and it had not been—some of the particles would misreport their positions and characteristics to any device that attempted to scan them. It would not harm the original actuality, but any duplicate would have imperfections.

"Are you saying Fajo's actuality might not work?"

"I dinnae know. I'd want to study it more—but it looks like Glake's attempts to make more copies went for shite."

I had no idea Glake was so industrious, Rios thought. *If I'd been this oblivious in Starfleet, I'd have topped out as ensign.*

A chime. Ian looked to the side. "There's a call."

Rios raised an eyebrow. Hails and most calls should have been reported to him by the ship's systems. But this looked like a call placed directly to the console in engineering. He stared at the display. "No identifier. Who'd be calling Glake?"

"It's a wild scheme," Ian said, "but you might try answering."

Rios did—but only after first suppressing the comm system's cam and mic. "This is Glake," he typed.

Palor Toff appeared on the display, looking seriously annoyed. *"Why can't I see you?"*

Startled by the identity of Glake's caller, Rios quickly recovered. He tried to compose something that sounded like the Nausicaan had sent it. "Interference. Ship in nebula."

"You're not supposed to be on the ship at all. You should be on a flight to Lya IV!"

Rios had a brainstorm. "Change of plan. Freighter is faster. When Rios left the ship, I stole it."

"That's delicious," Toff said, going from relief to delight. *"To art theft, add piracy. My friends would be so amused—if I ever told them!"*

The outlines of their dealings became apparent. Glake, having learned of the enormous price that third-highest bidder Toff had offered for the actuality, had given him another chance at it. Maybe the second copy he was trying to make was for Liselle, Rios thought, or another bidder. Why stop at one? But the copy protection Ian had found had thwarted Glake.

"I need the actuality right away," Toff said. *"You've made me wait too long as it is!"*

He decided to roll the dice. "What's the rush?"

"Oh, no. If I tell you that, I'll never see you—or it—again," Toff said. *"It is well beyond your ability to comprehend. So stop asking questions and bring it here, as you agreed!"*

Rios thought for a moment—and quickly sent a message back. It took a while to receive a response, but the collector finally assented before signing off.

"What did he just agree to?" Ian asked.

"I told him to wait for Glake at the casino bar on Lya Station."

"A nice place, is it?"

"As soon as somebody opens one, I'll tell you."

55

La Sirena
Pergazia System

In Santiago, it was the night before Christmas—and on *La Sirena*, nothing was stirring. Since Benzar, Rios had been completely alone whenever the holograms weren't active—and while he had welcomed his first solace in more than a year, worry had clouded his thoughts.

He wasn't concerned over Palor Toff or Glake. The former had attempted to call repeatedly, and Rios had not bothered to answer. It was enough to know that the snotty would-be baron was wasting his time.

Rather, his worry came from his repeated calls to Cynosure. None had resulted in a chance to speak with Ledger, and even his attempts to reach out to Wolyx in the Convincers had gone nowhere. Rios had taken a few menial jobs in the meantime, enough to stay current with Arkko—but Picard's warning and Fajo's actions had been on his mind.

That afternoon, after a truly distasteful assignment—hauling the corpses of four hundred Pergazian emigrés back to their homeworld for ceremonial interment—he decided he'd had enough. His customer's "good news," that the weekly undertaker run was his if he wanted it, had barely registered with him. His next flight would be back to Argelius II. If Ledger was there, he'd find her himself.

Rios had only started to set coordinates when a Convincer dreadnought dropped out of warp at the edge of the system and without any notice. While it was still quite distant, there was no question those aboard had spotted him.

A hail followed. *"This is* Sockdollager*! Izzat you, Rios?"*

"You know it is, Burze." Rios wasn't surprised to see the Iotian on the main viewscreen. Ledger had long ago explained that the street hierarchies Iotians were accustomed to did not translate easily to the operation of starships; mob captains were rarely worth a damn as ship captains. Instead, the Convincers treated their largest vessels as oversized flivvers packing lots of heat, with their drivers enjoying no special status at all. It was how Burze, a traveling salesman, had appeared now and again on deck as spokesman. Speaking for *Sockdollager* required nothing more than a big mouth.

"What's the story?" Rios asked, eyebrow raised. "I'm current with you guys."

"This ain't that," Burze replied. *"Just heave to or whatever you call it. We need to talk."*

"We can talk right here." He'd been dropped in on enough by the Convincers to know it never went well. He minimized Burze's image and yawed *La Sirena* gradually, so as to stop closing with the dreadnought. "What do you want?"

"A sit-down. We'll be there in a minute. Smoke 'em if you've got 'em."

Yeah, right. Somebody was going to get smoked, and checking his sensors, Rios had a good idea who it was. Two more dreadnoughts dropped out of warp—and then two more—and two more.

Seven. He'd never seen the Convincers send so much muscle before.

This was going to be tricky. The Iotians were smarter than Seejee's mercs had been at Argelius. The six new dreadnought arrivals weren't closing in; rather, they were moving to take stations a million kilometers equidistant from *La Sirena* on all three axes, boxing her in while *Sockdollager* made her approach. If Rios bolted for deep space, one of the snipers would get to take potshots at him while he tried to jump to warp.

But there remained room in which to operate—and that gave him an idea. Rios studied the region, muted the comm, and called to the air. "*Ian!*"

The engineer materialized. "Aye, Captain?"

"You know where the Convincers' tracking device is?"

"Aye. I let it be, like you said."

"I want it to lie its ass off. You get me?"

Ian smiled. "I'll have it talking oot its fanny flaps." He disappeared.

Rios had been instructed not to remove the tracker while he still owed the gang money, but he assumed all bets were off—and now, the device could work to his advantage. He pointed *La Sirena* toward the gas giant Pergazia orbited—

—and realized he couldn't do what he intended to do alone. He'd have to break another promise to himself.

Might as well do them both. He inhaled deeply. "Activate Emergency Helm Holograms!"

Two figures sprang into being in the seats ahead of Rios.

To his right, the Emergency Navigational Hologram looked like him, albeit with differently combed hair. The ENH smiled. "And would there be a navigational emergency you're having?"

And we're Irish, Rios thought. *At least I can understand him.*

That was a mild surprise compared to the Emergency Tactical Hologram. The ETH was a Rios, as expected, but with mussed hair, tattoos, and a generally bedraggled demeanor.

And he appeared to be completely hammered. "*¿Qué deseas?*"

The words had been a drunken drawl. Rios blinked. "Are you all right?"

"*Ay, que caña que tengo.*"

Caña? It was Chilean slang. *How can a hologram have a hangover?*

The ETH rubbed the side of his head and squinted at the navigator. "*Hay demasiado gente en este hotel.*"

The navigator stared—and looked back to Rios with concern. "This fella thinks there's too many people in this hotel."

"I heard," Rios said. He felt the same way. "Well, now I know which one of you I created *last* that night."

He directed them to the problem: Pergazia Prime, looking orange and ominous as it filled their viewports. "We're going to make like a meteor."

The ENH frowned. "D'you think that's a good idea?"

"No, but we're going to do it. Find me an atmospheric layer least likely to pulverize us." He turned to the tactician. "I'm going to want to know where the dreadnoughts are at all times. *Comprende?*"

A grunt in response. That was good enough. Rios gave the command—and *La Sirena* dove for the turbulent cloud tops. Already slammed by the gas giant's magnetic field, the freighter now felt the fury of the planet's eternal storms.

From the dreadnought, Burze spoke with alarm. *"What are you doing? Are you nuts?"*

Rios unmuted long enough for a single announcement. "Good-bye, cruel world!"

The orange haze went to brown—and then completely black, as *La Sirena* raced through regions in search of a corridor. It finally leveled off in a zone where frequent lightning illuminated immense pillars of clouds, each a tornado capable of swallowing a moon.

"Here we are," the navigator said, with some trepidation. "As long as this pocket doesn't collapse in on us, we could manage not to die horribly for, oh, two, maybe three minutes."

"All I need. Map us a circumequatorial route around those storms—at full impulse."

The hologram did a double take. "*Full impulse?* Are you daft?"

"I'm decided." Rios punched controls, revving the ship's new outrigger engines. No freighter could really be optimized for what he was intending to do, but *La Sirena*'s new configuration was good enough.

The ship began to race through the murk. Rios called to the EEH. "Ian, how's that tracker?"

The hologram's voice resounded overhead. *"She's ready for her lines."*

"Wait ten seconds, then beam it fifty meters off our port bow. We like this place so much, we've decided to stay. Got it?"

"Aye!"

The engineer called up when it was done. Rios's attention then went to the dreadnoughts. He didn't expect the Iotians' sensors to be much of a match for the interference, and *La Sirena*'s weren't doing much better. But the tactician, despite his appearance, seemed more than capable, coaxing a few updated dreadnought positions as the freighter raced along.

It's working. Rios saw that the closest vessel, *Sockdollager*, had moved to a position above where the tracker was making its arcing descent to the depths. Three of the other dreadnoughts, more remote, had moved off point to join her. Rios directed the flight crew to find an escape path out of the range of those that remained.

La Sirena erupted from the atmosphere on the far side of the planet so fast the clouds in its wake luminesced, creating a blazing contrail. It was something else for the Iotians to gawk at besides the freighter itself, which found a lane.

"Warp five," Rios declared—and the trap was slipped.

It was just a short hop, enough to get clear; with the hated tracking device crushed to its component molecules, the Convincers had lost their squealing rat. He wasn't surprised when a subspace message came through: Burze would certainly have learned of the ship's survival from the other dreadnoughts by now.

Against his better judgment, Rios answered. "What now, Burze?"

It took a second for the visual to come up. *"I know I'm whispering, but I hope I don't sound like* that *idiot."*

He blinked. "Ledger?"

She appeared on the screen before him and spoke in a rasp: *"I hear you've been trying to reach me. I've got news for you—and you'd better listen!"*

56

La Sirena
Deep Space

The freighter's main viewscreen was so large that it almost looked like Ledger was standing in a new addition forward of the bridge. This was no office in the backroom of a packing plant; rather, it resembled a skyscraper corner executive suite at night, with windows looking onto a moon-filled night sky. She stood beside a wide antique table that doubled as a desk; it held an ornate lamp at each end, providing dim lighting.

"Volume down," Ledger ordered in a low voice. Rios could tell she was speaking not to be overheard. She started to say something else, only to pause when she noticed the two holograms seated in front of him. *"Wait a minute. You've got two more?"*

"Ignore them," Rios said.

"Are you starting an army?"

"I'm getting rid of them."

"You can't if they've got names." She pointed. *"Enoch, Emmet, glad to meet you."*

"Don't name them!"

"You might need the muscle—because I've got news." Her initial worried expression returned. *"Listen up. Arkko's sending her goons after you."*

"Yeah, I just ditched them."

Her eyes widened. *"How many?"*

"Seven dreadnoughts. I didn't know I was that hot."

"Buddy, you're on fire," she said. *"There's more. I found out that Fajo put a plant on your ship, long before we even met him."*

"I know. Yerm. He and I talked all about it. We're good."

"How did—" The news flustered Ledger. "*Whatever. I know* this'll *blow your wig. The Ferengi brothers—"*

"—were both poisoned by Fajo, using the ship's replicator and Romulan wine."

"Good heavens, what don't *you know?"*

"Why you're not on Argelius." He recognized the satellites he saw outside her room from his visit to Theta Zibal III. "You're on Mount Fajo."

"Yeah, when he brought the actuality here, he moved the management of all his operations with it. He and Arkko are in business together—it's the only way he can afford her price—and they can't cooperate in the open. That's how I've heard all this." She looked surreptitiously around. *"It's a creepy place."*

Rios explained that he'd been trying to reach her. That he'd learned from Picard that Fajo had kidnapped Data and murdered his aide, Varria—and that anyone who worked for the collector might be in danger.

"That stuff's nothing in my world," she said. *"I can handle it. But I thought you'd better know Fajo got Arkko to set the hounds on you. You've got something he wants."*

"So that's it." Rios reached beside the seat and brought the golden apple into view. "Guessing he's looking for this right here."

This time, Ledger's arms jerked backward in an expression of shock—jostling the lamp beside her in the process. She grabbed it quickly to keep it from falling. Setting it aright, she looked back at Rios. *"Is that the real McCoy?"*

"Your question suggests he knows he's got a fake." It felt good to be a little ahead of the game. "How long has he known?"

"Long enough," announced another voice—and the lighting in Ledger's room grew somewhat brighter.

She turned to her left. *"Boss—I didn't know you were still up."*

"Of course. We all work late here." Fajo entered the frame, accompanied by a meek-looking Romulan elder. *"I have a lot to keep tabs on—including outgoing communications."*

Ledger straightened. *"This isn't—"*

"Pishposh," Fajo said, waving his hand to forestall her explanation. He faced forward. *"Ah, Rios—and more darling little Rioses. It's very late, Captain, but I appreciate that Ledger's gone to the trouble of contacting you."*

Rios started to slip the puzzle out of sight, only for Fajo to raise his hand. *"Uh-uh,"* he said briskly. *"There's no reason to hide that, Captain."*

"Guess not," Rios muttered. He brought it back into view.

"That's better." Fajo smiled and indicated the old Romulan. *"This is Bonnalo, an expert in Parch actualities—much like your friend Professor Quimby. For weeks, he'd been telling me I had the real actuality—yet our study of it kept*

hitting dead ends. We never would've known if not for a bug I planted in Palor Toff's luggage when he left your ship." Fajo leaned against the table in full view and crossed his arms. *"It seems I've been swindled."*

"Not by me."

Fajo tut-tutted in his usual way—a response Rios had come to hate. *"Captain, I don't wish to assign blame. Forgery and the old switcheroo, to use Ledger's word, are time-honored parts of the hobby. I admire your intrepidity."* He studied his fingernails. *"Still, what are we to do?"*

Rios straightened. "Well, we—"

"I'm sorry—that was rhetorical." Fajo glanced back at the moons. *"The last week of the year in your calendar begins tonight, doesn't it?"*

Rios didn't respond. He kept his eyes on Ledger, who stood frozen, watching Fajo. Calculating, as always.

"We're about to hit that big century mark in a few days. 2393: a hundred years after Chang's false dawn. I want to have the real actuality here, in my hand, by then." He clapped his hands together. *"So what's it to be? Another auction, I suppose. You'd like latinum, I assume."*

"The way I hear it, you don't have much to spare."

"A momentary handicap—and there are other units of exchange." Fajo raised his finger to the air. *"Tell you what. Bring me the actuality, and I'll give you the job you wanted."*

Rios barely remembered it was something he'd once desired. "Just flying?"

"If that's what you want. You and your metal mermaid can swim the seas together, with never a thought as to where your next cargo run is coming from."

Rios couldn't see doing that—not now, given what he knew. And between Fajo and the Convincers, he expected he'd wind up dead. "No sale."

The collector seemed nonplussed at the rejection. *"All right. To be honest, I'd have lost a bit of respect for you had you taken that."*

"You have respect for me?"

"More than I once did." Fajo strolled behind the table and looked out at the stars. *"Perhaps there's something else you want. I hear you used to be a member of Starfleet—but were tossed out because of something so bad or so secret that even I can't find out what it was."* Fajo faced Rios and raised an eyebrow. *"Maybe I can get you back in."*

The offer startled him. "You . . . don't have that power."

"Don't be so sure. Oh, you may all act like—what's Ledger's term?—Goody

Two-Shoes, but Starfleet's made up of mortals. They have wants of their own—and respond to pressures, correctly placed. Even General Chang found someone to work with."

Rios scowled. "I don't believe you."

"Just a second," Fajo said. He strolled back in front of the table, where the Romulan handed him a padd. *"I have a couple of lists here. One includes high-placed collectors. Some of my best clients don't even know they're dealing with me. And then there's a nice* new *list from Arkko of people they've crossed paths with who have . . . shall we say, habits to hide."*

Rios's mouth went dry. Starfleet officers certainly had succumbed to outside pressures before; he'd wondered if Vandemeer killed his guests to keep something from being found out. But making a starship disappear from the records was huge, and he could hardly see Fajo buying someone off with a knickknack or the Convincers blackmailing someone else. "You're wasting your time," Rios said.

"Am I?" Fajo leaned against the table. *"I bet there's names of officers on your discharge certificate—your* dishonorable *discharge, I would imagine. Let's just see how many admirals and captains I can find on this list. I'm guessing we've got a few names in common."* He grinned. *"For all we know, it could be a clean sweep!"*

Fajo began examining the padd—and Rios felt his heart pound. The offer couldn't be real. He couldn't get near it.

And yet—what if there were names on Fajo's lists? What did he owe them?

He stood and faced the holographic flight crew. "I'll be back. Anybody shows up, go to warp. Any questions?"

"One." The ENH raised his hand. "Am I Enoch or Emmet?"

"Shut up."

Rios dashed back to his quarters. The trunk was there, with his gear from Starfleet—and the dreaded isolinear chip. He knew there were names on it: the names from the secret meeting, the cabal that had done him in.

He skidded to a stop before the trunk and knelt. The open shutters cast light across the locks. Glancing to the right, he saw a glistening blue orb not far away. It wasn't Earth, of course—and yet for the first time, he felt like it might be close. Earth, San Francisco, his commission, and his whole life.

It had all vanished in a cloud of deceit. *So what* if he got it back in the same way? *Serves the bastards right!* He opened the chest and brought the chip into the light.

Something over his head caught his eye. The blue light glinted off one of the mermaids on his shelf. Two had come from Fajo, including the first one; he'd found more, since. He paused to catch his breath—and remembered what he'd read of Andersen's fairy tale, so much darker than later retellings. The mermaid, her love unrequited, had been given the chance to get her form back by slaying her intended and his new wife. Her sisters had even traded their hair to a witch to give her the magic knife.

And the mermaid had thrown the knife into the sea, dissolving as she did.

Outside, he heard Fajo's faint call. *"Captain, where'd you go?"*

Rios glanced again at the mermaids before turning and marching back out onto the bridge, chip in hand.

"There you are," Fajo said. He held up the padd in triumph. *"One hundred sixty-eight!"* He beamed with confidence as he waved it around. *"Someone here is your way back in. I guarantee it."*

"You guarantee it," Rios repeated, picking up the actuality from his chair. Holding it in one hand and the chip in the other, he seemed to balance them.

The chip weighed a lot.

Fajo gave the padd back to Bonnalo. *"Bring me the actuality, Captain, and I can get the ball rolling. You'll be wearing drab uniforms and eating lousy Starfleet food again within a month, tops."*

I never minded the food, Rios thought. Closing his eyes, he couldn't deny that it would be nice to be back. But he'd made his decision. He opened his eyes—

—and threw the knife into the sea. "Pass."

Fajo looked startled. *"Seriously?"*

"Is there a problem with the connection?" He let the chip fall to the deck. *"Pass."*

Fajo's head tilted slightly. His jaw set, and he began to pace. *"I know what's behind this resistance. I heard part of your conversation earlier—about what that busybody Picard told you."*

"Indirectly."

"It couldn't be indirect enough. He's a nasty little nothing—living his years out in much-deserved obscurity. But you mentioned Varria. You're right: when Data tried to hold out, I sacrificed her. Cast her from my collection, as it were. So you know I'm fully capable of doing so again."

From the folds of his garment, he produced a small handheld weapon.

Ledger, who'd been standing like a stone, chortled. *"Sale on popguns?"*

"Oh, no," Fajo said. *"It's a Varon-T disruptor. It was hard enough to find the first one. The second one was murder."*

He smiled eerily at her—and then spun. He fired the weapon at Bonnalo. The old Romulan screeched as he was consumed from the inside, and the blaze from within lit the room. Seconds of agony later, he—and the padd Fajo had been reviewing—were gone.

Weapon in hand, the trader shrugged. *"Academics are cheap. He should have caught the forgery earlier."* A wry smile crossed his face. *"Now just imagine, Captain, how I would have reacted if Bonnalo had secretly called the man who robbed me, trying to warn him. Tell me, what should I do in a case like—"*

Rios saw it happening before Fajo did, but said nothing so as not to give away the fact that Ledger had lifted the lamp from her end of the table. She brought it down toward the back of the Zibalian's head—

—only to be repelled backward in an electric flash. She was thrown to the floor along with the lamp, which shattered beside her.

"Ledge!" Rios called out.

Fajo looked back not at her, but the fragments. *"Those lamps are valuable, you know."* He patted his chest. *"So's personal protection. I was able to get my shield device back, too, after my unfortunate holiday. It's a smaller version of what protects this whole mountain."*

Seeing Fajo looming over her with the weapon, Ledger struggled to sit up. *"Don't wave that thing at me. You touch a Convincer, you get war with all of us!"*

"Oh, I don't think so," he replied. *"Arkko wasn't happy I had brought you on board in the first place. She's already told me you're expendable. If I tell her it's to get the true actuality back, I'm sure she'd pull the trigger herself."* Fajo looked at Rios. *"Maybe* she *would be worth making a deal for, hmm?"*

Ledger laughed. *"You've got the wrong number. I'm nothing to him."*

"Which is why you reached out to warn him?" Fajo smirked. *"My dear, you forget: I was aboard his ship for days. I watched him at the banquet—and when the Ferengi attacked. Women are* never *nothing to Rios. Under that festering scab of a personality sits a true knight errant."*

Somewhere in the room, a grandfather clock chimed. Fajo glanced in that direction.

"It's Christmas," he said. *"You have seven days—and you know where I am."* He winked at Rios. *"Come on, Sir Cristóbal. Chivalry, you know. Tallyho."*

57

La Sirena
Orbiting Theta Zibal III

"A starship is a time machine," Alonzo Vandemeer had told him once. "Give an ensign any task, and you'll see what forever is like."

Rios had no ensigns, but he did have five holograms that required no sleep or sustenance. And he had something else: an extremely fast ship. So it was that he got more done during the week he had been given than he'd ever imagined possible. When *La Sirena* did make its return to Fajo's homeworld, his greeting was well prepared.

Boss Arkko really had set up shop in this system far from the Convincers' usual territories; five dreadnoughts guarded the planet, including *Velvet Glove*. That reinforced the value she put on her arrangement with Fajo—just as the fact that an even larger number of dreadnoughts had hunted Rios down underscored what price they'd put on finding the real actuality.

Rios had been summoned to Fajo's planetary doorstep, but he'd calculated that the collector wouldn't dirty his hands with what came next. Why set foot on the hated freighter one more time when he had members of a race of violent henchmen at his disposal?

When *La Sirena* entered orbit over Theta Zibal III, it had offered no response as Arkko's vessels circled it. The Convincers had boarded him twice before; Rios figured they were getting accustomed to having the run of the place. That was something he could use.

Boss Arkko either hadn't gotten a new desk to ride around on, or had decided not to bother with it. It wasn't the occasion for half-clad bearers in any event; she had already transported a dozen hoods onto the freighter with more to come. She had liked Mr. Hospitality, so Rios made sure she was satisfied with who met her at the transporter pad.

"Oh, sweets," she said after materializing. Arkko stepped up and tickled the chin of what she thought was her favorite *La Sirena* hologram. "Hello, doll."

It was Rios who smiled back, wearing clothing replicated to look like Mr. Hospitality's. Flanked by Stench and another gun-toting thug, Rios gushed, "Welcome back to *La Sirena*! It's such a joy to see you again."

"I thought I told you to lose the shirt next time," she said.

"Why?" Stench asked. "He's already frisked."

"That's not what I meant."

Rios clasped his hands together and tried not to puke over being so cheerful. "Will you be needing a stateroom? Something to nibble on?"

"I'm dry, darling."

"One martini, specialty of the house," Rios declared. The concierge system responded, and a cocktail glass materialized in his hand. "One olive or two?"

Arkko was delighted. "We never should have sold this ship." She took the drink and sipped. "Top-notch, Holo Boy."

Stench waved his heater about. "No sign of Rios, boss. We're starting to fan out."

Rios tilted his head. "Is there something I can help with?"

"We're looking for the dingus," Arkko said. "The puzzle thingie. Fajo says your boss pulled a fast one on him."

"Oh, dear. That doesn't sound like him." Rios looked to Stench and his wingman. "But I believe I *did* see something like what you're describing."

Arkko's bracelets jangled as she waved. "Lead on, MacDuff. I'll be right here, waiting for you." Rios made sure she got a spare drink before he left.

Stench hadn't wised up to the hospitality hologram's true identity earlier, and still had not. That had worked out well for Rios. The Convincers this trip were well aware of what *La Sirena*'s bulkheads did to bullets, and they weren't going to risk getting air-conditioned over a lousy hologram—or at least that's what Rios heard one of them say.

Downstairs, Rios encountered Emil. The medical hologram stepped toward them, prompting threatening moves from the hoodlums. Rios raised his hand. "Relax. He's the doctor."

Stench's buddy guffawed and pointed between Rios and Emil. "They look alike!"

"Of course they do, you idiot," Stench said. "Are you a dunce or something?"

As the toughs looked him up and down, Emil appealed to Rios. "What's the problem?"

"These are the ones I told you about," Rios said. "You know, from the ship I mentioned?"

"Ah," Emil said. He looked at the intruders. "Iotians, I see. Well, even for you, bolaphagic fever is an incredibly dangerous condition."

Stench snapped at Rios. "Hey, what's he talking about?"

Rios shrugged. "It's just a doctor thing. Does anyone *ever* know what they're talking about?"

Emil surveyed Stench's expression and shook his head. "Aggression, too." He looked to Rios. "Shall I?"

"For the safety of the ship, by all means."

Moving quickly, the EMH produced a hypospray and applied it to Stench's neck. His partner gawked in shock—giving Rios time to grab hold of his gun. Emil stepped in quickly and applied a dose to the second Iotian.

"What'd you do?" Stench asked woozily. Rios reached for his weapon as well, and it slipped from the Iotian's limp hands as he slumped to the deck.

Emil knelt over the pair and spoke. "Very sorry to have acted so abruptly, but there was little time to waste. Muscle use causes the infection to spread. You must cease movement for four hours, until the virus is rendered inert."

Rios opened the bottom drawer—ironically, the one Stench had been trapped in months earlier—and tossed in the machine guns.

Emil examined the now-sleeping thugs. His brow furrowed. "Are you sure they have bolaphagic fever? It's a Gorn malady, and quite rare."

But it does exactly what I need it to do, Rios thought.

"It would be against my programming to act offensively against anyone," Emil added.

And that's why I picked it. "Worry about diagnosing them later," Rios said. "As captain, I'm declaring a biohazard emergency. These guys are rifling through the cargo bays and the staterooms. I want you winking in and out, neutralizing anybody you can find—that's not me or Arkko, that is."

Emil seemed convinced of the need, but looked with concern at his hypospray. "I haven't enough serum for everyone aboard."

"Just get who you can—and leave the main deck to me. If anyone challenges you, dematerialize and go someplace else!"

He needed to do the same. He ran back upstairs. Arkko was standing, directing her troops. "Did we hit the jackpot?" she asked when she saw him.

"They're getting a look at sickbay from the ground up." Rios swiftly changed the subject. "Oh, I'm so thoughtless," he declared.

She watched as he hustled over to Ledger's old room and carried out a comfortable chair. "While you wait, my queen."

"You're the tops." Arkko thought that even more when he ordered her another martini. "See if you can find some of those little pastry things I had last time."

"Right away." He trotted away like a waiter in a rush—only to pivot and dart quickly into engineering.

Dinky was there, another of Rios's "old friends" from Verex III. The massive Iotian's mission: to keep the black-capped hologram from doing anything with the engineering controls. Rios gave him a hospitable grin. "Can I get you anything, sir? A snack, perhaps? A side of beef?"

"Get me something better to do," Dinky said, sullen. "This job's a yawner. This here guy don't even say anything."

"He's the latest in a line of silent engineers," Rios said. "He's just bothered that you're in his domain." He acted as if an idea had struck. "I know! Just take him for a walk. Nothing can happen here if he's with you."

Dinky eyed Rios with suspicion. "Yeah, but what about *you*?"

"Sir!" He laughed. "I'm the hospitality hologram. What would I know about engineering?"

The hood seemed to chew on the notion.

Rios sweetened the deal. "I had just replicated a cake downstairs when you arrived."

Dinky's eyebrow went up. "Pineapple?"

"What an amazing coincidence!"

Rios stood aside as Dinky prodded his holographic hostage from the room. Certain they were gone, he stepped behind an obstruction and called out, "Activate Ian."

The true engineering hologram appeared beside him. "I don't think Mr. Hospitality much liked wearing me tam."

"Keep your voice down." Rios peered over the console and through the window to the main deck. "Remember what to do?"

"Aye. Target their personal comms one by one as I can, and beam the gadgets into space." Ian's eyes narrowed. "Why can't I just send the *people* elsewhere?"

"First things first. You depopulate this ship now, they'll just send reinforcements." Rios patted Ian's chest. "Stay low. Anybody comes back here, dematerialize until they leave."

Rios stood and began walking to the exit, only to stop. He summoned a tray of canapés from the concierge system and carried it with him.

Convincers were hurrying back and forth on the main deck, some chattering about how comrades of theirs were turning up knocked out cold. *Emil in action,* Rios thought.

"Here you are," he said to the seated mob boss. "Sweets for the sweet."

"You're a prince," she said, reaching for one. Rios found a small stand so the tray could sit beside her as she directed her underlings. He took her empty glass from her. "Oh, you're dry again."

She squinted at him. "That's good stuff. Are you sure you didn't slip me a Mickey Finn?"

"I would never do such a thing," Rios said, "in part because I have no idea what it is." He provided her with another drink, which she took. "I'll see again if I can help your friends find the captain. He must be here somewhere."

He bowed and stepped toward the port cargo area. As he did, he overheard her say something that delighted him: "Anybody seen my comm unit? I could swear I had the damn thing . . ."

58

LA SIRENA
ORBITING THETA ZIBAL III

As tactician, Emmet—Rios had adopted Ledger's suggested names for simplicity's sake—was the only one of the holograms he'd activated that had a security role. The others could only passively resist—or be tricked into acting offensively, as Emil had been. But the ETH could do more, and as a commotion came from farther in, Rios could tell he was doing it.

Three Convincers had surrounded Emmet. They leaped at him—only to crash into one another when he dematerialized. He popped back into existence a dozen meters away, right beside Rios.

"*¿Qué pasa?*" the hologram asked, only mildly interested.

"You're doing fine." Rios had ordered Emmet to play cat-and-mouse with the Convincers shipwide, eschewing tougher tactics until he understood the numbers involved. "Who's still upright?"

"*Nueve.*"

Nine was more than Rios wanted to contend with at this stage, even if Emil managed to catch a few more. But it was also a low enough count that he thought his next stage would work. "Head for the Alamo. Run, so they can see you. I'll be right behind you."

Emmet complied—even as the fallen Convincers began to rise. Rios affected his Mr. Hospitality airs. "Can I get you anything?"

"A way to shut that damned holo down," one said.

"Only Captain Rios can do that. He's on this deck, in the last starboard compartment forward. My colleague was just headed in that direction."

That was all they needed to hear. The Convincers bolted for the main deck, with Rios jogging along behind.

Emmet had done a good job of attracting attention as he went, just as Rios had intended. Convincers emerged from staterooms and took off after him—and as Arkko looked in the tactician's direction, she couldn't believe what she saw. "Izzat Rios?" she asked drunkenly. "Jeez, he's gone to pot."

The tactical hologram broke from a scuffle and ran forward along the starboard walkway lining the pit to the galley deck. Another Convincer appeared from the bridge area, and Dinky could be seen ascending the stairs. The hologram had only one place to go.

It was time. Rios tapped his communicator. "Ian, I'm ready. Put me in there!"

The transporter brought him from one end of the upper deck to the other, such that he was standing in the holodeck even as Emmet arrived. He heard shouts from approaching Convincers outside. "He's trapped! We've got him!"

The thugs barged through the doorway—and gawked as they found themselves standing in a barroom, confronted by many Klingons of legend. And if they did not recognize whom they faced, the Iotians certainly read their expressions.

"That's them," Rios declared to the Klingons. "*They killed Verengan!*"

With angry cries of vengeance, the holograms launched themselves at the newcomers. Verengan had turned off the safety protocols in the *Sto-Vo-Kor* program, meaning that the Klingons' fists were hard, and their blades were sharp. The Iotians had been in bar fights aplenty—but that, to use another of Ledger's expressions, was bush league.

"You slew our greatest friend," Kahless shouted. "Now feel our wrath!"

Rios stayed mostly out of the fray, passing a bottle or weapon to a Kang or a Koloth. L'Rell and Azetbur took turns battering Dinky. Emmet, with nothing to do, ambled behind Kahless's bar as if it belonged to him.

Taking a head count seemed less important by the second, so Rios flipped over an unconscious Convincer and peeled off his overcoat. He grabbed the hat from another—wardrobe shopping off the floor of *Sto-Vo-Kor*. Satisfied, he stepped outside and called to the overhead. "Ian, do you have all the communicators?"

"Aye, Captain!"

"Beam everyone down—whether they're walking or not!"

From the corner of his eye, Rios saw Arkko staggering toward him. "You louse!" She pulled a pistol from her ankle holster. "We shoulda come in guns blazing to start!"

"Ian!"

If the engineering hologram answered, Rios did not hear it. But the glowing light that carried Arkko away was confirmation.

He hurried back to engineering. "Where are you putting them?" he asked Ian on arriving.

"Middle o' the Zibalian desert, like you suggested. But I—"

An intraship call interrupted the engineer. It was Enoch, the navigator, confirming that the helm was free—and that more company was arriving. *"Our pals from Pergazia—all seven of 'em. Edge of sensor range."*

Seven dreadnoughts. He'd guessed someone would arrive to reinforce *Velvet Glove*'s flotilla; the fact that the force was large was no impediment to his plan.

In fact, it helped.

"Enoch, I'll be right there." He looked to Ian. "Bridge me."

Rios rematerialized seconds later beside the navigator—and looked out upon *Velvet Glove* and two of its escort dreadnoughts. The other pair were aft of *La Sirena.* "Have the locals seen the new arrivals yet?"

"I doubt it," Enoch replied. "Haven't detected as much as a sensor sweep from any of them. Whoever's running that squadron is making a right hash of it."

"Good." Rios stretched open the overcoat. "Put this on."

The hologram did not struggle as he was being dressed, but neither was he happy about it. "Cap'n, I want to say again this is *not* within my operational parameters."

"You handle comms when I'm not around. You're going to issue the standard greeting to Iotians that we rehearsed."

"But I'll sound barmy."

"Quiet," Rios said, jamming the fedora on the hologram's head. There was no time to delete the ENH's mustache and beard—none of the Iotians seemed to wear them—so he flipped up the jacket collar so it obscured the lower portion of his face. "You're on. Hail *Velvet Glove.*"

Rios dashed to the side, out of range of the pickup. On the screen, the cigar-chomping hood who served as acting mouth for the flagship appeared. *"What the devil's going on over there?"* He squinted as he looked forward. *"Who the hell are you?"*

"Shut yer gob!" Enoch shouted, laying his accent on thick. "Ye'd better talk to me with respect!"

The toughs on *Glove*'s bridge looked at one another and laughed. *"Get off the sauce and off the comm, before Arkko hears you. She don't have time for boozehounds."*

"I don't think she'll be objectin'. I've rubbed out the old bat!"

The tough dropped his cigar. *"You clipped Arkko?"*

"That's right! It's time for new blood!" Enoch looked uncomfortably at Rios in the wings, who urged him to continue. "Now, listen here. My pals are coming in now. *Sockdollager*'s the new flagship, you get me?"

Velvet Glove's bridge erupted with chatter. *"Those bums did this?"*

"Yeah—and they'll pop you, too, if you don't knuckle under and get in line. What do you have to say about *that*?"

The clacking of automatic weapons answered. Rios made a slashing gesture across his neck, and Enoch cut the transmission.

Removing the hat, his navigator looked puzzled. "You're *sure* that's how Iotians greet one another?"

"Probably more often than you think."

The lead pair of dreadnoughts from the Pergazia encounter screamed toward Theta Zibal III, with the others in a shambling formation behind. For several seconds, Rios wondered if the gambit had worked. Then disruptor fire stabbed out first from *Velvet Glove* and then its companions, targeting the approaching group.

Delicious chaos ensued, as Convincer turned against Convincer over fissures that Rios assumed had to have been there already. "You might not be able to turn Romulans or Klingons against one another," Ledger had once told him, "but an Iotian without a boss around would start a war over a fish sandwich."

La Sirena was happily situated, for the moment, with the two forces moving to square off against each other. But Rios wasn't done. He slipped into the captain's chair.

"All hands on deck, report to duty stations," he declared. "We're taking the war to Fajo!"

59

La Sirena
Theta Zibal III

"Arkko! What's going on?"

Fajo had asked the question several times. Rios hadn't felt the need to respond. The only reason he'd heard it at all was because Ian had missed one of the Convincers' comm units; it had been recovered from the holographic debris in *Sto-Vo-Kor*. Artificial crewmembers could indeed make mistakes, particularly if you gave them things to do that were outside their normal duties.

That said, the quintet had played their parts well—and they were continuing to do so. Enoch and Emmet were directing *La Sirena* on a screaming odyssey through the skies of Theta Zibal III. Amid the confusion of internecine warfare, the crews of a couple of the Convincer dreadnoughts had kept their heads and had directed their vessels to pursue. That had allowed his holo flight crew to show its stuff, using the freighter's improved configuration to dive into and out of an atmosphere riddled in places by colossal sandstorms.

La Sirena had even fired phasers at its antagonists occasionally. Rios had no expectation that her weapons would do much damage to the dreadnoughts, but he had no way of seeing the results. He sat before a different sort of controls, in a place where the few sensors he had were of no use.

But they would be.

"Approaching insertion point," Enoch said from two decks above. *"Expect we'll only have ten seconds on the surface before we have to go."*

"That'll be enough." Rios cracked his knuckles—and looked down at the Convincers' comm in his lap as it buzzed again. This time, he answered. "What?"

Fajo sounded apoplectic. *"Arkko, what's going on? I'm seeing fighting all around up there!"*

"Why don't you walk outside and take a better look?"

A beat. *"Rios?"*

"Speaking."

He could hear Fajo sputtering. *"What happened to Arkko?"*

"She took a powder. Or went to the powder room. Some shit like that." Rios acknowledged another signal from Enoch before he spoke again. "I'm just here to bring back something that belongs to you."

More shock. *"The actuality?"*

"Not quite."

La Sirena touched down hard, an impact that traveled through its landing gear into the fuselage—and through the fully restored Tucker 48. Having started its engine on Enoch's previous call, Rios put it into drive even as the ramp it sat on hydraulically descended.

A heavy thump, and he was on the desert floor, gunning the engine. In the rearview mirror, he saw *La Sirena* lift back off, getting quickly underway.

Within seconds, he was racing across the blazing sands at a hundred twenty kilometers an hour, the vehicle bounding over ruts and leaving a curtain of dust behind. Above, he saw *La Sirena* race past, a dreadnought on its tail. Handling that challenge was going to have to be on Enoch and Emmet. For Rios, it was all about picking up speed—ever more speed, while avoiding spinning out in the shifting sands.

He would not have yelled "*Yee-hah!*" had he not noticed the comm unit blinking as Mount Fajo came into view. He did so entirely for Fajo's benefit.

"That's my car," Fajo declared in shock. *"But it was destroyed!"*

"Holographic restoration experts," Rios shouted over the engine. "Try 'em sometime!"

He wasn't exaggerating. Ian had finished the work he'd started in no time at all, drafting the others in to help with the heavier work. Mr. Hospitality had cleaned the windshields and mirrors—and had even suggested the new silver stripes that gave the maroon sedan a sportier look.

An explosion ahead to the right sent a tower of debris into the air, and announced that one of the dreadnoughts was onto him. He swerved—only to see the Iotians bring to bear a unique weapon in their ship's arsenal: machine guns mounted on its underbelly. A ribbon of lead tore into the surface, forcing Rios to change course again.

"Where are you guys?" he growled as the strafing continued.

The answer came quickly, as *La Sirena* swooped in, striking the attacker's bridge head-on with phaser fire. The dreadnought's pilot overcorrected hastily, clipping a nearby mesa. Disabled, it limped out of Rios's view. A hard landing resounded moments later.

He couldn't look. His focus was entirely on the looming tower ahead, part of the network that kept Mount Fajo's protective shield operating. Wherever he was, Fajo's eyes were clearly on it too.

"You're wasting your time," the collector said. *"My force field is—"*

"You talk too much," Rios said. He clicked off the Convincer comm unit and slammed on the accelerator again. Then he toggled the communicator the engineering hologram had affixed to the dash. "Ian!"

There was no answer for several seconds. Then *La Sirena* soared again overhead. *"Ian here. We had to shake the eejits."*

"I'm almost there," Rios said, fingers digging into the steering wheel. "Are you sure about this?"

A brusque laugh. *"It'd be a pretty poor time to say no, now, wouldn't—"*

"*Ian!*" Rios shouted.

"All right, all right. Yes. After the boom, we'll get about five seconds, maybe ten. I know who we're looking for."

"And don't forget me!"

Rios had delivered many cargoes since buying *La Sirena*; he was delivering another one now, this time for an old customer. That was because Sovak had returned to Irtok to reclaim control of the ranch he so wanted to escape. Getting Rios's request a few days earlier, he had responded by providing the one thing he had left to offer: *yashivoo* dung.

It was, as the Sylvus Project knew, a great fertilizer. But it was also raw material for a particularly high explosive, and Ian and Emmet had done the work necessary to transform it while on the way from Irtok to Theta Zibal. The automobile's forward-facing trunk contained not luggage, but a veritable warhead, set to detonate on impact. *La Sirena* carried no torpedoes; the Tucker *was* one, finally true to its nickname.

Rios leaned over and propped the strut he'd brought against the accelerator. There was no need to count down: his "crew" knew his position exactly. The Tucker, which weighed almost two metric tons without the payload, hurtled angrily toward the immense metal base of the tower.

When the gray wall had completely filled his view, he clicked open the channel to Fajo again. *"Happy new year, asshole!"*

He raised his hands in front of his face the instant before the transporter effect began. In the next moment, he was on *La Sirena*, falling backward onto the transporter pad. The freighter tossed violently, having been caught in the shockwave from the detonation of the Tucker's cargo. Ahead, he could see the pillar of flame outside the forward viewscreen. He quickly turned over on all fours and looked at engineering, where Ian was fighting to remain in place over his console.

Rios glanced to the left, and the empty pad area beside him. "Did you get her? Did you get her?"

Painful moments passed. He was rising to help Ian when the glow began.

Ledger stood, looking stupefied and bedraggled. She wore her clothes from the night a week earlier and had a massive armload of books clasped to her chest. She had a pencil in her mouth, which fell to the deck as she saw him.

He stepped over to steady her. Mount Fajo had not been the focal point of the blast, but it had still felt the impact when the shielding failed. It took her a few seconds to talk. "I've b-been locked in his library," she finally stuttered.

Rios looked down at the volumes she held, some of which fell to the deck. They seemed pretty old. "You stole *more* books?"

"I've been trying to figure out what to take." She gazed up at him in all earnestness. "I had to. No severance pay now—and my luggage is all back there."

He stared at her—and when she started to laugh, he tried to give her a hug. It resulted in him holding all the books—and that made *him* laugh.

"Well, we're not going back for the luggage now," he said, turning. "Enoch, get us out of here!"

She beamed. "You used my name for him!"

"His idea. Not mine."

Enoch called back in response. "*Where to, Captain?*"

Rios had planned many moves ahead—but not that one. He looked to Ledger. "Where to?"

"If you've got the real actuality," she said, "*it* will tell *us*." A devilish grin formed. "Wait until you get a load of what it *really* is . . ."

☿ ♃ ♂ ♄ ♀

— 2393 —

THE CHAINS OF THE COWARD ANGELS

*In which **Cristóbal Rios** finds the river of death—*
and gets taken for a ride

60

La Sirena
Deep Space

Rios stared at the puzzle in his hand. "You're telling me this thing is *a treasure map*?"

"That's what Fajo thinks," Ledger repeated. "It's what it's all been about, this whole mess."

She had told him the same thing earlier, before absconding to her quarters to spend an hour cleaning up. She'd spent the hour after that eating whatever Mr. Hospitality brought to the mess table. Her imprisonment on Mount Fajo had been a peculiar form of house arrest, as the place had no holding facilities. She'd been locked in the library and its adjoining rooms with food beamed to her only rarely, when someone remembered she was there.

Late in the ship's night, she sat wearing a nightgown and sipping hot cocoa in the galley while Rios, across the table from her, stared at the golden apple.

"They *all* think it's a map," she said. "It's why Palor Toff wanted to swipe it." She shook her head. "Glake—I never figured him for a thief. It's always the quiet ones."

"Yeah, well, *you* hired him."

Fajo's experts, Ledger explained, had operated on a secure lower level of the facility they were never allowed to leave. She hadn't seen inside, as only Fajo and Bonnalo could come and go from the place, but her doing the budget for the organization had made it clear there had to be at least a dozen people residing on the floor, trying to find the hidden meanings in *Chang at the False Dawn*.

"I got the idea a couple of weeks in that there were features missing. Some of the detail we saw when it opened during the auction wasn't showing up. It made Fajo crazier and crazier." Once he knew he had a forgery, he hit the warpath and she realized Rios was in great danger. "I should have known he'd be tapping the office comms, as paranoid as he was."

None of it made sense to Rios. "What kind of treasure would be worth ten thousand bricks of latinum?"

"Quimby, Bonnalo—all the scholars—are convinced that when Parch went underground, the final actuality told where the artist could be found."

"And that's valuable?"

"Brother, *is* it. Parch was rumored to be an obsessive collector—somebody to beat Fajo and the rest at their own game. Add to that all the gifts that came from the muckety-mucks who sat for Parch—and you've got a treasure trove these people would die for."

"And kill for."

"That's why I keep telling you," Ledger said. "We need to solve it, and get the treasure ourselves!"

"Solve it? All those scholars couldn't do it. You said Fajo had a roomful."

"Yeah, but you opened the thing, right? You can do it again. For that kind of dough—"

He put up his hands. "I'll do it—but not for the money. It doesn't matter whether I have this thing or not, trouble's going to follow me around until somebody puts a stop to this insanity."

La Sirena hadn't been molested on the way out of the Theta Zibal system; the dreadnoughts were still all busy battling one another. It was coming sooner or later, Ledger had said. But he didn't know what had happened to Arkko, and Fajo was still out there somewhere. The madness wouldn't end any time soon—unless he did something.

"I'll take a look at it," he said, putting the puzzle down. "Maybe if we prove it's a myth, that'll be that."

"Or find the treasure."

"Or prove it's a myth."

"*Or find the treasure,*" she repeated more emphatically.

Rios shook his head. She didn't want to let it go—and he didn't, either. "It's always money with you, isn't it? You're quits with the Convincers. You can go anywhere, do anything, be whatever you want. Why do you need to find the treasure?"

She sighed. When she talked again, she spoke quietly and firmly.

"Cris, you just don't get it." She ran her finger around the lip of her mug, working out what she was going to say. "You crossed the stars to go to Mount Fajo. You spent a week getting ready. You risked your neck fighting a war on the ship. You nearly *blew yourself up*—and all you came away with . . . was *me.*" Ledger stared into the cocoa. "Why'd you do that?"

The question startled him. Yes, a holographic Klingon had told him to perform a great deed, but that wasn't an appropriate answer. He had never really thought about what he was doing; he'd just done it.

"Well," he finally said, "I can't really—"

"Hush." Ledger kept looking down. "Now, if we decide you came to find me because I knew the actuality was a treasure map, that's one thing. But if you did all that for *me*—well, that's *something else.*" Her eyes met his. "You're not ready for something else. Are you?"

He stared at her for a few moments—and sank a little in his chair. "No."

"That's fine. We'll leave it where it is." She stood up. "Tomorrow morning, first thing, we hunt for treasure."

"Why not start tonight?"

"I'm beat—and besides, I'm on a case of my own." She picked up her book from the table where she'd left it.

"What're you reading?" he asked.

"Some rare book Fajo had. A supposedly lost novel from a detective series. I was in something called the *noir* section when you showed up." She waved the volume. "I swear, if I hear another Earthling make fun of Iotians for being obsessed with your ancient gangs, I'm going to throw the book at them. Or a whole lot of them."

Rios read the name on the spine. "*Dixon Hill.*" He'd heard of it, but he couldn't remember where. "You're really reading it?"

"I already know the fantasy's more fun than the truth—and besides, I thought I'd find out how the players on the other side lived." She snickered. "The detective guy's all right, but the women in here are dumber than a sack of rocks."

As much time as Rios had put into opening the puzzle, he had not thought a lot about what the actuality depicted. Yes, he knew that it showed a scene from a hundred years earlier featuring General Chang—but that had only interested him as it connected to how Verengan got the actuality. Once Gorkon filled in the blanks about the old trader's parentage, he'd put it out of his mind. He had his own Starfleet conspiracy and wasn't in a hurry to think about another.

But outside the excitement of the auction, he found himself marveling at how much detail the vignette depicted. He opened it on *La Sirena*'s main deck, suitably darkened for the occasion—and he had brought in his holographic reinforcements.

Ledger sat in an easy chair, looking on with amusement as the six Rioses stepped around the life-sized imagery. "This is the daffiest thing I've ever seen," she said.

"Yeah, well, it's working." Rios had found that the themes he'd encountered in the puzzle's solution were repeated within the content of the actuality. There were symbols from Klingon, Romulan, and Earth history on the apple's exterior dials; the details evoking those cultures were embedded within Chang's surroundings.

And there was something else, which Ledger said she'd never heard a whisper about on Mount Fajo.

"There was audio," Ian said, reporting a finding from his scans of the device. "It appears to have played a single file only once—and permanently deleted its content. Seems a waste."

Several volumes of Quimby's masterwork lay strewn about the deck; one was open in Ledger's lap. "Says here Parch did a few talkies," she said. "Always a computer-generated voice. Poetry—even birthday greetings and party invites. But there were fewer as time went on."

"Well, we've got one." Rios was disappointed to learn that the recording couldn't be restored, but the fact it had existed added something. Was it just noise from the Praxis explosion reverberating through Chang's ship—or was it something else?

He'd continually returned to the Wuxing elements—and the cycle that solved the puzzle. There was no water in Chang's environment that he could see; the bloodwine was the only liquid. But wood was present.

"The table he's sitting at," Rios noted, standing within the image. "I'd expect everything on a bird-of-prey to be metal, but Chang was weird."

"Or maybe Parch made it a wood table," Ledger said.

"*Oye*," Emmet muttered. Leaning against the bulkhead, the tactician had appeared his bored, disheveled self—but he'd interjected an occasional observation. "*El papel proviene de la madera*."

"I don't savvy," Ledger said.

"He says paper's made from wood." Rios looked more closely at the book on Chang's table. "And it's not just open to *Macbeth*. It's open to the Birnam Wood scene. Wood from wood, on wood."

Fire was easier. It was in the braziers—and everywhere, once Praxis exploded and the sequence ended in fanciful flames. But earth was the bear. There appeared to be no soil in the room whatsoever.

"Could be a reference to the Earth in the window," Enoch suggested.

Rios looked back at the navigator, who'd said almost nothing until now. "What are you talking about?"

"The Earth." Enoch stepped into the actuality and looked keenly at the starfield outside Chang's window before the blast. He pointed at a shining yellow star. "It's Sol. No doubt there. Spectral class is spot-on."

Rios squinted. "Are you sure?"

"If you get in real close, you've got quite the little orrery here. Jupiter, Saturn—even a tiny blue pinprick. It's definitely the Sol system."

"Would you be able to see that from near Praxis?"

"Not a chance." Something else caught Enoch's attention. "And what have we here?" He pointed. "*Romulus!*"

Rios gawked. "The Romulan star and Sol shouldn't be in the same sky in a window that small."

"Don't have to be a navigator to know that," Ledger said.

"Pretty big mistake," Enoch observed, stepping back.

Rios shook his head. "Parch doesn't make mistakes. It's like Quimby said."

Ledger chuckled. "You just love saying her name, don't you?"

He disregarded her—and ordered Enoch to keep looking for stellar features that didn't belong.

"We need metal now," Rios said. Of course, it was everywhere—in the deck and bulkhead—but as he focused on the image as it cycled, he saw more things. "Chang's blade."

Emil stepped closer. "And those rivets in his eyepatch. I can't say as I approve of his surgeon's choice there."

Rios frowned. "But the cycle begins and ends with water." He stared for several moments. "I just don't see it."

His shoulders slumped. They'd been going at it for three hours.

Ledger hopped up from her chair. "No mistakes, right?"

"Right."

"Let's find some." She picked up the Wine-Stained Folio, which had remained aboard after Sovak rejected it. "The one in the actuality was open to the page where the stain is, right?"

"Yeah." He watched her as she brought it into the actuality near the virtual folio, just as had been done during the auction. "We did that already. We know it's the same book, the same pages."

"Then tell me why the page numbers are different."

Startled, Rios walked over to join her. The copies were indeed identical, including their page numbers. But as the vignette cycled, the page numbers in the actuality copy changed, just for a second. "I never noticed that before."

"No one did," Ledger said. "It's right after the blast. Who's looking at the book when that's going on?"

Rios made a note of the numbers—and of the correct ones. "What do you have when you've got two sets of numbers?"

"That's an easy one," Enoch said, looking back from Chang's window. "Surface coordinates."

"But on what planet?" Rios looked to the portal. "Found any other stars where they're not supposed to be?"

"No, everything's in its right place." The navigator gave a little laugh. "Just not in its right time."

"What do you mean?"

Enoch called something up on a padd and showed it to Rios. "Except for Earth and Romulus, it's all in a position you'd expect from a vessel in Klingon space near Praxis. Except it's a starfield you'd have seen about forty days later."

Rios studied the padd. "They'd have known better back then for sure."

"Forty days after the explosion," Ledger said. "We've got coordinates and a time. Maybe it's another party."

Yeah, but on what planet? Rios turned again to the idea of water—and took a closer look at the wine. "Mr. Hospitality, get over here."

Ignored until now, the hologram hopped over with glee. "Some refreshment for your research? Some tea to help you think—or, perhaps, some brain food?"

"Bloodwine," Rios said.

The hologram was taken aback. "Not something I was going to suggest, but it is a choice."

Rios tugged at his jacket. "That bloodwine," he said, pointing to the bottle on Chang's table before the explosion. "Tell me about it."

Mr. Hospitality studied it. "A Klingon label, of course."

Interested, Ledger walked over to join him. "The hooch we bottled at Verex III wasn't the same kind of stuff, but we never messed with labels. Why would they?"

"Ah. That's because it's from Sherman's Planet," the hologram said. "There was a competition between Federation and Klingon colonists on that world—and agricultural produce leaving the planet had to be labeled."

Rios's eyebrow went up. "I didn't think the Klingons lasted there very long."

"True, and the vintner there was short-lived." Mr. Hospitality looked up. "I'd tell you whether this vintage was any good, but it didn't exist."

"What do you mean?"

"This date: 2269. There was a drought in the Klingon sector that year. No wines were produced." He tsk-tsked. "I'm afraid this image is in error."

Ledger and Rios looked at each other—and mouthed the words at the same time: *There are no errors.*

He clapped his hands. "Class dismissed. Enoch, set course for Sherman's Planet, top speed!"

61

La Sirena
Orbiting Sherman's Planet

"Wood stands for something else," Ledger muttered as she stepped off the transporter platform. "Barking up the wrong tree."

With every light-year they had traveled toward Sherman's Planet, Rios had begun to doubt his choice of destinations. But he couldn't warp to a nonexistent Romulus, and he figured it would be years before he'd be willing to go near Earth. That left only one world indicated by his interpretation of the actuality.

The problem was, the Sherman's Planet of 2393 was much different from the place it had been a hundred years before. It was more populous, and no permutation of coordinates suggested by the pages from the folio appeared to be home to any kind of secret refuge. All they had found at one site was a café run by an Andorian who had been very confused by their questions, but had served them delicious pastries nonetheless.

"Maybe Parch retired to make quality baked goods," she said, wiping the sugar from her lips. "That's the only treasure to be found."

"It'd serve everyone right," Rios said. But as nice a find as Clovo's Confections was, the establishment was not a secret worth killing for. Or ten thousand latinum bricks, for that matter.

He exhaled in aggravation as he looked at the actuality again. It was crazy to have thought the two of them and a bunch of holograms could've figured the thing out. It all presumed there even *was* an answer.

Or maybe there's more than one answer.

"Water referred to the wine, but there's got to be more than one reference." He remembered his Derrida reading: words having multiple meanings. "Maybe it doesn't have to do with water, the element—but water, the symbol."

Ledger watched as he picked up one of the books from the deck. "If you can send us to a nice seafood place next, I've had a hankering for—"

"Yes!" Rios said, slapping the page of the book. "In Wuxing, water is associated with the planet Mercury—and its astrological character is on the puzzle."

"You want to go to Mercury now?" She chuckled as she followed him to the bridge. "How are the restaurants?"

"This system has a rocky inner planet of its own," Rios said. He looked to the navigator. "Am I right?"

"Aye," Enoch said. "A recent capture from another system, astronomically speaking. Bit of a runaway."

"What's its name?"

"Not very creative, the settlers here. They called it Outcast."

Outcast. The chase had lost its capacity to surprise Rios. "Set a course."

"It's no place you want to go, Captain. There's nothing but—"

"That's an order."

Impulse drive started, *La Sirena* left orbit—and he and Ledger began poring over database records of the barren inner world. There were no artificial features of any kind on the surface; just craters battered by hellish radiation.

"Makes Verex III look like a ski resort," she said.

Rios had moved on to the subsurface surveys. "There were some attempts at mining, but they stopped." He looked up at her. "Around 2290. Interesting timing."

She gave a tired sigh. "I know you and the holo boys are a bunch of geniuses, but are you sure you're not leaping at—"

An alarm went off. "*Nuevo contacto,*" Emmet mumbled. "*Muy grande.*"

Rios soon understood just how *grande* as a colossal vessel emerged from warp almost dangerously close by. It was a ship he had seen before, but not in this configuration. Large domes and networks of magnetic shields protected gardens and forests for space travel.

"*Sylvus Bestri.*" He watched as several interceptors exited a landing bay.

"Here we go again," Ledger said. "I thought you and the princess had a sit-down to sort things out."

"We did." Rios frowned as he accepted the hail. "*La Sirena.*"

Royce Claggett appeared in *Sylvus Bestri*'s command center. *"We meet again, Commander."*

"It's still *Captain*. What do *you* want?"

"I'm not allowed to do what I want—lucky for you. I'm here to tell you to leave the system."

"This is a Federation system, last I checked." Rios's eyes narrowed. "What are you even doing here?"

"Some work on one of the outer worlds. We don't want you around."

That didn't wash. "You only help nonaligned worlds."

"Change of policy." He clapped his swagger stick against the palm of his hand. *"We don't want you anywhere near our operations. The squadron's going to escort you out of the system."*

"We're in space, *amigo*. I can lose your fliers without even—"

"Cristóbal," said another voice.

Rios watched as Liselle stepped into view. "*Marquesa.* What's going on?"

"I need you to do as Royce says. I can't explain. It's just that—" She paused, as if searching for how to phrase things. *"It's just that what you're looking for will not help you—and it can only hurt others."*

Rios's eyes widened. Ledger tugged at his sleeve and whispered, "She knows! It's why she bid on the damned thing!"

"It is," replied Liselle, having overheard. *"It's what's right, Cris."*

"Right for *you*," Ledger retorted. "Charity not working out?"

The Iotian's words antagonized Claggett. *"My people are going to blow you from the sky."* Liselle took umbrage to his remark, and she took him aside, muting her audio feed while they argued.

Rios did the same—and watched in wonder. Claggett had been his underling for a brief time; Liselle, his lover for an even shorter while. Yet they were in a heated argument over what to do, in front of their own crew.

He looked to the right—and saw Enoch beckoning. "What?"

"Beggin' your pardon, but I've scanned Outcast at your coordinates." The navigator demonstrated his display. "There's a large void down there—a system of caverns, or mines. Appears to be between 2,260 and 2,280 meters beneath the surface."

Astonished, Rios added: "Or 2269."

"Aye, that number *is* between 2,260 and 2,280." The response appeared to baffle Enoch. "I can suggest a few others—and still more if you don't mind decimals."

Ledger had gotten it. "2269 was the vintage of the bloodwine."

Rios nodded. *An elevation—below ground.* He gestured to Enoch. "Get ready to get us there, fast, on my mark. Outcast's on the other side of the sun—we ought to get a few minutes' lead time." He glanced at the fliers outside the starboard portal. "Tactical, I'm going to want to lose these guys in the process. But don't kill anyone."

Something between a grunt and a groan came from Emmet.

Onscreen, Claggett stood back, abashed. Superior authority had won out, Rios supposed. He opened his audio channel. "*Marquesa*, I'm committed here. Things won't—"

"Just a second," Liselle said. She stepped to the left side of the view onscreen—and helped back in a much older-looking Duke Javen. *"My uncle would like to speak with you."*

The Valtese elder squinted. *"Is that the book thieves?"*

Javen's appearance startled Rios. Since their last meeting over a year before, he appeared to have withered. "Duke, I'm sorry about your books."

"Hush up, and listen. I don't give a damn about the books. That'll be that." He looked directly at his listeners. *"Just go."*

Rios could only think of one way to respond—and it wasn't a yes or no. "Why?"

"You can't ask that. But I'll give you whatever you want. Your own hortiporter, your own planet."

The offer took Ledger's breath away, and she clutched Rios's arm.

"Just walk away from all of this," the old man said. His eyes opened wide. *"And don't you tell a soul. Ever."*

Those were the wrong words to say to Rios.

"I'm sorry, Your Grace. You too, *Marquesa. La Sirena* out." He spoke to the holograms. "Punch it."

The freighter lurched, and Ledger left his side. Rios slipped into his command chair and called up a display, prepared to help the holograms if he needed to. But they did their job admirably, evading the interceptors with ease.

The respite allowed Rios to switch to a different interface. *La Sirena* could run a battery of scans before it ever reached the planet, telling him something about what awaited beneath the surface.

Once he had all the answers he expected he was going to get, he rose—and headed for the alcove where he'd started a small arsenal during his months on the run. He selected a phaser and hurried aft.

He met Ledger as she stepped out of her quarters. "Where'd you go?" he asked.

"Didn't have the right shoes for a dungeon. And I wanted *this*." She brandished her pistol.

Rios shook his head. "I can do this alone. We don't know what's down there."

She stepped onto the transporter pad beside him. "Stop talking. Time is money."

Dixon Hill and the Recluse's Web

Tracy Tormé, 1937

(Excerpt from Chapter 32)

I counted how many bullets I had left as the cab sped over the bridge. Lenny, the driver, was a drinking pal from the old days; I could trust him not to bark at the sight of a piece in the mirror. It didn't stop Alice from shivering—or from burying her pretty face into my shoulder.

What had started with Alice LeGendre looking for her father had turned into a sordid tale of treason and betrayal, with bodies strewn from Seville to San Francisco. In my pocket was the photograph that had started it all, more deadly than any pistol, more lethal than any machine gun. A thousand doughboys had gone to their deaths in the Great War because of the secret meeting it depicted—and the Recluse was making sure nobody ever said a word about it.

The trail had taken me to places where the name of Dixon Hill meant nothing to anyone. From posh rooms and swank shops where nobody spoke English, to some of the seediest dives the world had to offer. Now the road had circled back home—but it was far from over.

The brown recluse isn't like other spiders, which spin webs as traps. It's a hunter, going wherever its prey is. Its web is a retreat: always in a cold, dark spot where no one would ever look. That suited my quarry perfectly. The Recluse wouldn't be in a gaudy mansion, but rather deep in the shadows. I was pretty sure I knew where to look.

That didn't suit Alice, who'd been to hell and back with me and wasn't keen on having to go again. "Please, Dix," she said, blue eyes full of tears as she squeezed my arm. "Let's just leave things as they are. It's already cost so much."

"You can't walk away now, any more than I can. Until we find the Recluse, it's just going to go on and on."

"But—"

"Shhh." I put my fingers over her lips. "And don't kid yourself into thinking there's another way." I patted my pocket—the one with the deadly photo in it. "We can go over to the bridge, tear this up, and throw the pieces into the bay—and our lives still won't be worth a plugged nickel. We've laid eyes on it. That's enough. We see it through, or *we're* through."

It wasn't about the payday—not anymore. It was about getting clear, about cutting loose from the past. One way or another, it had to end.

"You're right," she said in that silken voice, barely more than a whisper. "You're always right."

"Now you're talking."

The car hurtled into the night—and toward destiny.

62

Outcast

Rios didn't know what all seven of the wonders of ancient Earth were, but he imagined they were lauded for their engineering as much as for their artistry. A strange thing about living in the twenty-fourth century was the number of even greater, more recent engineering achievements one encountered—many of which had been abandoned due to obsolescence.

Underground chambers on distant planets, for example, fused centuries of mining knowledge with astronautics and environmental science. All that activity, with important noteworthy exceptions, was simply no longer necessary. Magnetic shielding had eliminated the need for subsurface habitats in all but the most hostile of places. Replicators had not fully eliminated the need to mine for raw materials, but they had considerably winnowed the list of compounds for which it was worthwhile to cross space and dig a big hollow.

It was not surprising to Rios to find a large network of connected enclosed spaces beneath the surface of Outcast; the fact, detected from orbit, that it had a breathable atmosphere also came as no shock. But it was quite unusual, more than two kilometers beneath the infernal surface, to find daylight, a cool wind, and a flowing stream.

Ian had detected matter that might interfere with a clean transport in all areas but one, so he had deposited Rios and Ledger in a cavern off to the side of the main system. Light from a tunnel had drawn them to an enormous domelike chamber, where a forested island sat across rushing water. At first glance there appeared to be a normal, if unearthly, sky above. Only by squinting did Rios notice the presence of lights, recessed into the roof that was coated with some kind of fluorescent substance.

The stream, too, was artificial. Standing at the bank, he looked downstream to where, fifty meters away, a waterfall went *uphill.*

"Antigrav," he said, pointing. "The river's a circle. It's recycling there."

Ledger snapped her fingers. "There's something this way."

Upstream, she'd found a series of engraved markers rooted to the rocky surface. Each had a saying that repeated in the characters of different languages. In addition to Standard and Latin, Rios recognized writing in Klingon, Romulan, and Vulcan.

"This is some cheery stuff," Ledger said, beginning to read from one. "*This miserable way is taken by the sorry souls of those who lived without disgrace and without praise. They now commingle with the coward angels, the company of those who were not rebels nor faithful to their God, but stood apart.*" She looked to him. "What *is* this?"

"I think it's Dante."

"What's that mean?"

"That this isn't a great neighborhood." Rios read from another stone, clearly a Standard translation of an equally dire Klingon saying. "This one's about those who are unwelcome in *Sto-Vo-Kor*."

"That's because they didn't pay the cover charge." Ledger was no fan of Verengan's holodeck program.

They continued to walk. The shore, ringing the circumference of the chamber, was miserable and barren, but what lay across the stream didn't look so bad. Rios had been looking for a place to ford it when they spied a dock, mate to another that existed at the island. A cable stretched between the pier and the one on the other side. Rios noted the presence of a flat-bottomed boat attached to the cable.

"Manual propulsion," he said as they reached it. He stepped into the boat. "All aboard."

"Thanks, Captain." She climbed in and gestured to the wheel attached to the cable. "The helm is yours."

Rios gave the wheel a push—and realized it was going to take a heave. With effort, he got the wheel moving, and the boat slipped into the current. "This thing hasn't gone anywhere in years. We're just going to creep along."

"Yeah, well, it's all creepy."

He didn't disagree.

One revolution after another brought the vessel farther across the black water, rushing beneath. Ledger looked all about. "The cost of this must have been enormous."

"I'm gawking, you're budgeting," he said. "Did you get any of our mythology on Sigma Iotia?"

"Nothing that didn't involve running numbers."

"Well, if you see a big three-headed dog, bark."

Minutes later, they landed on the other side. A path led through exotic trees, and as they walked it, the place felt much less alien.

"It's all a big grotto." What struck Rios most was the silence. By the stream, there had at least been the sound of the water. Here, the breeze—artificial, he knew—barely rustled the foliage, and there were no animal sounds. It almost seemed like a holodeck program where things had been left out—but, it could not be that. The space revealed by his orbital scan was far too large.

Ledger stepped faster. "There's something ahead."

There was, in a clearing at what Rios reckoned was the island's center. A small, ivy-covered ranch house stood amid topiary bushes of green and blue, each sculpted into fanciful shapes. Here and there, too, were bases upon which sat three-dimensional holographic paintings. It was an artistic medium that stretched back far, Rios knew; on a visit to Vulcan as a cadet, he had seen works done by Spock as a young lieutenant on *Enterprise*. These were large, some two meters tall.

And at the side of the house stood the artist, working with her hands to shape some kind of gryphon, made from light.

She looked human, with wrinkled dark skin contrasting with long white hair. She had tied it off several times, and still it went halfway down her back. Her smock was a patchwork of patchwork; if she had no replicator, she clearly had the crafting skills to improvise. Indeed, she appeared to have made do with just about everything. Her sandals were carved from some kind of wood, bound to her feet with what appeared to be ropes of hair.

If she noticed them, she made no indication—even when the newcomers circled her.

Ledger stared at her. "What the hell?"

"We are but at the *gates* of hell," the artist replied in a grave voice that cracked. "This place is for the angels who stood by." She looked up at them, suddenly less solemn. "Didn't you read the damn signs?"

Rios goggled. "Are you Parch?"

"You're trespassing." She turned back to her work, shaping a wing.

Ledger sighed—and tromped back into the woman's view. She brought the Chang actuality out of her pack. "This is our invite, toots. You sent for us."

"I certainly didn't send for *you*." The artist's eyes were wide, determined, and full of life—and they landed on the golden apple for just a moment. "That invitation went out a century ago."

"Then you *are* Parch," Rios said.

"Sure, why not?" She waved to the trees. "If you're looking to settle here, there's an open patch across the stream by the air processor. But you'd better be a vegetarian."

It wasn't the way he expected her to answer, but he took it. "How long have you been here?"

"Since they left. Since *he* left. Since it happened." Unhappy with her last strokes, Parch glowered at the gryphon.

Rios turned back to face the house—and noticed crops beyond it. "Have you been here for a *hundred years*?"

"Everything runs on automatic," Parch said. "I don't remember how all of it works anymore. It was built to last two centuries—I'm surprised any of it made it this long." Disappointed with her work, she attacked it with her hands. The gryphon turned to digital dust and vanished. She faced the visitors. "I suppose you want something. I don't do interviews. I never did."

Ledger looked about to say something. Rios forestalled her. "We just want to understand."

"Pilgrims, then." Parch let out a deep sigh. "I'm not your guru. I don't have any secrets."

"You damn well do," Ledger said, crossing her arms. "Nobody climbs into a cave for a hundred years without them."

Rios was afraid Parch would bolt then—but instead she looked coolly at Ledger, and then at him. "I like this one," the old woman said.

"That's why I bring her along." Rios gestured to the ranch. "Maybe show us around?"

63

OUTCAST

Hot tea was not Rios's drink, and while the concoction Parch poured for them at her kitchen table was not tea, it was in the general beverage vicinity. But he did not complain, because, hosting her first visitors in years, the artist had opened up.

"Why the name?" Ledger asked. "Why 'Parch'?"

"I was living in a world of plenty—of magnificent excess, in fact. Yet I was dying of thirst, as one in the desert." Parch walked to her window, outside which purple flowers grew in artificial light. "It was never considered seemly for one of my family's station to be a working artist. We were to be patrons, no more. Dilettantes."

She stepped close to the door, where a cloak hung on a peg. "So I went incognito, to protect the family name—and worked only with subjects who would agree to preserve my identity." She ran her fingers over the cape, feeling the fabric. "Somehow, that only made me more famous."

The kitchen did not seem to Rios like it belonged to a superstar. It was simple, with only a modicum of technology. Yet she was clearly facile with it—and when she took the golden apple from the table, she spoke about her work.

"Holography in those days had stalled out. The technician class thought it was too much trouble, that it didn't add anything. I felt it could be made to do so much more—that tremendous meaning could be invested in it, if you made the effort."

"Holograms *have* come a long way," Rios said. "You'd be surprised."

"Yeah," Ledger said. "His serve him drinks."

That drew a blank expression from Parch. "I don't want to know," she said. "I haven't wasted a day wondering how the universe has changed. I left for a reason."

"What reason?" Rios said.

"You don't know?" Parch seemed genuinely surprised. She displayed the apple. "I'm holding it."

She had depicted many of the greats of politics, philosophy, and the arts during the 2280s, she explained, but Klingons were stubbornly resistant to her appeals. She'd focused her efforts on General Chang, whose interest in the literature of other cultures gave her a possible in.

"He was difficult to meet—and would never have sat for one of my portraits. But I tempted him with something he greatly desired."

"The Shakespeare folio," Rios said.

"Correct." She rose to pour herself another cup. "I was his guest on his ship for almost a week. He would never let me depict him on the bridge; he thought other officers would think it vanity. So for six days I sat in silence, recording him as he read, looking to find the transcendent moment that would capture the man."

"And it found him."

Parch blanched—and dropped her teacup. Worried she would faint, Rios helped her to her chair.

"It was astounding," she finally said. "And frightening. It was amazing that I was recording then—and immediately after, I forgot all about the portrait. First, I feared the ship wouldn't survive; then, I thought we would never disembark. Only when we went to Qo'noS did I realize the scope of what had happened."

Rios remembered seeing a record of the blast recorded by *Excelsior*'s sensors—and imagery taken later on from within the Empire. It was a sign of how dangerous the operations on Praxis were.

"While on Qo'noS, I learned of Chancellor Gorkon's idea to reach out to the Federation. I offered to help in any way I could—and told Chang. I hoped to speak with Gorkon. But it was the general who approached me, asking my help in setting up a meeting with the other powers. Klingon politics were always unruly; he said it needed to be done privately."

She was the perfect third party to reach out, Parch said, because she understood discretion: just as her subjects protected her identity, she could be trusted to serve as a quiet back channel. And she already knew several of the people Chang hoped to reach.

"Admiral Cartwright from Starfleet, I knew from a diplomatic conference I visited. He was a fan of the commemoratives I did for the Klingon War. Then there was Nanclus, a Romulan ambassador with the praetor's ear. He had sat for me a decade before."

"Wait," Rios said on hearing their names. "You mean *you* brought them all together?"

"I don't know that I was the first or only contact," she said. "It was never clear, and it was so long ago. All I know is I approached them after leaving Qo'noS, under the guise of offering them copies of the Chang actuality. When they expressed interest, I sent copies to both of them and the general, with an agreed-upon time and location embedded within."

"So Earth and Romulus in the window—they weren't mistakes."

"Have you ever seen my work?" Parch chuckled. "They were *attendance confirmations*." She considered the golden puzzle. "It felt exciting—like being a spy!—but I feared my little flourishes would be over their heads."

"That's why you included an audio file," Rios said.

"So all three could interpret the clues." She sighed. "I even had to provide instructions for opening the puzzles. I liked my fun, but I'm told Chang found it all very droll."

Rios nodded. He couldn't see any of the power brokers being entertained by it, though it made sense they were looking for secrecy.

Ledger was troubled by something else. "Wait," she said, pointing to the apple. "Do you mean there were *three* of these widgets?"

"Yes," Parch said. "Which one did you find?"

"Chang's," Rios replied. His head was still swimming from the artist's earlier revelation. "Did you say the actuality indicated the meeting place? Ours led us here."

"Sherman's Planet was a border system, so it made—" Parch stopped, and rose from her chair. "Perhaps it's better to show you. I did one more actuality after that one—after which I gave up the craft forever. Come with me."

She led them into the next room, a library with shelves on three walls and an inactive fireplace on the fourth. Rios had seen a chimney outside; it hadn't seemed necessary in this temperature-controlled underground pocket, but then, every reading room needed a fireplace to be complete.

"The kitchen table used to be in here," Parch said. She approached a shelf and pulled down an alabaster bookend. "Pull those shades."

Ledger and Rios complied. Parch placed the bookend on the floor, in the center of the rug. Then she triggered something and stood back.

The table that holographically appeared was the same size as the one in the kitchen, but it had a fancy cloth draped over it—and fine candlesticks atop. Three guests sat in the chairs, making a toast.

"I don't recognize these men," Rios said.

"I only invited one of them." Parch was standing aloof, by the shaded window. She did not look at the imagery, but gestured precisely as if she knew where every element was. "Nanclus came in person, but Chang and Cartwright didn't attend. The human with the mustache is Colonel West."

He remembered now. "Cartwright's co-conspirator." He was out of uniform, unsurprisingly for a secret agent whose stated rank seemed calculated to obfuscate his true position. "And the Klingon?"

"A general," Parch said. "His name was—"

"*Grokh*," Rios said at the same time.

Ledger looked to him. "You've seen this guy before?"

"Never." But it made sense, such perfect sense. "He was Verengan's father. That's how his son wound up with the actuality."

"Which is one-third as rare as we thought it was." Ledger pointed to the display. "And it's not even the final one after all. That one is!"

He glanced at her, ready to explain to her the historical importance of the moment being depicted. But he turned to Parch, who seemed to be wilting near the wall.

"Hey," he said, crossing to her. "Are you okay?"

The old woman blinked back tears. "I haven't activated this in years."

Rios still hadn't determined what she had known. "What did you hear them say here?"

"I wasn't allowed in the room. I wasn't even to take an image—but I was vain, and greedy." She wiped her eyes with the back of her hand and gestured to the toasting conspirators. "I hid my imager in the room so I could capture the visual when galactic peace would prevail. Here, under my roof." She choked up. "And instead . . . *instead* . . ."

"So it *is* true." A familiar voice came from the door to the kitchen. There stood Liselle, with Claggett behind her. She stared at the actuality. "*It's all true.*"

Claggett pointed his disruptor at Rios and Ledger. "Step over there, Commander. We have something important to discuss."

64

Parch, astonished to see so many people in her home, looked to Liselle. "Do I know you?"

Rios watched as Liselle approached the old woman. For a moment, the *marquesa* simply stared, taking in Parch's appearance. "You do not know me," Liselle said in a gentle voice, "but I know you. Therrey was my grandmother."

"Therrey is my sister," Parch said. "She was a child when I left."

"I am sorry to say she is departed—as has her son, my father. But your brother yet lives."

Another voice from the doorway. "*Avaleth?*"

Parch looked over—and, for a moment, said nothing, as if disbelieving her eyes. "*Javen?*"

The old man stepped forward, staring at the sibling he hadn't seen in a century. For several seconds, they stood, frozen—statues from the past.

Then they hugged, stunned expressions in place of tears.

The others' attention momentarily drawn away, Ledger reached into her pack and removed her pistol. Claggett spotted her out of the corner of his eye. "Stop!" he shouted, redirecting his disruptor.

"*You* stop," Rios said, his phaser now in his hand. "It's a piss-poor security chief that doesn't check for weapons."

Liselle snapped at them both. "This isn't necessary!"

"I think it is," Claggett snarled, his aim still on Ledger. "You told me what this means to your uncle."

Javen released Parch and glared at Rios. "You just couldn't let it alone. You couldn't let this woman be."

"I wasn't doing anything," Rios replied. "I just wanted to know what the hell was going on—and to put a stop to the madness!"

"I've been trying to do that since before your parents were born."

Javen sighed loudly—and began to explain.

"When we inherited the family business, I did my best to make the lives of Avaleth and little Therrey as comfortable as possible—as anyone *could* be on Valt Minor when the Klingons still ran the place. Avvy wanted to be an artist, and I did what I could to help."

Parch gestured to the ceiling. "All this—this house, this haven—he created for me."

"Most of the firm's activities were in mining then," Javen mused. "This grotto was my first attempt to plant something that would grow. It gave her what she wanted—a retreat, for when she wasn't traveling. And it made me happy that she was beyond Klingon space."

Rios's eyebrows met. "You were in mining. Were you—?"

Anticipating the rest, Javen looked down. "We mined Praxis for the Klingons—as did a dozen other firms that owed them fealty. It was their own people working lower down who caused the disaster—that's the only reason my firm survived. But we lost a lot of good people, and I share the blame."

Rios saw Liselle was listening intently. He wondered how much she'd known.

"I was still handling recovery efforts when Avvy called me from Qo'noS," Javen continued. "I was horrified to learn she was there—and went immediately to pick her up. It was then that she told me about the peace plan."

"And the idea of meeting here," Rios said.

"Well, it sounded insane to me—and that's saying something. I knew Chang, and wasn't sure he could be trusted. But I also knew the Klingons couldn't recover from the ecological disaster without outside help."

"Those weren't the only reasons you went along," Parch said in a low voice. "Tell him the rest."

Javen did, with reluctance. "There was a lot of finger-pointing after Praxis—some of the operations that survived the accident were wiped out in the purge that followed. Worse, I'd opened my mouth about Valtese freedom to Gorkon at a public event the year before. I was terrified they'd shut the firm down, accusing me of incompetence—or worse. In my worst nightmare, it could threaten Valtese people everywhere. I figured doing Chang a favor would protect us."

It was Javen's vessels that ultimately delivered the conspirators to Outcast for the meeting, he explained—and it was he who returned in a panic, after their role in Gorkon's assassination came to light.

"I was horrified. She was *devastated.*" He looked to his sister. "I told her it wasn't her fault, that she didn't know. But she wouldn't accept that."

Tears streaming, she raved at the holographic villains displayed before her. "That these . . . *peacemakers* could have threatened the galaxy, after sitting at my table. Drinking my wine. Toasting their evil!"

She stepped into the actuality, waving her arms, as she had in dispelling the gryphon earlier. But this was not that kind of medium, and the ghostly images remained.

Javen hurried over to embrace her again.

"She wanted to leave," he said. "To tell people her role. I said she couldn't, she shouldn't."

Parch pulled back from him. "You just wanted to save the company!"

"There was that," he said, weeping himself now. "I admit it. But I also did it to save you. I knew you meant well. *You were not one of these people.*"

Parch looked back at the images, eyes widening. "I *was* tempted. By vanity, by the promise of relics, by excess."

"So you chose exile," Rios said.

"I gave Javen the stained Shakespeare, which Chang no longer wanted. And then I told him never to come back."

Teary-eyed, Javen looked to Rios. "I had never seen inside the actuality—I didn't know it depicted the folio, or I never would have let Hain think he could have it. I'd already had second thoughts when you arrived with him. I'm sorry he's dead—and I'm sorry I cheated you, Captain."

Ledger shrank. "We did the same to you."

Javen looked down. "I honored her wishes by never coming back here—and I committed to helping clean up Praxis, and everywhere else. It's been a hundred years alone—but I've tried to do right, Avvy. I really have. You should see the great things we've done."

Parch looked up at him. "I'd like to."

For moments, nobody said a word.

"You can see," Liselle said to Rios, "why it has been vital to keep this secret. My uncle and I thought it *was* secret. Chang, Grokh, and West were killed at Khitomer. The Romulans were said to have executed Nanclus. Cartwright died a broken man in prison—yet no word ever emerged of this meeting. We assumed that all three had destroyed their copies of the actuality."

"It'd be the smart thing, intel-wise," Claggett said. He shook the disruptor. "Setting this meeting up with *toys* was not smart."

"I don't recall asking you," Parch retorted. "And it seems to me you boys with your guns were the real problem."

"Whatever. It's a liability, now—to the Sylvus Project." He waved the disruptor around. "It's my job to protect it—and your family."

"You dolt!" Ledger said. "You shoot me, Rios shoots you. Do the math!"

Rios spoke quietly. "Wait."

"Iotian trash!" Claggett replied. "I might shoot you on general principle!"

"Wait," Rios said louder.

"Go ahead and try," Ledger said. "You'll prove what a—"

"*Wait!*" Rios said. He made a show of redirecting his phaser toward the toasting traitors—and lowered the weapon, aiming downward. He fired once, destroying the emitter—and ending the actuality.

Ledger gave a start. "What did you do?"

"What needed to be done." He threw the phaser on the floor. "Javen's right. The work he's done—saving dozens of planets—more than atones for the role he had." He looked to Parch. "And you did harm without meaning to. But you've repented—and his work has redeemed you."

Liselle stared at him, eyes full of wonder. "I like how you put that."

"Well, I read a lot." Rios walked to the center of the floor, where the actuality had been. "You didn't want anybody to know. Fine. Everybody doesn't have to know everything. People sure don't have to die over it."

Then he turned suddenly on Claggett and shouted in his most commanding Starfleet voice: "Put that weapon down, Lieutenant!"

"Yes, sir!" Claggett lowered his disruptor. The sheepish look that followed showed he'd acted reflexively, without thinking. Humbled, he holstered it.

Liselle approached her great-aunt. "This means you're free."

Parch looked up and around. "I don't remember anyplace else. I don't remember a real sky."

"Our home is under a different sky every year."

The old woman smiled. "I might like that."

Liselle turned to Claggett. "Wait outside. That's an order."

Claggett grudgingly slouched to the doorway. He stopped and peered at Rios. "Can you really keep your mouth shut?"

It's not my first cover-up, Rios wanted to say. "I promised the *marquesa*." He looked to Liselle. "Good enough?"

"Good enough," she said.

Claggett exited, and the three Valtese began to follow. They stopped when Ledger shouted, "Hold up!"

All eyes on her, she tromped around the room. "We were told you had a collection here—a treasure. It damn well better not be that last actuality, because Rios just annihilated it. Now, where is it?"

Parch waved indifferently. "Oh, that." She whistled a ditty, and the fireplace, mantel, and wall behind it vanished. Behind the holographic barrier: an entire storeroom filled with paintings, statues, and other artifacts.

Looking back, Ledger lost her balance—and Rios had to catch her to keep her from falling.

Javen addressed his sister. "Avvy, you shouldn't be giving all that away."

"I don't want it," Parch said.

Liselle, as astonished as Rios was, looked to him. "It *would* be helpful to fund the project."

Ledger sputtered. "Wait, what?" She pointed. "She just gave it to us!"

Rios had an idea. "Tell you what. There may be a way some good can come from all this, after all. But you'll need to hire me for just one more job . . ."

65

LA SIRENA
SHERMAN'S PLANET SYSTEM

"I can tell you're leaving something out," Raffi said over the comm. *"Maybe a lot of somethings."*

"Yeah, well, maybe I'm not much of a storyteller." Rios sat in his quarters on the deck at the end of his bed. He idly threw the golden apple against the floor, where it caromed off his Starfleet trunk and then back into his hand. In addition to being a devilish high-tech puzzle inviting the greatest villains of the previous century to a group treason session, the actuality made for a surprisingly resilient baseball. Parch's genius truly knew no end.

"You're not still bent out of shape because I helped the admiral find you, I hope? I only did it because she was worried about you."

"Not a problem, Raffi. In fact, it's come in handy."

"How?"

"Can't say."

"You're so aggravating."

"The story's not over yet." He caught the actuality on another bounce. "How's *your* story going?"

"Not so hot." She didn't sound so hot either. *"Everything lately is in a haze."*

"Get off the leaf, Raffi."

"Are you off the aguardiente?"

"I haven't had *time*." He smirked. "Maybe that's the secret."

"Not for me. I've got too much time." A pause. *"Well, I'm glad I was able to help you fill some of yours."*

An alert chimed, and Rios made his last catch and stood. "Better days, Raffi. Take care."

Outside his quarters, he stepped up to the bridge long enough to confirm what he'd been alerted about. There was no hurry, he saw, and he wasn't planning on responding. He casually wandered aft.

Ledger sat at a round table in the common area, playing cards with all five of Rios's activated holograms. He didn't know how she had talked them into it or what they were playing for, and he remembered her saying she rarely gambled. There weren't any honest games where she came from. But here, she appeared to be doing well.

She laid down her hand. "Full house, fives full of sixes." She collected her chips while Mr. Hospitality picked up the cards. She looked to him. "Your deal, your choice."

"Wonderful!" Mr. Hospitality gushed with enthusiasm. "Let's play fizzbin."

"Not again." Ledger put her hand on her forehead. "*Why* do you keep calling for that?"

"It's an Iotian game, and you're our guest."

"It's a ridiculous game, and a reminder that I come from a species that can be talked into any damn fool thing you can imagine."

Mr. Hospitality shuffled like a professional. "It's night, so queens and fours are wild."

"Bollocks," Enoch said. He pointed behind him. "What's that big star out there, but daytime? Kings and twos are wild."

Emmet burped. "*Yo tengo shronk.*"

"You can't have a shronk," Emil said. "We haven't started playing yet." He looked to the others. "Is it *shronk* or *sralk*?"

"Enough!" She ripped the deck from Mr. Hospitality's hand and passed it to the hologram's left. "Ian. Your deal."

"This'll require a wee bit o' thought." The engineer scratched his beard, before beginning to deal. "Texas fizzbin."

Ledger snarled, "There is no Texas fizzbin."

His eyebrows went up. "You hear that, everyone? This lassie's a rookie!"

Rios could have watched the game all night, but there were other priorities. "It's time."

She tossed her cards away. "At last. May I?"

"Be my guest."

"Dismiss holograms." The five disappeared, leaving their cards to drop to the table. "If Kirk needed a diversion, why couldn't he have started dancing?"

She rose and joined Rios near the transporter pad. He rubbed the golden apple against his shirt. "Should be any—"

Before he finished his sentence, five transporter effects appeared behind him. He saw the four mercs with disruptors drawn first—and then their leader, Seejee.

She chuckled to see him. "Told you we'd meet again, dear."

Rios raised his hands, and Ledger did the same. "How'd you get the drop on us?" he asked.

"I'm surprised myself. Sending unencrypted messages saying you were here—sitting around with nobody on the bridge? You're losing your touch. Too bad—because our client has a real grudge." Seejee tapped her communicator bracelet. "Send him over."

Another transport later, and Kivas Fajo walked off the pad. He looked haggard—and angry. "I swore I was never going to set foot on this damned ship again!"

Rios greeted him. "Where's my mermaid? You always bring mermaids."

"You reprobate—you're lucky I don't have you cut off at the knees." He spied the apple in Rios's hand. "Give me that!"

"In a minute," the pilot responded. "But maybe you want to check out the other goods first."

Fajo turned to look about. Port and starboard from the transporter pad, multiple displays stretched off into the cargo areas, just as had been the case during FajoFest. Only this material was new to Fajo.

Or rather—he knew it all, but had never expected to see any of it.

"Kavaj's portrait of Surak. Cleopatra's last will and testament. Molor's *mek'leth*!" Fajo staggered around the displays as if in a dream. "The crown jewels of Kavadda III!"

Rios looked to Seejee. "Should I call my medic? He's hyperventilating there."

Fajo pulled at his hair. "What is all this? Where did you get it?"

He turned back to see Rios, arms still raised, wiggling the actuality in one hand. "*You found Parch's fortune?*"

"What can I say? Good with puzzles."

Fajo chortled—and then he laughed out loud. "Yes, that's very good." For a moment, he seemed uncertain of where to start. Then he addressed Seejee. "Tell your vessel that we need to transport everything across."

Seejee shrugged. "Why don't we just jack the whole ship?"

"Even better," Fajo said. "A fast freighter is always useful—after we dump the pilot."

"I heard him say that," Rios said to Ledger. "Did you hear him say that?"

"Clear as a bell," she replied.

Fajo stared at them. "I don't get it. What's going on?"

Seejee's comm bracelet sounded. *"Company!"*

Her companions had only started to react when Rios, hands still raised, explained the situation. "That would be the *U.S.S. Galadjian*. It's an engineering vessel, but it can burn your Britches in a hurry."

"I like that one," Ledger said.

"Good, huh?" Seeing Fajo looking about in panic, Rios called to him. "Here!"

He tossed the golden apple to Fajo. Instinctively, the Zibalian grabbed for it—and was still holding it when a dozen Starfleet security officers materialized, phasers drawn.

Fajo looked to Seejee. "What is this?"

She had no answer. But the next person who materialized did.

"Kivas Fajo? I'm Admiral Marta Batanides of the *U.S.S. Galadjian*. The Sherman's Planet system is in the Federation—and I'm here to place you under arrest for suspicion of piracy."

"Piracy?"

Ledger tapped the device at her hip. *"A fast freighter is always useful,"* Fajo's words repeated, *"after we dump the pilot."*

"Add to that, grand theft," announced someone from the side. Liselle emerged from a port stateroom and gestured to the display items. "I hired Captain Rios and *La Sirena* to transport this material." She stared down the stupefied Fajo. "I accuse this man." She turned her eyes to Seejee. "And also his accomplice."

The mercenary, hands behind her head, looked about innocently. "I don't know you, lady. I'm just a passenger." She glanced to Rios. "Tell her, baby!"

"Her name is Choda Garrol," Liselle said. "She runs the Core Breaches, an outlaw band." Liselle stepped over to the admiral. "A full accounting of the goods aboard is being prepared, should you need it for evidence."

Hands also up, Fajo stammered. "This—this is nonsense! The recording is fabricated. I didn't take anything."

A shit-eating grin on his face, Rios pointed up. "Look at your hand."

The collector brought his right hand down—and looked at the actuality he'd caught. "No, I bought this. This is no evidence—this is mine!"

What happened next surprised even Rios. A localized transporter effect began—and when the light dissipated, *Chang at the False Dawn* was gone from Fajo's hand. "What happened to it?"

Rios didn't know, himself. He looked to Marta. "Your people?"

She was as puzzled as he was. She touched her combadge. "Did anyone on the Core Breaches' ship just transport something from here? Did *we*?"

"Negative, Admiral. And there's nobody else about."

It made no sense—but Fajo was willing to make use of it. "See, there's no evidence of theft."

"Damn," Rios said. "We'll just have to go with murder then." He gestured to the admiral. "I sent her *La Sirena*'s records and Sovak on Irtok has submitted testimony. There's also a victim in Professor Bonnalo, back on Theta Zibal III." He turned to Seejee. "As to you—better luck next time."

"I can't wait." Scowling, she nonetheless blew him a kiss as she was marched back to the transporter pad with the other perps.

Fajo said nothing as the officers prodded him forward. He looked once to the left and once to the right at the riches from Parch's personal collection. His head was hanging in despair when the beam whisked him away.

66

LA SIRENA

SHERMAN'S PLANET SYSTEM

"We'll take your statements over the comm," Admiral Batanides said to the three remaining on deck. Specifically to Liselle, she added, "I'm very sorry you had this experience in our space. Starfleet is working to make the spacelanes safer."

"I'm sure you are, Admiral." Liselle shook her hand. "You have my thanks."

"No, you have mine. A lot of people in the Federation greatly admire the Sylvus Project. You're doing valuable work. I hope we're able to help you out in the future."

"Thank you. Good things are happening." Liselle gestured to the displays. "We'll be converting the antiquities in this shipment into resources that should keep the project going for some time."

Shifting awkwardly around the Starfleet officer, Ledger acknowledged the mention. "I'd better get back to that inventory." She headed off, accompanied by Liselle.

Rios stepped over to shake the admiral's hand. "Thanks for answering—and for that other time."

"I was surprised to hear from you both times. I take it that Jean-Luc's message helped?"

"It did." Rios remembered something. "I almost forgot," he said, stepping to the side. He approached her with a box.

"More evidence?"

"Just some old stuff. My friend back there's lost interest in it. But maybe you'll know someone."

Marta peeked inside—and smiled. "I just might." Then she looked at him. "It *has* been good to see you."

"It's good to be seen. Sometimes."

She had beamed away when Liselle approached from the cargo area. "You were right," she said. "Ledger got half that material indexed just while we were waiting for Fajo to show."

Rios knew why she was working so hard. "Did she share her idea with you?"

"That she handle the sales of my aunt's collection? Yes, just now."

"You could do worse," Rios said. "She was just working for the biggest pawnbroker in the galaxy—and she knows her onions, as she would say."

"True," Liselle said, gazing far off into the cargo area where Ledger was tabulating away. "But she was still a criminal—and you know how I am about scandal."

Rios watched her. "Yeah, I know."

"Well, that's that." Liselle faced him again and smiled. "The duke and duchess are certainly doing fine. He's back on *Sylvus Bestri*, constructing a house just like hers in the glade."

"Beats being outside the gates of hell."

"I've also taken to heart what you've said about Claggett. I don't think cashiering him again would be at all helpful for his next employer—or those who'll serve under him. But I think I can maneuver him to a position in the organization where he'll do little harm."

That wasn't an idea Rios could argue with.

Her comm unit buzzed. "I expect my life is about to get even busier."

"No doubt."

Responding to the tone in his voice, she took his hand. "You may be tired of all the 'madness,' as you put it, associated with our little family drama. But I do hope you will drop by for dinner sometime, if we are ever in the same system."

"Thanks for the invite."

She released his hand and strolled away.

She was partway across the deck to her quarters when he called out, "*Marquesa!*"

"Yes?"

"How'd you know Seejee's name?"

She paused and glanced back. "Who?"

"Seejee." Rios approached her. "Our mercenary back there. You called her Choda Garrol."

"Oh," Liselle replied mildly. "I'm sure you said it, while we were preparing for their arrival."

"No. I didn't. I didn't even know *Seejee* was a pair of initials."

"Then it must have come up in one of Claggett's reports. You had said she was one of the mercenaries pursuing you on our behalf."

"You see, that's the thing." Rios slowed as he stepped closer. "Claggett is a vindictive jerk. But he was Starfleet—and a security officer. He knows intel procedures." He stopped before her. "If he was sending them to kill me, he never would have let you know who he hired. For your protection."

She opened her hands in apology. "Cristóbal, I'm sorry they attacked you. But we were only interested in getting the duke's collection back. If anyone Claggett hired tried to kill you—"

"They exceeded orders?" Rios shook his head. "Nope. No way. Seejee's too much a pro for that. Her people lobbed photon torpedoes at me in the Yadalla system. Javen's books wouldn't have filled a teacup." He reached for her wrist. "You know Seejee's name because you hired her. Personally, but indirectly—she didn't know your name or face. But she got her orders from *you*."

She stared at him, eyes widening—and looked away.

Details that had nagged at him came forward, puzzle pieces locking into place. "I'll tell you what you did, *Marquesa*. When we escaped *Sylvus Bestri*, you had it out with your uncle—and discovered what he was trying to protect. You assumed that we had an actuality and that it—and the book Hain wanted—would lead us to finding out about Chang's meeting. And your aunt." He gripped her wrist tighter, drawing her eyes back to him. "And then you tried to destroy the evidence. *And me with it*."

Liselle stared at him. Her eyes glistened—but she did not cry.

"I was afraid of what was in the actuality," she said quietly. "Of what it would say. Of what my aunt would say, if we found her."

"But Javen had told you everything."

"He had only told me some—and in his mental state, I could not know what to believe." He released her wrist, and she looked down at the deck. "You see, a businessperson—even one running a charity—has to consider all possible outcomes, all potential threats to the organization. And the story my aunt told of brokering a single meeting for the conspirators, while bad, is not the worst thing I had imagined."

Rios blinked—and understood. "*You thought Javen destroyed Praxis.*"

"Or that he had a hand in what happened, in some way. It had always been assumed it was the Klingons, with their lax safety, who set off the explosion. But they had many slaves—and corporate helpers like my uncle. He had a motive—freeing Valt Minor—and there would have been opportunities." She looked up at Rios. "Causing *that* would have been a stain that a millennium of good works would not erase."

"But he said that didn't happen. It wasn't his doing."

"Before you, and me, in the grotto." She nodded. "That was a great relief. But he would not answer my questions before that. What's more, I had worried that Avaleth—Parch—suspected him, and *that* was why she disappeared."

Rios remembered. "That'd be something worth going underground for a century for. But it didn't sound like that was the case."

"No, it was not as bad as I feared. But I had to protect the project—and those I loved—and you were caught up in it. For that, I can never apologize enough." Liselle clasped her hands before her, ready to accept his judgment.

Rios wanted to respond with compassion—but then he recalled that until a few minutes ago, she had never intended to apologize at all. "We're both in business," he finally said. "Businesses offer make-goods, when deals go wrong. Do you agree?"

"Yes," she responded with a curious stare.

"Here's what I want." He pointed back to the far cargo area, where Ledger was still tabulating away. "You're going to take Ledger's deal. Bring her in. She's going to handle the sales of this trove, and she's going to take a cut. And if she makes off with a crown jewel or two, you're not going to squawk—because you literally only have this stuff to sell because of her."

"And you." Liselle took a deep breath. "If that's what you want—yes. It will be done." She offered him a weak smile. "Thank you, Captain. You know, you *will* become a successful trader."

Maybe, Rios thought. *Stranger things have happened.*

She opened the door to her quarters—only to pause and look back. "What caused you to suspect me, if I may ask?"

"You mean besides paranoia and a persecution complex?" He chuckled. "Dixon Hill."

"Where's that?"

"It's a person, not a place—and not a real person, at that. Ledger had a few old mystery books that I looked through. Every damn one, the high-class lady is always giving the hero the shiv."

She grinned. "You're starting to talk like her."

"I know. I hate myself."

—Epilogues—

THE BIG GOOD-BYE

In which a king loses to a queen after dark, holy grails find homes—
and ***Cristóbal Rios*** *gets back his metal*

67

Thionoga Detention Center

"Prisoner Fajo!"

Seated on the bunk in his cell, Kivas Fajo did not answer. His fingernails had grown approximately three micrometers in the last hour, and he was afraid that if he looked away, he might miss something.

A uniformed Tellarite appeared outside the force field. "Is that *Kivas* Fajo?" The jailer squinted at him—and grinned. "I'd heard it, but I didn't believe it. Old Fajo, back again."

"Old Ghuva, rocketing to the top." Fajo hated that he remembered the guard's name. "Does it disturb you, madam, to have the same menial job you had twenty-seven years ago?"

"I'd rather be on this side of the field than your side. I thought you moved up and out of here years ago." Ghuva chortled. "I presume you're starting off with another hunger strike?"

"It's not a hunger strike. I just refuse to eat anything prepared by someone whose culinary training was at a bioweapons facility."

The Federation had joined with nonaligned powers in the construction of the Thionoga space station well over a century before, during one of its flirtations with new methods for rehabilitation. Following various scandals and incidents, the Federation had distanced itself from the detention center several times—but an aggressive five-year reform plan had put Thionoga back in the mix. Fajo had served much of his previous sentence here, and his return had underwhelmed him.

He knew from his previous stay that at the cost of a few slips of latinum to the prison officials, any of his messengers could get in to see him in a chamber free from surveillance. It had been the one bright spot years ago, helping the king of collecting to feel as though he were granting audiences. He expected that even a reformed Thionoga was still Thionoga, but his current financial situation was much worse. His lawyers had departed soon after he left processing and were not due back anytime soon; his coffers were nearly empty.

So it surprised him when Ghuva said a visitor was waiting. "Looks like it's starting already," she declared, opening the screen. With nothing better to do, Fajo rose and followed her into the turbolift.

The renovated Thionoga wasn't just cleaner than it once was: all the lighting had been fixed, meaning that it was daylight all the time. Every surface and furnishing in the interview chamber Ghuva led him into was a bright white, causing Fajo to sink into despair. He had always said that "Hell, for collectors, is knowing someone has something that you don't." He realized now that hell was more likely a room with absolutely nothing noteworthy in it.

A slight-looking Iotian entered, carrying a large satchel. His belongings and person had been scanned on the way in, and as the door closed behind him, he sat across the table from Fajo. The collector recognized him as one of Ledger's assistants in fencing Duke Javen's books. "Mister Wemyk, I presume."

"Wolyx."

"Sorry for the confusion. There was a Wemmick in *Great Expectations*."

"I have read it."

"He also was sent by his master to talk to convicts."

"I have no master—not anymore."

Fajo had been wondering about that. "What happened to Arkko? She must have escaped Theta Zibal—she was gone when the Federation conducted its raid." He corrected himself. "Its *extralegal invasion*, I should say."

"Yes—well, as I expect you know, the rest of the Convincers scattered without her in control. There wasn't much for her to do after that."

Wolyx explained that Arkko had gathered her remaining supporters and drawn on some rainy-day assets to retire somewhere. Fajo knew that due to her homeworld's murder-filled past, nobody really had any idea what the life-span of an Iotian was. He figured Arkko's chances of finding out were a lot better now that she was out of the business.

"I was given an assignment and was en route to your world to see her," the Iotian said. "I don't know where she is—and I don't know what to do now. So I came here."

"Ah." Fajo spoke quickly, to get the meeting over with. "I'm afraid, Mister Wolyx, that you've found me at a disadvantage. Cynosure's board has voted me out, the ingrates—and the Federation has pressured the Zibalian government into seizing my collections. If they act as they did in 2366, what the Federation doesn't impound as stolen property, my fellow citizens will pilfer for themselves."

"I'm afraid you don't—"

"Not only was the greatest treasure of all time taken from me, but the key to it, which I mortgaged practically everything for, literally vanished from my hand. There's someone else in the game, and I may go to my grave never knowing who it was."

"Sir, I—"

"Don't be ashamed for coming here looking for work, Mister Wolyx. But I'm trying to tell you that everything I have is going to pay my attorneys—or to make my life bearable. There is no job, no opportunity, no anything to be found in coming here. Sorry that you've wasted your time. Farewell." Fajo bolted to his feet and prepared to leave.

Wolyx was rattled. "Sir, that isn't why I'm here at all." He heaved the satchel onto the table. "I'm here because I have a book to show you."

"A book?" Fajo paused and peered down. "Show me."

Hands shaking, Wolyx drew the large volume gingerly from the satchel. "I'm almost afraid to touch it."

The collector saw it—and immediately lost any interest he had. "*Chicago Mobs of the Twenties*. What of it? Your people have made countless copies of 'the Book.'" He spoke the last two words disparagingly.

"Again, I'm afraid you don't understand." Allowing his hands to hover just above the surface of the cover, Wolyx whispered: "*It's not a copy.*"

Fajo's eyes bulged. "It's the original?"

Wolyx nodded—and described a caper he'd been sent on that, to him, verged on sacrilege. "Arkko had learned that the Iotian Syndicate Assembly was in talks to transfer their original copy of the Book to the Federation, to commemorate their long ties of friendship. I gained entry to the facility where it was being prepared for travel—and switched it with a replicated one."

Fajo sat back down. "Provenance?"

"A nonreplicable microtag, fused to the binding."

"Oh, those are very good," he said. "I helped fund their design, years ago. It's in a collector's interest to know a thing is truly rare." Using the tool Wolyx handed him, Fajo confirmed the book's authenticity.

Wolyx explained that Arkko had intended to hold the true volume as leverage against the assembly, in case they came down on her for anything, but she was gone by the time Wolyx arrived with it. He looked to Fajo. "I'm afraid I don't know what to do with it."

"You didn't consider returning it, did you?"

"Sir!" Wolyx declared. "An Iotian *never* returns stolen property!"

"I apologize. I meant no offense."

He slumped in his seat. "Even if I wanted to, I couldn't. Half my people would want me punished for belonging to the Convincers. The other half would excoriate me for turning myself in. I lose either way."

"You're no loser," Fajo said. "This may be the single most important copy of a book in the known galaxy." He raved over the precious volume. "Earth had its holy texts, its Magna Carta, its various constitutions. But none of them *began* as books. The *U.S.S. Horizon*'s copy of this otherwise unremarkable history transformed an entire planetary society." He looked up. "It might be the most valuable single copy of a book in publishing history. You've done very well, Mister Wolyx."

The praise seemed to assuage Wolyx's nerves—but only a little. "What good is it to you? You can't very well sell it."

"Sell it? Oh, perish the thought." Fajo sprang from his chair and pranced around the room. "It's far too dear an object to besmirch with commercial negotiations. No, a book like this—it serves as a centerpiece for collections in my world. Nay, almost a magnet." He gestured grandly. "It attracts more valuable objects to it *just by existing*. Collectors will come to view it—surreptitiously, of course—and will beg to have their own precious things displayed in the same place."

Wolyx looked at the bare bulkheads. "But you can't do any of that in here."

"I've been in places like this before—and I won't be here forever. While I am here, though, what I will need is a *curator*."

"A curator?"

"Someone to help build the collection anew." Fajo calculated. "I can't simply hire from the conventional art world—no academic would do. My curator has to be comfortable working with sources that may operate outside the law—someone whose love for the articles in question transcends considerations of property, and who doesn't mind being a part of what some might call the underworld. Such a person would be very difficult to find, I'm sure you'll agree."

Wolyx tentatively allowed his fingertips to touch the book. "The curation job—is it available?"

"Not anymore." Fajo offered his hand. "Welcome aboard."

68

THE BIG HOUSE

RISA

"Naw, naw," the pit boss said, leaning over the trainee dealer's shoulder. "Them cards ain't wild. It's kings and deuces."

The trainee looked at the cards in confusion. "But it's after dark, Mister Burze."

"That's local time. It's what time it is in the capital, back home on Sigma Iotia." He jabbed a stubby finger in the dealer's face. "Unless it helps the player—then, it's the reverse. House rules. House wins." Burze grabbed for the chips.

"This is an extremely stupid game," replied the player on the other side.

"Who cares what you think?" the pit boss snapped. "If you don't like it, lady, find another game!"

She decided that she would. She rose, her emerald-colored flapper dress catching appreciative glances from other gamblers as she made her way back into the teeming crowd. It was odd finding a speakeasy in the style of Prohibition-era America on Risa, where very few vices were prohibited. But the new establishment had done a pretty good job of capturing what the actual places had been like.

Vash knew. She had been there.

That experience in fact came up when she spotted an elderly lady in pearls and a fancy yellow dress. She appeared to be the hostess—and Vash definitely had seen her before. "Boss Arkko?"

"Nobody here by that name."

"Sorry. It's just—*you're* the owner?"

"What of it? You think it's strange to see a dame running a joint like this?"

"Oh, no," Vash said. "Several women ran them in New York—Belle Livingstone, Helen Morgan, Texas Guinan." She paused. "No relation to the other Guinan, of course, though I did see her at the El Fey once when Chaplin and Swanson were there." She thought back happily on that memory. "I just wondered if you recognized me."

"I don't know you—and I don't know what you're jawing about. I do know you need to get a drink in your hand, or get out." Arkko turned away. "This ain't a museum."

Vash had seen her share of museums. Some she'd filled by selling relics she'd discovered; some she'd robbed. Others, she had visited in the distant past and far future during her sojourn traveling through space and time with Q, a being of extraordinary power.

She had met Arkko the year before, but that time it was Vash who was operating under a different name. She had spent several years disguised as Professor Xandra Quimby, a woman with a much different appearance but whose initials winked at her secret identity.

X.Q. was Q's ex. A joke only a handful of people would get, none of whom she'd seen in years.

Vash had left Q's side after losing patience with his petulant behavior. Being adjacent to omniscience was also nowhere near as interesting as she'd thought it would be. Much of what she'd loved about fortune hunting was the chase, the solving of mysteries. Flipping to the answers in the back of the book wasn't much fun at all. And besides, she already lived in a day and age in which it was possible to traverse great distances both quickly and invisibly. One didn't need to tag along with an annoying immortal to do that.

However, one did need a partner. "I'm done here," she said to her communicator. "Beam me up."

Moments later, she rematerialized aboard *Prospero*, where she saw her cohort for the last decade. "Thanks, Glake."

"My pleasure," the Nausicaan said, not drawing his words out as he had aboard *La Sirena*. "Were your entertainments satisfying?"

"Seen one dive that serves rotgut, you've seen them all." She ditched the heels and padded across the deck in her stocking feet. "Cloak still running?"

"As you requested. The best security system of all."

Glake was the smartest engineer she'd ever met—and he'd been game to take part in many of her operations. This last caper had run a little too long, straining their relationship. He'd put more than a year into his surveillance of *La Sirena*, and the erudite intellectual had kept his mouth shut for almost the whole time. *Such patience.*

She'd been even *more* patient, working for Fajo for years in hopes that Cynosure would lead her to interesting and valuable artifacts. Fajo was a ghoul, but he had sources—and through him, she'd learned that one of the greatest finds of the century, the possibly final Parch actuality, had been discovered by one of her oldest rivals: Sovak.

Sovak's fortunes had fallen far in the time since they first clashed, but he was capable—and the only way to keep him from exploiting the actuality was to make sure she got to it first. Believing, as Fajo did, that it was aboard Verengan's old freighter, she'd directed Glake to sign up with Rios on Alpha Carinae II. He had lasted longer on *La Sirena* than Fajo's agent had; he'd even acted imbecilic, to buy more time to continue searching. But Glake had still not located the puzzle when the collector found another excuse to board *La Sirena* himself: his auction.

Since Vash still worked for Fajo, it had been easy to tag along, though she'd been forced to hustle to avoid encountering Sovak should her disguise fail her. She'd expected to find the actuality; what she hadn't expected was Cristóbal Rios. Far more than a simple pilot, he'd solved the puzzle.

What had followed was one of the unfortunate things that happened in her world sometimes. Greed and frustration had driven Glake to offer a copy to Palor Toff, and that had delayed her getting it. But she couldn't really blame him. In her line of work, the occasional betrayal didn't have to torpedo a good working relationship. He'd returned chastened, and willing to be helpful again.

While *Prospero* had been too slow to get her to Sherman's Planet in time for whatever Rios was doing there, its cloaking device had allowed her to get in close enough for Glake to beam the actuality right out of Fajo's hand, even as a Starfleet vessel waited nearby. Fajo's victims got justice; she got her prize. At last.

Vash stepped into her parlor, where shelf after shelf was lined with knick-knacks—each one hiding a Parch actuality inside. *Chang at the False Dawn* sat in its new home, at the end; she picked it up. They had been her main drive in the years after her partnership with the Ferengi entrepreneur Quark had ended: collecting them all. She'd always been fascinated by the objects, but they held an additional status for her.

They were stories she hadn't spoiled for herself.

During her time with Q, Vash could easily have learned everything about Parch's identity and whereabouts—yet it was one subject area she stubbornly left unexamined, for reasons she never fully understood. Perhaps she'd already known she was going to walk away from Q, and would need something to fill her time. Or, perhaps, she'd admired the efforts that went into Parch's art, and to ruin that would have been an act of disrespect.

The books she'd written on Parch's actualities had been real. There were dozens more of the devices suspected to exist; the hunt for them could keep her engaged for some time. If she ever did want to crack the solution of the final actuality, she knew she could do that—but there were so many other things to find first. *Why ruin it?*

She put down the apple and walked to the port. She looked down at Risa, far below. She'd tangled with Sovak there, years before, when she met Jean-Luc Picard. He and Rios could hardly be more different, and yet she had found both of them immensely appealing. If she had the powers of Q, she might understand why—and she'd know whether she'd see either of them again, and if those meetings would be worth having.

But what would be the fun in that?

69

LA BARRE, FRANCE
EARTH

Jean-Luc Picard put aside the manuscript. Another story completed; another crisis at hand.

What to do next.

I don't like to write, but I like having written. Picard had heard the expression attributed to Dorothy Parker, but he had also heard its origins were earlier. Either way, it had never applied to him. His pages, lately all adventures in which people with youth and energy ventured out against great odds, were the only place he had any fun anymore.

Then the books whistled off into the void, leaving him with nothing to do.

Laris and Zhaban, his Romulan assistants, were going into Paris for the evening. "It's raining there, too, you know," Picard said when they checked in on him in his study.

"Contrary to all my people's intelligence reports," Zhaban said, "Earth's restaurateurs appear to have discovered how to construct roofs over their establishments."

"Go ahead, abandon me." It was seventy-five percent playful.

"You're in a mood," Laris said. "I hate to leave."

"You do not," Picard replied.

"Well, perhaps you'll like this." She stepped toward him with a parcel. "This just came for you."

Picard squinted at the name on the package—and brightened at once. "It's from *Marta*!"

Zhaban repeated the way he said her name, mildly mocking. "Old flame or colleague?"

"Depends on when you ask the question." Picard remembered getting the message from her asking about Fajo some time back. "I wonder what this is about."

"Find out," Laris said. "It beats sitting there moping all night."

"Go. Have fun." They transported away.

He brought the package to his table and opened it. Atop a small bundle was a handwritten note.

Jean-Luc—

I've been remiss in thanking you for the information regarding Kivas Fajo. I doubt that the news has reached you, but he indeed did offend again, and I was able to arrest him. Your warning to my friend was timely and helpful, and it prevented further harm.

In appreciation, please accept from me the enclosed, which I was given by the friend in question. If I recall correctly, it will be of particular interest to you.

I hope you are doing well.

—Marta

Picard set aside the letter and undid the wrapping. His breath caught.

Dixon Hill and the Recluse's Web.

He ran his fingers across the cover, marveling—and could not help but speak aloud: "It exists!"

Collector legend held that this entry in the fiction series had been pulped by its publisher after a very real political conflict. *Recluse's Web* was rumored to have been Tracy Tormé's answer to the rise of fascism in Europe, baked into a story about a cabal of World War I conspirators. The author was too prescient: an isolationist America under the Neutrality Acts was unready for it, and Tormé had never gotten the rights back. In recent decades, many had come to believe that the book had never been printed. While still in Starfleet, Picard had made a standing request that any located copies be digitized and added to *Enterprise*'s database, but he'd never expected it to come to fruition.

Here it was. Using just two fingers, he carefully opened the book. It was real. He chuckled in spite of himself as he read the colophon and copyright information. "Nineteen thirty-seven—earlier than anyone thought. *Remarkable.*"

But it was what was on the title page that made him gasp. A scrawling signature—along with an inscription:

Might be the only one I'll ever sign. Them's the breaks. Enjoy.

—T.T.

Picard spoke in a small voice: "My word."

He sat back, wondering whom the author might have given it to.

His heart raced. He knew he needed to alert D. S. Whalen, an expert in Earth history specializing in fiction of the time period Tormé wrote about. The Federation's archivists would certainly need to be informed—as would the society in San Francisco that held the author's papers. And there were countless other fans who would love to hear of the find.

But he was damn well going to read it first.

Picard settled back into his chair and addressed the bulldog waddling about. "Get comfortable, Number One. I won't be going anywhere for a while."

70

Sto-Vo-Kor

Verengan opened his eyes.

To the best of his recollection, the Klingon had been drinking—and it had been a long drunk. He did not know if it had been a good drunk, if such a thing were possible, or if there was a reason for his drinking. He just knew that he had awakened in a tavern—and that those around him looked very much like great Klingons of legend.

Kor. Koloth. L'Rell. Kang. Azetbur.

And at a table, across the way: Gorkon.

Verengan shivered at the sight of the chancellor. He knew his father had participated in the conspiracy to kill Gorkon, and he quickly turned, shielding his eyes.

It was then that he saw the bartender. He resembled the clone emperor, and that meant he resembled Kahless the Unforgettable. And something in his mind told him that the Klingon before him was the latter, instead of the former.

"Forgive me," Verengan said, standing and averting his eyes yet again. "I do not know what goes on here."

The barkeep spoke kindly. "You are at a tavern." He beckoned to the hairy-faced human at the end of the bar. "Another?"

"I'm good," the man said.

Verengan looked about as if in a daze. "These people are dead."

The human gave a little wave. "I'm not. Not yet."

"This is *Sto-Vo-Kor*," Kahless said, wiping the bar.

Verengan was horrified. "*Sto-Vo-Kor* is not a saloon. It is a place for the honored dead."

"I am glad to hear you know that now, at least." Kahless reached over and put his hand on the old merchant's shoulder. "But this is also a place for the dead, as you say—and you are one of them."

Verengan blanched. "This is so?"

"It is so." Kahless nodded to the human. "Rios here learned of your death—and of your life. And he learned you had visited this place many times before. He decided you should join us."

Startled, Verengan looked at the human—and then back to Kahless. "But he did not know me."

"*This place* knew you—and it is from its knowledge of you, and the things you said here, that you were created."

The concept puzzled Verengan. "I do not understand. Tell me how—"

"Ho! Here but moments, and you would know all the secrets of the universe, before having a single drink." Kahless smiled. "You will be an amusing addition."

Verengan looked about the room at its occupants again—and felt completely out of place. He turned back to the bar and drooped. "I do not belong here. I had no great deeds." He choked up. "My father—"

"Is of no consequence to my judgment," Kahless said. He pointed to Rios. "Or to his. Verengan, we can speak many long nights of things past—but you might think first to greet your fellow captain, who brought you here."

Verengan watched as Rios sidled over. "You too are a freighter captain?"

"That's right," the human said. "I fly a Kaplan F17."

"I also!" Verengan beamed. "It is a trusty vessel."

"Has been for me." He gestured with both hands. "Try adding outrigger propulsion. Speeds it up."

Verengan laughed. "Why would a freighter ever need to be so fast?"

"Depends on what you're running from." Rios looked closely at him. "I understand you've done this a long time—flying cargo. Sounds like a rough life."

"It was not easy."

Rios watched him. "Would you do it again?"

Verengan looked down for a few moments before answering.

"My life was filled with small acts," he finally said. "But they were many. There were conflicts—and victories, and losses. I made my way as I could." He looked up. "Had I to do it over, I would have carried fewer things, and more people."

"That's your advice?"

"That is my advice."

The human stepped back from the bar. "I'd better get to it."

"Rios," Kahless said. "Before you depart, there is something for you."

"For *me*?"

"The noble Verengan is correct about not valuing things; Klingons do not believe in taking trophies. Our deeds are all that is important. But you entered the recent fray without a weapon, and it is right that you should have one."

Rios chuckled when Kahless brought the long bundle from behind the bar. "Really, I don't need a *bat'leth*!"

"It is not a Klingon weapon," the bartender said, undoing the cloth wrapping. "Indeed, it is yours." He handed Rios a sheathed sword.

The human looked amazed. He drew it from its scabbard—and noted the engraved *R* upon it. "It *is* mine. Is this real?"

"A woman entered here before you did—and asked me to give it to you on your next visit. I do not think she expected that would happen for some time. But it was asked, and I keep my promises."

Rios showed it to Verengan, who read the inscription. "*Awarded for an ancient battle.*" The trader nodded with approval. "I collect old things. That is a good one."

"*Gracias*," Rios said. The human smiled at Kahless and Verengan and stepped toward the exit.

Someone called out to him before he reached it. "Rios!"

Verengan turned to see Chancellor Gorkon standing at his table. He addressed the human. "You are ever welcome here. Will you visit again?"

"Maybe."

Gorkon raised his cup in a toast. Then his eyes fell on Verengan. "There is a seat open, friend. Will *you* join me?"

Verengan looked to Rios—and then to Kahless—before facing the chancellor. "It would be my honor."

71

KRELLEN'S KEEP
VEREX III

She's leaving again, Rios thought. *But then, she was always going to.*

Back when she was working for Fajo, helping to coordinate the operations of Cynosure and the Convincers from Theta Zibal III, Ledger had run a few side hustles of her own—and had memorized the numbers and passcodes for several accounts the Federation investigators had never found. That, and the deal Rios had made with Liselle, had allowed her to sweep up the remnants of Fajo's legitimate pawnbroker operations.

To those, she had added something novel—and necessary: field recovery teams, who went into abandoned areas in Romulan space to bring out whatever they could find. Intentionally or not, Fajo, through Cynosure, had created the most comprehensive directory of evacuees held by anyone. Under Ledger's scheme, the company profited only a little from what it found: the rest went to funds for refugees. Meanwhile, items of obvious personal value were held in trust while Cynosure reunited them with their owners.

The firm's advance work had additionally allowed Sylvus to begin operations on the Romulan side of the former Neutral Zone, armed with data from Ledger's fortune hunters. They had even found a role for Sovak's ranch; Irtok was relatively close to many of the candidates for planetary restoration. His *yashivoo* would be busy doing what *yashivoo* did.

The amazing thing to Rios was that Ledger had arranged almost all of it remotely, from her office on *La Sirena* in the days after Fajo's arrest. Liselle might be able to move mountains from her workspace, but Ledger had just benefited multiple sectors of space with nothing more than her comm unit. She was truly amazing.

All that time, Rios understood the job she was creating was somewhere else—and that her days as a passenger aboard *La Sirena* would be ending. She had stayed aboard for a return trip to Verex III, where the freighter's exterior had just gotten a makeover to go with the one its interior had received.

The emergency holograms had suggested Rios replicate their custom paint scheme from the Tucker onto *La Sirena,* making it dark red with a jangle of whitish stripes; he'd seen no reason not to. He couldn't argue with the cost, at least. Verex III had been Ledger's old haunt. He wasn't surprised someone owed her.

That wasn't the only reason she'd asked to return. She'd spent the day visiting her flop and gathering her things, and waiting for a charter to one of Cynosure's new worksites. Rios was heading in the opposite direction, in search of different scenery.

But there was time for one more cigar.

He walked down the ramp. The air in Krellen's Keep actually smelled decent tonight, with just enough of its volcanic ground fog to make its drab spaceport look moody and mysterious. Ian had already transported Ledger's luggage over to her place. She could have gone with it—but after their previous dockside parting, she'd wanted a do-over.

"Did you have fun with your Klingon friends?" she asked from atop the ramp.

He looked up to see her in fashionably cool clothes for the weather: a white skirt and light blouse, with a wide-brimmed hat. He pocketed the cigar without lighting it. "Only minor property damage this time."

"You're slipping." She strolled down the ramp, valise in hand.

"The sword was a nice touch." As she stopped at the foot of the ramp beside him, he looked to her. "How?"

"I checked in earlier today with what was left of the countinghouse. The Convincers never sold your sword. It was collateral, remember? Turned out it was in the one safe nobody cracked." She put on a glove. "It helps to remember combinations."

"*Nobody* took it? Don't they blow safes open?"

"It was marked as holding weapons, and they have plenty of those. You might as well have the thing anyway, because there's no counterparty to your lien." She pulled on the other glove—and paused to smirk at him. "Now don't tell me you're so thick you think the *sword* is the big news here."

He stared. "*La Sirena* is mine?"

"*La Sirena* is yours."

Rios laughed, unbelieving. "Even with Arkko gone, I thought *somebody* would pick up the note. You can forget a sword, but a freighter?"

He could see the hint of a smile on her face.

"You—?"

"I have certain powers." She gestured. "And speaking of, look behind you."

He did—and saw a mermaid, looking down on him. Nose art, atop the new paint job. He laughed. "You did that?"

"The detailers threw it in. I just figured you needed one mermaid that didn't come from Fajo."

He grinned. "*Gracias.*"

"*De nada.* Did I get that right?"

"Close enough."

She looked into the night and breathed deeply. "This new job is going to be a big deal for me."

"I'm glad," he said. Seeing her expression, he corrected himself. "I mean, I'm not glad you're going. But you're cut out for a lot more than keeping track of one tramp freighter." He smirked. "I think I heard you say that a time or two."

"Or a thousand. And you don't need anyone keeping tabs on you."

"Except when I do."

She grinned. Then her expression turned more serious, and she touched the side of his head, turning it so she could look in his eyes. "Are you going to be okay, chief?"

"Yeah. I just have a thing to work out." She withdrew her hand, and he shrugged. "It's complicated—I can't talk about it." He scratched the back of his head. "Could take a while."

"Well, keep your nose clean. Because I'll be in a position of authority, you know. I could even see throwing some business your way someday—*if* you can demonstrate a record of dependability. I *only* work with the best."

"Of course."

She offered her hand, as she had when they first parted, long before. He shook it—and was startled when she pulled him toward her and planted a kiss on his lips.

Rios had no sense of how long it lasted, a second or a minute; only that his mind had only begun to register it when she pulled away and released his hand. He blinked repeatedly. "What was *that*?"

"Test flight." A bemused expression on her face, Ledger pushed down the brim of her hat and picked up her valise. "Take care, sailor. Give my regards to the mermaids."

With that, she strutted across the tarmac and into the haze.

He watched until she was well out of sight. Then he took out his cigar, lit it, and turned back to look up at the painting on the freighter.

Just you and me, kid.

ACKNOWLEDGMENTS

Having written two very different *Star Trek* novels in successive autumns, I wasn't expecting to do a third in a row. Then a good thing and a horrible thing happened in succession: I saw Cristóbal Rios and *La Sirena* in *Star Trek: Picard*, and daily life everywhere was transformed due to the impact of COVID-19.

So when my editor Margaret Clark asked if I was interested in doing a *Picard* novel, I asked to write about Rios—and when I spoke with series co-creator Kirsten Beyer, I said I wanted to write a novel that would be completely fun, for a world that needed a break. Both readily agreed, and I am grateful to them both for helping make this book happen.

I'm further thankful to the rest of the *Picard* creative team, including production designer Todd Cherniawsky, whose *La Sirena* video set tour and blueprints were of great assistance—and, of course, to Rios actor Santiago Cabrera and Fajo actor Saul Rubinek for performances that provided plenty of inspiration. Words in that regard also go to the memory of Christopher Plummer, who passed away the week this novel was completed; his General Chang remains one of *Trek*'s greatest villains.

If you believe in destiny, there's some significance to the fact that fizzbin and I were introduced to this planet at the same time. I was about four hours old when the world first saw the streets of Iotia in "A Piece of the Action," and if I missed the episode then, it captured my imagination later on. I'm greatly appreciative to the work of teleplay writers David P. Harmon and Gene L. Coon, as well as the folks behind all the other episodes and films my story drew elements from.

Other inspirations came from real life: it was nearly thirty years ago that I attended a lecture given in English by the late philosopher Jacques Derrida. His discussion of the story of Abraham and Isaac directly inspired the passage here.

My thanks as always to John Van Citters and his crew at ViacomCBS, as well as to Ed Schlesinger at Gallery Books, Dayton Ward, and copy editor Scott Pearson. Also appreciated was proofreading help from Brent Frankenhoff—and from Meredith Miller, Number One on my bridge.

This story celebrates the importance of books, which have, in the last year, been a refuge for many. Writing this one was certainly a haven for me. It's my hope that this volume finds its readers well—and in a better, healthier world.